WHAT IS
GOING TO
HAPPEN
NEXT

WHAT IS GOING TO HAPPEN NEXT

 A NOVEL

KAREN HOFMANN

NeWest Press

Library and Archives Canada Cataloguing in Publication

Hofmann, Karen Marie, 1961–, author
What is going to happen next / Karen Hofmann.

Issued in print and electronic formats.
ISBN 978-1-988732-06-0 (softcover).
ISBN 978-1-988732-07-7 (Epub).
ISBN 978-1-988732-08-4 (Kindle)

I. Title.

PS8615.O365W53 2017   C813'.6   C2017-901285-1   C2017-901286-X

Editor: Anne Nothof
Book design: Natalie Olsen, Kisscut Design
Author photo: Julia Tomkins

NeWest Press acknowledges the support of the Canada Council for the Arts, the Alberta Foundation for the Arts, and the Edmonton Arts Council for support of our publishing program. This project is funded in part by the Government of Canada.

#201, 8540–109 Street
Edmonton, AB T6G 1E6
780.432.9427
www.newestpress.com

NEWEST PRESS

No bison were harmed in the making of this book.
Printed and bound in Canada
1 2 3 4 5 19 18 17

For stragglers and strugglers: late bloomers everywhere.
For the ones who are bridges.

Before

THE SAME COPS THIS TIME as the ones who came in June, which is a bad thing, she thinks. She imagines them saying to each other, *Not those people again.* But a good thing, too, because everything doesn't have to be explained all over again. They don't ask, *Where's your mom?*

She's been trying to say what happened, but Che and Cliff talk at the same time, interrupting, so nothing can be heard. The older cop says, Get those two out of here, okay?

So then it's just her, Cleo, talking. She's holding Bodhi, and they're sitting on some short logs, there for the purpose, in front of the house. It's early; the sun hasn't quite crested the cedars, and the clearing around the house is chill.

The younger, guy cop says, But don't you need a....

Take them away, says the older cop. His uniform is of thick, shiny material, green-grey-blue. Not organic looking. His hair greying like Dadda's but cut short, bristles at the temple and nape.

He doesn't want any of them in the house while the ambulance guys – the paramedics – are working.

Cleo didn't know that when you called an ambulance for this, the police came too. Will Mandalay be mad? Maybe she should have waited for Mandalay to get home from school.

But it's Mandalay's fault this happened. So she can't be mad at Cleo.

Anyway, if she, Cleo, had waited until Mandalay got home to call, she might have got into trouble with the police. When she goes to Myrna Pollard's to collect Bodhi, the television is on and it's often a detective show and people get into a lot of trouble if they don't disclose information right away. A police car has been sent to get Mandalay. A squad car, on TV. Dispatched. Cleo wonders if it has arrived yet, if Mandalay is being told, if she is shocked, crying. How long for the squad car to get to the high school, in Port Seymour? She sees Mandalay getting off the bus, the police officer waiting there, saying her name, the other kids turning to look at her. Mandalay pausing, foot still on the lowest stair. But no: Mandalay must have arrived before the call, logically. She changes the picture: The knock on the classroom door, Mandalay called out into the hallway, the rows of orange-painted lockers, the scuffed beige linoleum. Mandalay in the back of the police car, weeping.

She looks over to the squad car parked in their front yard, Che and Cliff wrestling over the steering wheel, the younger cop's face.

The older cop says, Now, walk me through it all again.

Cleo is afraid she will contradict herself. She knows from the detective shows that you can get into trouble for that, too. I went to get Dadda up, she says. It was eight forty-five and we needed to leave for school so I went to wake him up to drive us. She keeps the image in her head now firmly glued to the clock beside her bed – her clock that she had asked for and got for her birthday, the only clock in the house – and the boys sitting in a row on the bed, all dressed properly and clean, forbidden to move.

That was the deal. Some mornings Daddy just needed to sleep in. Had a bad night, his back was killing him. Give me ten minutes warning, he said. So Mandalay would leave, running down the driveway to catch the high school bus for Port Seymour and Cleo would get herself and everyone else ready, the boys into their jeans and T-shirts and jackets, and herself into whatever was in the basket, which might not be much if she hasn't done some laundry the day before and if Mandalay has beaten her to it. Mandalay doesn't remember to do laundry and she wears what Cleo was planning to wear. Dadda says, Don't do all of the laundry, let your sister learn the natural consequences of her actions. But he also says, No personal property in the form of clothing. So there isn't much choice.

Get herself dressed in whatever is semi-clean and mended and then wake up Dadda and he would put on his pants and find his glasses and the truck keys. And if Dadda was going to be working that day, Bodhi needed to be dropped off at Myrna's. So all of them climbing into the cab, and Bodhi on Cleo's lap.

But this morning.

A great tiredness washes over her, like sand-warmed waves at the beach. The tide coming in. That feeling, the whole ocean seeping into to the bay, the water warmed and lulling.

So you tried to wake your dad up, the cop prompts. What happened then?

Bodhi wriggles away from Cleo and goes after the cop. She should get those diapers washed out. Dadda does his own and the boy's laundry. Even Bodhi's diapers, usually. He takes the wet clothes out to the line, his height meaning he doesn't have to stand on a stump like Cleo does, and pins them up. He says, hanging out clothes is an art, Cleo. You want to put your attention into it. You want to find the Zen of it.

Come on, Cleo, says the cop, plucking Bodhi up at arm's length, sort of like he's lifting up a muddy dog. I know this isn't fun. But just run through it for me one more time, and we'll be done.

I'm *twelve*, Cleo says, meaning, don't talk to me like I'm a baby. She sees the cop's face sag, lose some of its resolution.

Twelve. That means Dadda was forty-two when she was born. And Mam twenty. And Mandalay is almost fourteen now, which is four years away from eighteen, what Mam was when Mandalay was born. How much older Dadda is than the rest of them! If you add up Mam's age now and Cleo's and Che's, you get Dadda's age. Or instead of Cleo's and Che's ages you could put in Mandalay's and Cliff's.

Her mind running along on two tasks, then: One playing with the numbers of their ages, like beads on an abacus, and the other replaying, for the cop, what had happened that morning. It is the wrong thing, she knows: She's not paying enough attention. Dadda always reminds them to be mindful. Cleo is getting better at it. But she can't do it now — her mind skitters around the edge of things, won't look at them, won't let them in.

She says again what she said before, on the phone and to the cops and the ambulance guys when they first arrived, coming in the door and then the younger guy cop bolting out quite quickly to throw up under the red-osier dogwood. The smell, he said, coming back in, but she guessed it wasn't just that, the open bucket of Bodhi's cloth diapers, which were getting a bit rank, but also the bucket of chicken guts and heads, which they hadn't put outside because of the bears, and which she should probably bury pretty quickly.

He didn't wake up. I tried shaking his shoulder and talking real loud. Then Che did. But he didn't open his eyes. So I felt his chest, but nothing.

And then finally she is done and now her mind is quiet and she can ask some questions, which are: Is someone going to tell Mandalay? And, what will happen next? Though not the questions burrowing away inside her, burrowing away at some internal organ like her liver: *Did we kill Dadda? Did we?*

Mandalay's fault because she didn't wash out Bodhi's diapers like she was supposed to and Dadda pretty near bust a gut when he saw the bucket still in the kitchen, reeking, haloed with flies. Him yelling, his face like bricks except for the birthmark patch on his left cheek that looked like the map of Poland and now pulsed purple. Mandalay was supposed to do it when she got home from school, was supposed to wash out the diapers and hang them on the clothesline. Only the clothesline was gone because Che had taken it down again to tie some branches together for a tepee, so Mandalay had said she wouldn't do it, wouldn't wash the diapers, though she, Cleo, had pointed out reasonably that they could be hung on the fence.

No, Mandalay had said. They won't dry fast enough. Which was dumb because they'd dry faster than not washing them at all, and they were nearly out of clean diapers.

Mandalay's fault for being stubborn. And Che's fault for taking the clothesline again.

And then, no dinner till very late because there was nothing in the freezer to cook and Dadda had to kill a chicken and then he did a few more because it was coming fall and better to get the mess over with. Feathers and guts all over the kitchen, and the dog going crazy. Dadda with the axe and sweat darkening the silver hair at his temples to iron and sitting down suddenly.

What's the matter, Dadda?

Just give me a minute.

Then Che jumping off the dresser, he did that kind of thing, and hitting his head, and Dadda trying to hold him down to see if the cut needed a trip to the doctor.

Just a small one. It'll clot up.

And Che howling, howling, so that the house itself seemed to be pounding with a headache and she burnt the potatoes.

Not her fault, with all of that noise.

Cliff crying too, out of hunger or sympathy, you couldn't get a word out of him when he was like that, and falling asleep before dinner, like Bodhi. And then waking up in the night: Get me a sammich an' some milk, Cleo. And herself pretending to sleep, because she didn't want to be birthed yet out of that warm bed into the cold kitchen, and Dadda getting up to feed Cliff and Bodhi, who was awake, too.

Not *her* fault, though. She had done everything she was supposed to. She, Cleo, had got herself and Cliff dressed and off to school that morning before, like every morning, with a jam sandwich each, had found Bodhi's shoes and Che's homework and made Cliff wash his hands, had fed and dressed Bodhi while Mandalay only had to get herself ready and run for the high school bus.

Then after school she, Cleo, had made sure Che and Cliff got home, rounding Che up from the playground where he was with a huddle of grade seven boys who were pretending to dribble a soccer ball while passing around a joint.

Hey, Cleo, one of them had said. Want to suck on it?

But she had grabbed Che and found Cliff still in his class-room, trying to finish his day's work — Cliff worked so slowly, he needed learning assistance, his teacher said, but Dadda had said, he's in first grade, for god's sake, let him learn at his own pace. Only this was Cliff's second time in grade one, and he wasn't keeping up even though she, Cleo, made sure he missed hardly any school now.

Making sure Cliff and Che got going toward home, and going down the road to collect Bodhi from Myrna Pollard's place even though Myrna said, as usual, Are you sure you won't leave him till your dad gets home, Cleo? He's no trouble.

But he was her brother. Her and Mandalay's responsibility. Her job to get him home, and she had done it, carrying him on her hip up the road and down their long driveway, balancing the weight of him against her book bag, which swung against her thighs – the strap was too long.

And that was the best part of the day, walking up the road from Myrna's, with Cliff – Che usually went off by himself, got home before them – with Cliff and Bodhi. Herself, with Cliff and Bodhi, telling Cliff a story to keep his feet moving, singing with him one of the grade one songs, like *Five Little Ducks*, which he felt confident about, this time around.

She did this, every day, after school. It was her job. She had not let Dadda down.

Not her fault.

WHAT HAPPENS NEXT is that the social worker comes. This woman is someone they have not met before. She goes into the house and then comes back out right away, her little gauzy scarf with its splashes of red and pink poppies pressed over her mouth and nose. She has a lot of long curly hair, like Mam, only it's silver-grey, and she's wearing a jean skirt and an embroidered top that Mam would have admired. Cleo feels sad about this, but can't decide why.

The social worker's name is Jean. She speaks more quickly, briskly, than people Cleo knows; Cleo thinks she must be from Vancouver.

Five children? Where are the others? For about a second Cleo hates her, but then Jean picks up Bodhi, dirt and all, and puts him on her hip in a comfortable way.

Lewis is entertaining the two boys in the back of the car, the older cop says. We've sent another car to pick up the oldest from the high school.

Great, Cleo says. Three-quarters of my siblings in squad cars at this moment. Then she blushes, because that was a very non-mindful and also inappropriate thing to say, and the older cop and Jean the social worker look surprised. But the cop only says: We don't call them squad cars in Canada.

She knows that. It was a joke. It was from the police dramas on TV at Myrna Pollard's. She has watched a lot of these. It isn't useful — they are only reruns and not currency for school conversations. It's Che really who likes to stay and watch — she just does because the TV is on, and Che likes to see them.

They've never had a social worker but she knows what they're for. Dadda said that they didn't need one, at the hospital when Mam went in. He said he could manage fine on his own. I may be an old hippie, he said, but I can manage fine on my own.

That's what Dadda always called himself: an old hippie. When Che asks, as he does about fifteen times a day, why they can't have a TV, Nintendo, why Dadda doesn't have a job in town, but worked odd shifts at the mill, does odd handyman jobs, Dadda says, I'm an old hippie, as if that explained everything. Which it doesn't. Being an old hippie means you don't need the same rules as everyone else, because you are self-sufficient and smarter. But lots of Dadda's friends, leathery-skinned, grey-haired men and women — lots of them work at regular jobs and have televisions.

When Mam wants to go to a party or shopping or move into town, Dadda says, God, Crystal — I'm an old hippie. You knew that when you shacked up with me. And when they make too much noise, the boys ricocheting around the cabin and over the sofa and beds, he says, God, you gang. I'm an old hippie. Can we have a little peace and quiet? You are driving me crazy.

When Mam had gone to the psych ward, Che had asked, on the way home in the old station wagon, Did we drive her crazy? And Dadda had said, No, your mother has an illness. She's in reaction to her own toxic upbringing, and they had all nodded, their heads bouncing up and down just out of rhythm with the bouncing of the car seats over the broken highway, and then when they got home Che had climbed up the shed roof and fallen off and broken his arm.

They'd all gone along to the hospital to see Che's arm put in a cast, because Mandalay was in hysterics and wouldn't stay at the house and Cleo didn't want to, either. At the hospital, Che had asked if it was the same hospital where Mam was, and if they could go visit her, but Daddy had said she would be sleeping.

Now Daddy's going to be in the hospital himself. Will someone tell Mam? Cleo is surprised that they will take him to the hospital, but Jean says that's where the morgue is.

Then she asks Cleo to spell their names for her forms, and give their birthdays.

Mam got to name the girls. Mandalay, because she'd heard *On the Road to Mandalay* on the way to the hospital when Mandalay was born. Mandalay was supposed to be born at home but after forty hours of labour their neighbours had said Mam had better go to the hospital. Cleo was Cleopatra, Queen of the Nile. That was from an old movie, Mam said. Then Dadda had named Che. What do you expect? he had said. I'm an old hippie. And Cliff: Cliff was named after Dadda's father, who had died, far away in a state called Indiana. They had never met him, not even known they had a grandfather until Dadda told them he was dead. He was ninety years old, Dadda said.

What about Dadda's mother?

She died when I was younger. She was born in 1900.

Indiana is in the United States. That's where Dadda was born.

Then Bodhi. After the Bodhi tree, of course.

Cleo is spelling the names, and remembering the years that they were all born in, and doesn't see them wheel Dadda out, doesn't notice until the ambulance doors shut with two bangs, and then the ambulance leaves, quite quickly, but without any lights or sirens.

Will someone tell Mam?

THEN MANDALAY IS BACK, and things shift. Mandalay, when the second police car arrives at the house, leaps out and hugs everyone, weeping, and then changes Bodhi's diaper and makes him a bottle, so that it looks like *she* is the one who takes care of Bodhi, not Cleo. Then Mandalay pulls some chairs out of the kitchen, and sits with the social worker and the older cop and tells them everything, everything Cleo has not. And they decide — probably right there — to let Mandalay have Bodhi.

Cleo could have told the social worker things, but she does not. She hears Jean asking things about Mam, and she sees Jean's face, at the replies: It does not go saggy, like the older cop's, but rigid; only the skin around her eyes softens and thins, and her eyes darken, as if she will take in everything that is told her, and nothing will come out of it. But Cleo knows better.

She hears Mandalay telling about the axe, but she doesn't confirm what Mandalay is saying, nor does she spill the beans about the rest. She wants, she wants to have Jean look at her with those dark, absorbing eyes: *Not your fault.* But she does not say, because of Mandalay taking over the telling, taking over Jean.

Mandalay tells how through January and February Mam had lain in bed smoking and staring out the window at the rain. And about in March and April when Mam constantly took them on adventures, shaking them awake at dawn, come on, come on, let's pack a lunch and hit the road, Mam's eyes and voice full of laughing, and so the younger kids had jumped out of their bed, Yay! We're going on an adventure! And there would be no school that day unless she, Cleo, managed to hide the car keys, though Mandalay doesn't tell this part.

Cleo had used to go along, had used to get caught up in it, but not now. Now, she knew, missing a bunch of school only meant falling behind, getting confused, getting more work to do. And Mam's adventures were exhausting, more than fun.

In April, they had gone hiking on Knucklehead – Mam driving them up in the old station wagon to the park gate, then leading them out onto the trails, where they had got caught in a late snowfall, and Daddy had come crashing through the bush, twigs in his big grey beard, looking for them, finding them where they were huddled in some fallen logs, where they would have goddamn frozen to death.

Found them only because Cleo had thought to leave a note on the kitchen table: *Gone to hike Knucklehead.*

After that, Cleo hadn't gone along – to the mushroom-picking, to the turtle-catching, to the pirate day. And Mandalay hadn't either – she had by then got a group of friends at the high school, and preferred hanging with them.

Mam had been mad – not at Mandalay, but at Cleo – for not joining their expeditions. *Oh, get the stick out of your ass! Teacher's pet! Think you're so smart, eh? Think you're better than the rest of us?* And she had gone back to bed all of May.

Dadda said Mam's problem was that she thought she was one of the kids. She didn't want to be responsible. Instead of being nurturing, she was in competition.

And then it was June and school nearly over for the year and Mam had got up, all lardy-assed and stringy-haired, and chased Mandalay around the house with an axe. And Mandalay had called the police.

Mandalay's fault, for calling the police, then. Crystal couldn't run nearly as fast as Mandalay.

Mandalay's fault, for telling the social worker all of this. Cleo had not told.

While Mandalay is crying all over the social worker, Cleo takes a shovel and digs a pretty big hole in the garden where the soil is soft enough to dig, and she tips the pail of chicken guts and heads – the eyes, filmed over and milky, now, but still staring, into the hole, and the pail of diapers, too, and fills it all in. Then she comes back to the house to find Bodhi asleep in the car seat, and Jean the social worker says, *Don't touch him. Don't wake him up.* As if Bodhi wasn't Cleo's baby brother. As if she didn't take care of him every day of her life.

So Dadda is taken away in the ambulance, dead because they have all worn him out with their fighting and not taking care of chores, but it is not Cleo's fault.

She sits on the short log while Mandalay talks to the social worker. Cleo is so tired, now: She feels that she has been tired for years, and that she will never not feel tired again. She thinks about Dadda: that he is gone, never coming back. She puts her face down in her lap and wraps her arms around her head so that nobody will see her face, and she thinks about that: Dadda is gone. No more. Gone. All of the fact of him, the bulk of him standing between her and the rest of the world, the kindness in his face when he was not tired, the ways he knows Cleo, as nobody else in the world does.

What is she now, without Dadda? She thinks: Mandalay does not understand this, or the little boys either — that Dadda is gone. And that is the real problem, not what everyone is worried about now, which is what is going to be done with all of them.

What happens *next* next, as Che would say, is this: Jean the social worker divides them all up. This is a shock to Cleo, who had assumed they would just stay, and neighbours would help out, at least for the present. That they would continue on as before. But no.

Che goes home with Myrna Pollard, who is suddenly in their yard, wringing her hands and sniffling. When Cleo hears this being arranged, she asks, Why not Bodhi too? He's used to Myrna. But Jean says Myrna Pollard's place isn't suitable for a very young child. Cleo can see that. There aren't railings anymore on her second-floor deck — Myrna's husband Keith took them down a couple of years ago to replace the rotted boards, and hasn't got them up again — and there's also a large hole in the Pollard's yard where Keith took out the old septic tank.

But Myrna has been babysitting Bodhi since spring. And she's handy, right next door.

What Cleo hasn't thought out, hasn't realized, is that she, Cleo won't be at this house. She wouldn't be near Myrna Pollard's place, even if Bodhi were there.

Then she understands that Mandalay has been nailing the future shut for all of them. Telling her stories, enjoying the attention, not seeing, as Cleo can see, that she is making sure that Crystal will never be able to come back. Cleo can see it in the social worker's expression. Mandalay doesn't get it. She doesn't see that they need Crystal, that without Crystal, they will not be able to live here again, ever.

Jean says that for now Mandalay and Bodhi will stay with the family of a friend of Mandalay's, in town. And Cleo and Cliff will be taken into temporary care: which means, to go live with strangers. This is all being decided by Jean and Mandalay.

Cleo says, Why can't we just stay here? And at that Jean makes a squinchy shape with her mouth and says, No, that wouldn't be possible. Even though Cleo has been taking care of everything already, even though it could be okay if Mandalay would help out more.

Mandalay says, *Cleo.* How can we take care of everyone, without parents? And then crumples prettily, like someone in movies, into tears again.

THERE HAD BEEN temporary arrangements, and then more permanent ones. They had not had much choice in what happened to them, though they had made things worse for themselves, definitely, by what they had done after Dadda's funeral. You've really cooked your goose now, Myrna Pollard had said, that day.

And of course Mandalay hadn't got to keep Bodhi after all. None of them had.

It Could Always be Worse

THE MOUNTAINSIDE on which Cleo's house sits is sloped on two planes, so that all of the streets are pitched, and the sidewalks fall in cataracts, with stairs built into them. Twice a week, in mid-morning, she descends this fish ladder, weighted and off-balance, a small child holding one hand, taking the steps one at a time, a smaller child strapped in a pack on her back. They drop down through the tiers of houses – rows and rows of pastel, vinyl-clad, variations on a theme of jutting garages and small windows – to the elementary school, which itself is arranged on two levels, the upper, where the school sits, an octopus of arms radiating from the gym, and the lower, where the field and playground have been occupied, most of the winter, by a pool of water.

In one arm of the octopus is the Community Room, where classes are held for small children. Twice a week, in mid-morning, she makes the descent to the school, to this room, and twice a week the trek back up the mountain without the larger of the two small children, and then in early afternoon, she makes the descent again, with only the smaller child, and the second ascent, with both.

There is a route without stairs, but it is much longer, and involves walking along a thoroughfare noisy and stinking with trucks loaded with fill, with earth-moving machinery, with cement and lumber and pipes. If she has time, though – if the smaller child feels heavier (he seems to change density, day to day) she will take the longer route, on her second trip, so that she can use the stroller, and the larger child can ride shotgun on the way back up.

On occasion, on the second descent of the day, she has carried the stroller, with the smaller child in it, down the fish-ladder stairs. But then two weeks ago there had been invisible ice, and she slipped and bumped down a dozen concrete steps on her tailbone. She had not let go: She had held the stroller in front of her, upright, and the child had not even been tipped. But she had decided not to risk falling again. (Possibly she should have seen a doctor, but the bruising is already less painful than it was. Getting to a doctor had seemed impossible to arrange.)

It is not designed for walking, this neighbourhood. It is designed to funnel working people in cars out of their driveways and onto the thoroughfare in an organized and efficient way, to channel them like cattle to the highway, and then to deliver them back again at the end of the day.

She does not have a car. Or rather, her husband drives the car to his workplace, as the transit system isn't very efficient in this suburb. If she is willing to wake the children up and dress them and put them in the car, she can drive him to work, and then pick him up again at the end of the day. It is an hour-long return trip. She doesn't often do it.

There is always fog, or cold currents of air that flow down the steep streets like invisible rivers. The rivers cannot be seen, but they are tangible: She steps into them, they are a force at her back, pushing her down the hill, or resisting her climb upward. She can smell them, their freight of blue clay, their top notes of iron and dust. The real river can be seen only in glimpses, five hundred metres below her house, a ribbon of brushed nickel.

There is a bus that goes down the main road, past the school, all the way to the plaza where there is a Safeway and a Zellers, a branch library, even a small café, but she does not take the bus.

It is February. It is the last year of the century, and of the millennium. Well, maybe not: Trent keeps telling her that the new millennium doesn't start until 2001, technically. But it is the last year of the 1900s.

The children are her own. The older is four; the younger a year and a half. On some days she doesn't remember their names: She speaks to them using only pronouns, because it is just the three of them together all day, and there is no need for the distinction of names. *Do you want juice? Can you give him the ball?* Only when they are among others, for example waiting outside the Community Room, does she use their names, *Olivia, Sam,* and they sound false, arbitrary.

Herself she refers to in third person: *Mommy has to put her boots on now. Mommy needs to go to the bathroom.* As if any distinctness she has, any function separate from them, is a necessary but inconvenient aspect of the three-ness of them.

At the school, in the hallways outside the Community Room, she rarely speaks, or is spoken to. She doesn't always recognize the same people from one day to the next. They seem paired off: speaking in other languages, often. Or they are speaking English, but what they are talking about is incomprehensible. (No, not quite incomprehensible; she recognizes that they are talking about the plots of TV series. She recalls this sort of exchange from high school, her own willing exclusion from it.)

Some of the waiting adults are very young: twenty-ish girls who speak to each other in a language that she decides is Polish, because it isn't Latinate or Germanic or Slavic. Some are elderly, and speak to their charges in Punjabi (she guesses) or Cantonese, and to each other not at all.

In the waiting area, in the corridor with its children's artwork and posters ("You can be anything you want!") she feels suspended and anesthetized and incomplete, as if she's waiting for a limb to be reattached, an organ transplanted. Often, she isn't certain that when the door opens, her child will be on the other side of it.

When at last the door is pushed open, in a controlled way, by unseen hands, the children are waiting inside in a line, wearing their paper crowns or clutching their finger-painted sheets of paper. Then they are anonymous for a few seconds, very small humans in bright clothing, diminished by the height of the room, the row of adults. There is a time lapse while her eyes travel down the row, light on the child that is hers, identify her, reclaim her.

Then a sort of scrum, because these are very small children, and must be zipped into their coats, have their mittens and boots pulled on, have their small backpacks, with their Disney motifs – *The Lion King, Pocahontas, Toy Story* – plucked from hooks and attached to their shoulders.

Olivia does not have a Disney backpack. She has one from a mail-order company, with Beatrix Potter characters. She has expressed a desire for a Snow White backpack, but she will have to make do with Mrs. Tiggy Winkle and Jeremy Fisher.

During the scrum Cleo waits while Olivia puts on her own boots and jacket and backpack. She believes in cultivating Olivia's independence, in things like this.

Is the playground dry yet? Olivia always asks.

No.

Then their ascent, either up the steps (there are one hundred and seven) with the weight of Sam on her back, or along the thoroughfare, which is also steep in sections, with both children in the stroller. She feels during these trips that she is shouldering more than the normal amount of gravity, that the fog or the cold drift of air are adding resistance. It's a trek, an arduous expedition. Her back muscles, her thighs, ache. Every time there is a point at which she wants to stop, to sit down in the middle of the sidewalk.

And then do what?

These are the good days, days that have a shape to them.

Things really aren't that bad.

It's just the problem of time.

It is not that there is too little or too much, but rather that it presses and stretches erratically. She is unable to predict or adapt herself to it. The days are endless, but there is no time for her to read or go shopping or just be in her head. She is always waiting, trying to fill long stretches of time, but also always hurrying, feeling that something is slipping away from her. Then she feels guilty: She is not on top of things, not organized, not prioritizing or taking charge, but also not being in the moment and present. She is not appreciating this time, which is precious, fleeting, a gift.

The walk down to the school and back up the hill fills time. But it is generally monotonous, and not salubrious. The landscape is grey with concrete and dust and the general leaflessness of trees. It is cold: not cold like Inuvik or Winnipeg, but damp and chilly, so that her bones recoil from it; she feels her body tense, her spine curl inward. Sam and Olivia grizzle, complain. The air smells of iron and clay, from the construction going on further up the hill. They often see nothing living, other than crows.

Once, in the winter before, she'd tried to catch the city bus, which looped through the subdivision only one street over from hers. She'd propped Sam, still a small baby, on her hip, folded the stroller with one hand while Olivia jumped around in excitement. The bus had nearly been empty — only a couple of teenaged boys at the back. As she'd started down the aisle, the driver had released the brake and taken off with a lurch. Olivia had gone flying, had banged her head and knees and howled. Cleo herself had stumbled, nearly fallen, nearly dropped Sam. The boys at the back had yelled at the driver, who had snarled back.

She had been speechless, so shocked at what must have been either gross incompetence or stupidity or almost criminal malice that she hadn't known how to react. She had not attempted the bus again. She had understood the driver's message, or, if she wanted to accept it as an accident (which Trent, when she told him, assured her it must be), then fate's message, as surely as a horse's head on her pillow. Whoever these mostly empty buses toiling up the mountainside were meant for, it wasn't her.

It is her own fault. She has chosen this.

WHEN THEY ARE HOME, they go downstairs, Olivia and Sam to play, herself to fold laundry in the adjoining room. She turns on all of the lights, the baseboard heater: the downstairs room is gloomy, chilly. It is where the television is, the larger one, and the VCR machine and the children's toys. Trent complains about the lights, the electric heat, but they must have light and heat.

The pleasure in simple spatial labour done at her own pace. She folds and stacks onto the table Trent's striped and checked button-down shirts, his khakis and jeans, his white athletic socks and his knit boxers, with her own white cotton bikini briefs and her Playtex nursing bras in their mesh laundry bags, her T-shirts and her jeans and pajama bottoms, Olivia's jumpers and tights and tees, her tiny bright underwear and nightgowns, Sam's overalls and sleepers, the organic cotton onesies, the tiny socks rolled in pairs (She never loses any; Cleo can't imagine how people lose socks in the wash), the striped and fruit-patterned kitchen towels and dishcloths and pot-holders, in their rich Provencal colours, the thick terry facecloths and hand towels and bath sheets, in their rich wines and teals. When the table is stacked with all of the week's laundry, clean, fabric-softener scented, accounted for, sorted for ripped or worn-out items, which will promptly be mended or replaced, she feels a small sense of well-being, of contentment, of purpose, of virtue and virtuosity both. It's a little ridiculous. She wishes she could tell someone about it, though. The goodness of it, and the sense that it is trivial.

This phase, this era of her life will not extend indefinitely. When Sam is three and Olivia starting grade one, she will return to work. So really she has only two more years at home to fill — to enjoy. She should be enjoying them. Olivia and Sam will never be small again.

Already, she is aware of how fast they are changing. Already, she has put away boxes of Olivia's baby clothes, weeping over them as she folded them up, checking for indelible stains of spit-up milk. The little pink terrycloth sleepers, size three months, she had folded with trembling fingers. It was not the sleepers she was mourning, of course, but Olivia, with her wide drooling grin, her alert round eyes, her tufty hair, dark-brown fading to blonde, as if she'd dyed it as a disguise and was letting it grow out, her clinging warm little body. That baby, subject of her every thought, her needs indistinguishable from her own, attached through every cell of Cleo's tissue, tuning-station for each of her senses — gone, lost forever. Even in the past few months they have changed, Sam walking now (though not talking — Olivia at his age had talked); Olivia reading a bit. They will grow up so quickly. She ought to learn to love, to fully immerse herself in, each second of this time. Not resist it, feel such panic and guilt about it. And after all, what is required of her, but time?

She carries the folded laundry upstairs to put it away. In the bathroom, she draws up the slatted blind that shields the small window, and sees, over the roofs of other houses, forest, or at least clumps of trees, and beyond them the scrap of silver ribbon that is the river. It's a view of a far-off land, a land of openness and freedom:

Her mind pulls toward it as if it would cajole her body out of the window, into the air.

She lingers, gazing at the far-off treetops, the glimpse of water, thinking of paths and green and birds. And hears, before she's finished putting away the towels, Sam's wails from the family room. When she comes around the corner, Cleo sees that Olivia has made a kind of box around Sam with the sofa and armchair seat cushions, the pillows, the throw. He is wedged in, a barnacle in his heap of foam, waving frustrated wet outstretched fingers. Cleo plucks him up, balances him on her hip. Olivia looks at her sideways, her new separate considering look.

Sam doesn't like to be trapped, Cleo says. Please pick up the cushions now and put them back on the sofa and chairs. She speaks calmly, firmly, as she has taught herself to do. Olivia ignores her, except for in the set of her mouth.

Now, please, she says. Do you need to go to your room? she says.

The sidelong glance, testing her. Olivia will not go to her room without such a flailing and wailing that both of them will be battered, exhausted. And why should she go to her room? Cleo thinks. She has been playing, amusing herself and Sam; now the play has collapsed, but she is not necessarily done with it. Cleo can see into her mood. I have tried to please you, Olivia is thinking. I have been entertaining Sam when I would rather have had your attention. Now I am to be punished.

Cleo can see the scattered furnishings through Olivia's eyes: great unwieldy blocks. What have they to do with her? How have they got there? Her play has been intruded on; what is it to her that Cleo wants the room tidy? What Olivia wants is for Cleo to retrieve the current of pleasure, to lift her back into that transcendence of play. Cleo can do this, easily, by softening her voice, by entering the game, by suggesting another game, something they can do together.

But she has not finished the laundry, has not (more importantly) had ten minutes to herself, to her own thoughts. The irritation rises in her. She begins, crossly, to put the sofa back together. She has to put Sam down. He clings; he wants to nurse some more. It's only for comfort, and he has just nursed, not an hour ago, but it's easier to give in than argue.

She sits on the floor, her back against the stripped sofa. Sam latches on, eases into the space he goes to when he nurses, a right-brain space of complete relaxation, connection, contentment. She relaxes into the letdown, the flow of milk. A child Sam's age is easy to breastfeed. He knows the ropes. He can do it on his own, practically. She needs only to show up, unhook the front of her bra.

She reaches with her free hand for Olivia. She has to make a great effort to do this sometimes, as if the nerves and muscles in her arm have atrophied, as if she's suffering from some devastating degenerative disease. She has to speak, too, from a great distance, with great effort. Come, she says. Tell me what you're building.

Nothing, says Olivia. She has evidently decided to sulk, to punish Cleo. But she is not good at this yet. It will take her time to develop that distance. For now, she can't resist watching Cleo out of her round grey eyes. She can't resist crawling over to Cleo, to sit next to her. Her hair is light, wispy, falling in fine loops to her shoulders. Trent's fine hair. Baby hair. Some of the girls in the preschool class have thick, glossy hair falling to their waists, already.

A cave? A house for a mouse? A space ship? Her brain aches, as if she is forcing it through a too-small aperture.

Olivia shakes her head. But she is drawn in, she can't resist Cleo's playfulness. Even when it is given with half of Cleo's attention, even when Cleo is not really trying, Olivia will be pulled in, opened, to Cleo's attempts.

It's a prison, Cleo guesses. For a big bad baby brother.

Olivia nods, happily. He kept knocking over my house.

He does that.

I told him not to. He did it on purpose.

What should we do with him?

She can see Olivia considering. Sell him, Olivia says. At a garage sale.

The distance between them annihilated. This time.

Should we sell you, Sam? She asks. How much could we get for you?

Olivia can be seen to be reflecting. Too little, and she'll lose the drama; too much, and she risks overvaluing the thing she is rejecting. It's as if Olivia was born understanding economics. Five dollars, she says, finally.

Wow, that much, Cleo says.

Sam falls asleep, and Olivia says, Read to me, and she leaves the ironing, the folding of clothes, to lie on Olivia's bed with her and read.

She reads to Olivia, and to Sam, every day, for hours. She buys books when she can afford it, and goes to the library and to garage sales and thrift stores. She gets a complete set of Dr. Seuss and *Where the Wild Things Are* and *In the Night Kitchen* and *Are You My Mother?* They acquire all of the Disney copies of *Snow White* and *Cinderella* and *Lady and the Tramp* and *The Aristocats* – the classic fairy tales and the other movies, which are also classics, she supposes – and VHS tapes, which are also useful on long rainy days. Mandalay and other people she knows do not approve of the Disney books, but they are easy to come by. She also acquires more beautiful, imaginative, elegantly retold and fabulously illustrated versions of the classic stories, and of new ones. She buys Margaret Wise Brown's *Goodnight Moon* and *Scuppers the Sailor Dog* and *The Runaway Bunny*.

Olivia wants the same books over and over, and she learns her letters, and by her third birthday can say the alphabet and identify any capital letter she sees, and by her fourth birthday can print her name and words like cat, Mom, Sam, Dad, and can read *Green Eggs and Ham,* though everyone says she has just memorized it, which she has, but she recognizes all of the words from the story if she sees them elsewhere. (These accomplishments please Trent very much.) More than this, her vocabulary is varied, complex, plastic. In her play, in her interactions, her conversations, Cleo hears empathy, flexibility of perspective, self-awareness.

It is astonishing to see language and cognition unfold in her children.

She has nobody with whom she can talk about it. She has lost track of most of her friends from university. A couple of them have email, but their communications are always along the lines of *Crazy busy here!* She is not close to either her foster parents or her biological mother. And Mandalay isn't married, doesn't have kids: She doesn't get it. But she feels, intuitively, that she is right. About this one thing, she is right.

The rest, the complicated business of how to raise children, is a mystery. More than a mystery: a quest, a journey of delicate importance, for she knows, she has read, that mistakes can be fatal. It is not that there is too little known, but rather too much: too many books and articles and conversations and pieces of overheard, remembered advice. She is lost in a forest of conflicting information. And at the same time, she is all alone. She has nobody to talk to, for Trent won't talk about the details of it; he's bored by it.

Her sister Mandalay says: Why do you live out there? Those houses are terrible. They're a waste of space and resources, with their own little yards. You don't even play in the yard. You have to go everywhere by car! There's no sense of community. Wouldn't it be more fun somewhere like Kits, where there are lots of playgrounds, and a library, and cafés?

We can't afford a house in Kits on one income.

Really? I see lots of young women with strollers and babies, in the café.

Probably nannies.

Anyway, why not an apartment? You don't need so much living space if you get out more.

But she wants space. She wants space around her sometimes.

When Olivia was a baby, before Sam, they had lived in two different apartments. One, the upstairs of an older house, had been lovely, with original mouldings, leaded glass windows, a turret with a window seat. The kitchen had been a bit funky, built into a closet, but she had loved that place, had loved the neighbourhood, the walks to the library, meeting friends.

Then that house had been sold, and they'd moved to a townhouse complex, in a good location, but where the units were narrow dark spaces with open stairs, where the baby gate hadn't really worked, and the complex had a communal playground where the tough preschoolers, beefy, foul-mouthed four- and five-year-olds, appropriated Olivia's toys, her sandbox bucket and shovel, her ride-on tricycle, her rubber balls and her miniature plastic shopping cart, before Cleo could stop them, and broke them.

In that playground she could sit – on the grass; there were no benches – and talk sometimes to other parents. She had been hopeful.

She remembers a woman with a boy Olivia's age and a girl a little younger – a woman who had seemed educated and normal, but then had asked Olivia's gender (Olivia dressed, at two, in her OshKosh denim overalls, a green sweater) and said that her son played with trucks and her daughter with dolls, and that's the way she liked it.

Then a woman with two small girls, one around Olivia's age, the other a little older, who was planning to home-school. Cleo was interested in the possibilities of home-schooling, had wanted to talk about pedagogical theories, but the woman explained that she was a Christian, and she was afraid of the values that her daughters might pick up in the public school system. Do you know, she said, solemnly, in the hushed voice women sometimes use to mention sexual deviance, they even expose the children to *meditation*?

Later a new family moved in, and there were two bright and gentle children around Olivia's age who played nicely with Olivia in the play area on the weekends, and whose father would sit on the railway ties and talk to Cleo. The father told Cleo all about his job as an archeological consultant to the city, about the quirky strange things that happened. She knew a little about the field, from her grad work, and up the long stairs from the cellar of her brain she had dragged the ability to ask semi-intelligent questions about policy and ethics and legalities. He was a good storyteller, and a good conversationalist, and it brightened the weekends, or an hour or two of the weekends, to sit and watch the children. She'd looked forward to it. She'd thought of this neighbour, Mark, as a friend. That he was a guy was kind of awkward, but it was all just friendship, a meeting of the minds.

Then he wasn't there, and when she saw the children outside again with a woman, obviously their mother, Cleo talked to her instead. She mentioned the children's dad, that he'd told her about his job. The woman said, pretty calmly, that her ex-husband wasn't an archeologist at all. He worked as a stock boy at RadioShack and was a pathological liar. He'd had visitation rights with the children but he was working weekends now and never made it over.

She still thinks of Mark, sometimes, not with rancour or concern, but with curiosity. His own version of himself, oddly, seems more real to her than his ex-wife's.

She'd been already very pregnant, loaded with Sam, when the resident caretaker had mentioned to her the four-year-old boy, James, who was left outside in the playground sometimes for hours on end, sometimes while his single mother went off by herself. The caretaker lived next door to the boy and his mom; the caretaker's wife brought the boy inside sometimes, if his mother wasn't home, fed him, let him warm up. The caretaker said, sometimes when she's home, and the boy's outside, we see several different men come to visit the mother in one afternoon. They stay about fifteen minutes and then leave.

Fifteen minutes! Cleo had said. The caretaker, in his sixties, had seemed embarrassed then, said no more. Cleo had taken to bringing out Olivia's lunch, sharing it with the boy. She noticed other moms did too. But she had said to Trent: We need to move. We have to have our own house and yard. And so they had emigrated far out of the city.

ON THIS FEBRUARY AFTERNOON she reads to Olivia and then starts supper while Olivia draws at the table and talks to her: there is more time to fill entertaining Olivia. They have read a new book, one picked up at the library on Saturday and hoarded for this day. It's a folktale Cleo remembers having heard sometime in her own child-hood – at school? – called, she thinks, *The Crowded Noisy House*. In this version it's called *It Could Always Be Worse*. In it, a man complains about the crowding and noise his wife and mother and children make in the house, and is advised by the rabbi (in Cleo's memory, it was a wise old woman) to take in the chickens, the pig, the goat, the cow – until the house is unbearable – and then toss them all out, at which point his house with only his family in it seems spacious and peaceful.

What is passed down in folktales, Cleo thinks, is that it could always be worse.

Olivia draws the animals from the story; she still draws as a young child does, impressionistically, not symbolically, and her draw-ings are strange and dreamlike in their figures and composition. She has drawn a cut-away diagram of a house with many separate rooms, each containing one human or farmyard animal figure. There is room for all. It's optimistic.

Then Sam wakes up, and nurses – he is down to three times a day now – and she and Olivia read some board books to him. (He remembers what comes next, Olivia says, and she thinks Olivia is right: They are lucky to have each other, Olivia and Sam. They see each other as full people, already.)

She cleans up after supper so that Trent will have time to play with the kids but he doesn't, really; he turns on the TV and keeps half an eye on them. Once she has finished the dishes and wiping the counters and sweeping the floor, he takes his attention from them completely, like a teenager released from a babysitting stint, and she gets them ready for bed. If she asks Trent to put Olivia to bed, he forgets to brush her teeth or read her a story, leaves her clothes where they fall. If she reminds him, his voice gets hard and petulant: Why is she always criticising the way he does things? She doesn't need to control everything. Don't sweat the small stuff, he says. Let it go. But that just means she'll have to do whatever it is herself, when Trent has gone to bed or is watching TV. Or she'll have to deal with the consequences.

If she puts Olivia to bed first and leaves Trent to take care of Sam, he just ignores Sam, lets him get sleepy, doze off without nursing or a diaper change, so that he'll then wake up around midnight, hungry and wet, and Cleo will have to wake up and look after him and try to get him to go back to sleep. When she remonstrates with Trent, he says: My mother put me to bed at Sam's age with a bottle and didn't hear a peep out of me for twelve hours.

She doesn't say that this sounds like child abuse to her. She doesn't want to fight in front of the kids. There is nowhere in the house that a raised voice cannot be heard.

Sometimes it seems that Trent is missing some important organ or part of his brain. He doesn't really seem to pick up on the needs, the emotional tenor, of the kids.

One of the books she has read says: If you want your man to help out more, don't criticize his efforts when he does. Another one says, like Trent: Don't sweat the small stuff. This is not helpful.

If she complains about things when they happen, he says she is picking on minutia. If she waits until something escalates into a pattern, a problem, and then mentions it, he says: Show me examples, and then, You should have mentioned that at the time, not waited until you were mad and then ambushed me.

She reminds herself that Trent is working hard, that he has long and demanding days, that the weight of the mortgage and car loan, everything they spend, rests on him.

She nurses Sam until he gets sleepy, sucks only sporadically. His mouth finally relaxes. She puts him into his bed, his little crib. Soon he will try to climb the bars, and they will have to take off the side rails and convert the crib to a tot bed.

Then she goes back downstairs and finds Olivia leaning up against Trent, both watching a crime drama in which characters are assaulted and shot and in which the dialogue is violent, full not only of adult language, but hate-filled, vicious.

Do you think she should watch this?

Ah, if she's old enough to understand it, she's old enough to deal with it, Trent says.

She puts Olivia to bed, which requires forty-five more minutes of stories and singing: Olivia is nervous, anxious.

When she goes back downstairs, she says: Don't let Olivia and Sam watch that crap. They understand more than you think.

Trent gets up, puts his arms around her. You're right, he says. I was just zoning out, I didn't think.

Come and watch TV, he says. I haven't seen you all day. Let's watch some TV.

But she doesn't want to watch TV. Her mind has been in a crowded and cold shed all day, harnessed to work that tires but doesn't satisfy. She needs to read. She has a new book, one she had requested for Christmas, and she climbs into bed and delves into the book, which is thick and full of theory for her mind to chew over, and references that she will write down and follow up. The book is on urban theory, a subject which is not (she thinks) connected with her life in any way, but which takes her out of it, transforms her so that she is once again whole and autonomous, and can forget her maternal role. She feels her brain stretch and leap and forget itself: It is just seamless graceful movement through the landscape of the book, its ideas and examples, its language.

After a while Trent comes upstairs and undresses and falls into the bed and lies there, a dead weight, eyes closed, letting her know with his heavy silence that he wants to have sex with her, but she pretends she does not notice this, and she keeps reading, until she can tell from his breathing that he is asleep, and then finally puts her book down and turns off the light.

Aloft

PARVANEH SAYS: Checking for the mail again, Mandalay! You will not hurry your fate that way. She says this in a light way, teasing, so that Mandalay isn't supposed to take offence. And she doesn't. She says, playing along, putting on a girlish voice, I want to see it! I want to see it!

You are hopping like a flea, Parvaneh says. You shouldn't get your hopes up. It might not come today.

Yes, Mandalay says. But I want to see it. They said it would be out today, and I want to see it.

You don't want anyone else, all of those passengers, knowing what it says before you do yourself.

Exactly.

It's amazing, how well Parvaneh gets her. How well they understand each other. They're really attuned. It's lucky; it's so good to work with someone who is always on the same wavelength. It's really rare, and lucky. And it's why they've been able to collaborate so well and achieve so much. It's so lucky.

You know, Parvaneh says, when it comes, we will be unhappy with the photographs: You will complain that they haven't caught your best side, and I will complain that they have given me a double chin, and we will find so many mistakes in the writing, and will be shaking our heads. But all the while she says this, she is smiling.

Mandalay says, I love you, Parvaneh!

You should go home, Parvaneh says. We're past the lunch rush, even.

It's true. She should leave now; she's been at the café, as usual, since five in the morning, and she won't have much time before she has to come back in to close, but the mail has not come yet.

Go, go get your nails done and look at the new spring coats, Parvaneh says. If it comes I will put it in your box. Nobody else will see it.

It's a fantasy that Parvaneh elaborates on, that Mandalay has nothing to do but have manicures and go shopping when she's not at the café. Parvaneh, of course, has a household and kids, and splits her shifts so that after the morning baking she goes home, gets her kids up, gets the older one off to school. Then she leaves the younger with her mother-in-law, comes back for the late morning and lunch rush, cleans, goes back home to collect her children. And then does the bookkeeping after they go to bed. Mandalay always says, I don't know how you do it, and it's true: She can never quite imagine it, the chores and demands that must fill Parvaneh's day.

But she doesn't have a life of leisure herself. She bikes, she does yoga. She also has to do things like clean her apartment and do laundry and pay bills. And she'll be back in the late afternoon to do inventory and ordering and close. Then she has to go to bed horribly early, by nine, so that she can be back at five.

She works hard too. They both do. But it's just fun. As the cliché goes, she can't wait to come to work every day. And it's lucky, again lucky, how she and Parvaneh have made their schedules dovetail so well. They have one server come in for the early morning traffic, and two for the lunch rush, a couple of extra on the weekends, but it's amazing how well they manage, how they have coordinated and adapted to each other so well. What an amazing thing they've made of the café.

She's grateful, so grateful.

She says goodbye, finally, slips out the front door, turns onto Fourth, walks along in the early spring sunshine past the kitchenware and clothing boutiques, the noodle houses, the Mexican restaurant. Garnishes of daffodils and primroses in the planters along the sidewalk; hits of pistachio green on the trees. She is so lucky to have her job, to be living in Kits. Luck is on her side, right now. She's almost afraid to think about it too much, but that's superstitious: She needs to cultivate this, enjoy this good patch. Or maybe it's bigger than a patch. Maybe it's a whole field, a meadow, of things going right for once.

And living within walking distance of the café; that's another occasion for gratitude. It's just around the corner, really. A right onto Larch and then a left onto Third, and here's her home: what she'd always hoped for. Only a studio, but she has her own entrance, and a tiny balcony a foot wide, with a wrought-iron railing outside a big window, and the corner of a view of the water. Inside her apartment, high ceilings, original hardwood floors. Every day, even when it's raining, the apartment feels lofty, uplifting. The tall window is a beautiful architectural shape, and lets in lots of light.

It's true that her bathroom is miniscule and lacks a tub, and her kitchen is barely big enough to make toast, and there is no storage. But she's been lucky; she's been able to scrounge crates and planks, and an old dresser with carved decorations that looks almost antique, painted white, and she's covered her bed and the walls and floors with amazing rugs and scarves and pieces of textiles. Everything's a bit faded, a bit dusty, a bit ragged, but when the sun is shining, like now, the colours look like a Vanessa Bell painting, and at night, with only the lamps on, the room glows.

She lets herself in, goes to the sink and runs a glass of water, drinks it down. That's her rule, before doing anything else. She's learned to work these healthy rituals into her daily life. Now she unrolls her yoga mat, though her body is full of electricity, and doesn't really want to do yoga. She knows it's even more helpful when she's feeling nervy like this. She needs to ground herself.

She does three vinyasas, one after the other, concentrating on the stretching and flexing of her joints, the precision, balance, the flow of energy through her body. The stretch upward, skyward; the folds; the plank and the lunges, the downward dogs, cobras and the warriors. The stretch skyward again. The skittish energy in her head becomes more channelled, more connected. She sees a crow leave the branch of a tall tree in a neighbouring yard. The crow lifts; she feels the push of its lift through its feet and wings. The branch reverberates a little; she feels the precise balance of the branch's swing to the crow's lift. The crow is clutching a bouquet of sticks in one of its feet, and she feels the stretch and tension of the crow's toes and claws around the sticks, the subtle alterations it must make with its wings to compensate for the weight of the sticks. The crow flaps past her window and its glance meets hers for a microsecond, in which she sees its curiosity, its observation of her, reflected in its obsidian eye.

Now present and calm, she drinks another glass of water, and eats an apple. She rarely needs to cook; she can eat the seconds at the shop, the turnovers that lose a corner coming off the pan, the quiches whose edges crumble too catastrophically, the last piece of a batch of spinach pie, or spoonful of chickpea salad, which can't be put out in the morning. It's all delicious, though a little high in the fat and carbs.

Thinking about the shop again, she feels the anticipation coming back, the nervous energy. She needs to get some exercise, to move. She'll bike over to Granville Island, check out some of the students' work, choose some more pieces for the shop, pick up some supplies for herself at Opus. That will keep her tethered for the afternoon.

IN THE EVENING, the magazines still haven't arrived, but she's able to keep riding the wave of happiness about it. She's not allowing herself to be squashed down by Parvaneh's lack of ability to enjoy the moment. It's not her problem, Parvaneh's repression or whatever it is. No: she won't allow negative thoughts of Parvaneh. They are great together. Her vision and fearlessness; Parvaneh's attention to detail. That's what works. She needs Parvaneh, and Parvaneh needs her. She has to appreciate and embrace her difference. That's all.

But she really wants someone to celebrate with. It's too bad that the article is only going to be in an airline magazine. Nobody she knows will see it. (Well, maybe her ex-boyfriend, Andrew, whom she hasn't seen in ten years. She thinks he's still touring, but that the band isn't doing well enough, anymore, to hire private jets. She imagines him in First Class, though, thumbing through the airline magazine, maybe recognizing her photo, her name, maybe thinking about looking her up.)

It's a farfetched fantasy. But she will get some extra copies; she can give some to people she knows.

She telephones Cleo. It should be a good time, she thinks. Cleo will have finished dinner – they eat early – and won't be putting the kids to bed yet. She should be able to talk.

Cleo is excited. Cleo gets it, the excitement of it. She wants to see the magazine right away. She wants a copy right away. Save me one, she says, and I'll get it next time I'm in the city. Or mail me one.

Cleo lives only half an hour out – maybe an hour, if the traffic is bad – and has a car, but she hardly comes downtown anymore. It's as if she is hundreds of miles away. How can she can stand it? There's nothing but suburbs of identical vinyl-clad houses and malls out there. Cleo says she doesn't like it, either, but when she asks Cleo why she and Trent don't get a condo in the city, she says it wouldn't work, with kids. Mandalay has pointed out that there are lots of young families in

Kits – she sees moms with strollers in the café every day. You wouldn't really have that much less space, she has pointed out. Your main floor isn't that big. And you don't really use your basement. And how much time do you spend in your yard? But Cleo doesn't seem to think it's possible. She's stuck, somehow.

Cleo says, Tell me all about it; tell me what it says. She's seen the café, met Parvaneh, discussed with Mandalay some of the menu and even the art pieces, and she asks the right questions, remembers details. Cleo gets that it matters more than almost anything else to be creative. Cleo is on her wavelength, when it comes to creative stuff.

She wants to tell Cleo more, now, about how she can see the café expanding, and how she might be able to parlay her curatorial work in the café – which the article really picked up on – into a job at an art gallery. She'd really like to work at an art gallery. It would be her dream job. (That, or writing for a lifestyles magazine.) She knows she's at a disadvantage for those kinds of jobs, not having a university degree. But in some areas that could be seen as an advantage too, right? Right? She would have more unique ideas. She wouldn't be cut from the same cookie cutter as all of the other visual arts students.

Yes, yes, Cleo says. But suddenly Mandalay can tell she's not listening. There's a lag in her replies; they're not connected anymore to what she's saying. She can hear her niece Olivia's voice now in the background, a little bit whiny, and Cleo answers her, hardly turning from the mouthpiece, so it's like she's saying in Mandalay's ear: *Just go. You don't need me to help you. Just go do it.*

Is this a bad time? Mandalay asks. Do you have to go? No, no, Cleo says, but the intrusions get more frequent and louder. Mandalay waits while she's interrupted again and again, by Cleo's other conversation. Finally, there's a wail in the background, and Cleo says, hastily, I have to go now.

How long has it been since she's been able to have a phone conversation with Cleo that lasted more than fifteen minutes? Cleo laughs about it; she says that the telephone ringing is a signal for her kids to have crises. They can play quietly for an hour but if she gets on the phone, they instantly need her attention. But surely she has to have some time to herself. Rules or something. And why doesn't Trent help out more?

She can just call someone else. She has friends: lots of friends. But of course it's hard when you start thinking about the last time you talked to someone, or the things that might have to be mended between you before you can tell them about something exciting that's happened to you. There are people with whom she's shared houses or apartments, or been in classes with or worked with. She spent quite a bit of time with some of them, before they drifted apart. She might still have phone numbers for some of them, or at least know people who'd know.

The woman with the dark bob, from her sociology class, a couple of years ago. Diana? They'd gone out for coffee a lot, worked on a project together.

No: Diana had been friends with Christopher. What about the woman from the yoga class, the one with the dreads, Yasmin? They'd talked a lot; Yasmin had been interested in doing some painting classes together.

But now a sinking feeling that she'd been the one to drop the relationship, that she'd been supposed to call Yasmin about a favour, something she'd said she could get Yasmin, a ride or the loan of something, or maybe a shared house that had an opening for a roommate.... That was it. And she hadn't done it; she had let it go.

Honestly, it's hard to keep up with people. Everyone moves on. Some of the people she knew were really just associated with where she was at the time: her jobs or courses or housing, and she's moved on so much.

What about someone from the art college? She has a contact there, one of the instructors, who helps her choose the student art for the wall at the café. She has her work number, anyway.

No answer; just the machine, asking her in a kind of distracted way to leave a message. She can try again, but it's not the sort of thing you need to say on an answering machine.

She could call her mom, Crystal, but Crystal only ever talks about herself, can't hold onto the thread of what Mandalay's trying to say for more than a few minutes. Then she just goes vague. Plus with Crystal there's always this undercurrent of jealousy; she can't let Mandalay have rich experiences or shine. She always has to compare herself or start talking about how she, Crystal, didn't have any opportunities.

There's not really anyone else. It makes her sad, that people can't maintain totally open, unselfish connections with each other.

Maybe that's been her own fault, a little. She has to admit she's put most of her social energy, since she was in her late teens, into relationships with men. And she hasn't stayed friends with any of them, as some women she knows are able to.

Tomas, an international student from Brazil, colourful, self-confident, larger than life. Ponytail, dashing clothes. Late nights discussing art and politics and philosophy with his cosmopolitan friends (French, Bosnian, Nigerian, other Latin American). Mandalay had met him at the café she worked in then; he came in all of the time, looking like he'd been worked over in a very interesting way, asked for coffee as if he were dying and only she could save him. He'd got her reading, thinking, listening to the conversations. He'd taught her about clothes. Canadian women, he'd said, dress like they've just left a Mennonite colony. He'd taught her about Lycra and waists. The waist is not the true erogenous zone, he said, but it is necessary: It creates the bosom and the bum. Without the waist, nothing. He'd taught her to wax and to wear high heels – she won't thank him for that when she's fifty — and to wear her clothes tight, like a second skin. He had never expected her to clean up after him, though, or not respected her ideas or wants. He liked talk and sex and music and food. He'd liked people, their minds and bodies. He said people were the same, all over: They had the same feelings, the same dreams. When he had gone back to Brazil, though, he had not asked her to come along. She'd suggested it and he'd said: You'd hate it. It's not the country for you. Then he'd written her from Brazil, on a postcard: He had got married, to the daughter of old friend of his family, a long-standing engagement.

But first there had been the musicians. Three of them: Danny, Clive, Andrew. Each a little more successful, each a little more talented, a little more driven, but a little less human or kind or happy. Like falling down a staircase, slowly, those years.

Danny played guitar, and other things, in a punk band that had played a bar in Butterfly Lake. It was that small and unimportant a band. All of the musicians had other jobs, and did gigs on the weekend. Danny had been stoned much of the time, but not all of the time. In between times he'd written some decent music, and had good philosophical conversations with her. She'd followed him, when he moved to Vancouver to try to get better gigs, and he'd made her finish school, get her GED. And he'd been honest that he wasn't going to be exclusive. Though he'd kept letting her clean his apartment and do his laundry and cook him meals. (She had chosen to do those things, of course.)

Clive had been next: a cellist with the symphony, witty, well-read, sensitive, mannerly. He'd also been in a string quartet that rented practice space in the same converted warehouse that Danny's band did. He'd come and chat with Mandalay, commiserate with her. You deserve something better, he'd say. She had liked to listen to the quartet practice, and had known just enough about one of the composers they'd been playing — thanks to a set of books she'd read over and over as a child, *The Great Composers* – that she'd sounded to Clive that she knew what she was talking about, which she didn't. She just knew how to keep the conversation on the topics she knew a little about, and to smile when she thought he wanted her to agree with him, and raise her eyebrows when she thought he was trying to provoke her. He'd been so self-deprecating in his humour that she had misunderstood the depths of his neediness. She hadn't been living with him for more than a couple of weeks before she saw him spend half a day giving her the silent treatment because she'd bought the wrong kind of orange juice. Then it was two days curled in fetal position in bed after a negative review. And otherwise, tremendously articulate, gentle, sensitive, self-deprecating. Yes. That had been seductive enough to keep her sympathizing for almost two years.

Then Andrew: Andrew had been in a real band, a rock band that people had heard of, a band that was being played on radio stations several times a day, that toured. Andrew, though he screamed into the mic and thrashed his guitar with the best of them, had had a classical music education, and knew Clive from his music school, and had been obsessively jealous of him, though Andrew was more successful. He had deliberately, she thought later, set out to appropriate her from Clive. She'd gone on the road with the band, which had been a lot of fun and then hadn't. Andrew had worked very hard, and when he wasn't working, he practiced being an asshole. He'd been mean to everyone – critical, sarcastic, manipulative – but it had been worse for her: She had cared about him. (She can still, if she imagines his face, the way his hair fell in one sweep over his violet eyes, the way he pouted, feel pangs of sexual longing for him.) She'd also liked staying in nice hotels, in being backstage, in swaggering from the bus to the hotel or venue with the band, in a vintage leather coat she'd found, in very high heels – swaggering past the crowds of girls her age, girls who wanted to be her.

And then one day Andrew's manager, who was also his dad, had taken her for coffee, given her a plane ticket back to Vancouver — they'd been somewhere in Ontario — Hamilton? Kingston? — and a check for five hundred dollars, which was a month's rent, and told her to make herself a better life.

She'd been pissed off, mortally offended: had assumed she was being bought off. It had taken her years and years to realize that the gesture had been motivated, at least in part, by kindness. Someone looking out for her. Then there had been Tomas, and then Horst.

Horst she thought of as a grown-up. Her first grown-up man. He was not actually that much older than Clive or Andrew, but he behaved like a grown-up. He was a chef at a good restaurant, where she had got a new job. He talked about when they would marry. He made her go to school, to improve herself. He would not have an uneducated wife. He was bossy to a degree of bossiness that didn't have a name in Mandalay's vocabulary until she took sociology and psychology courses. He'd hated her body-fitting dresses, wanted her to wear printed cotton dirndls, to plait her hair and wrap it around her head. She'd thought about introducing him to Cleo. Cleo was the girl he wanted, she thought. She still thinks they'd have been a good match. But Cleo had gone east by then, to grad school.

The more she had learned, the less Horst had liked her. And the more he had clung, tried to control her every move, her every thought.

Christopher was a fellow-student, smart and ironic in the classroom, quick to pick things up and use them to make the other students, and even the prof, feel less smart. But he was only alive in company: Alone with her, he had nothing to say. He made banal comments about shows, books. He seemed then blank, shallow. She could have done more with him, she thinks now. He had a sweetness, he was smart. He had become a prof. But back then she hadn't known how to fire him up. Christopher was almost it. She had wanted so badly for him to be it, to feel any passion for him, but he gave her almost nothing, only a sort of hopeless longing. She had started seeing him to dislodge Horst, to prove to Horst her lack of viability – he wouldn't take her word for it that she didn't want him – and had had silent, not very good sex with him. Then he'd asked her to marry him, actually proposed, and she'd almost accepted, because she could have had the life she wanted then, or most of it. But she had been appalled on two accounts: one, that she was even considering marrying someone she couldn't orgasm with, and two, that he knew her so little that he thought they were at the point when a proposal would not seem bizarre. (She imagines, sometimes, that Trent was Cleo's Christopher, only that Cleo had succumbed to her longing for an SUV and a house in the suburbs.)

She'd been so appalled – and maybe so in danger of succumbing – that she'd turned on Christopher with undeserved meanness, calling up shades of Andrew. She'd almost killed him, she'd heard later. He'd had a nervous breakdown, had almost not finished his degree. But how had he not ever shown her that depth of feeling?

Then Benedict, her Swiss doctor. She'd met him at a bar in Thailand: She'd saved up and gone to Thailand. He'd been intense, a piece of burning phosphorus: an adept, focussed, full-on lover, fiercely committed to his work or play, whatever he was doing at any given moment. She'd watched him stitch together torn-up teenaged guerrilla soldiers, then, half an hour later, lounge in the bar laughing uproariously at some story. He rode his motorcycle as if he didn't care about living, went across borders, into the jungle, to treat patients, as if it were just some huge adventure. He would eat or drink anything. When he got dysentery – they all got dysentery – he'd laughed.

He had a fiancée back in Switzerland, whom he said he loved and respected. She believed he did, when he was with her. When he was with Mandalay, he loved Mandalay. He'd *got* her, had understood her in a way that she knew had more to do with him having known so many people and being so open to every experience than their being especially connected. She had no illusions that they would stay together, but later she heard, from a Canadian doctor whom they'd known in Cambodia, who'd come back to Vancouver, that Benedict, on a layover in Frankfurt, had met a Russian woman, had changed his plans to fly to Moscow with her and had married her there.

Danny, Clive, Andrew, Tomas, Horst. Christopher, Benedict. She can divide her entire adult life up into sections by the periods of time she spent with each of them. All of those relationships and each had really been a dead end, in a way, though it didn't seem very compassionate to think of people that way. She had given her life over to them, though: that was it. And when things ended, she had to start a new life; she'd changed where she lived, and jobs, and everything.

Would any of them see the article? And would it be a good thing if they did?

She has foresworn men, for a while, since Benedict, who had really shaken her confidence, though that had been karma, maybe for the way she had treated Christopher. After Benedict she had decided not to get involved for a while, to do more yoga and detox her life and make some money.

It's still working for her, this plan. She has to stick with it.

She is thirty-three.

WHEN SHE GETS TO THE SHOP the next afternoon at four, she goes right to the office in the back, and there's Parvaneh, smiling, and a little stack of copies of the magazine, still wrapped up in brown paper, on the desk.

You didn't open it? She can't believe that Parvaneh has come back when it's not her shift, but not touched the package. Parvaneh shakes her head, still smiling.

I can't believe you waited, Mandalay says.

Parvaneh's daughter, the four-year-old, comes out from under the desk, now. *Noushin*! Mandalay says. She hardly sees Parvaneh's kids; she doesn't bring them often. They're shy and look at her with shining eyes and small, solemn smiles.

Noushin means sweet, Parvaneh has told her. And Parvaneh means butterfly. Such unabashedly soft feminine names.

She is so shy. Is it a cultural thing? Mandalay thinks that other children are not that shy, not that well-behaved.

And then Parvaneh says something in Persian, and then in English: Go play now, and Noushin folds herself back under the desk, and Mandalay turns to the package of magazines.

The writer had come to the café a few times before approaching Mandalay at the counter. Mandalay had noticed her, not because of her notebook — the café is populated at any time of day by young women with notebooks — but because of her attentive air, the way she looked at everything closely and long. Mandalay had thought she was a health inspector, or a potential competitor, but Parvaneh had said, food writer, and she had been right, or almost right. A freelance lifestyles writer, she had said, and Mandalay had simultaneously been excited for the café and struck by jealousy: She wanted to be a lifestyles writer. It was exactly what she wanted to be, and would be good at.

So she had given the writer a lot of time outside her working hours, a lot of attention, a lot of information. Parvaneh had been a little more reserved, but had agreed that publicity was good for the café. It had been a little disappointing that the article was intended not for the Saturday pages of the *Sun* or *Province*, or even *The Georgia Straight* or one of the little Vancouver magazines, but an airline magazine was nothing to look down on. It would reach more people, over a longer period of time. Mandalay had just thought: I won't see it on newsstands. People I know won't see it.

The writer had said she would get some copies for Mandalay and Parvaneh. And here they are: a package of six.

She passes one to Parvaneh first, and then opens the second one, her hands actually trembling.

Aloft/Volant, Parvaneh says, reading the cover, smiling.

Mandalay runs her fingertip down the table of contents, finds the article title: "A Trendy Café in Vancouver's Kitsilano District Bridges the Old and New." That's it. That's it. Page fifty-four, she says to Parvaneh, who is still admiring the cover.

And there it is: the article, the photographs of the art wall curated by Mandalay, the counter with Parvaneh an impressionistic blur moving behind it, a close-up of a couple of their specialty dishes, Mandalay and Parvaneh outside against the steel and glass exterior, and, in a really surprising and appealing photo that she doesn't remember having been taken, Mandalay alone at a table in the soft light of one of the hanging Murano glass flutes, reflected in the darkened window, her head tilted slightly over the journal in which she noted the day's popular items, her hair loosened and trailing across one cheek, her nose ring, slightly out of focus, gleaming. It's an amazing picture: She's never seen such a beautiful image of herself. It's like a studio photograph of a model or actress. Mandalay stares at the angles of brow and cheekbone and jaw, the sweep of lash, the curve of her lips.

It has caught Parvaneh's eye, too. Oh my god, she says. You look like a movie star here, Mandalay.

Oh, delight. Oh joy. This is the best day of her life, possibly.

It's well done, after all. Of course the writer had described to them the angle she'd be taking. New café represents trendy side of Vancouver, and she's managed to get the details right.

Hm, hm, Parvaneh says, having taken Mandalay's invitation to read it to mean read it aloud.

The Seagull, a trendy new spot in Vancouver's up-and-coming Kitsilano district showcases the unique flavour of this neighbourhood. Since the early seventies a village of alternative restaurants and artists, Kitsilano is lately blooming with sparkling steel-and-glass high-rises. The Seagull shows a happy cohabitation of both. Co-managers Parvaneh Inosh and Mandalay Lund have combined a savvy new take on healthy lunch with the fast pace of the new young urban professional in an exciting international swirl of flavours and artwork.

Oh, they got our names right, Parvaneh says. She reads precisely in almost unaccented English – she's been in Canada since the late eighties. But Mandalay is impatient, wants to read ahead, to race through to the end.

There it all is: the descriptions of the clientele, the food, the art, which is for sale, which Mandalay chooses and sells on consignment for emerging artists.

You are happy with it? Parvaneh asks.

It's good, she says. Better than I expected. It will put us on the map!

What will happen, Parvaneh says, if so many people read this and want to come here that we run out of food and don't have enough staff or tables?

Then we expand, Mandalay says. We hire more staff and lease the space next door.

And then when we aren't a trend anymore?

But you can't think like that, Mandalay says. You have to seize the moment! Sometimes she feels that Parvaneh is decades older than her instead of the same age.

Parvaneh smiles. You are right, she says. Worry about getting too much business if that happens!

We should photocopy this and put it up on the wall, Mandalay says.

Or just tear it out, Parvaneh says.

Oh, no! We can't do that. We want to keep these.

But there are six copies, Parvaneh says.

Only three for each of us.

What will we do with all of those?

Give them to friends and family! Mandalay says. Three each won't go very far.

Oh, you may have all of them, Parvaneh says. I will just keep one to show my husband and my mother-in-law.

What about the rest of your family?

I don't know if they would want to see it. Parvaneh's smile is a little fixed now, and Mandalay knows she's pushed too far.

Is it a cultural thing?

There's nothing wrong with feeling proud of what we've done, she points out. And the publicity can't hurt. Business is business. This is free advertising.

Parvaneh says then: Oh, maybe some handsome and very wealthy businessman reads this article on his flight from Toronto, yes, and he falls in love with your photograph and comes to find you and marry you.

Mandalay puts her palms together and rolls her eyes upward, playing along. *Pray to god*, she says, using a Persian phrase that Parvaneh often utters when they're trying a new recipe.

But Parvaneh is closing off from her now. She scoops Noushin out from under the desk, speaks a little sharply to her, and within seconds is gone. She takes only one copy, leaving the other five for Mandalay.

Acquisition

WHEN YOU HAVE SOMETHING, people are hovering over to take it off you. Cliff knows this like he knows not to eat Chinese food from dumpsters or to try to jaywalk Kingsway at five in the afternoon or to reach under the mower to dislodge a stuck cone when the motor is running. Not because the worst has happened to him, but because he can so strongly see it happening that it is a foregone conclusion that it will happen. It feels inevitable, a law of nature. He can see it, a diagram with arrows and equals signs, in his head. He knows that when he takes his money and goes to buy it, the thing, people will smell it on him, will track him down, advance on him, try to snatch one or the other away, either by force or tricking.

He thinks he has a right to have some money and go into a store and buy the thing and take it home, but he knows that many people will not care about his right – which makes it only a wish – and they will try to get it off him, the money or the item. He knows they will be clever and try some ruse. He can be careful beforehand about the force part: if he goes in daylight and walks straight from the bank with the cash in his wallet which he will keep his hand on, straight to the store. And then he has put two good locks on his room, now: Nobody can get in.

He won't let them see what he is bringing back, either. So nobody will think it worth trying. Though some in his building he knows will go in other people's apartments out of habit, or on spec, just making their rounds in case there's anything to pick up. He's lost a couple of small things that way: tapes, library books. His dad's watch, which Mandalay hasn't forgiven him for losing. But now he has two good locks, installed himself, to foil the casual scavenging. And if he is careful about bringing the thing in, so nobody knows it's there, it should be safe.

He has planned it out. But the issue is still getting it from the store to his building. He won't be able to carry the thing that far. If he had a cart? For a second he contemplates borrowing a wheelbarrow, to which he has easy access, but he sees an image of himself wheeling a garden wheelbarrow six and a half blocks up Main and discards the idea. Too conspicuous.

If he knew someone with a car? Well, he does. Guy he works with. But he tried that. He had asked Ray at work, when they were crowded together in the shelter of a glass house, fogging it with their breathing, their sandwiches and coffee, well, Ray's coffee. Rain drizzling down the panes, the sky grey smears on lighter grey. They weren't supposed to work in the rain but they did: The rain didn't let up long enough. They took breaks during the worst downpours.

Ray had said: What do you want a new one for? Things depreciate soon as you get them out of the store. I've got one you can have. It works fine. Like new.

Like new?

Well, one knob's a bit loose but you don't need it, anyway. Pair a plyers will do it.

Does it get all the channels?

Many as you need.

How old is it?

Ah, not that old. Colour picture.

Why are you getting rid of it?

Got too many now. Got a new one for Christmas.

This, Cliff knew to be a falsehood. Ray had told him his family's gifts. Caution now cramped his lungs. Careful, careful. Ray was tricky.

Tell you what, Ray said. Give it to you for a hundred.

A hundred dollars?

Well, do you think I'm going to give it away? Now Ray sounded hurt, aggrieved. Cliff felt guilt settle on him. His neck grew warm.

It's a great deal for a kid like you, Ray said. What are you going to spend on new? Few hundred? And not get anything better. Worse, to tell you the truth. They don't make goods like they used to. Cheap Chinese junk.

Cliff said, I've saved up for new. Thanks. He heard his voice, small. He was not sure now that he did not owe Ray something. And he might be spending foolishly. He had saved up for six months. Now it would be all spent, and what if he got a lemon?

Disgust in Ray's voice now. Yeah, you young kids. Think you can just go around spending big bucks on toys. No thought for how the rest of us are trying to make a bare living.

Cliff had got up, zipped his coat, still damp, higher at the throat. Even when the rain stopped, the cedar fronds still delivered rivers of cold water under his cap, down his collar, whenever he brushed them. He had picked up the hedge-trimmer, slung its unbalanced weight over his shoulder. He had said in his head: I need to think.

You got the cash on you now? Ray had asked.

Then he had seen it, the dark birds circling. That had been his warning, had cleared his mind.

Nope, he had said. And then forced himself to turn, look Ray in the eye. Haven't really got it saved yet, anyway, he said.

Ray had growled, spat.

When he had started working there was more crew. It was summer. College guys worked for the summer, and there was more work: the gardens and the mowing. Then they all were laid off except Cliff and Ray and a woman, Nicki, who worked through the winter, doing what there was to do: trim trees and hedges, sweep up branches broken in storms. Clear leaves from drains. Shovel up snow if there was any. This was Cliff's third winter. Nicki was in the greenhouses this week.

Nicki had warned him: Nicki had said, don't trust Ray far as you can throw him. He'd forgotten. He oughtn't to have told Ray about his purchase. He shouldn't have let Ray know. Ray was too good at weaseling out things. He'd just asked, can you give me a lift from a store, and Ray had been on him for the details. Now he had to get out of it, hope Ray would forget. And he had to find another method of transport; that was for sure.

IT HAS TAKEN CLIFF YEARS to find a place of his own. He'd been in shared houses before: Often, he'd been able to afford only a mattress in a corner of a room shared by two other people, who themselves shared kitchen and bathroom with another couple, on a floor in a house cut up into similar floors. Smells of toilets, always, and cooking, burned grease that seemed to coat the walls, mildew in floor joists, cat pee in carpets. Laundry in the basement (also inhabited, every square inch), machines always in use or broken. Doors that no longer fit. Nothing could be left unlocked without someone helping himself to it. (Accusations, always, of theft, of breakage, and fights.) Twenty-five or even fifteen-watt bulbs put in by landlords who were waiting for land prices to rise, waiting to buy whole blocks of old houses, who were not willing to put in any more time or money than necessary into repairs, who weren't often appealed to anyway, because there were always more people sharing the space than the lease allowed, always more people looking for a space to live.

Two of the places Cliff has lived in have since been razed. Completely erased, the space they occupied, along with adjacent spaces, now filled with concrete and glass high-rises. Boutique shops on the street level, condominiums above. The city is remaking itself from the centre outward.

Cliff had known, almost instinctively, that he could find more space, more affordable space, by moving outward, ahead of the expansion, moving out of the downtown, but he had clung to it as if it had been a village he had always lived in, a village his ancestors had inhabited for generations. He had understood that the city core was becoming more and more expensive, that it consumed its denizens with its overpriced stores, the convenience stores that charged double for a carton of milk as the bigger stores a kilometre out, that the noise and smog, the fouled sidewalks, the fortressed new high-rises sprouting up, growing, like bull kelp, metres every day, gobbling the sunshine – had understood that these elements were sucking out his money, his health, his spirit. But he had not been able to venture out of the city's core. It was his home territory. It was as if an invisible ring of markings kept him from venturing.

He had stood on the sidewalk and watched one of his habitations smashed by heavy balls on cranes: the wrecking ball knocking out walls so that a room he had lived in for months, with its thickly-layered paint and discoloured wallpaper, the plaster behind them, the lamp-cord wiring and patched lead-soldered plumbing, the cracked lino, the shredded carpets, the rotten plywood and sturdy oak and old-growth fir beneath them – were suddenly raggedly torn open, exposed, with a terrible revelation, like an x-ray of some broken creature – and then, in the next swing, gone. Dust.

How a space you had lived in – filled with your possessions and your music and your thoughts – could be eliminated, cease to exist. That was the strange thing.

He had applied at different apartment buildings further out, east, along Main and Commercial, even Renfrew, leaving so much of the application forms blank that he knew he would never be considered. But then, after he had been working for the landscaping job for a few months, he had suddenly got a call from this place off Main, so far south he didn't know the bus route. He had moved up the waitlist. He could move in.

It was a studio suite, which meant no separate bedroom. He had hoped for a separate bedroom. Then it would feel like a real house. But there was a bathroom, with a working toilet, a sink, a bathtub with a shower, and a kitchenette, with an actual working stove and refrigerator. And it was all his.

After he moved in people he had known kept tracking him down, saying they needed a place to stay for a few days. But he did not let them in. He had longed for his own space for so many years that he was resolute.

The bathtub and the toilet and sink were a strange pink colour, like the insides of ears, and there was pink and white hexagonal tile on which grew a variety of moulds and fungi and algae. There were bugs in the kitchen that could never be got rid of, that taught him quickly to keep his food in jars with tight lids. The stove was yellow and the refrigerator was green, and then when that one stopped working, almond.

It was all his.

He'd got a bed from Goodwill, with only a few stains on the mattress. A real bed with a frame and box spring. No room for a couch but he'd found an armchair in pretty good shape in the alley. Table and one chair from someone's garage sale. Dishes, the same.

For a while it seemed that there was no end to things he needed to acquire for his apartment. Sheets and blankets. Lamps. Cooking pots. Cleaning things. For a while, he had felt dizzy with the proliferation of things he owned. He would come back from shopping expeditions with a bag of items to wash and put away, and he felt a kind of disgust, a surfeit. He slept long, heavily, then: ten hours a day, more on weekends.

But he had found most things for a nickel or a quarter. There was nothing in his place that he had not found and brought back that he did not know intimately. Everything was catalogued and described in his mind. Everything glowed in his imagination with its own selfness.

He bought cleaners and a scrubbing brush and cleaned everything. He washed all of the cloth things and dried them in the big front-loader dryers, feeding in more and more quarters, staying to watch nobody removed them still damp to appropriate the machines, waiting until they were over-dry, too hot almost to touch. Then, he thought, they were really clean.

ONE DAY HE HAD NOTICED someone on his floor was steam-cleaning their carpets. You were supposed to do this before you moved out: if you didn't it was deducted from the damage deposit. But the cleaning never seemed to have been done when people moved in. Someone was cleaning, though, an older lady, and everyone opening their doors and grinning, like she was throwing money away. But Cliff asked her: Could he borrow the machine for twenty bucks if she had time left on the rental, and she said yes, suspiciously, afraid of being scammed, of course. Yes if he would carry it down the stairs for her after and put it in her car. Which he did, after he had steamed the heck out of his carpeting and the armchair, years of dirt making a black soup in the collecting tank of the machine. Had gone over the rug again and again, till he was afraid the water – it wasn't really steam, but hot water with some sort of detergent in it – would start dripping through the ceiling of the suite below his.

He'd got his first TV at a yard sale: It was very small and not all of the channels worked. But cable was included in the rent automatically so it felt like a kind of economy. Then he had started watching nature shows and cooking shows, crime dramas and BBC dramas and sometimes old movies in the evenings and on weekends and his life had grown richer and rounder, as if he'd moved to another country.

He does not bother with soap operas – he is at work anyway – or sitcoms, where people stand in a row and say stupid things to each other, and then a group of unseen people laughs hard. He doesn't like the sound of the laughter in his place. He doesn't watch sports, because he doesn't see the point. And because Ray at work always wants to talk about the game. If he watches the game he will be able to say something about it – he sees the other guys do this – and then Ray will argue with him, tell him he is wrong. He does not see the point of that.

He rides his bicycle to work and locks it in the shed at work and in his apartment when he is home. The building manager had showed him, when he moved in, a place where he could keep a bike: in the basement of the building is a room full of mesh cages with locks where things can be stored. The front door key unlocks this door also, the manager had said, taking him down some steps where rainwater was pooled, showing him a side door, painted army-truck green at one time but dented and graffiti-splotched. Inside a room full of cages. They had numbered tags attached: 313 belonged to Cliff. Same as your apartment, the manager had said. He seemed friendly – old, with white hair sprouting from his ears – but the cages made Cliff nervous. There was some stuff in the cage marked 313, and the manager said, I'll have to get some wire cutters and get the lock off. You need your own lock. The manager had said, don't leave anything in cardboard boxes that could be eaten. We got mice here. We got rats. There's openings, ventilation openings, they can get in. The manager showed him a way to get into the cage room from the back stairwell, the fire exit. There was a door at the back of the room that led to a corridor full of turns, past the electrical room, under ducts and conduits, to another door that opened to the stairwell. If it's raining, you can come this way, the manager said, but Cliff did not think he would want to.

Cliff was worried that the previous owner of the boxes and oddments inside the locker would blame him if they came back and found the stuff gone. He didn't have anything to put in the locker then, and when he bought his bike, he was too afraid of the room with the cages – he didn't want to leave it down there. He didn't want to find his way through the maze of underground passages, with their possible rats and mice, either.

So he rides every day, even in the rain, and he carries his bike up the stairs to his apartment. It doesn't fit into the elevator.

His rent takes two-thirds of his paycheque, sometimes more if the weather is poor and there isn't a lot of work, but that is okay because he doesn't need much else. When he has money left over, he saves it. He saved up for the bicycle. He has saved up for a new television to replace the yard sale one, which doesn't work very well. He is saving for a rainy day, so he will never have to beg anyone for a corner of a room again.

He keeps mostly to himself. That is important, to keep safe by not letting anyone know too much about him, not letting them into his place. He feels – in his bones, he says to himself, but that's not quite right, it's really somewhere at the very back or core of his head – that someone is going to try to move into his place, to take over his stuff and his space. He doesn't know why he would feel this.

He has let only Cleo see his place. She had phoned him to go for lunch and then had come inside and knocked on his door; the buzzer wasn't working, she said. It sometimes wasn't. Then he had tried to come out into the hallway and pull the door behind him but Cleo had pushed the baby at him and slipped by. Cliff, she said, I really need to use your washroom. So she had got in and then she had stood and looked around and said, It's really nice, Cliff; you've fixed it up really nicely. You should put some pictures up on your walls.

Can't, he said. The manager said, No nail holes in the walls. It will come out of my damage deposit if I ever have to move.

They all say that, Cleo said. You put some filler in. But it's really nice, Cliff.

He had seen, from her narrowed eyes, that she was thinking about how she would fix it up. The next time he saw her, she had given him a cushion, a big square green cushion. For your place, she had said.

He did not want a cushion from Cleo to be in his place, but then Sophie had taken to sleeping on it, so he let it stay.

THE SALESMAN IN THE STORE is about Cliff's age, middle twenties, and Asian. He doesn't have an accent, though, and his cheeks are plump, smooth, shiny. Would he have a beard? Older men you see in Chinatown have thin, wispy beards. Cliff doesn't have much beard, but he doesn't shave very often, either, so his skin is never smooth. The salesman is wearing a red pullover sweater over a checked shirt. The shirt collar looks tight. Cliff feels a tightness at his own neck, has to run his finger around the neck hole of his T-shirt. It's not tight but he can feel it as if it is.

He knows which one he wants. He has spent the last six months researching. You can get the books at the library, reference section, where you look up the consumer ratings. He has looked at all of the flyers that pile up in the mail closet, saved and compared. Now this one he had decided on is on sale, this week only. He had been afraid there would be none left when he got here, but there are two boxes, beside the display one.

The store's motto is: We don't sell, we help you buy. The sales guy doesn't seem very interested in helping him buy a television, though. Even this one, which is not the cheapest, and has a built-in VHS player. Even after he points out what he wants, leads the guy over to it, the sales guy says, hopefully: Looking for a new computer? Car stereo?

He doesn't have a car, has never had a computer. He would like a computer but he doesn't have the money for that. Anyway he can use the computers in the library. But the sales guy's disinterest or redirection has him doubting himself suddenly.

Does he want a TV?

Yes. That is what he wants. He has looked at flyers and saved up for months.

Also he has already got rid of his old one, the Sally Ann one with the 13-inch screen that was mostly snow now, carried it down the back stairs before dawn this morning and to a dumpster a couple of blocks away so nobody would notice him getting rid of it, ask questions or guess.

Maybe it's a really good deal and the sales guy doesn't want him to buy it because he won't make any commission. That would be devious, but too bad. Cliff has a right to buy the TV. But it's a reassuring thought.

He knows not to take the one in the box that's been opened and re-taped, but to ask for the one behind it. And then to ask for the box to be opened and to check that everything is there: the cords, the manual. The sales guy carries it to the counter. Then there's the handing over of the cash from his wallet: six fifties, two twenties. He's remembered to have enough for the tax. He's never had that much cash on him before – or given it into someone else's hand – but it's a relief too. He feels lighter, now that he doesn't have to worry about his wallet, the sense he had that it was sending out signals, some kind of high frequency whistle or smell, advertising the presence of the money.

He turns down the offer of the extended warranty: He's read about that. The paperwork. He signs. Then carries the box outside.

He'd hoped a taxi would come soon but it doesn't and the box is too heavy to keep holding in his arms. He has to put it down. It starts to rain and he sees the water puddling on the gum- and bird-shit-spattered sidewalk and lifts the box up a little, balances it on his toes, so only one edge is touching the ground. He should have asked the sales guy to call him a cab, maybe. He's nervous, the crowds of pedestrians pushing by, the big box advertising its contents.

After a while the sales guy comes out of the door. Hey, man, he says. Are you going very far? I'm leaving in about five. Give you a lift if you want to wait inside?

It's said casually, in a friendly way, but Cliff thinks: Not a good idea. He shakes his head.

When a cab does come, East Indian driver, it stops before he can wave it down, and then he worries: Was it looking for him? Did the sales guy call it? But it's raining hard now, and dark, and the box darkening, and against his instincts, he lets the driver lift with him the box into the trunk and gets in. Edge of his seat all of the way, watching the route, but the driver stops where he asked and lifts out the box with no alarming deviance from what should happen.

Two-and-a-half flights up. Cliff finds he can lift the box a couple of steps at a time, set it down, lift it again. Thirty-five stairs. They are carpeted, and he moves steadily but without rushing. He doesn't think he has made a sound but on the second flight the door from the hallway opens and she's there, the skinny girl with the sunken eyes, the butterfly tattoo on her neck. She stares at him for a moment, then retreats. He wishes she hadn't seen. Wishes he'd put his coat over the box, hid the printing.

Now his floor. Out of the stairwell, holding the spring-loaded door open with his back while he shuffles the box through. Now his door. His keys. Imagines the corridor listening. Shuffles inside, re-bolts. Flips on the light switch. Sophie sitting there in the middle of his room, watching. Seeing him in the dark.

Home safe.

You're going to like this, he says to Sophie.

Nature

ON A MAP CLEO HAS SEEN that there is a park greenspace near their house, only a few streets over and a little higher. It's not on a street they walk or drive, but it's not far. On a sunny day she packs a picnic and finds their rubbers and they set out, with the stroller.

Will there be animals? Olivia asks.

Good question, she says. Maybe. Birds, anyway. She's afraid of getting lost in the cul-de-sacs but the park is easy enough to find, the entrance marked with a split-log rail and a sign. There are trees, there is underbrush. She can see the new leaves. Birds are singing. Now at its mouth, though, she's afraid to enter the park. The streets of this neighbourhood seem empty, the houses uninhabited. There is no one to see where they have gone.

But Olivia has run ahead, is running as if wound up, full of green energy, and Sam bouncing in the stroller, calling out. She wonders, belatedly, about bears and cougars.

In Butterfly Lake, once, when she was ten or so, she had come face to face with a cougar, on the path. She had walked backward, keeping her eyes on it, the tawny-grey velvety huge catness of it, until around a corner, and then had run.

There are likely no cougars here. Or bears. Just houses.

There is a trail paved in chips for the first hundred feet or so – just until the bend, where it can no longer be seen from the street – and then dirt. Or, rather, mud. It's very damp, the ground soggy, with little pools. She can see why: The forest slope above is running with rivulets. It's beautiful, jungle-like, thick with cedar and fir and salal and swordfern, the ground swathed in almost bizarrely thick and bright green moss. But the path is very, very wet.

Another hundred feet, and she has to admit the stroller isn't going any further. (It's the wrong kind of stroller; she had needed one of the new jogging strollers, with a strong, lightweight frame and large wheels, but Trent's family had given them this one. Trent had not wanted to exchange it.)

The stroller won't budge. It's halfway up its little wheels in mud.

She says, trying to get into the spirit of a challenge, We'll have to go on foot, soldiers.

What if someone steals it? Olivia asks.

She's thought of that already. We'll buy a new one, she says.

She puts on the backpack containing the picnic, lifts Sam out of the stroller. He can walk, even in the mud. He's wearing Olivia's old boots, but they're just a little too big still, and they come off, and he is covered in mud before long, not that he seems to mind. But then it's too rough going for him, and he won't walk any further. He wants her to pick him up. She doesn't want to – she'll then be covered with mud too. She makes him keep walking, and he grizzles.

It occurs to her that if a cougar (bear, pit bull, serial murderer) were to come along, she would not have many options. She can't move very fast at all. She calls Olivia, over and over, to stay closer to her, but Olivia is impatient, wants to run. I'm full of running today, she says.

Hold Sam's other hand, she says, and Olivia does so for a while, but then skips off again.

Olivia! she calls. She can hear her voice getting sharper.

It would be her and Sam, or Olivia. She could take on whatever came around the corner, and Olivia could make a run for it, but it would get Sam, too. Or she could pick up Sam and run, probably as fast as Olivia, even burdened, but whatever it was would catch up, and probably pick off Olivia as a smaller, weaker catch.

Sam sits down and refuses to walk further.

The forest path is beautiful, the light streaming green through the treetops, the new-leaved maple and alder. The moss glistens. It's a kind of paradise.

It's not for her. It's not for her, not today. She picks Sam up, mud and all, calls Olivia once more, trudges back to where she has left the stroller. Nobody has stolen it.

She tells Trent that she needs the car one day and drives into the city and takes Olivia and Sam to the science centre, which has, she is surprised to find out, many interactive displays for small children. She feels a kind of gratitude.

Nipple teeth, Cleo reads from the placard over the display. I totally know what those are. Sam has those, don't you, Sam? But maybe when those teeth emerge, it's time to stop offering the nipple. Don't you think, Sam?

The tooth in front of them has cone-shaped projections. Not nipple-shaped at all, Cleo says. Some unmarried Victorian naturalist's idea of a nipple. Breast-shaped, maybe. Anyway, doesn't "masto" come from breast? As in "mastectomy" and "mastitis" and so forth? So it's really breast-tooth, isn't it?

Pointy, conical breasts: symbols of power. She wishes she had someone to make that observation to. Someone to have a conversation with.

It's a mastodon tooth, a fossilized tooth, which the placard says is thirteen thousand years old. The tooth is broken – a couple of its roots snapped off. The top surface is not ivory or yellow, but deep amber marbled with carbonized black, and very glossy, like polished stone. The top, the surface part, has eight bumps or cones, each with a corresponding root. The whole thing is a little longer than Cleo's hand, and about as deep, and as wide as her palm.

A baby's tooth, the placard says. The mastodon ate tree branches and leaves. The teeth kept growing as they were worn down.

Photographs of mastodon skeletons and artists' renditions of mastodons are displayed on large posters. A skull with tusks, too, but it's a cast.

And the correct name is *Mammut*, not mastodon.

Olivia is up to her elbows in a bin of fossil pieces that has been placed at small child height. There are posters inviting children to match the shapes of pieces with the type of fragment they might be, but Olivia can't read, and is absorbed in rubbing the knobs and stumps and hooks of bone in her hands. She is humming, a sign she's concentrating. But when she sees Cleo, she points to the label on the bin. What does it say? It's almost an automatic gesture with her these days. What it must be like to suddenly be awake to the world as a place of signs you can't decipher.

Let's sound it out, Cleo says, and Olivia does, laboriously, with Cleo's participation. Olivia knows nearly all her letters, and identifies the sounds that the letters make.

The sign says *These are fossilized bone fragments*. It takes them a very long time to sound out the words. Olivia gets bored halfway through *fossilized*, and runs off. Maybe Cleo should have started them with *bone*.

She does not know how to articulate what she's thinking: her quick ephemeral sense, back there, of the fragility of connection to the physical world. Of how small children have it, unmediated, and then it's gone.

Can I see a mammoth? Olivia asks.

No. They are all extinct. They don't live here anymore.

At the next table, the skull of a cat, its fangs as long and as thick, at the base, as Olivia's arms. I met a cougar once, in the bush, when I was a little girl, she tells Olivia. I had to remember not to run away from it or it would chase me. She'd been lucky.

Wow, that was so brave, Olivia says.

A basket of fossilized fish skeletons, black and bony and broken. These from the mouth of the Mackenzie River, in the far north. The placard tells them to look for marks on the bones – marks made by tools, by knives cutting fish up for food. The bones, ancient table scraps, are thirty thousand years old. Ten million days.

Her foster family had not believed in evolution. She was allowed to watch nature shows, but the Giesbrechts would get upset if anyone said, this plant has been around for millions of years. You couldn't have a conversation about it. Once she had said to Mrs. Giesbrecht, what about all the fossils? And she had replied, God must have made the earth out of bits and pieces of other planets, and those bits had fossils in them.

Mrs. Giesbrecht had been making pie: She had squeezed together a ball of scraps, then opened her hand to show Cleo the shapes of the scraps pressed into the ball.

SHE TELLS TRENT she wants the car again, and takes Olivia and Sam down to the market by the river, to the mall, to the petting zoo. There are pygmy goats, with baby pygmy goats, only days old. The goats smell barnyard, ammoniac, not too unpleasantly. Their fur or hair is coarse and their legs short and they look primitive and industrial at the same time: low-slung, basic, functional. Their mouths look mildly discontented, or sneering.

The children are allowed to come into the pen and pat the goats. Olivia enters into this activity with enthusiasm. Olivia pats the goats on their backs and tries to move them around by pushing them, like her toy trucks. She wants Cleo to tell her the goats' names, to read them from the sign over the shed. She wants to sort them into families. Which babies belong to which mom? Where are the daddy goats? The kids are cat-sized with soft blunt muzzles and gangly legs, like fawns. They butt at the nannies' udders, hard, and keep butting while they lip the teats. Sometimes the nannies don't seem to notice and sometimes they bleat, a hard hoarse sound, and suddenly trot away, as if offended.

One of the nannies is pregnant, loaded with a kid or maybe two: They mostly seem to have twins. Her sides bulge like panniers and the kids jostle, inside, and Cleo can see ripples and nudges through the goat's hide.

Cleo has been carrying Sam on her shoulders and sets him down to look at a goat. But Sam whimpers, won't touch the animals, shrinks from them. A kid approaches Sam from behind and licks his fingers, and Sam screams and holds his hand out toward Cleo. Cleo looks at it closely. I don't think it bit you, she says. Just saliva. He looks up at Cleo, somewhat anxiously. I don't think it bit you, she says again.

But Sam is sobbing now, and Cleo picks him up and takes him back through the gate. You can stay for a while, she tells Olivia. But Olivia loses interest quickly, without Cleo to interact with. She sees Olivia try to attach herself to a preschool group, but grow frustrated: The other kids aren't interested in conversation at her level, yet.

Look, Cleo says, when Olivia comes back out of the pen: Look at the goats' eyes.

The pupils of their eyes are odd, horizontal bars that flare slightly at each end, bone-shaped. Letterbox. Does it affect their vision at all?

What do you think the world looks like through those pupils? she asks Olivia.

Food, Olivia says.

The eyes look evil or at any rate like primitive talismans, symbolic shapes whose meaning has been lost for millennia. Of course, primitive is a dubious word. Does she mean pre-industrial?

She needs someone grown up to have conversations with. She needs someone grown up.

▼▼▼

CLIFF'S FAVOURITE PROPERTY to work on is a big estate in West Vancouver. When they go it's for a whole day and with a team, as it's an expedition just getting there, and the place is so big. They take three vehicles: Ray drives the big truck with the mower and the other equipment, Nicki drives the small truck with the buckets and refuse bags in the bed and Fong and Fazil, the two new guys, labourers, in the cab, and Cliff drives the van with its shelves of sprays and dusts and concentrates in locked cabinets.

The client is a movie producer, Ray says. Loaded. They go four times a year, extra for doing the lawns in the summer. There are gates: They have to be buzzed in. Cliff thinks that the gatehouse would be a sweet place to live. They drive up the long curve of asphalt past the house, which is built of cedar and glass, with cantilevered parts, and looks about the size of Cliff's apartment building.

In front is a sweep of lawn ringed by trees: fir, maple, blue spruce, ornamental cherry, with a lower layer of elder and cotoneaster and red-osier and smoke bush, so that it looks like a painting. In fall it takes his breath away. They'll spray the trees for Anthracnose, the lawn for moss and leatherjackets, today. The movie producer says no chemicals, but it's all chemicals, Cliff knows. He means no fancy names, Ray says. Call it copper and lime treatment.

Behind the house, the slope has been landscaped with terraces and outdoor rooms with walls of cedar and stone and even metal. Each room is a little different: The Japanese garden with its small pond and round stones and mosses and azaleas; the Van Gogh, which in later spring will be all blues and yellows: jostaberry and iris and tulips, and open to the view of the sea, so that it seems to hang on the edge of the land; the Lovecraft, where twisted, bulbous, bizarre-looking plants grow out of polished black river stones. These plants are almost all tropical, and live in pots buried under the gravel, and are taken out in the winter and kept in the green house. He can see that this room is supposed to be a kind of nightmare or bad trip. Nicki thinks it's funny: She calls it the Twisted Garden.

But the best part is beyond the terraces: the wild acre. It's not really wild. Cliff must go in two or three times a year and rake leaves, prune back branches and vines, snub off plants trying to push through the paths, clean benches with lime. More, even: Remove a branch here and there to let light splash on a pool of bluebells or lady's slipper; augment moss or ferns where something has rubbed or scratched too much ground bare.

Mrs. Cookshaw herself had taught him how to take care of the wild acre. She said: Ray is too heavy-handed, he'd make it look like a city park. And Nicki wouldn't do enough. Someone would break his neck in there. You're the one with the right touch, Cliff.

They had sat on a stone bench, warming themselves in the sun, Mrs. Cookshaw resting her hands on the head of her cane, which was carved with an owl's face. It's a secret, Mrs. Cookshaw had said. You don't talk to Mr. Edelman about the maintenance of the wild acre.

Doesn't he know we do it? Cliff had asked.

He knows.

Cliff had nodded, but felt confused. He doesn't want it to just be left natural?

He knows, but he doesn't want to know. He doesn't want to think about it.

Then Cliff had understood. He wants to imagine that it's really wild.

You've got it, Cliff, Mrs. Cookshaw had said.

Mrs. Cookshaw doesn't come out to the jobs much anymore. She broke her hip, the winter before last. And she's nearly ninety, Nicki says.

Cliff's other favourite place is quite different: an older house right in the city, with big grounds. It's all very structured, and unified: *Italianate*, Mrs. Cookshaw had told him. Everything is lined up, spaced evenly, planned, even the kitchen garden inside its stone walls. When he's here he feels his mind finding a new way of seeing. It's different than the work of seeing the wild acre double, seeing both what is there and what could be there, at the same time. In the Italian garden he feels his mind floating on the expected, regular, symmetrical patterns of the walls and pavers and plantings. It's as if a net – or a hammock – is holding up his brain so that it doesn't have to worry about keeping upright or afloat or in motion, and can then go somewhere else. It can relax into a different place.

In the Italianate garden he feels his mind finding new openings, sending tendrils of thought places it has not gone before. Questions, maybe. But not the usual questions, like is Sophie safe, or why is Ray mad at me now, or should I sharpen the lawnmower now or is it going to rain soon? Instead, new questions: Does Sophie think about me while I am gone? What is her thinking like? How could I ever find this out? Do alliums and periwinkle and club mosses think? How could we know? And: What was the first thought?

Which are pretty pointless questions, he guesses. But as long as he is doing the work, snipping or digging or raking up, at a good enough clip, nobody minds.

The labourers go at the lawn and trees, mowing and spraying, with Ray supervising them, and Nicki is dealing with the ponds and Cliff moves into the wild acre. He finds here that he needs to use another set of senses, kind of like a different pair of glasses, except it feels more like they're inside himself, like smelling and hearing. He uses something inside himself to get a sense of how everything looks, and how it should look, at the same time. The vegetation is coastal forest: western red cedar, Douglas fir, broadleaf maple as the apex trees. Some trees have been removed, though, so there are light wells, and in the understory, trailing blackberry, mock orange, ocean spray currant, hazel, salal. Then sword fern, and this time of spring, False Solomon's Seal, Queen's Cup, trillium, violets.

It's natural, but just a little bit prettier than a real forest.

As he walks through, he sees a vireo, a warbler, a lazuli bunting; hears the hairy woodpecker on the snag they've left for it.

He has his loppers, his pruners, his knives and scrapers, his bags. Under the trees, he slips into his listening: senses the breathing of the cedars, the slow attentiveness of the maple, the clock-rotation of the sun wells, the dancing of insects. He listens with his augmented senses, and what he hears or sees or smells is *balance*, he thinks: light and dark, height and breadth, matter and space, coolness and warmth. He takes them in and his brain sorts them in a way that he can't explain, and his hands move to excise a root here, scrape off some excess moss there, disappear a clump of opportunistic hawkweed, lop off a small branch. In this state, he breathes in the forest, becomes it, moves in it, as if he belongs.

On his new television he watches *Nature* and The Knowledge Network and Discovery Channel. He watches shows about plant repro-duction, about orchids, about sharks and stingrays, about Kermode bears and bower birds and penguins and jaguars. He has watched shows about Jane Goodall and her chimpanzees, and about Koko the sign-language-using gorilla. He has watched shows about all the parts of the planet, the seas, the deserts, the tropical and temperate forests, the arctic regions.

His favourite are the ones about tropical reefs, about coral reefs and all of the fish and other creatures that live there: lobsters like fancy jewellery, long-spined sea urchins, giant clams, octopus. All of the creatures that look like plants but are really animals: sea pens and sea squirts. Sea turtles, of course. And the fish: the striped and spotted, the black-and-white and the neon, the box-shaped and the tube-shaped, the parrot-beaked and trumpet-headed. He's watched them so avidly that he can now recognize them on the screen: yellow tangs, convict fish. One day – maybe not till he's pretty old – he'll go snorkelling or skin diving in some tropical sea. He'll save up for that.

There is a man, suddenly, behind him on the path. He has on a yellow pullover sweater and butterscotch-coloured loafers and sunglasses propped on his silver hair. He says to Cliff: Ah. I'm so glad to have found you. I want to show you something.

Down the looping path to where the section of a fallen cedar has been left to rot and become a nurse log, just like in nature.

There the man says. Wet.

It's a seasonal pool. The wild acre is always a little boggy there, in spring. Cliff nods.

It would be fantastic, the man says, if it were a little more *dramatically* wet.

Like a little pond, Cliff says, finally figuring it out.

Yes. The man waits.

What is he supposed to say? He has realized who this must be, and guesses what he's asking, but how much can Cliff suggest? He remembers Mrs. Cookshaw's warnings.

The client is swaying a little now. Cliff's guts clench. Well, he says. There is a natural depression. It could be deeper.

The man nods.

Pond vegetation might grow there, Cliff says. It might need – another source – of water. For when the spring or whatever dries up.

The man waits. He has stopped swaying.

Cliff swallows, involuntarily. Maybe – it could be a little larger?

Make it so, the movie producer says. He slides his sunglasses back onto his face, though the wild acre is quite shadowy, and melts back along the path.

When Cliff relays the request to Ray, Ray swears, then says, Yeah, we'll find out from the staff when he's going to be gone for a couple of months, then bring in a bobcat. Should be able to get some new growth started, the damage covered, in that time. We'll go in on our hands and knees and plug in some ferns and moss.

How do you know he'll go away for a long time? Cliff asks.

Ray says: You think he lives here? No. He only comes for a few weeks out of the year. Tops.

▼▼▼

PARVANEH SAYS, There he is again. Different time today.

It's seven; they've just opened, and the first customers — accountants and bike couriers, Mandalay always thinks — are materializing from the greyish early morning streets. To the south and east, salmon-coloured streaks have made an appearance in the sky, a transparent wash against the blue-grey that she'd like to fix in her mind. Rain later. But it's clear now.

Different time? she asks. She's bustling to get a last pan of croissants out of the big oven, Parvaneh decanting brioche. They've had more traffic the last few weeks, have to bake more. Out in front, Josh is keeping the espresso machine going at full speed, Katie has the cash register ringing non-stop, and Leila can't serve from the counter fast enough to keep pace with the lineup. She needs to get out front right away.

He came the last three days, Parvaneh says. On your day off and in the afternoon when you aren't in.

Ha, Mandalay says. She tightens her buttocks to avoid brushing against Parvaneh's, makes her way to the counter. Leila sees her, says,

Thank you, and subtly adjusts her rhythm and movements to give Mandalay space. Next, please, Mandalay says. The man Parvaneh has pointed out from the kitchen door is now two behind the customer who steps forward to order his latte and cinnamon loaf. She glances at him a couple of times, briefly, while she calls the coffee order to Josh and puts the thick loaf slices into the toaster. Not a regular, no. Tall, fairly lean and muscular. Bald, or shaven, like so many men now, so it's hard to tell his age: early forties, maybe.

The latte-and-cinnamon customer moves down to the cash end and the next customer is Leila's and the next after that steps up. Black coffee, fruit salad, oatmeal porridge, egg. That will take her some time. Parvaneh's mark will go to Leila. But when she looks up, she sees he's let the customer behind him go ahead, so that Leila serves her, and he's waiting for Mandalay.

He's suited, like most of their clientele this time of day, but lacking raincoat or briefcase, and his suit is of a different cut and texture than those of their usual clientele. Different colour, even: a colour between grey and black, lacking the undertone of green or blue or brown that charcoal suits always seem to have. Not an accountant or shop clerk, she thinks. His face young-old: some lines at the corners of the eyes but the skin still taut, lacking those deep parentheses from nose wing to mouth, or the sags and pouches that begin to accumulate in the late forties. His eyes are quite strikingly blue, and his gaze pretty direct. She thinks: I bet he gets a lot of mileage out of those eyes.

He orders an Americano and says: So, up with the crows every morning? And she says, Every morning except Thursday, five to one, and there's the tiniest of flickers in his eyelid in response. It's too busy for more than that. When he has his coffee he says, Have a good morning, and moves to one of the small round metal tables and it's too busy for her to do more than note him sitting there, and she doesn't notice when he leaves, only looks up finally to his absence.

Parvaneh, out the door at eight, mouths *See him?* And Mandalay nods and puts more brioche on plates. She thinks: Not a food writer as she'd hoped. Lawyer, maybe. Expensive suit, aura of casual authority. Parvaneh will have romantic notions, but first off, he's not Mandalay's type.

If he's back at one, though? But he's not. Doesn't matter. She lingers maybe five or seven minutes, collects her bag, puts on her raincoat, slips out. Things to do. People to see.

Parvaneh is always hoping for Mandalay to meet a nice man. She gets very emotionally invested, which is to say almost offensively involved, when she notices a customer's attention to Mandalay, or if Mandalay says she's been out for dinner or to a movie, anything that could be construed as a date. Mandalay always says: You can't stand it that I'm free! You want me to be tied down and miserable like you! And Parvaneh says, Thirty-four this year; you are going to be too old soon. Tick tick tick!

It's all said with affection, of course.

Sometimes she is aware of time moving along; that is, she acknowledges that the time for certain things is finite. Having a child. That is certainly something that would have to happen in the next ten years. Or six or seven, maybe. But she's not even sure she wants to have kids, and the window for other things is closing, too. For having a career as an artist, as she's always dreamed. For certain trips she wants to make. For buying a house or having a pension. All of those things, in descending order.

But time is a sort of illusion. She's only aware of it in a scarcity model when she thinks too much about the future. If she remembers to live in the present, she doesn't feel it at all. She doesn't feel any older than she has for the last fifteen years or so. In her body, in her soul, she feels exactly the same. And though she knows she'll die one day, everyone is mortal, the thought that she'll age and get decrepit and wrinkly doesn't seem credible at all. It's not something that's important, or that she should give any room to.

Are there things she'll regret not doing? Probably. But that's true for everyone. And she has done lots of interesting things. She has really lived in the present, really had some rich experience. The Seagull, for example. That's been huge. She's put so much energy and time and imagination into it, and it's a big accomplishment. It's really rewarding. And she knows it can't last forever, but she'll know when to walk away. When the time comes she'll know: She'll start feeling like she's done all she can, or it will start feeling humdrum to her, or something else will come along – something new and fascinating and challenging that she'll want to give her energies to. Because life is all about growth, having rich experiences. She truly, truly believes that.

And maybe even one day – she doesn't long for it now but acknowledges that one day it might be right for her – one day, maybe even a long-term relationship, a shared place. Sometimes when things are really hectic she envisions a cool, white, high-ceilinged studio space, the comfort of simple domestic routines with a familiar partner, someone with whom she's burned through all of the heat and excitement of a new relationship, someone who is just comfortable. But that's way in the future.

He's there the next day, at one o'clock, at a table by himself. He's got a laptop computer out and a mobile phone, but when she looks up from the counter and sees him – somehow he has come in and got coffee without her noticing – he nods at her and closes the lid of the laptop. So what can she do, once she's taken off her apron, gathered her bag and coat, but walk over to him.

He pulls out a chair, and she sits. Duane, he says. And you're Mandalay.

So he did see the article, has come looking for her, perhaps.

So, he says. His voice is pleasantly deep, has a timbre of playfulness, of relaxed confidence. Mandalay, eh? That's a city in Myanmar.
Burma. I've been there. Have you?

In fact, she has. She doesn't know anyone else who has. Myanmar
is not a safe place these days to go. Three years ago, she says. She'd
gone in a little plane from Rangoon, with Benedict, her Swiss doctor
working for *Médecins Sans Frontières*. He's said that it wasn't safe,
but that it was her own head. She'd met him in Thailand, had been
determined to go to the city she'd been named after. She tells this
to Duane.

He nods. He had been three years before that. Heavily guarded
expedition, he says. Some Canadian mining exploration company.
They'd decided not to invest, after all. At the time.

One part of her mind pricks up at mining exploration. Bad, of
course. Exploiting natural resources, third world countries. Environ-
mental piracy. So you're a — mining engineer? she asks.

Nope. Just a lawyer. Corporate law.

It's very hard, she thinks, to have a friendly conversation with
someone when everything you've known about them is bad, according
to everything you believe in.

And so you have already decided that I'm a terrible, rapacious,
irresponsible, exploitative person, Duane says, easily, pleasantly.
He might even have a twinkle in his eye.

She knows how this story is supposed to go. At fourteen, she'd
been in a foster home with a woman who had a room in her house
completely full of bookcases of Harlequin Romance novels. Mandalay,
basically under house arrest, had read through not all of them but a
pretty good swathe, averaging about two a day. But since then she's
done some women's studies courses and she knows exactly what's
wrong with the story, too. Why it doesn't work.

Are you? she asks.

He says, If you've been here since five you probably want to get out. Do you?

She doesn't need to glance outside to know it's raining.

I have a very large umbrella, he says. And there's a decent Thai restaurant three blocks from here if you want to trip some sensory memory.

There is no logical reason for not doing this. She can feel Parvaneh's eye on her as she moves through the door he's holding open, holds it open in turn for him while he unsheathes the black umbrella.

Climbing

DINNER AT THE HOUSE of one of Trent's colleagues. Cleo is pleased about it. She has not been to a social event, she thinks, in nearly a year. They had missed Trent's firm's Christmas party because they'd all had the flu. What a holiday that had been — they had been sick, one after the other, all month, and by Christmas Eve she hadn't got dressed for a week, and Trent hadn't got out of bed for two days. On Christmas Day Mandalay and Cliff had come on the bus and Mandalay had made soup and done load after load of laundry — the children had been vomiting — and made Cleo have a hot bath and sit over the steamer, and Cliff had watched kids' shows all day with Olivia and Sam: *Frosty* and *Rudolph* and *A Christmas Carol*, all of it, while Trent and Cleo had got some sleep. Though sometimes, secretly, she thinks of it as her favourite Christmas ever: No gift-opening, except for Olivia, who'd brought the flu home from preschool and was over it the most quickly, and no cooking a big meal, just Mandalay and Cliff in the house, but without the obligation to entertain them, and the quiet, and Mandalay's soup. In the hot bath, she'd been able to read for an hour. Trent hadn't been very happy, though.

Now on this Saturday she hasn't been out for so long she actually feels anxious. Should they bring flowers or wine?

How about dessert, Trent asks. There's never enough dessert. Make that chocolate thing.

No, she's pretty sure you don't bring dessert to a dinner party unless it's pot luck. Anne will have planned the meal out, she says. It's kind of insulting to bring something.

Besides, for once, just once, she would enjoy not having to cook.

Are you getting dressed up, Trent asks. I don't think we need to dress up, do we?

She has put on her one pair of nice jeans and a blue and purple paisley shirt. She would have liked to wear a sort of flowing knit dress she has, but she knows Sam will want to nurse, and she can't very well do that in a pullover dress. She regrets the dress, though – has imagined herself elegantly seated in an armchair, with a glass of wine. The shirt will have to do. She has curled her hair under, put on a little mascara, eyebrow pencil.

She says, What do you mean, dressed up? I'm wearing jeans and a button-up shirt. Should I go in my baby-spit stained sweats?

You don't have to get so angry, he says, angrily.

On the way to his colleague's house he says: At least Anne and Doug don't have a big fancy yard, and Olivia won't fall into the pond.

Anger flicks at her again. Last summer, they'd been invited to a barbecue at the house of one of Trent's senior partners, Andy. The house had been in a part of Vancouver that Cleo didn't know, a neighbourhood of grand, older, well-kept-up houses with large lots and mature, expensive, finicky trees – magnolia and thread cedar and Japanese maple – and laurel hedges and fishponds and mosaic-tile terraces. The whole office had come. At one point, Cleo had been sitting in a deck chair having a glass of wine and feeding Sam and talking to one of the junior partners, and she'd had the feeling that something had shifted, and had looked around for Olivia, who wasn't there. Excuse me, Cleo had said, standing up, pulling down her shirt under the shawl, but before she was completely on her feet, there was a splash at the pond, the sound so distant and tiny that it might have been a water drop falling.

Somehow she had passed Sam off to the junior partner and run very quickly to the pond, which was quite far away: It was a big lot. Olivia had gone right under, but she had already regained her footing, was trying to climb out. She can still see her, the scene imprinted on her memory. Duckweed in Olivia's hair, and she had been clutching the pink blossom of a water lily. Cleo had grabbed her, hauled her out roughly, and Olivia had started to cry. Trent had walked up then, hissed at her, white-lipped: Why weren't you watching her?

She can't believe he would bring that up. Maybe this time you'll take your turn watching Olivia, she says.

What's that supposed to mean?

So they arrive in a fugue of suppressed snarls.

This house is less grand than Andy's where they'd had the barbecue (she remembers the white tile on the floor, the sea-colours of aqua and blues on the walls, the pretty mullioned windows of the bathroom in which she had changed Olivia into the spare outfit she always brought along in the diaper bag), but grand enough, with cedar siding and two big decks, vaulted ceilings and enormous view windows and a kitchen into which Cleo and Trent's entire main floor could probably fit.

They're the first to arrive, except for the older single colleague who's always first. (Why had Trent chivvied and rushed them to get going?) There's a bit of an awkward time, as Doug and Anne are still preparing some food (Why invite people for six, if you don't really want them to come till seven?) but then the rest of the guests come. There are no other children there but Anne and Doug's own two, teenagers. The boy disappears quickly, after being made to say hello, but the girl, older, stays around, plays with Sam a little. Anne and Doug make a fuss of Sam and Olivia; we're starved for little kids around here, they say. Cleo does not believe this.

They have gifts for the children, or Anne does: items that Cleo sees add up to about three times what she has spent on the flowers she has brought. There are books for both of them, a clever board book with mirrors for Sam, a pop-up illustrated fairy tale book for Olivia. There is a brightly-coloured toy for Sam, the kind you get at home educational toy parties, with parts that move and rattle and slide into each other: It's perfect, Cleo has to admit. And for Olivia, a beribboned gift bag full of small items: small sparkly hair clips and bracelets, sticker books, clear plastic cases that open to release tiny scented dolls, pastel-coloured ponies with tails and manes that can be brushed with miniature brushes. Olivia is enchanted; she says, Oh! Oh! Oh! in a breathy voice. Cleo has never thought to give Olivia things like that herself. She almost has to repress a little jealousy.

The talk at these parties is largely work talk, though there are partners who aren't in the profession. Talk about local politics does interest Cleo, and she tries to join in, to ask intelligent questions. She has nothing at all to contribute to the other conversations, which are about where people's children are going, or planning to go, to university, about their own university days, during which they seemed to do little but party, and yet which culminated in dozens of appealing job offers, their trips to Hawaii or Mexico or France, their kitchen renovations. They're all about ten or fifteen years older than her and Trent; the firm had not hired for some time before Trent joined it.

She thinks: They are a different generation, the baby boomers; they come from a golden age that won't appear again, likely. It won't appear for her and Trent, who have begun working too late, had their children too late, bought into the now inflated housing market too late.

She enjoys being out, though. Trent's colleagues are kind to her. They are friendly, they have good manners, they make sure she is included, they remember her interests.

Sam is passed around, exclaimed over, dandled and played with. The most severe and unsentimental of Trent's colleagues plays round-and-round the garden and something called fly-away dickie-birds with Sam, who looks back over his shoulder at Cleo, his face anxious. She's beginning to see an anti-social personality emerging in Sam: Whereas Olivia is outgoing, and becomes mannered, almost too graceful and adult, in public, Sam is very shy, very clingy, hating to be the centre of attention. She sees Trent's colleague give him up to the teenager quite quickly. She should probably go rescue him. She will, in a few minutes. After she's been able to sit with her glass of wine, just a moment more.

And then there's a thud, a crash, a too-long pause and a wail, Sam's wail, on a note she's never before heard. The thud replays itself in her head almost instantly: the sound of flesh and bone on something hard.

Sam has climbed up on a kitchen chair, tipped it over backward, hit his head on a corner of a wall on the way down. He has a furrow like a dent in the middle of his forehead, a vertical indent that wasn't there before, and he's screaming at an unfamiliar pitch and volume. Doug gets to him first, picks him up, hands him to Cleo. Trent tries to take him from her. Someone passes Cleo a package of frozen peas (frozen peas?) and says to put them on Sam's forehead. There are a couple of nervous jokes, but everyone is surprisingly calm. After a while, one of the wives, a nurse, asks to have a look at Sam. See there, she says. Bump coming up nicely. That's what we like to see.

We do?

Swelling outward, not inward, she says. She is very, very calm. They are all discussing whether Sam should be taken to emergency, very, very calmly.

Sam's screams subside, then turn into sporadic hiccupping sobs. He begins to nuzzle; Cleo carries him to a quieter corner of the living room, sits, opens her shirt. Tears flow down her face with the milk let-down. She has seen the end of things, the cataclysm has passed by in front of her eyes. How can she survive this?

That's some house, eh, Trent says on the way home. He estimates what it is worth, what the taxes are, the cost of the lawn and garden maintenance, the heat bill. She thinks he's trying to transform something, to turn his admiration for the house, his desire to have a house like that himself, into something else: something like disdain or scorn.

I don't know why, she says, more expensive houses have better-proportioned rooms and windows and nice wide baseboards and trim.

Because, Trent says, they're more expensive.

No, she says. I mean, those things can't cost that much more. Why not put them in smaller, less expensive houses? Why not think out cheaper houses a little more, make them look a little more appealing?

They're cheaper because they're not as nice, Trent says.

No. I mean, why are they not as nice? Why do they have to be less attractive? Why can't they just be, oh, a bit smaller, use less expensive materials? Why do they have to be – stingy – too?

Well, if you want a fancy house, Trent says, his pleasant tone vanishing again, you'll have to think about getting a job again soon.

That is not what she meant, not what she meant at all. But it's pointless to keep it going.

After a while, he says, What were you doing off in the corner with Andy Dalgleish?

Nothing, she says. He brought me my wine, when I was having to comfort Sam.

Did you ask him to?

No, he just did, she says. He was just being kind.

He wanted to see your boobs.

She had predicted that statement so accurately that she congratulates herself.

He's losing his edge, old Andy, Trent says. He's letting the big stuff go to the other partners, the juniors, now. He's wearing out, I guess.

There's nothing to say to this.

After a while, she says, I talked to Kate Jensen about work.

Oh yeah? Trent sounds interested.

I told her, I was looking for fall the year after next, and maybe for part-time, at first.

Now why would you do that, Trent says angrily. Why would you do that? Do you want to live in poverty forever? Do you want me to work my ass off supporting you? You always said you'd work. Were you lying? I'm warning you, you'd better get your act together. Maybe you should look for a job at the mall, or something.

She's aware that Olivia and Sam are both awake, listening, in the dusk inside the car.

Please don't use that tone of voice to me, she says, neutrally. We'll talk about this later.

There's a wailing, then, behind them, of a siren, the flashing of lights. Trent pulls to the side, but the vehicle pulls right up behind him, stays there as Trent swears, pulls right over, stops the SUV. The red and blue lights pulse through the windows.

Were you speeding, Dad? Olivia asks, in her clear, almost adult voice.

Just the marriage police out again, Trent says, before he presses the button for the window to open, and Cleo snorts in spite of herself, and suddenly remembers why she had agreed to date him, to sleep with him, to marry him.

▼▼▼

ONE OF THE NEW CLIENTS walks up to Cliff while he's trimming her lawn edges and says: This big whack of lawn, it's such a waste of space and water, don't you think?

He doesn't know what to say.

I thought maybe you guys would have some other ideas.

At this point he should refer the client to Ray, he knows that, but because of his encounter with the movie producer, and because the day before he was dreaming in the Italian garden, he forgets this basic rule, and he says: Well, you could put in a sunken terrace, about two-thirds of the way down, like *here*, about so big, with pavers and big pots of herbs and orange and fig trees, and a couple of benches.

And the client's face just lights up then: She gets it. And the energy of her getting his idea is like someone's flipped on some stadium lights in his brain. He says, though he knows he shouldn't, Do you have a piece of paper? And she goes into the house and comes out with a pad of graph paper and a pencil, and he draws it, counting off squares in his head, imagining a berm here, a tall, light, airy tree – cascara, maybe? – here, calculating the angle of the sun, the heat that would collect in this spot, if it were recessed into the ground, if it were partially shaded.

When Ray comes up to them, he says, in the softest voice Cliff has ever heard him use: What are you doing, Cliff? And his heart almost stops, and then starts in like a pavement cutter. Because he knows that he's in that much trouble.

Only in the truck, afterward, of course.

You do not do that, Ray screams. You do not ever do that again. You do not dream up stuff for clients. That is not your job, and it never will be. If I see you do that again, you'll be out of here so fast that it'll take your nuts two days to figure out which way you went and catch up to you. *Capiche*?

He is sorry. He is not sorry.

Mrs. Cookshaw comes out to the sheds in a taxi. She says, Clifford, the client likes your idea. But you can't do this. You have to take smaller steps. You can't jump up just because you feel like it. And you can't antagonize Ray.

He says he understands.

Ray says: We had planned to design a maze for the client, in that space. A labyrinth, in yew. They're big now, and we can do a lot more planting and then there's the pruning that will be necessary, and we can make a lot more money out of this place. Your ideas, those, they don't bring in money. They're useless. Got it?

He gets it.

I wouldn't say *useless*, Mrs. Cookshaw says.

But Ray would. Anyway, he gets it.

▼▼▼

THERE'S A SONG Mandalay keeps hearing on the radio in shops and cafés this spring. It's very much a pop song, with a quick bouncy tune and catchy, but inane, maybe silly lyrics. She hears people sing it under their breath sometimes. She has to disapprove of the lyrics. They're cheeky, playful, but they also represent some deplorable sexism. The singer, or the singer's persona, is articulating a pretty blatant promiscuity, listing the names of his girlfriends as if these women were so many accessories or toys.

Mandalay hears Duane singing an adulterated version of it almost under his breath as he's opening his car door for her: *A little bit of Mandalay in my life*. She has to make herself scowl at him.

What's the matter?

Sexist?

Ah, it's just playful.

If a woman were singing it, she'd be called a slut.

It's tongue-in-cheek.

That doesn't make it okay.

It's making fun of male fantasy. Listen to the lyrics.

I think you're wrong.

I think *you're* wrong.

All of this said smiling at each other from the comfortable leather bucket seats of his car. He hasn't started the engine yet, or even put on his seatbelt; is just sitting there half turned to her. She would say his smile is goofy, but she's aware hers is probably a reflection of it.

The thing about Duane is his personal or social honesty, which isn't the common, uncouth disagreeableness that most people think of as honesty, which is really just a blunt instrument of aggression, another way to package their projections and insecurities, their jealousies and resentment and lack of generosity.

Most people, Mandalay thinks, who pride themselves on being brutally honest in the social sense – people who will say they don't like moussaka, when that's what you've made for dinner, or tell you that your outfit isn't flattering, or that you hurt their feelings last week when you made that comment about Georgia O'Keeffe – those people aren't really that invested in being honest, but rather are trading off the social contract which allows all individuals a little bubble of comfortable delusion for the pleasure of putting someone down. That's all.

Real honesty, on the other hand, requires two things: first, a really clear, unflinching knowledge of one's self, one's hang-ups, fears, motivations, neuroses, triggers – and second, the ability to genuinely not give a fuck. Which in itself requires a certain amount of self-acceptance.

That's what she's learning about Duane. It takes a certain amount of getting used to.

She asks him if he wants to walk along the seawall, Sunday morning, and he says No: too many people. She asks if he'd like to have dinner at the Naam. And he says, No: good student food but I like things more nuanced now. Dinner at her house? No. No point, he says, unless you're a really fine chef, which I assume you're not, and even then I don't want to watch you cook. Breakfast, maybe, he says. If I sleep over. Almost a wink. Movie? Maybe, he says. I'm choosy.

String quartet at the Queen Elizabeth? No: no chamber music in large public venues. Even though we have amplification these days? No: it's about style and tone, not volume.

No to a picnic in False Creek: all goose shit and diesel. But yes to ripe strawberries and brioche from *la Baguette and l'Echalote,* eaten in his car on Grouse Mountain. Yes to the symphony, or some performances of it. No to the opera. Not here, at least. (She thinks of Clive, the classical musician she had dated for a while, and sends a little mental bubble of gratitude toward him, for educating her a little bit about music. Leaving her with some cultural capital, as Christopher, another of her boyfriends, would have called it.)

You're a snob, she says. It's all very well, when you can afford only the best.

It's not about money, he says. It's about quality of experience. Sometimes that costs more.

Almost always, it costs more.

Possibly. For me it's really about time.

Time?

There's only so much of it. Why spend it on things that aren't really great experiences?

I guess, she says, that people enjoy different things.

True, he says. But for me, there's a difference. Quality.

Isn't that subjective, really? Don't we just assign values to things?

Well, he says. Think about these strawberries. Good, yes?

They are really good. Sweet, more intense of flavour than she's had for a long time.

Where do you think they came from?

Someone's garden?

Ha, he says. You're right. And where do most strawberries come from?

Huge farms. Here or in California. And they're bred for fast growth and size and keeping time, and picked before they're ripe.

Exactly. And what do they taste like?

Well. Sometimes better than others. Not as good as these.

Yes. And these strawberries, I got from a man who grows them in his yard, and sells them for about five times as much as supermarket strawberries, and you really have one day, maybe two, after they're picked to eat them.

And you can afford them because you bill your time at six hundred dollars an hour.

Just for starters, he says, grinning. But anyone can buy good strawberries. If you're going to eat strawberries, eat the best straw-berries you can find.

But that's – elitist or something.

Is it? What if everyone just started refusing second-rate straw-berries?

But that's just what she thinks. Everyone should eat better-quality, locally-grown food. Only there's something missing, a place she can't quite put her finger on, where his argument doesn't hold together completely.

Mandalay expects a modern, minimalist, self-consciously mas-culine steel-and-glass tower, but his building is slightly older, not as high. He lives on the twentieth floor. There's only one above him, the penthouse. There are tall, wrap-around windows, but the walls are painted a sort of café-au-lait, and framed in wide white trim. The floors are darkish wood, and the sofas have a softness to them – they aren't the rolled-arm, tufted and studded monstrosities of Trent and

Cleo's house, but they aren't all hard lines and steel tubing, either. The leather is aged-looking, a sort of darker grey-brown, like an ancient motorcycle jacket, maybe. There are some large paintings — abstractions that look like city skylines with water reflections, if you were squinting at the skyline, or seeing it through rain. Or tears. There are pillows and a rug in browns and greens and greys. From the windows she can see half the city, it seems: the lighted globe of the science centre, the Granville and Burrard Street bridges, the ships off English Bay, the sails of Canada Place, the great dark swath that is the park.

Go ahead, he says, laughing. Look around.

The kitchen and bathrooms are not ostentatious, but have sturdy, simple-lined cabinets, lots of lighting. There are two bathrooms: an ensuite and another full bathroom. Two bedrooms: The smaller contains a desk, a couple of bookcases, a computer. In the larger bedroom there's a walk-in closet and a king-sized bed. One wall is papered with a black-and-white graphic of leafless trees, and the bed is covered with a duvet in a soft, mossy green with light in it: not olive, but brighter. At first she thinks it's mottled, but then sees that there's a pattern of tiny leaves. The bed linens are very white.

Are you going to tell me what you'd change about the place? he asks.

What? No, she says. It's beautiful.

She's picked up the warning in his voice: Other women before you have made this mistake; don't do it. There are some strange models out there, she thinks, for responding to a man's apartment. There's the women's porn model, where everything is incredibly luxurious and desirable, but too hard-edged and masculine. The woman has to appreciate the money but envision her own things in place. There's kind of a pathos, a Jay Gatsby angle to this, too: I was so poor, and I've raised myself up by my own guts and smarts and sweat,

KAREN HOFMANN

▸ 99 ◂

and now look at all of the pretty shirts I have, and the fine closet to store them in. Then there's the horror version: Bluebeard's castle, which these days probably just means a dungeon in the basement, or the evidence of complete slobbery that emerges: weeks' worth of crusty laundry that's been stuffed into the closet, under the bed. The woman doesn't notice it until too late, and then she's expected to deal with it.

It's an odd experience, as a woman, to come into a man's place and admire it but not want it, not expect to move into it, to have to make it her home.

You don't want me to put up some prettier art? A painted armoire in the bedroom? Some little carved African tables?

There's an edge in his voice that makes it difficult for her not to react defensively. I'm not those women, she wants to protest. Or: Why do you care so much about your precious space? She's been standing; she sits, now, on the sofa, whose leather seems buttery to the touch. Smiles up at him. Definitely, she says, the little tables. There's nowhere to put pieces of driftwood or the glass elephant I was going to get you. And some nice plates with cute pictures of cats would soften up your kitchen, don't you think? And what about a crocheted cover for your spare toilet roll?

It's not what he's been getting at, she knows that. She's deflecting like crazy.

He looks at her quizzically. He's made drinks, brought them over to the couch. Old-fashioned, he says. I only seem to ever have the makings for one kind of drink in the house at one time.

So this is the drink of the week?

Of the month, sadly, he says. I don't entertain much.

She says, I like your place. It's clean and has appealing colours and lines and is – definite. It feels like you.

Then she says: Way too tidy, though.

A little inclination of his head, then, as if something he has been expecting or hoping has been confirmed. He touches his glass to hers, deliberately, then puts his down, on the low table, and takes hers from her hand, and puts it down also, and then pulls her to her feet by her hands, slides his hands up to her bare upper arms, holds her just apart from him, meeting her gaze, holding it.

The Prodigals

SHE DOESN'T GO to the Giesbrecht's often. Trent is bored by them, their dilapidated farm, their conversation about livestock and people he doesn't know. The Giesbrechts adore Trent: They think he is brilliant, well-mannered, hard-working, sophisticated. It is a class thing, she sees, though there aren't supposed to be classes, in Canada. They defer to Trent. They think Cleo has made a great catch.

She can only take so much of them. She is working on separating herself, on seeing them just as people whom she used to live with, whom she isn't like, now. She should stop going to see them, but she has got in the habit: They like to see the kids, the kids love the farm, the few chickens and ducks and goats that are left. It is a place to go where she feels she is wanted. She works on visiting just enough so that they complain too much about her not visiting enough, but not so little that it would seem ridiculous to pretend to have a relationship, and not so much that she will be in the constant state of irritation that visits put her into.

She usually makes Trent come along, for protection, but this time he refuses.

It's a day trip, only an hour's drive. They are so happy to see her, to see the children. Olivia and Sam awash in hugs, in exclamations over their height, their beauty. There is lunch, which is a little worse every time – Mrs. Giesbrecht is falling down in her cooking, she's getting old. Or maybe she never was a good cook, and that's why she needed Cleo. The meat – oven-fried porkchops – is overcooked and dry, the potato salad somehow a little runny, the blueberry pie undercooked, and maybe not sweetened enough. Mrs. Giesbrecht laments the absence of Trent to do justice to her cooking, though in truth Trent doesn't like her cooking: complains about it in the car on the way home.

There are baby rabbits, this time. Cages of rabbits. Olivia is enchanted. Cleo catches Mrs. Giesbrecht's eye, and they communicate silently: Don't tell her they're for meat.

She mentions Cliff and Mandalay, what they're doing, though Mrs. Giesbrecht doesn't seem much interested. Cleo doesn't give much detail: Oh, she's taking a break from that. Well, she has her own business. He's living downtown.

Mrs. Giesbrecht says that Mandalay ought to get married, that she is getting old for having kids. That Cliff ought to move back out to Abbotsford, buy a farm. The Giesbrechts congratulate themselves, Cleo knows, on steering Cliff into horticulture, to his landscaping job, but had thought he'd stay in the community.

They are delighted in the children. They have none themselves, no grandchildren, except that some of the foster children they've raised – those delinquent youth they took on for nearly thirty years – some of them are married now, with respectable jobs and kids, and these they dote on, as they dote on Cleo and Olivia and Sam. Mrs. Giesbrecht shows them pictures. She does not see any of them much.

You'd think of all of those kids, one would have wanted to stay, take on the farm. But no. And some of them – some of the boys Cleo remembers – have come to bad ends. She remembers to ask about them. The Giesbrechts do not take children in anymore; she and Cliff were the last.

For almost thirty years they had taken in delinquent boys, worked them on the farm, made them go to church. (How? By making it more unpleasant not to go than to go. Sometimes the boys had run away, but mostly they had stayed.)

In the late eighties they had stopped. The trouble boys are in now, Mr. Giesbrecht had said. Twenty years ago it was skipping school and fights and drinking too much beer, a little stealing. Now it's hard drugs and burning things down, cutting each other up with knives. And they don't want to work at all! That's not so easy to deal with.

They are hurt, she thinks: perpetually wounded, by the number of their boys who do not come to see them. Which is another reason she does. They are wounded, but you can't say to them, you were so *hard*. You gave those boys good food and a clean and healthy place to live and self-respect through work, but you gave them no affection, no real kindness. Why would they want to visit? They see only that they gave of themselves (of course they were paid for it; they had stipends for it, and they worked the boys hard on the farm as well). They cannot see what they didn't give. They wouldn't be able to see it.

It's for small children, only, their affection, their delight. And for Cleo and Trent, who are such model citizens, hard workers and producers of small children.

But she can navigate that. She can maintain a relationship at this node, this juncture: the delight in small children. She chatters about Sam, about Olivia. She tells the Giesbrechts, over lunch, about Sam's fascination with books, his surprisingly big attention span. She talks about Olivia's preschool, her cleverness. She talks about the great playground at the school and Trent's colleagues' beautiful houses.

If she is bragging a little, if she is casting some shadow on the Giesbrechts through comparison, she knows it is minor. It will be forgiven.

It has been so long since she has been here without Trent that she has forgotten what to be on guard for, and so it catches her by surprise, as it always used to. They have almost left; they've had their coffee and coffee cake – supper is a small affair, here, a small, late affair – and Olivia is playing with Mrs. Giesbrecht's doll collection that: Mrs. G. had started buying for herself in her middle age, since she was not allowed them as a child in Germany. Sam is napping. She's just about to wake him up, to get the kids into the car, when it comes.

Of course, Mrs. Giesbrecht says, you don't live a very godly life, Cleo. It makes me very sad to see you without spirituality. It makes sad that you are depriving your children of a life of faith. Every day we pray for you, Poppa and I, that your heart will be softened again. Christ is our Lord, Cleo. I know that. You know that too. I only wish for you to come back to Him.

She's defenceless against this. The things she says – I don't believe; you are welcome to your beliefs but please respect mine – make no impression. Mrs. Giesbrecht smiles as if Cleo were a child, an obstinate child.

It is not fair, what they do. She would never do it to them. She can't even summon the anger she needs to protect herself from them, because she is so unable to hurt their feelings. She says, politely, that those are their beliefs, and she respects that, but she doesn't agree, even when Mrs. G. is nearly shouting in her face. Her cheeks burn. She can only gather the children and flee, but not too quickly, not so it looks at all like she is running away.

At the Giesbrechts', Cliff and Cleo had shared a room. She'd taken him to school, picked him up, supervised him or hung out with him most of the time. He'd seemed fine – thriving, for Cliff. Not exactly sunny, but calm, content. When she moved out, he'd been fifteen, and had chosen to stay. He'd liked it, he said. He had his 4-H, friends. He'd been worried about Mr. and Mrs. G, who were getting older, not up to all of the farm chores. The older boys had all left by then. Cliff had told her that they needed him to hang around for a few years, while they sold off the stock. He had thought he might even want to keep living with them and running the farm.

Then, at eighteen, he'd suddenly moved out. She didn't know why. She'd been getting ready to move, to leave Vancouver and go to Ontario, for grad school. She'd offered to take him with her, but he'd said no. He'd found a job, a place to live.

That was another thing, worrying about Cliff while she was in school, thousands of miles away. Long distance calling had been so expensive then, and Cliff didn't have a phone, half the time.

She hasn't called Cliff in weeks, she thinks. She is too busy, with the kids. She can't be responsible for Cliff, now.

But she has to. She has to. Because of what happened to Che. What she let happen to Che.

On the way home Olivia complains she's hungry – still hungry – and Cleo doesn't want to stop because Sam's asleep but doesn't want to do a fast food drive-through. She sees a convenience store deli at a gas station – there will at least be sandwiches there, apples, bottles of milk. What to do about Sam, though?

She'll leave him in the car. It's a cloudy, cool day. She'll lock the doors, leave the window open a crack. She'll be in the store five minutes, and she'll be able to see her vehicle through the store's glass front the whole time she's inside.

She's standing at the cash desk, three minutes later, paying, when she sees the women standing by the suv, looking in the window at Sam, pointing, talking. The expressions on their faces make it clear that they're disapproving, even very angry.

She waits a moment, till they move off, then grabs Olivia and makes a dash for her car. She's shaking. All the way home she expects a siren behind her – expects that the women have called some authorities, reported her.

▼▼▼

IT IS AN EARLY SPRING DAY and it has been good: Ray not more than usually nasty and he had got some planting done faster than he expected, and Nicki had said, You are amazing, Cliff. He cycles back to his apartment and for once it's not raining and he does not get splashed. Home, he flicks the light switch on and calls Sophie, though she's usually at the door before he opens it. A small breeze, a flow of cooler air that he follows to the window, which is open too wide, the catch at the second notch instead of the first. Had he left it loose or had she forced it? The first notch is stripped and doesn't always catch anymore; it has to be wiggled into place, made secure, and even then she works away at the window, nudging at it with her wedge-shaped head until it pops along its tracks and she can weasel out, skull, shoulders, hips in descending widths negotiating even this narrow opening. He has meant to bring home a stick of wood to lay in the track and stop the window but he has forgotten.

Now he opens the window further, puts his head out, calls her name. No answering meow, though he listens intently, straining through the baleen of his senses the *hoosh* of traffic on wet pavement, the dripping of the rain's aftermath, the various growls of engines, the random blurts of horns and shouts. She's done this before and he has found her by going out into the alley under his window, and he makes his way there now, but she does not come to his call. That has not happened before.

Visions of her cold, thirsty, frightened, mangled, crying for him. Trapped. Too soon to think that. Not useful. He goes back inside. On the stairs he sees the basement door has been left open and wonders. He puts his face through, calls her again. Nothing. Back in his apartment he leaves his door propped open to the hallway. She could find her way back inside. He had found her once inside. Someone had let her in or she had found her way through a vent. Maybe he will cook some meat and the smell will bring her, but he's suddenly not hungry. He goes to the window, calls again. A man's voice outside laughs, says, She ain't coming back, dude.

A soft tapping at his open door and there's the girl from the floor below, the druggie one or maybe hooker, with Sophie in her arms. In a fluster trying to secure Sophie and not slam the door on the girl, he almost pulls her inside.

He thought the girl had a bald patch on her head but he sees now that it is shaven, just one side of her head up to the top of her ear, and the rest of her hair is there, but thin, kind of matted, with that dull look hair gets when its rubbed too much, or chewed. There seems to be *stuff* in her hair, too: coloured streaks and yarn woven in, bit of knots or beads, glints of metal. Feathers, too: striped and mottled feathers, grey and cream and burnt brown, of some wild bird. Grouse, maybe. He can't tell if they are just woven into her hair or also hanging from her earlobes. Her eyes are dull and set deep in her skull and there is bruising around them like the stains wet leaves make on the sidewalk in fall.

She's dressed in layers of things, as if she has dressed herself from a bag left in a Goodwill box: what appears to be an undershirt, a satiny green evening dress, a sheer, sparkling vest, another vest, or maybe it's a denim jacket with the sleeves cut out, a couple of scarves. There is the butterfly tattoo on her neck, a professional one, and some jagged, amateur lettering on her arms. A Tibetan symbol, maybe. On her lower half she's wearing leggings and a raggedy, dirty bit of tutu, or something like that. Her feet are bare, and their tops covered with an elaborate pale brownish design. A kind of ink, he thinks. Her toenails are trimmed and pale pink and look very clean – perhaps the only part of her that does look clean. Her fingertips are stained yellow-brown. Her arms are bare, and he can see the goosebumps, the little hairs standing up.

She says her name is Ellie. He sees that she is a kid, really. Not more than twenty, though her face is so thin, her eyes so old. Underneath the huskiness, her voice is faint, her sentences flat.

She's still holding Sophie, who isn't even struggling, but giving Cliff a slit-eyed smile: Come and get me. He takes the cat, now, trying to scoop her from the girl's arms without touching her person. He thinks he ought to give her something, for bringing Sophie back. Feed her, maybe.

Do you want to smoke, she asks, then, and his mind whips so fast into another place that he feels he has been slapped inside his head.

No, no, he says. Her face smooths itself out and only then he hears his own harshness.

No thanks, he says, trying to soften it. I can't....

Probation? she asks.

No, he says. Trying....

Well, good for you, she says.

Sorry.

No, she says. I mean it. What you're trying to do, it's good. She touches her hand to her lips, to the top of Sophie's head. Bye-bye, sweetheart, she says. Stay out of trouble.

He locks the door and checks that the window is completely shut, fills Sophie's food and water bowls. Little stupid, he says. Scaring me. You could have got hurt. You could have been lost forever.

He feels that old childish swelling in the throat that precedes tears or sickness, and realizes he's shaking. He sits on his bed for a minute and then lies down, drawing himself into fetal position. There's a feeling like a roaring in his head, like a wall of dark water coming at him, but the roaring is a feeling of force, not a sound. He hugs his knees but can't stop trembling.

He won't think about her. He won't. But he does.

The other girl, the girl from when he was younger, eighteen.

Her eyes, which he had thought of as doors to some sort of beautiful place in nature, like a field with sunlight and wildflowers and butter-flies. She had on a white top: white embroidery on it, and little buttons with tiny perfect loops, and a string at the neck, with tassels. The top couple of buttons undone, and the tops of her breasts showing. Her eyes laugh at him, saying, I know what you want and it's cool because I want it too. Her eyes had been really blue, mountain-lake-blue, and he'd thought, I could swim in them, and also: She knows me, all of me, already, and she's cool with it all.

Up close her skin had been soft and taut as a baby's. He could see that she had black stuff thickly pencilled around her eyes and he wanted to take the corner of a soft cloth and wash it off. Her hair made little wisps the colour and texture of milkweed fluff around her forehead. She was a meadow that he could lie down in and be safe and be part of nature. She was like him. She had not been scuffed up, burnt up, yet.

He should not have gone with her but it had been so clean and light, and she had asked him. That is no excuse, though, and he should not have. He should not.

He realizes he's still lying curled on his bed, clammy with sweat and breathing like he's been running hard. He's disoriented, looks at the clock. He's lost a couple of hours.

Sophie is kneading his back, making those sucking sounds she makes, dreaming. She wasn't weaned properly, he always thinks.

Focus on holding each breath back a little, then a little more. The door in his mind slides shut on its tracks, the meadow and sunshine snapped off. Gone.

He feels so tired, as if he's run up a mountain, and his muscles are now crying out for nourishment though his stomach has made itself into a locked fist. He has missed a program he wanted to watch on Kodiak bears but there's one just starting on sea turtles, their long lonely journeys. The females heave themselves up beaches to squeeze their glistening soft eggs into scraped-out holes. The cameraman has used some sort of infrared camera and the turtle and its eggs seem on the screen to be made of gleaming wavering dots. They seem ghostly, or like space messages. He watches the eggs glisten, distorted, at the end of the turtle's opening, and then pop out and fall, regaining their rounded shape, into the nest. He feels in his shoulders the effort of hauling his mass up the shore, in his forelimbs the effort of scraping the sand. He feels in himself the pressure on the egg and the release.

Turtle, eggs, nest: they are all containers. Boxes inside boxes. What is the turtle thinking, hunkering in the alien sand, weeping silvery mucous? Is she aware or is it all instinct? She knows to choose the right night of moon and tide, the right beach. She knows to bury the eggs. But is that all instinct? Is there nothing going on in her mind about her babies? No worries or thought about their safety?

By the time they hatch she'll be hundreds of miles away. She'll never see them. Most of them will perish.

And yet, not knowing about them, she has provided for them.

Cliff sits, Sophie in his lap, until the program ends. Another starts, on deserts. Sophie gets up to eat, meows to remind him to leave out her treat, which she only gets at night. When he opens the fridge, he feels hungry now himself. Not for chicken, though. Or eggs. He prepares a package of pasta with cheese-flavoured sauce. Does not eat it from the pot, but puts it into two bowls, and eats one, and then the other.

Sophie sits beside him, watching him, never blinking her large, light, protuberant eyes.

▼▼▼

THE BOY OR YOUNG MAN is giving close attention to the paintings on The Seagull's gallery wall. He's dressed in the usual Gore-Tex and baggy earth-coloured hiking pants that students favour. His hair isn't long enough, his little beard is trimmed too neatly, to identify him immediately as a potential consignor, an artist.

Mandalay drifts over, as unobtrusively as she can, to ask if she can help him. He turns at her approach. He looks slightly familiar. A regular, perhaps. Not likely a customer for art: too young. And though she has the sense that she knows him from somewhere else, not the café, he's twenty-two or three at most, too young to be someone from her past. He still has that roundness, that downiness, to his cheeks.

He says, Mandalay? And takes a step closer, looks at her as if he's trying to place her.

She says, Can I help you? And he goes pink and then pale and says, I think you're my sister.

So very little drama for this moment that she has dreamed and rehearsed and polished over in her imagination for the past twenty years. Here it is, the sky casually splitting open. She says, her voice cracking a little: Bodhi.

He nods. I was, he says. I'm called Ben now.

Is it possible? She has carried the image of a toddler in her memory for all of these years, even knowing that her brother must be growing up. But she can see aspects of both Cleo and Cliff, even of her own face, shining at her with such obviousness, now, that she doesn't know how she could have been blind to them.

He holds his arms out, then, in that gesture that men use in awkward social situations: We might as well hug. And so she steps in, and embraces him, in the tentative way of strangers embracing.

It is her baby brother, returned to her after all of these years. And it is, at the same time, not.

He says, I saw your photo in the airline magazine. He has the page with him, ripped out, folded to fit in a wallet.

She's staring at him too intently. She has to do something, say something. How did you know I was your sister, though?

He says: I've known your name for a few years. You registered with the agency.

So she had, back in the mid-eighties, when it had become possible. For a few years? she asks.

Now he flushes, again, wings of pink staining just the tops of his cheeks. Yeah, he says. My parents told me about the registry when I was still in high school, when I was about seventeen, but I didn't know what to do with the information. I guess I wasn't ready.

Four or five years, he's known. And hasn't tried to find her, or register his own information. But she needs to remind herself that he is very young: barely a young man.

He says, I was flying back from Maui during reading break when I saw the article with your picture. I nearly freaked out. I thought, I have to do this now.

They sit down at one of the round metal tables. She remembers to smile at him. Wow, she says. Four or five years. It's hard to reconcile you, all grown up, with the baby brother I last saw.

The flicker of discomfort in his eyes, now. Had she intended to cause that?

I was afraid, he says, you know, when I was younger, that you might turn out to be — well, if I contacted you. Someone who was....

She waits.

My mom works for legal aid, he says. She tells me about stuff.... I wasn't ready to take on someone with a lot of problems.

Now she hears in his word choice, his inflection, an older adult speaking. His adopted parents, of course. If she were them, she probably would have also cautioned him.

She says, So you're a university student.

Yeah. Third year of my degree. Then law school probably. But I might take a break first to do some travelling.

Law school, she says. It's as if she's interviewing a potential new barista: Her mind has stopped functioning except to pick up the most obvious pieces of information.

Yeah, he says. Both of my parents are lawyers. It seems I have no choice.

There's no apparent nervousness, other than his paleness and occasional flushing: no stammering or stumbling over words. And this is a joke he's made often, she can tell, to smiles and laughter. It's the kind of thing she hears the students who frequent the café, that is to say, the better-off students, say. What it really means is not that he has no choice, but that he has too many choices, and for now he's taking the default option in order to postpone a decision.

Where do you live? she asks. Did you grow up here? Do you have siblings? She can't think, can't process. He has Cleo's eyes and colouring – except for his lighter hair. The same quick pink under the skin.

He says, I'm an only child. My parents – we – live in West Point Grey.

Of course they do.

I still live at home. He's laughing. I mean it's kind of embarrassing, right? But it's close to campus.

There had been a time in her twenties when she had taken to bicycling around the Point Grey neighbourhoods, looking at the estates, the mansions, letting the conflicting currents of envy and disdain build a frothing riptide in her, a sort of anarchy fueled in equal measure by her own observations of social and economic inequity and her frustration at being excluded – as far as she could tell, forever – from possession of one of the truly beautiful houses she sometimes saw.

So her lost little brother, her stolen little brother, had been ensconced in that place of exclusion. While she had been bicycling around, grinding her teeth, she had not guessed that behind one of the driveway gates, the *Architectural Digest* homes, her little brother was an unwitting prisoner, an illicit treasure.

She has to shake herself: She let go of all of that toxic envy and judging long ago. No need to revive it now.

She asks him and he says he likes to snowboard and to surf (when I'm at my parents' condo on Maui, he says). To read, but he doesn't read enough. She predicts he likes to hang out with his friends and listen to music, and sure enough he says that next.

And then, like the well-brought-up boy he is, he asks her politely about herself.

She has to carry her answers through that strange tide of resentment or anger, then. It's as if she's struggling through a swirling muddy flood holding over her head something she doesn't want dirtied. She says, trying only to elaborate on the article, fixing her attention on that rosy, tidy, safe portrait of her, that she has done part of a visual arts degree, that she's worked at quite a few jobs, that she sort of fell into the job at the café, that she lives now in the neighbourhood. That she isn't married, has no kids.

He asks, then, about the others. She'd put only her own contact information into the registry, but he knows – has been told – that he has other siblings.

Cleo, she says. (She thinks: Cleo's going to be shocked. She doesn't know if she'll be happy.) Cleo, she says, lives in Coquitlam. She's married. Has two little kids.

Really? Bodhi/Ben seems excited by the prospect of small relatives. Maybe Cleo is who he really wanted to find: a sibling who would bring him more connections. Or maybe he's like her, at a loss, looking for something to connect with.

Cleo's son Sam is a year and a half, Mandalay thinks. The same age as Bodhi when. She doesn't mention that.

And Cliff, she says. He lives here too. Off Main. Somewhere around there.

He's close to my age?

Yes, she says. (How much has he been told? Had his adoptive parents been provided with a lot of information about Bodhi's biological family, while they had got none about him, where he had ended up?)

Cliff is twenty-six, she says. He works as a landscaper.

Landscape architect?

No, she says. For a landscaping service. Kind of a gardener, I guess.

Bodhi/Ben nods. His parents would employ a landscaping service, Mandalay realizes.

I think he does well at it, she says. I think he enjoys it. Being outdoors, and so on.

Cool, he says. She thinks: He's trying to get his head around all of this new information, around Cleo and Cliff. They're not real to him. What can she say about them, though, without reducing them to a few symbolic phrases? It's too early for family stories. Even if those existed. Even if that was what he wanted.

And you see them often, Cleo and Cliff? he asks.

She says, not often. If he's after a new family, a close-knit one, he's out of luck. We were in separate homes from the time Cleo and I were twelve and thirteen, she says. Then Cliff ended up with Cleo. We hardly saw each other for ten years or so. We've all grown up different people. It's kind of surprising how little we have in common.

Why has she said this? She isn't even sure it's true. It's as if she's trying to discourage him, to wall him out, or maybe she just doesn't want him to get his hopes up too much. Or maybe she's trying to make him feel less excluded — not as if they all were a comfortable unit and he on the outside.

Where did you grow up? he asks.

Various places.

Butterfly Lake?

Mostly.

And — I was told I had two older brothers, not just one.

She says, flatly: Che. He was killed in a work accident a long time ago. Ten years ago.

He nods, looks solemn, but she knows that information will just be an abstraction to him.

It's kind of funny we've all ended up here, though, he says. I mean it's weird, isn't it?

Not given that half the population of the province lives in the city, Mandalay thinks, but she says: Not if you're from Butterfly Lake. If you have any gumption, you leave Butterfly Lake. And Vancouver's the obvious place to go. The only bus out of Butterfly Lake goes to Vancouver.

I'd like to go there, he says. Butterfly Lake. I've heard about it but I've never been. Isn't the scenery supposed to be spectacular?

It is.

Do you go back?

Not very often, she says. She remembers, with a start of guilt, Crystal. Our mom still lives there, she says.

Ben/Bodhi seems shaken, disturbed. He pales, then reddens. Cleo's complexion's like that, a pond open to whatever passes across the sky.

Our mom?

Your birth mother. Crystal.

My birth mother's still alive?

A little dull stab of anger under her breastbone, then. Not that she hasn't forgotten Crystal's existence sometimes for months at a time. But for her to have been entirely erased.

Yes, she says. She had a long illness when you were a baby. That's when you were adopted. But she recovered. She's very much alive.

And in Butterfly Lake?

Yes.

I don't fucking believe it, he says. I was always told....

He's unhappy, now. He's confused, and unhappy. And his unhappiness is going to get bigger, the more he processes, she thinks. She can see the white and red burning in his face.

It occurs to her then that Crystal might turn out to be the kind of relative that her brother was afraid of finding, but she's not going to be the one to say this. There's a little burn of righteous anger in her now that Bodhi was told that his mother had died. She knows that there might be a reasonable explanation, but she doesn't care. The little flame gives her a focus, now. She feels centred. She feels that she has a handle on the whole Ben/Bodhi thing. The reunion. It has been such a shock, so unexpected, so random, so disorienting, but now she's got an angle, a handle, a lens. She feels she knows where she's at.

Bodhi/Ben says he wants to meet them all.

One at a time or at once?

All at once, he says. She can see that he's choosing badly, choosing the difficult thing, but that he's agitated and reactive now and that he'll act impetuously. He won't be satisfied to take cautious first steps, as he has been up until now. He'll be impulsive. He'll go for the drama.

Just as she would have at his age.

It's only after he leaves — clutching the list of phone numbers she's written down for him — that she realizes that she has not drawn a full breath since she walked up to him. It feels like she hasn't breathed this entire hour and a half.

The Golden Gates

ON A BULLETIN BOARD in the school hallway Cleo sees the notice: Kindergarten Registration, and the date, and the times: an afternoon, an evening, doesn't pay attention to it at first, and then is struck by the rest of the notice. Children born in 1994. That's Olivia.

It's six months away, the start of school. She had not been thinking about it. She wonders, now, what would have happened if she hadn't seen the notice? But it's in the newspaper that week, too, and on the bulletin board at the library, and at the public health clinic.

She says to Trent, it's so funny: I never thought you would have to register children for school. It never occurred to me.

Of course you do, Trent says. How would they keep track? How would they know how many kids to expect?

It makes sense: It just hadn't occurred to her, and it seems strange, anomalous in some way. Maybe alarming, this early intrusion of bureaucracy into Olivia's four-year-old life. Or maybe it's just that she has carried with her a child's perspective of the educational system: that schools, or their personnel, are all-seeing, all-knowing. At her school, in Butterfly Lake, she remembers, all of the teachers knew who she was, knew her parents and her siblings, where she lived, from the first day. Maybe she had assigned that apparent omniscience to everyone connected with schools, then, not realizing that she was part of a very small community.

What about when you were living with your foster family? Trent asks, reasonably. You must have had to register at a new school then.

She can't remember. She can't remember most of that first year.

On the scheduled day — it's not a preschool day — she walks down the street to the school, Sam in the stroller, Olivia lollygagging, talking to her imaginary friends or just babbling — Cleo doesn't always listen that closely — crouching to look at rocks, plants, a bird. It is a long journey, but it doesn't matter — they don't have to be there at a specific time.

At the school she doesn't recognize any of the other children from Olivia's preschool class, nor their attending adults, in the large group milling around the gymnasium. It appears that a lot of the people here know each other, though. They're chatting and eating and drinking, ignoring the signs on the walls: No Food In Gym, and the couple of secretaries who are trying to corral them into a line. Cleo feels anxious, a little dazed, at first. It's like walking into a party as a stranger. She can feel Olivia hang back, too, and sense her trying to make herself invisible behind Cleo's legs.

Then a plump woman with a pleasant face and round glasses smiles at Olivia and says hi, and introduces herself to Cleo, and says, My boy is motoring around here somewhere — and then another and another. The room is full of women about Cleo's age, it appears, all friendly, all with four- or five-year-old offspring, many with infants or toddlers too. And men! Not a lot, but a few men, young men. One or two perhaps gay.

How is this possible? How has this group of likeable, friendly people come together, existed in her neighbourhood, without her stumbling upon it earlier? She feels dazed or stunned. She knows that later she'll have to figure out where she took the wrong route, how she has not discovered this country before, but their friendliness is astonishing. She has perhaps not spoken to that many adults in their thirties – most are in their thirties, she estimates, though there seem to be a couple of slightly older men or women, and a couple of women, one heavily pregnant, who are not past twenty-five – cumulatively, in her entire adult life.

She's bewildered also because at first there doesn't seem to be a line or anything happening, but eventually – after the secretaries harry and nudge for a while – people start sitting at tables, and filling out forms, and then start a line at another table, where the secretaries seat themselves.

There's a long paper form to fill out, both sides: It asks for information Cleo doesn't really have to hand: the telephone number of the family doctor, the family dentist (dentist?), an emergency contact. There are lines and lines she leaves blank: previous schools attended, medical conditions, legal guardianship, custodial parent.

A woman sitting at her table says, I wonder if this stuff is allowable, under the Freedom of Information Act? I think I'm just going to leave this blank. Or put NOYB. She laughs. Cleo is astonished: It would not have occurred to her to take a cavalier attitude to the form. The other woman sharing her table, who looks just a little older than Cleo and has a mass of long black-brown curls says, God, I'm always afraid that I'm going to put different information on this form than I did on the other kids'. I have no idea who I put before for emergency contact, or if I gave them Jim's cell number or his practice number.

Just put *Look it up on one of my previous forms*, the man sitting with them suggests.

It's a novel idea, not to be afraid of school staff, Cleo thinks.

How many is this for you now, Mira? the first woman asks.

The woman with the curls says, four. But this is it, thank God.

All in this school? the man asks.

Yes, says the curly-haired woman, Mira. Seven, five, three and K, next year. I've heard they're going to name one of the classrooms after us.

I think they'll name the sickroom after my kids, the other woman says. I think the mattress on the cot still has bloodstains from Jeremy slicing open his knee.

It's astonishing. It's like finding yourself at the cool kids' table in school, Cleo thinks, and not being told to leave.

The woman with the dark hair, Mira, asks her name, and Olivia's. Her daughter is entertaining Sam in his stroller, with a professional air.

Oh, Mariah loves smaller children, Mira says. It's a pity none of my others did. Never could get any of them to entertain their younger siblings. Only Mariah.

Such ease, such a casual humorous competent off-hand confidence they all have.

When Cleo's turn comes at the secretary's table, it turns out she has not brought the right documentation. She has Olivia's Care Card, which she always has in her wallet, but has not remembered her birth certificate.

Well, she's not going home for it. But what a nitwit she is. She resolves not to tell Trent.

Mira, behind her, says, Oh, you can bring it down anytime. They just want the number. Obviously your child exists.

The secretary says, I'm afraid we can't process the registration without it.

That's silly, Mira says, in a friendly way. I didn't even have birth certificates for two of my kids until a couple of years ago. The ministry accepts Care Cards.

We prefer to have the birth certificate too, the secretary says.

It's alright, Cleo says. I have it but it's too far to go home and come back right now. I don't have a car. Can I bring it this evening? She can feel the line of people, relaxed up till now, start to become impatient behind her.

The secretary purses her lips, then says, I suppose so.

When she leaves, Cleo says to Mira: You all seem to know each other. She thinks this might be rude to say and normally would just have gone on in ignorance, but it feels like what she thinks of as social propriety might be more relaxed in this room. She is emboldened.

Oh, that's from preschool, Mira says. A lot of us go to the same preschool, Kid Planet.

That's the other preschool, the one Cleo had rejected. She had seen that the ads for it said co-op and hadn't liked the sound of that, for some reason. Or Trent hadn't. And it was more expensive.

So she has sent her life, and Olivia's, down the wrong trajectory already by choosing the wrong preschool. She feels a sort of hopelessness and anger. How could she have known? Now it feels that she has made a series of bad choices, lacking some mysterious important information, and will likely continue to do so. She adds wrong preschool to a list that she sees contains *wrong university major, wrong neighbourhood*, and possibly *wrong husband*. It isn't fair. Why isn't she ever given the key?

But maybe there's some principle, some identifying characteristic, in choices like this: something lacking in her. She might just not be the kind of person who chooses the better thing. She might just not be worthy of the nicer things in life because she's lacking the better instinct. What is it? Some generosity or something.

And now she has the long push up the hill still ahead of her, and Sam is complaining about being in the stroller, and Olivia doesn't want to go: She's found some other children to play with, is running around the gymnasium like a crazed pony and when Cleo intercepts her, catches her elbow, she stares at Cleo without recognition, and says, *Let me go*!

On the way out of the school, both children are crying. Cleo sees the Community Room door open, some parents and children from the Kid Planet preschool group still hanging around in there. She sees, too, even as she marches Olivia and Sam out, the table and chairs set up in the Community Room, the table with the coffee urn and the plates of cookies. People standing around, like a little party. She has chosen the wrong thing, will be an outsider forever.

In the evening, she goes back, with the car and Olivia's birth certificate. Here is a new group, now: It is lined up, patient, docile. There are few children this time, but she thinks she recognizes two or three from Olivia's preschool class. The children are all patient and docile, too. The adults are all strangers – lots of women or couples, talking quietly, or not at all, as if at a formal event; more Asians and South Asians than in the morning. Most in their business clothes, still: severe suits, white shirts. They all look like accountants, perhaps. She ought to have brought Trent. There are no younger or older siblings here, just the few composed children.

The Asians and Indians are elegant, but she sees the Caucasian men and women are less so, their suits or business wear drab, not as well-fitting, the men's haircuts very short, the women mostly with severe practical hairstyles, little makeup.

The nerd's lineup, she thinks: But this is where she and Trent really belong, maybe, not with the cheeky convivial confident group of the afternoon. Perhaps she should have worn a suit. Or her University of Ottawa Engineering T-shirt.

She stands quietly in line like the rest, even though she doesn't need a form, needs only to show the card and see that the number is copied down. The secretaries from the afternoon are absent, and the registration is being overseen by a young-middle-aged man, and an efficient, perhaps officious, determinedly cheerful woman. Principal and vice-principal, she guesses. (Do elementary schools have vice-principals?)

She seems to be the last one in line – the others must have all been here when the evening registration opened – and then the gym door swings open and a slim woman in a smart dress and scarf, tall leather boots and designer handbag, and a haircut Cleo has only seen in *Vogue* sashays across the glossy floor. There's a stir from the others in line, but nobody greets the woman. Cleo turns, though, and gives her what she hopes is the right kind of friendly smile.

Oh my goodness, the woman says. Am I late?

At that the principal or vice-principal – whichever the male official is – looks up and beams.

Hello! the woman calls, in a tone that somehow manages to be friendly and mocking at the same time. She's really quite attractive, Cleo sees, glancing at her again. By far the most glamorous of the women in the room.

The woman turns her attention now to Cleo. I'm such a flake, she says. I came earlier today but forgot to bring Claire's birth certificate.

Me too, Cleo says. I mean, I did that too. She thinks of high school again; this time it's as if the prom queen (not that they had prom queens at her high school) had started up a conversation with her by mistake. She's grateful that she put on her decent pair of jeans and her good jacket before she left the house. Some makeup would have been a good idea, though. And she must own half a dozen scarves. Would it be so much work to wear one, once in a while?

I guess we just have too much going on in our pretty little heads, the woman says.

She's kidding, right?

She winks. Cleo laughs, a little too late.

You have a little girl too, the woman says. I see you walking sometimes, with your stroller. That's a good way to keep fit! You put the rest of us to shame. I always feel guilty when I go by you.

Her voice is so light, so brittle, or not brittle – glassy, like a wind chime, or like the sound of a crystal wineglass, rubbed along its rim. Cleo can't tell if it has malice in it, and her face, or eyes, seem sincere. She says her name is Lacey. Cleo asks if Lacey's child is also in the Kid Planet preschool, and Lacey says, Oh, who has time for that? Claire goes to the Parks and Rec one. I work those days and the daycare person takes her.

(The efficient woman with the triple stroller and two preschoolers, Cleo thinks.)

What does Lacey do? But she can't ask. Won't ask. Does she look a little familiar, or is it just that she has the kind of face that is instantly memorable? The other people in the line do not seem to speak to her, but then, they all seem intent on not noticing anyone around them, focusing on their own conversations, if they are in couples, or on their Blackberrys.

When she gets to the front of the line, Cleo tells the principal (it is the principal, it seems) that she has already filled out a form and is just bringing the birth certificate, and Lacey says, Me too! and the principal says, Oh gosh, you didn't need to make a special trip for that, you could have just brought it in the first week of school in September.

Then he pulls both of their forms – Look at that, he says, right next to each other, Lennox and Lewis.

And on their way to their cars, Lacey touches her arm and says, We should get together for a play date sometime!

Cleo says something like yes, then climbs into her car but just sits. She doubts that this will happen, somehow.

All of this social possibility has been going on around her, and she oblivious, or cut off by lack of a car, or by her house being on the wrong street, or something.

It could change now. She sees that. She remembers one of Trent's colleague's wives saying that all of her friends were people she met through her children: the parents of her children's friends. It will change. She has already met new people, been invited to their houses, for what it's worth. Things could be looking up, socially.

Though now as she sits in the car, in the chill spring evening, she remembers that it will be better not to be too hopeful. It is likely, after all, that she will be disappointed. If she does, in fact, get to know some new people, it is likely that they will turn out to be unsuitable: not capable, because of lack of education or innate smarts, of intelligent conversation, or radically adherent to some doctrine or cause, or possessing bizarre personality traits. She foresees the possibilities of boredom, discomfort. Perhaps it is safer not to bother.

What she misses, maybe, is work: the kind of significant work that will fulfill her. She has not had this for some time. Maybe, if she could get back to work, she would be less bored. And she'd have relationships there, too.

She and Trent had met just as she was finishing her Master's, and she had got pregnant with Olivia, married and moved with Trent, giving up the job she had lined up. She thinks sometimes, resentfully, that Trent had talked her into it, assuring her that she'd find work in her field on the west coast. But it is also true that, burned out from several years in school, tired from the pregnancy, she had maybe been relieved not to start a job right away, to let someone else make the decisions.

She had moved with Trent and had worked part-time drafting for an engineering company – she had taken some drafting courses during her Master's – until just before Olivia was born, her belly jutting against the drafting board. And worked again for a year before

Sam was born. It did not pay well, part-time drafting for the engineering company – not even enough to cover daycare for both Sam and Olivia. She had not been part of the social and professional fabric of the firm. She had done her work (and redone it, patiently, taking criticisms without comment) and gone home: she had not been expected to go to meetings, be part of consultations.

She had worked part-time, and summers, all through her years of university. She had not travelled. She had been poor and diligent. In her first year, her foster parents had loaned her money, but she had paid it back, had borrowed no more.

For the last five years, she has been partially or wholly supported by Trent, which neither of them had intended. (Well, of course, a voice in her head says. You've been home with very young children. And it's not him supporting you. It's your family income. But she does not believe this voice.)

She has heard Trent's colleagues say that they loved their university years – meeting different people, having all of those wonderful opportunities to learn and not much responsibility. They talk about their university years as if they were an extended adolescence: hanging out with friends, going to parties, travelling, learning a little bit.

Cleo had not had that experience. She had worked, she thinks now, eighty-hour weeks between her part-time job and her courses, supporting herself, keeping her scholarship. She had not gone out to dinner for six years, probably. She had not bought clothes or records or books new, had not gone to any full-price movies or concerts.

She had not been unhappy. It's only now that she feels she missed out on something. When she goes back to work, she knows, she'll likely be designing office buildings or malls, highway off-ramps. She'll be expected to put in sixty-hour weeks. She's not enthused. She actually can't imagine how that will work, with having two small children. (She imagines herself coming back to the house, late in the evening, standing outside, while inside a nanny is talking to, laughing with, a slightly older Olivia and Sam. Or worse – ignoring them: They sit, miserable, alone, in darkened bedrooms.)

She's not even sure that she wants to work at engineering. She had missed something, somehow made a mistake, though she can't put her finger on it exactly. Some early, foundational mistake. She had liked her courses well enough – she was good at math, good at spatial logic – but then, in her last year, taking her obligatory electives, something had shifted. She'd seen some other possibilities, felt her mind stretch and rouse itself in a new way, as if it had up to then only been pretending.

But it had been too late to start over.

And now. What now?

The car is cold, the parking lot emptying. Her hands on the wheel are stiff. She starts the car. She puts on the heater, though she knows it won't throw out any warmth, in the short distance back to her house.

Merger

THEY GO OUT FOR DINNER — or dinner and some sort of music or entertainment — two or three nights a week, mostly on weekends. They go to gourmet restaurants whose prices shock her, restaurants that are featured in tourism brochures. They have elaborate Japanese dishes where sashimi is sliced in front of them and arranged to look like coral reef creatures; multi-course Italian dinners beginning with plates of antipasto. They eat Salt Spring Island lamb and little crisp-skinned birds, tenderloin that seems to melt in the mouth, duck and venison and bison, salmon and swordfish and lobster.

Mandalay has been more or less a vegetarian for fifteen years, but she finds herself daydreaming about the tiny savoury portions of meat. They eat vegetables so young and tender that she imagines them plucked by hand out of a garden behind the restaurant: potatoes the size of grapes, multi-coloured carrots, button-sized squashes with their flowers still attached. They eat grains and mushrooms whose names she has never before heard. The foods and the ways they are prepared are an education, she thinks. She reads the descriptions carefully, she listens to, and then sometimes joins in, the conversations Duane has with the waiters. She eats slowly, pays attention. She thinks that she is learning to understand nuance and complexity.

She thinks that the restaurants are grossly overpriced, and then she doesn't.

She says, You always pay. I can pay sometimes. Or I can make you dinner.

He says, I appreciate your sense of fairness. But it's not necessary.

She says, If you pay every time, I feel like.... She doesn't want to say *mistress* or *kept woman*.

Like you're exploiting me? Or that I'm trading dinners and concerts for sex?

Well, yes.

Which? he asks. You can't have it both ways, you know. Both of those possibilities can't exist simultaneously.

That doesn't mean that one of them isn't true.

Look at it this way, he says. I would go out for dinner and to the club anyway. Your company makes the experience more enjoyable for me. As we've established, I don't mind paying more for a better quality experience.

Am I paying for it with sex?

I hope, he says, that our sexual encounters are mutually rewarding. I hope so.

Her mind and body are aroused by his dry innuendo. She has to grip the edge of her chair. She has to turn away, for a moment. What am I giving you in return for your always paying? she asks.

Look, he says. My income is so many more times than yours that it doesn't make sense for you to even think about paying.

She can see that. In her experience, though, there's no free lunch.

They go to the symphony, to performances in small public rooms of visiting, famous cellists and pianists, to clubs that she didn't know existed, where singers she didn't know were still alive sing jazz or blues. They hear the Vancouver Symphony and John Coltrane and Nina Simone and Pearl Jam and Lenny Kravitz. She listens intently: She must develop her ear. When she hears music on the radio, now, she doesn't hear it is a homogenous stream of sound; She hears the instruments, their individual notes, sees the movements of the musician's fingers. The music moves her, galvanizes her nerve endings. Knowing more helps her respond more fully – intellectually and emotionally – to the music.

After concerts the sex is intense, magnified, prolonged. If it's a weeknight, if she has to be at the café at five in the morning, she doesn't sleep more than an hour or two, and the next day feels like she has been electro-charged. Everything is heightened and radiant. She takes to sleeping in the afternoons, losing some of the time that she has for maintaining her private life. Some things fall away. She has a new life, she realizes, after a few weeks.

When they are not eating or listening or making love, they talk and talk. They talk in the car, walking between the car and venues. They walk to the market and talk; they talk in bed, before and after sex. There is never enough time to complete a conversation, and two days will go by and she will get into his car and they'll pick up the thread where they left off. They talk about the food and music, of course, and what they do at work. They talk about what is going on in the province or city – Mandalay has always skimmed the papers that the café gets for its patrons, but now she tries to do more than skim, and sometimes takes them home at the end of the day. They talk about books they have read, though they are not the same books. They see *The Matrix* and *American Beauty, Being John Malkovich* and *Fight Club, Buena Vista Social Club* and *The Hurricane* (but not *The Talented Mr. Ripley* or *American Pie* or *Eyes Wide Shut*). They talk about the movies.

They talk about their lives, though not as much as she has done in other relationships, where one's personal stories of family grievances, high school escapades, other relationships are construction materials for the new relationship, materials which will define, and possibly limit it, in the future. When they talk about their personal experiences, they transform them into something more public: still unique, original, but with more objectivity, more deliberation. They talk about their travels: Both have been to Southeast Asia, which is unusual, maybe. He's also been to Italy and France, and backpacked around Central America, when he was very young, he says. But she has travelled across Canada in a rock band bus, which he hasn't.

She thinks: There is so much more to us at our age. We have learned and experienced and felt a lot. We bring all of that to this relationship, and so it is more complex, with more connections. It is like a very strong web, and it seems that it can grow and expand and support itself indefinitely. And it must grow, to stay alive. It must keep growing, deepening.

Sometimes she wonders if *relationship* is the wrong word. There is no such thing as relationship, she says to herself. It is not a thing you build. It is always just two people, and what we've said and done, and what we do and say new every time we are together. It makes sense. There can't be attachment, expectations.

Only it seems right that they should open more and more to each other, and share more and more.

SHE SAYS: What if we got together with my sister and her husband for dinner? I think you'd like them. They're on their way to an opening in a new gallery on the North Shore, Duane driving. She'd mentioned the event to Cleo, and Cleo had said kind of wistfully that she'd like to go out sometimes.

Without looking away from the highway, Duane says, I don't do family dinners, nephew's first-birthday parties, Dad's surprise retirement parties. I don't do the guest thing at weddings. I won't go out for dinner or drinks with your friend Sue from high school and her husband Mike.

She has no friend called Sue, she thinks: a little lifeboat of thought bobbing on a wave of surprising dismay. She says: Unless Sue is a nationally-known radio personality and Mike is an astronaut, right?

Is she? Is he? He's laughing, though.

Why don't you want to do these normal social things?

Do you?

No, not always. But I have to. I should. I mean, if I don't, sometimes, I won't have friends. I won't have a relationship with my sister.

Well, you have to, then, he says. You've entered into a social contract in which it is necessary. But I don't choose to spend my time in social situations that are awkward or boring.

What about work parties?

What about them?

Don't you have to go to, like, your office Christmas social? Shower for your colleague's baby?

He laughs. Yes. Of course. Sometimes. It's part of my work culture. I have to do it to maintain relationships with my colleagues.

What's the difference, then? If you're in a relationship with a woman, don't you have to be part of her social network, to maintain a good relationship?

Ah, he says. But I choose not to. I choose not to have that kind of relationship.

And you have that choice, why?

Because I'm asking for it. I'm asking for that consideration, in my private social contract.

You're paying for it with all of those dinners and concert tickets, she says.

And is it worth it?

She's annoyed to find she has teared up. She didn't mean to. She doesn't want him to think he has hurt her feelings. She's not hurt, only – she's feeling something she can't name, something that feels like hot froth inside her throat. Anger, anger, she thinks. But she's curious: Where does it come from?

He has put his hand on her upper knee, or lower thigh, but now he pulls the car over, gives her his full attention.

Spit it out.

It's a kind of rejection.

Not of you.

Maybe. You don't know me well enough to know that.

You're absolutely right, he says.

A couple of moments' pause.

But you're not going to change, are you?

He says, Mandalay, I really like you. I really, really like your company. I don't want to go down the conventional relationship road. I've experienced it and it isn't for me. I don't want why didn't you pick dog food up on your way home and can't tell her I've never liked asparagus in case it hurts her feelings and we need to go to Home Depot this weekend and pick out a light fixture for the bathroom and why weren't you home at seven like you said you'd be. I don't want it. I won't do it. It's important that you understand that I'm telling you the truth.

Quality of experience.

She's so angry. But she gets it. She does understand what he's saying. And it's not so different than anything she's thought of herself. She's always said she didn't want a conventional relationship, marriage, two kids, house in the suburb, Christmas with the in-laws. She's always thought that. The things he's rejecting are not things she needs.

Whatever is making her angry is something else.

And then suddenly, all she's thinking of is that she needs to save face.

Goddammit, Duane, she says. You don't know how much you're missing out on, giving up listening to my brother-in-law talk about third party withholdings.

He laughs. That's actually something I know about, he says. It's actually something that has some interest for me in corporate law.

Really?

No, he says. It's boring as hell.

She laughs, as he meant her to. She doesn't know why she teared up. She still feels shaky, not in control. It's not how she wants it to be, between them. She is not this woman who cries because she is afraid of rejection, or because she doesn't get her own way.

She has imagined introducing Duane to Cleo and Trent. Has thought: They are part of his world; he'll see more of who I am, if he meets them. Now she's ashamed of that fantasy, as if she's been contemplating some sort of deception, a masquerade or some kind of exchange to gain some cachet, with either Cleo or Duane.

But still. It doesn't feel right, not to ever mention Cleo, or her kids, or sweet dopey Cliff, with his nature-show obsession, his cat. Or, especially, Bodhi, come back miraculously into her life. Especially Bodhi, who has reminded her of something, who has opened the door to something she had long given up on. Though she can't name it; she can't quite articulate it, it's there, a kind of empathy and openness that seems to have no place in her relationship with Duane.

You okay now? Duane asks, after a moment.

What can she say? They are pulled over beside a highway; there is a bridge ahead of them. She is wearing a new dress, a dark slippery shimmer of a dress. She wants to see this art show; it's important.

Sure, she says, and waits for the car to slip back into the stream of northbound traffic.

DUANE SAYS: You've gone shopping.

Maybe, she says. Is it permitted?

They're walking in Yaletown, en route to dinner. He bumps her a little with his hip. He hasn't done that before.

You look very elegant, he says.

She is lying by omission, perhaps. But she can hardly say, I had nothing to wear, and I just spent an entire month's disposable income on new outfits.

He says, carefully, Women seem to need more changes of clothes than men do. I never thought about it before, but I imagine having any kind of social or work life requires a certain level of — sartorial expense.

Is he implying that she has been spending too much, or too little?

He doesn't continue until they're seated in the restaurant, with drinks. Then he says, I'd really enjoy it if you let me treat you to some — feathers and furbelows — once in a while. He seems odd, formal.

I can afford to buy my own clothes, she says.

He just nods.

Unless, of course, you think I have really bad taste.

I think you look beautiful and elegant, he says.

Do you want to go shopping with me?

No, he says. Not my thing. Sitting in a shop waiting while women try clothes on. Sorry.

Okay, she says.

Look, he says, let's not beat around the bush. I know you probably don't have the kind of clothes women tend to wear out to decent restaurants and concerts and so on. I'm just realizing that it's probably a big expense. As you're going out to places I choose, I'm offering to subsidize you.

You're offering to buy me clothes to wear when you take me out for dinners or concerts.

Something like that.

But you're already paying for everything.

I have told you, it doesn't make any difference to me.

She's tempted. And thinks: If he buys me so much as a pair of socks, I'll have lost my autonomy. My dignity.

And yet she does not know why this should be true.

SHE SLEEPS OVER only occasionally: once a week. Usually one of them has to work early the next day. They end up at his place more often, but he usually drives her home quite early, around ten. Sometimes, if he seems really tired, she takes a cab. She doesn't mind: It makes her feel autonomous, sophisticated, a little dangerous, even. Like someone in a movie.

If there were any movies about women who were independent and self-reliant, who didn't end up raped and/or murdered, or turn out to be serial killers.

He apologizes sometimes: not for her having to leave, exactly, but for her having come to his place and then to leave. He says: We both need to wake up in our own space.

You could come to my place, she says.

I do.

Not very often.

Your bed isn't very comfortable.

It's true. She still has the double-sized pine slat-and-futon bed that she bought with one of her first paycheques, back in her twenties. She's used to it, but she has to admit his bed is of a different species entirely.

At first she assumes he'll ask her to move in one day. Or more likely, that they'll get a bigger place, together.

They don't have this conversation, but she's old enough and experienced enough to know that Duane's personal space is really important to him. She has known one or two men like this: They don't invite women into their space casually. They don't do sleepovers. They like their space, their routines. No slippery slope of leaving a toothbrush and then a change of clothes, a yoga mat, one's own brand of yogurt in the fridge. Women, too. Cleo was like that. When she had her own apartment, Mandalay had crashed there a few times, but Cleo always rounded up Mandalay's things, before she went off to her classes, put them in ziplock bags, handed them to Mandalay.

Of course it's logical. The irritation of some men she'd spent weekends with, picking up her stuff, or complaining about it. It makes sense, it does. It's just that she's never before been in a longer term relationship that hasn't progressed to the point of one of them moving in with the other. It seems just the way things are meant to go. Romantic relationships progress or die, don't they?

IT HAS NEVER OCCURRED to her before to wonder what a man saw in her. If he asked her out, wanted to date her, sleep with her, she just assumed it was because he was attracted to her. If she accepted, because she was attracted to him. She assumed that there were mysterious, inexplicable forces at play, deciding who found whom attractive — and she took for granted that she was attractive to most men — and left it at that. And when things went badly, she assumed that the guy had problems: He was too controlling, too territorial, too jealous, too lazy. He had a roving eye. He was cheap or immature or depressive or not ready to commit.

She had never thought *incompatible*. She assumed that she was compatible with most men. Obviously she weeded out the worst cases before getting involved — the drunks and users, the unwashed, the thieves and moochers, the hitters and yellers. It didn't really take very long to figure out who these were.

Women who say they found out their husbands were addicts or

abusers or con artists a couple of years into the marriage – she never buys that. She thinks that they are willfully blind. She's had a lot of bad boyfriends, but she always knew early on. The signs were always there from the beginning, she had to admit.

But with Duane. The delight in it, in the gradual unfolding of him, of herself, as if maybe billions of micro-hooks were meshing together, with billions of tiny satisfying clicks. Her brain tickles, fizzes, as if some new section of her is coming into being.

Do you *have* parents? she asks.

Yes, I have parents.

What do they do? Where are they?

They live in Ottawa. My dad's a retired civil servant. Tax department. My mom is a retired elementary school teacher.

Do you like them?

Sometimes, yes.

What are they like?

He says: Ordinary. My mother is kind and concerned about people and often obsessed with tiny details and a bit naïve. My father is cautious and self-critical. They are responsible and try not to offend and they don't do or think anything interesting.

Which could be a good thing, with parents, she says.

He laughs. Yes.

They must have some eccentricities. Quirks.

He says, They go to Florida every year, for four months. January through April. They stay in the same condominium every year, for which they pay exorbitantly. When the Canadian dollar is low, they fill their second piece of checked luggage with toilet paper and coffee and laundry detergent. Oh, and peanut butter.

This doesn't seem so very strange to Mandalay, except that she can't imagine how much it costs to stay in a condo in Florida for four months out of every year.

And do they bring something back in their empty suitcases when they come back?

I'm not sure, he says. I'm guessing Tommy Bahama shirts, as that's what my brother and I get for Christmas every year.

Every year?

You doubt me?

You must have an impressive collection.

I do, he says. I do. One day I'm going to sew them all together into a massive quilt and spread it out somewhere public. An art installation.

Like Christo.

Exactly. I'll wrap Siwash Rock in it. A statement against creeping US capitalism.

She's not sure if he's being funny, and if he is, what he's being funny about.

Do *you* have parents? he asks.

She says, My father was a millwright, sort of a hippie, too. He was a lot older than my mother. He worked himself to death, I think. He died twenty years ago, when I was thirteen. My mother's kind of a hippie, too. She paints.

How she edits. She says: Up the coast. Small town. She does not say Butterfly Lake, because people over a certain age have heard about it: Butterfly Lake was in the news so much in the mid-eighties, and most people have ideas about it already, which will shape how they will react to her story, to her.

He says, My wife died of cancer. I don't want to talk about it. I don't want you to flinch when someone mentions cancer in my presence. I don't want you to avoid mentioning cancer. One day I might tell you more about her, but not now.

He says she is right. That what they are for each other is a kind of seawall against loneliness. And if so, he says, the relationship needs to step up. We need more emotional intimacy. More knowledge of each other. More trust.

She thinks: It is still about intensity of experience. He has merely come to understand that his enjoyment of her time with him, even their sexual pleasure, will be heightened if there is more knowledge of each other. More sense of risk.

She thinks, Because he has changed his mind on this matter, he will change his mind about other things.

HE SAYS: Four or five nights of the week I work late. I want to come home and retreat inside of myself. I do not have it in me to be aware of someone else's needs.

Maybe it would be better, Mandalay says, if he hadn't had to work at the kind of job that depleted him like that.

Ha, he said. You're an idealist. But it's not possible for every job to be simply fun or to fit into shorter work week.

Why not?

And it's not always a matter of being depleted. I love my work. It's very interesting to me. It doesn't deplete me. It's just that it takes fourteen hours to get through it, sometimes, and then I am tired of thinking.

Why do you need to put in sixty-hour work weeks? Do you need to make that much money?

No, obviously not. Why do I? Let's see. Because my firm wants a certain number of billable hours. They get paid too. Because if I don't put the hours into my cases, they won't get finished in a timely fashion. If I started turning some of them down, I would start losing my reputation and my presence. The competition would not only take those clients, but others would stop seeing me as an expert in my area, because I wouldn't be producing as much, so I would get fewer cases, and not as interesting or lucrative ones.

IT'S NOT ABOUT THE MONEY, he says. But when she tells him how much she makes, he is shocked. But you are getting shares, then?

No. Just wage.

But you're running the damn place, and you co-created it. You're doing a management job, the hours you put in and the growth you've created. You're being remunerated at about the same rate as a barista.

That's not the point, she says. I like my job. I like the arrangement. There are intangibles.

Really? And you can put those into your retirement fund, can you? How much is the owner making?

You know what, she says. She's laughing, but she is starting to feel the prickle of anger along the back of her neck. It's my decision, so back off.

It's just that I know this world inside and out, he says. I see people every week in court who are getting screwed by management.

Okay, she says. Maybe you're right. But I do need you to back off.

Also, he says, it's not just about you personally. It's about economic and social parity. What you choose to accept affects what others can ask for.

I don't want to have this conversation, she says.

He's sweating heavily, from his head, as if he's undergoing a great physical strain. But he draws in breath sharply, over his teeth, and says, fine. Okay. You're right. Not my business, unless you ask me.

PARVANEH ASKS: Will he ask you to marry him?

I don't know, she says. That's maybe not what this is about.

Is he single?

Widowed.

That is the best kind. A wealthy widower. No kids? Truly, Mandalay, you won't find better. Do you love him?

I'm in it for the fun, she says. We have a great time together. We relax, we enjoy ourselves, we really like each other. We're happy as we are.

Ahhh, Parvaneh says. You are what, thirty-three! You should be thinking about marriage. You should always be thinking, Is this one that I could be married to? You should be thinking long-term.

I'm not sure I want to marry. I like having a career.

You should have children, Parvaneh says. If you don't, nobody will visit you when you are old.

Mandalay laughs. This isn't Iran. Women can have perfectly good lives without husbands, here.

That's another thing, Parvaneh says. Western women are free to choose, but they choose badly. I hear the afternoon women talking, you know. She means the young women with the strollers. They are already talking about how they hate their husbands, how they think they will leave them. About having affairs.

I think it's very complicated, Mandalay says. Women here are free to choose, but they get caught up in unrealistic expectations of what their lives will be like. That's what makes them unhappy.

She has just thought of that, and it seems a pretty good insight. It's something she wouldn't have understood, a few months ago.

And another thing, Mandalay, Parvaneh says. This isn't a career.

But Mandalay hardly hears her over the rumble of the bread machine.

THIS IS WHAT IT'S LIKE. It's like finding yourself on another planet and having an alien life form approach you and start humming your secret, favourite song.

It's like climbing a mountain and being able to see the world around you, and then looking back and seeing the whole of your life as a trail to this point — a trail that makes sense.

It's like having all of your cells and molecules replaced by better ones — ones they've always wanted to be. Mandalay feels that she has been transfigured into someone smarter, wittier, wiser, more perceptive, more hopeful. Also, more open, generous, kind. She feels the world is lit up now: everything transformed, beautiful.

SHE CALLS HIM, on his mobile phone, one evening when she hasn't seen him or heard from him for a couple of days — though they have plans for the weekend — and when the call goes to voice mail, she doesn't leave a message. When she sees him next, he says, You called me. It's a statement, not a question.

Is it not permitted?

He laughs, not spontaneously. Of course it's permitted. I wouldn't have given you my number otherwise.

Okay, she says.

Did you call for a specific reason?

No, she says.

Nothing urgent?

No.

I imagined not. Or you would have left a message.

I'm still getting the impression that I shouldn't have called you, she says. His honesty, she thinks, liberates her. She is able to be bluntly honest, too.

I am not implying that, he says. I just wondered why you called.

Maybe I called just to connect with you, she says. To say hi, how was your day? People do that.

You wanted to have a conversation about the events of my day, and then tell me about yours.

Yes, she says. Part of her is quaking, perhaps in humiliation, but another part is standing on a magnificent hill, vigorously flapping new wings.

Is that something you would like to do?

Occasionally, she says. I live alone, as you know. Sometimes I just want to say: I had this experience today. I think it meant this to me. Or to listen to someone say that to me. To listen while someone makes a story out of the events of their day for me.

It's a fairly common human interaction, she wants to add, but doesn't.

Were you lonely? he asks, and she can't pin down his tone as either mocking or sympathetic. It seems to be neither – maybe just curious.

Yes, she says. I was lonely.

She has really put herself out there now. She hopes that she sounded ironic, or at least incredibly blasé.

He takes her hand – he has been parking his car; they're going to eat at the new French restaurant – he takes her left hand in his left hand and lifts it to his lips. *I can't*, he says, kissing the tip of her index finger – *be* – he kisses the middle finger – *the answer to* – now the ring finger – everyone's *loneliness* (her baby finger). Then holds her thumb between his own index finger and thumb and runs the ball of it over his upper lip.

Then a smile that she doesn't know an adjective for – inscrutable seems clichéd, and not quite accurate anyway – and gets out of the car, and comes around – not to open her door; he doesn't do that, but to hold out his hand again as she steps out – it's a very low-slung car – onto the curb.

The next weekend he says: I feel it would be good to have some uninterrupted time together. Should we take a trip? Can you take a week off?

She feels first a surge of pleasure, excitement; then some doubt. He'll want to go somewhere she won't be able to afford, and he'll have to pay.

I've always wanted to go the Queen Charlottes, he says. Interested?

Haida Gwaii. Oh, yes.

I have a couple of ideas, he says. Maybe I could tell you, and you could choose.

The options are a sailing ship with a naturalist that travels the archipelago in a week, or camping and sea kayaking by themselves. Do you think you could handle the kayaking? he asks.

She has kayaked. But she can't decide.

He gives her brochures to look at. Take a couple of days, he says. When she has some time, the next afternoon, she goes to the library and uses the computer to look up the sailing tour company website, and the cost of renting kayaks at Skidegate. She's not adept, yet, at navigating websites, finding information on the computer, but she finds her way. The sailing expedition runs about five thousand dollars a couple. The kayaks are a few hundred for a week, camping equipment included. She thinks: He has been very, very sneaky. She calls him up, leaves a message, her first, on his voice mail. Kayaking, she says.

And then she tells Parvaneh: I need to talk to your uncle about my compensation.

An Education

CLIFF HAS BEEN ON THE CAMPUS, which occupies a large promontory of land to the west of the city, before. He had visited the anthropology museum after seeing a program about it, and had descended one of the very long wooden staircases, with its railings and resting platforms, down the cliff face, down deep into the rainforest, and walked along the beaches, even the nude beach (it had been early spring, so no nudes) and back up another zig-zagging set of stairs. The trip to campus had taken him two buses and over an hour. He had always meant to go back, but had not. It seemed a trip to another country, an island perhaps.

He had skirted the main part of the campus, then, afraid to wander in among the concrete and glass buildings, the manicured gardens. So he hadn't seen the campus, really.

Ben notes the names of the clusters of buildings they pass by: Earth Science, Forest Science, Life Science. The buildings named after people. Cliff feels the tug of curiosity. It is another country, he thinks. City state. Everything looks *intentional*. Students live there in the big towers but he can't imagine what that would be like. On the outskirts, clusters of optometrists' offices and pizza takeouts form a kind of village, and then there are the mansions where the profs and university administrators live, some with gardens like parks.

Cliff has worked in some of those gardens. He tells Ben this. Those places are worth a couple of million, Ben says. It's ridiculous. But Ben's parents live near here, too.

Ben picked Cliff up from his apartment and he sees now that this has meant an hour or more round trip for him. I was going to MEC anyway, Ben says.

Maybe we'll crash at my house later, Ben says. Folks are away.

Ben drives all around and through the campus, showing it to Cliff, and then parks and leads him between buildings to the pub. Cliff wonders if he would be able to find his way back, on his own. Or to find the bus platform.

In the pub it's noisy, of course, but really *clean*. It's not like a bar. The ceiling is high and there is an architectural grandeur to the room, beyond the clutter of chairs and bodies, the pool tables and the incessant banging and wailing of the band. There are columns and panels and other interesting structures. It's like a big public room, a library for example.

The people in the pub are mostly students, he guesses. Young people, mostly taller than him, except the Asian ones. Even some of them though. They have that different look that students have, at least in groups, than other young adults: more casual, more relaxed or at ease. They look like they still think of themselves as adolescents. Carefree? That might be going too far. Maybe something about the shoulders, the spine. They are all wealthy, he supposes, supported by parents or at least growing up with money. What says that? They are certainly all scruffily dressed, in frayed and faded clothes. He sees a lot of worn-in jeans, plaid flannel shirts, old woolen sweaters, thrift-store overcoats. Everyone looks like they need a hair trim – maybe even a shampoo.

Shabby, scruffy. Ray would have send him home if he turned up for work like that. Yet something about the students says money, privilege. Maybe it's a kind of healthy good looks: He doesn't see any bizarre, any ugly faces.

They haven't got far into the room before Ben is hailed, met with back slaps, even a handshake. Ben seems unembarrassed. He has a lot of friends. They're pulled to a table with four others right away. He introduces Cliff: my brother. The friends all say, enthusiastically, Hey, or Hey, man. Good to see you. He thinks for about thirty seconds that they're interested in him and then realizes that they are just like that. Ben says their names ironically, as if it's not cool to have names, and he forgets them right way. They refer to each other by nicknames that are different than the ones Ben told him.

The four other guys all look like Ben, though, or variations of him. One is taller, with a too-lean face and jutting jaw, but the same light hair and beard. Another might be Ben's double, but has darker hair. One has slightly longer hair and no beard, but a deep tan, and the fourth has really dark skin: Indian maybe, though he has no accent at all.

They are all interested in snowboarding. That is what they talk about. Cliff has never been snowboarding, though he's seen it on TV. He hasn't been to Whistler, where they snowboard. He can't join in the conversation, though he doesn't mind just listening and picking stuff up. And not having to be thinking of things to say to Ben, as he did when they were driving up to campus. Ben had kept asking him questions that Cliff couldn't formulate answers to quickly enough. He knew he should ask Ben things too, but anything he could think of wouldn't make sense to ask. He wanted to say: Do you notice we have the same hands? And: Do I smell like your littermate? And: Did you ever wake up in the middle of the night when you were small and think you were back home and then realize you weren't and feel like someone had pulled out a plug in you and you would just drain away?

He wants to ask these things, but he wouldn't even know how to find the right words.

The other guys, Ben's friends, are all talking about snowboarding but Cliff doesn't mind, and he is happy to half-listen and to watch the people around the pub and drink a beer poured from one of the communal pitchers. (Will he have to contribute one? Has he brought enough cash?) He's happy to listen to them talk about girls, a different category of talking-about-girls than what Ray does, which is body parts and what he's done to them, a catalogue of deeds. Ben and his friends do kind of the opposite, though their talk is no less dirty: It's like they're having a competition to see who is the least adept or lucky with girls.

Man, one of the guys is saying, she gave me a *look*, you know, that look, and my manhood kind of did a U-turn and crawled back up my pubes, whimpering. And another of the guys says, Yeah, my date! It was like having to write my calc three exam *again*, without studying. They all laugh, mocking but also not.

A competitive display of sexual inadequacy, Cliff hears a voice say in his head, in the awed whispers of David Attenborough. *Only in these isolated boreal islands do we encounter these s fascinating adaptations. Only here, where the male of the species don't need to compete for....*

But faux David Attenborough's commentary is broken off by the arrival of two girls. Perhaps they are the girls of the conversation: Cliff can't tell. The guys greet them with minimal attention. One girl leans over and kisses one of the guys fairly intensely on the mouth, but doesn't then drape herself over him, or giggle, or even sit next to him. They just all squeeze over to make room for a couple more chairs. The girls are both pale, naked of cosmetics except for apparent bruising around their eyes. He knows that's makeup. They are both skinny, not very big in the chests. Both are wearing tight low-slung jeans and little T-shirts that show their navels. One is wearing a grey ski tuque. The one who kissed, whose long hair is the colour of something familiar that he can't name, a brownish-tan colour, is sitting so near to him that their thighs are rubbing. He draws his leg away but she doesn't try to. She looks at him neutrally. Hey, she says. Or not neutrally, but with the look of a member of one species for a member of another that is neither prey nor predator. Like a deer looking at a porcupine.

After the girls arrive, the conversation shifts again, to a course several of them have taken, and then to what Cliff thinks at first is a discussion of a TV series, but then comes to realize is actually a group of real people, other students and teachers at the school they all seem to have attended.

The beer flows and flows. Cliff needs to go to the men's. He has drunk a lot of beer. A lot. When he stands up, he knows he is actually a bit drunk. He had better be more careful.

When he comes back, he can't find Ben or his table. It takes him a while to realize that he has lost them. At first, he thinks he has forgotten where the table is and mills through the crowd, expecting that some stranger's features will suddenly coalesce into a familiar face. That Ben will suddenly pop out of the background camouflage of people who look similar to him. But Ben doesn't appear. So maybe he's outside. Cliff recalibrates: He'll look for the table instead, for Ben's friends, Sam and – the other ones, whose names he can't remember. Only he can't quite remember what they look like. He circles back to the table he thought was his when he came back from the men's, and there is a group of three guys and a girl sitting at it. He isn't sure. He tries to walk past without slowing too much, to make eye contact without seeming to make eye contact. Do any of this party recognize him? But mostly they don't look up. One guy does, and Cliff thinks he sees recognition in his glance but when he stops, the guy opens his eyes too wide and raises an eyebrow, and Cliff wants to move on without speaking, but he asks, Have you seen Ben?

No, the guy says, too deliberately, I have not seen Ben. His full, red lips, moist with beer, emerge from a bristly light beard.

Cliff tries again. Is this Ben's table?

The guy laughs. I imagine it might have been Ben's table at one time, he says, but it is now our table. The girl beside him, long brown hair and oval face, says something to the guy, and he laughs again.

Do you know me? Cliff wants to ask. Do you recognize me? But how can he ask that?

He ambles on, makes another weaving, alert walk in a figure eight around the room, trying at look at people intently without appearing to be looking at them. Come on, moron, he says to himself. Remember something. Don't be so useless.

On his third round a burly guy about his age, mustached, in a T-shirt, stops him with a type of hip-check. Cliff doesn't want confrontation of any sort. He says sorry and sidesteps, but the man is there before him, is blocking his way in a manner so subtle yet effective that he must have been practicing for years.

You looking for someone? the burly guy asks.

Yes. My brother.

The guy smiles, shakes his head minutely. He must have a hundred pounds on Cliff. Cliff can feel all of his own animal defences awaken: His feet and hands seem filled with electricity, and the hairs on the back of his neck rise. Hackles, he thinks. But he knows that even to someone standing right next to them, the other man's actions might be invisible.

The guy watches Cliff: holds him in his gaze a minute too long. You don't look like you belong here, buddy, he says, finally. Still smiling. Just letting you know I've noticed you circling, eyeing people up. I'm going to give you some friendly advice. Keep your hands where I can see them and find your friends or get out of here really soon.

Cliff falls away from the guy – bouncer, he must be – as if released from a magnetic force. Crap. His face burns. Low anger begins its spring-thaw trickle, too late. I'm not a pickpocket, asshole, he whispers. Someone turns hearing him. He brushes past. Makes it to the door.

Outside, groups of people talking, laughing, but he doesn't recognize anyone. It's too dark. Ben would not have just taken off, ditched him, would he? But why not? He imagines Ben's face, remote, polite, kind of surprised. Hey, man. Didn't know I was supposed to let you know all of my movements. Didn't know you wanted your hand held. Old insults, the push and shove of adolescence, trickle up. He doesn't know: Are guys supposed to tell each other before they split?

In the cooler air his head clears a little. He's afraid to go back inside but he has to. He'll put his hands in his pockets, move around more purposefully. It would help if he were taller. Also he sees this now, his blue windbreaker is just kind of the wrong thing, though he can't put his finger on why. Also his cords and golf shirt. Nobody else is wearing clothes like his, though he can't say why what they are wearing, specifically, should be correct. Loose, dirty-looking jeans, plaid flannel, rock-band-logo T-shirts. Hiking boots. Things he would not think to wear to work.

Inside he tries not to look at people but he wants to keep an eye out for the bouncer who, he knows, will approach him with the lethal stealth of a large cat, a leopard maybe. He makes a circuit. Is that the same group of people at the table he thought was his? No Ben, though. What if Ben is looking for him, or thinks he's left, now? He doesn't have a sense of how much time has lapsed, so he can't judge if this explanation is probable. He should get another beer. He doesn't want another beer – his stomach is churning and he's still conscious of being drunk – but he should get one so he looks like he has a purpose. Does he have enough cash?

There's nowhere to sit so he edges his back up against one of the support columns. Its rough cold edges.

A hip-check again but this one lower, not subtle. He moves sideways, away, before looking, but it's a woman, and she's smiling at him, not with the bouncer's shark-smile but a real one. Eyes. Dimples and eyes and red lipstick. A little taller than he is.

She's at a table with two spots. She has saved a spot with her jacket. She says, sit. The metal seat still warm. Who has he displaced?

She's curvy, he sees. Well, fat. Big hips, arms and breasts, and a belly. But also long thick lashes and thick, lustrous hair. Her smiling makes him feel larger, like he has a right to be in this space, like something heavy and sharp-edged is being lifted from his shoulders.

He can see that she is not so young, and that her makeup is of a different style than that of the other women, the students. Shinier, more opaque. Her clothes are shinier, too: A red sweater stretches across her generous breasts and she's wearing a skirt and boots of something that looks like some kind of leather or leather-like substance, and they're shiny too, and maybe don't reflect light in the same way real leather does.

She is still smiling, her eyes crinkling at him in the corners. A genuine smile includes the eyes. What program had he heard that on? Her hair is a cascade of glossy curls, not like most of the other girls in the pub, with their lank, unwashed-looking hair. When she moves her head the big curls move around and shine. He tries not to look at her breasts again. He knows he's looked at them at least twice. She says a couple of things to him but he can't hear her in the din, which is worse sitting than standing, even. He nods, smiles. …friends? she says. …U2? That's a guess, but a U2 song is playing. He leans in closer. …work? she asks. He nods, smiles again. This is crazy. He should get up again, look for Ben. But here's a couple more beers in front of them, and when he takes out his wallet she holds up her hand, she's got this.

He doesn't actually like her smile, he thinks now. There's something kind of scary about the way her eyes, which are kind of small, it's the thick black lashes that made them look bigger, and her mouth, which is small, too, like a too-small door, a door leading under some stairs, disappear into the fat of her cheeks. When she smiles it looks like something is being squeezed off.

She shakes her hair at him again and some small hard thing he doesn't quite see falls out and strikes the table and falls to the floor. He wants to leave, at that point, but another beer has appeared in front of him, and he begins to drink it.

And there's Ben, suddenly, his hand on Cliff's shoulder, his arm around the girl with the tuque. Hey, man, Ben says. His voice is not slurred but relaxed, a bit slow. Hey, man, where did you get to? I was just looking for you. Think we're going to split now.

Cliff tries to get up but his foot is somehow pinned. No need, Ben says. No need. We'll hang out later this weekend, hey? He's a bit unfocussed, or focussed on something else. The girl seems to be holding him upright, at one point. Cliff can see the situation: He will only be in the way now. Ben has another trajectory now. He can see that; he isn't stupid. He knows what he has to do.

Yeah, catch you later, man, he says. Ben makes the telephone sign with his hand, taps Cliff's shoulder, and kind of lurches away, a three-step as he leans on the girl.

Cliff wonders what time the buses stop running. It's a good ten kilometres from the campus to his building off Main. The woman is smiling at him again, her eyebrows raised, her head slightly tilted. Her skin is very smooth and opaque; it seems to lack capillaries or pores. Her cheeks are perfect half-globes. She seems to be waiting for an answer to a question.

KAREN HOFMANN

▸ 159 ◂

My brother, Cliff says. The woman leans close, smiles again, shows her teeth, which are small and not very white. Do you need a ride? she asks.

IN HER BED she sucks him over and over. She straddles him and her breasts swing above him like fruit. Each as big as his head. She invites him to put his head between them, and his dick. She invites him to mount her from behind, but attempting this, he is reminded of a program he once saw where a very small dog, a toy poodle maybe, was standing on a little stool mounting a much larger one. Making the point about dogs being all one species. Thinking of this makes him laugh and lose his erection. She splays herself out on the bed and he thrusts happily but she is soon bored with that; he can see it on her face. He knows he is supposed to be doing things with his tongue but he isn't sure. He wants to but she says: You can pay me back later. Which scares the part of his brain that is still working but he can ignore it.

He stays through Saturday and Saturday night, and Sunday and Sunday night. There is no question of his leaving, it seems. He thinks that he has had more sex than in his lifetime up to this weekend. On Monday morning she says, I have to go to work and you have to go to work. But we'll have tonight. She covers his face with little kisses, *mwa mwa mwa*. He thinks now with guilt of Sophie. He's left extra food out, thinking he might stay at Ben's, but he's never left her this long. He doesn't have time to check on her before work though.

After he gets to work his thoughts come back to him like a photograph developing, and he thinks: I won't go back to Loretta's. I'll call and tell her not tonight. He does this. He goes back to his place and feeds and strokes Sophie, and calls Loretta from the pay phone.

Her voice is so strange. There's something in it of a small boat that's been cut loose but he can't tell after a while if the boat drifting toward the edge is her or himself. He hears in her voice that if he does not go over to her place tonight he will not be allowed to go over again. He rides over. She won't look at him or smile at first and then she says a lot of things about using her. He says he's sorry over and over and then goes to leave, but she lies on the floor between him and the door and holds his ankles, and then pulls him down on top of her. He bangs his elbow painfully, trying not to land with his full weight on her. When he sees she's laughing, he's so relieved that his view of everything changes: goes bright, shadowless. He stays.

KAREN HOFMANN

Letdown

CLEO SAYS TO MANDALAY: I love this house.

You always say that.

She does, though. She always feels a rush of pleasure in and longing for the house Mandalay lives in, its elegant architecture, its views of English Bay, of the city and the mountains rising to the north of the city: swashes of changing blues. It looks like it was built in the first decade of the century, and is probably worth half a million dollars or more, because of its location.

The house been cut into many suites, but Cleo imagines the original architectural beauty: the wide French doors between the former dining room and the living room (which are bedrooms, now), the hardwood floors, which, though scarred and yellowed, are warm and authentic, the high ceilings, the wide mouldings, the beautiful windows. She fantasizes about owning it, fixing it up. If it were hers! She sometimes walks through each room, in her imagination, sanding, re-papering, re-painting, putting in period tile and fixtures and handles and faucets ordered from period hardware catalogues, creating something out of this house, as some of Trent's colleagues have.

When she tells Mandalay what could be done to fix up the apartment, what it could look like, though, Mandalay is annoyed. She says,

It's beautiful as it is. And it is, sort of, with the shabby assortment of things Mandalay has, the little wicker tables from second-hand stores, the armchairs layered with shawls and scarves. But it could be so much better.

She had thought that she would have a house like this, when she married and started working. After she had paid off her student loans.

Her own house, a basic suburban builder's house, lacks distinction. It gives her no scope. Even the furniture is bland, monolithic: pale oak and puffy pine-green leather, furniture that was already out of fashion, likely, when she and Trent went to the store on the outskirts of the city and bought (thanks to a gift from Trent's parents) what they needed to furnish the house.

I just wish my house had some more character, she says.

Mandalay says: You could get slipcovers for the sofas and chairs. You could paint the furniture white. You could have the wall-to-wall taken out, and put in colourful patterned rugs.

Trent would never let me, Cleo says.

She's in town for her birthday trip — it's actually a couple of weeks past her birthday, but this was the first day Trent was free to watch the children. She had asked for a weekend off, a weekend to go into town, stay in town, visit Mandalay, do some shopping. Trent hadn't wanted her to. He had tried to dislodge her plan by first saying, Why don't we have Mandalay come here for the weekend? That would be easier. And then: Why don't we all go into town for the day? Maybe Mandalay could watch the kids so we could go out for dinner. She'd almost been defeated, almost given up. But Trent had to do it as her birthday present, all she had asked for.

And she had told his mother, on the phone, that it was happening, and Trent knew that.

She might have discovered a new strategy. She'll have to see if it works.

But here she is, having caught an early-morning bus — Trent didn't want to be left looking after the kids without the car for the day — here she is, with almost a whole day to herself. It is true that they have just decided to go clothes shopping for Mandalay, but she does not mind that. It will be at least a change.

Mandalay says: Why don't you try on some things, too?

I don't need anything, she says. Really, I'm at home with the kids all day. I never go anywhere.

But seeing the displays in the shops, she wants new things. Clothes have changed in the last year or so, she sees, and not just subtly, but radically: The baggy jeans and comfortable T-shirts, the flannel and the flowing dresses that she has been wearing the last decade have suddenly disappeared, and been replaced by snug-fitting jeans and tiny tops and short, ultra-feminine, little girls' dresses. And everywhere, snug black pants, yoga pants, she thinks they're called, but worn for every occasion. Snug in the bum and thighs, flaring out slightly at the hem.

Nothing she owns looks like anything in the shops. Of course, she has been pregnant or post-natal for the last five years. But still. She feels aggrieved, as if something has been kept from her.

Why don't you try something on too? Mandalay calls through the change room door.

If she starts, she won't be able to stop. Better to stay on the outside, just looking.

I thought you only shopped vintage, she says.

Styles have changed too much, Mandalay says. Or not enough. I can't find what I need.

In the past, Mandalay would have said *what I want*, not *what I need*.

It's kind of like stuff from the seventies, Cleo says. The tight flared pants and little shirts. You should just ransack Crystal's cellar.

It would be just different enough not to work, Mandalay says. Anyway, I don't think this stuff is going to end up in thrift stores. It's pretty cheap.

She can see that. The knits are flimsy, not well sewn.

I guess it's the new thing, Mandalay says. Disposable clothes.

Isn't that environmentally wrong? Who is buying this? Cleo wonders.

I don't think any of it would fit me, she says. The shoulders and upper arms and busts are so small, and nothing covers the middle. Nobody who has given birth could ever wear these things.

You have to work out, Mandalay says, her voice muffled now as if she's pulled something tight over her head. The waist is the new erogenous zone.

Anyway, I don't have any money, Cleo says. This is not quite true: She doesn't have any income herself, but Trent says she should buy what she needs. She's pretty sure he'd grumble, though, say that she should get a job, if she said she needed new clothes.

When am I going to meet your new man? she asks, when they finally leave the shop and are back out on the sidewalk.

He's not really into that, Mandalay says.

Into what?

Family things. Meeting the relations.

So you have a lot of mutual friends?

No.

So what do you do, then? Socially?

We go out for dinner. Good restaurants. Symphony, gallery openings, benefit parties.

Are you sleeping with him?

Well, duh.

So you're like, his mistress.

No. Why would you even say that?

I assume, the things you do, he's for paying all of it.

Mandalay doesn't answer: gives Cleo the silent treatment for the next two blocks. Cleo has perhaps gone too far. She has just wanted to understand the arrangement. She says this to Mandalay.

Why? Mandalay asks.

Why what?

Why would you want to understand my *arrangement*? You might want to know that your conventional house and two kids in the suburbs isn't everyone's dream.

Did I say it was? Cleo asks.

Her first day off, her first day to herself in months, and this is how she's spending it: trailing through shops watching Mandalay preen and listening to her put her down. Why does she always get sucked into this? She ought to have her head examined. Trent always says: The definition of madness is repeating actions and expecting different results.

And Bodhi hasn't called her. He has apparently called Cliff, but not her. She has to wonder if Mandalay even gave him the right number.

They are both silent. They walk shoulder to shoulder; they allow themselves to be separated by other walkers; they rejoin.

Why don't you call him? Mandalay asks.

Cleo says: He has to call me first. He has my number. I have to let him call.

That's weird. I know you think about him all the time, Mandalay says.

MANDALAY SAYS: His adoptive mother is trying to poison him against us.

Really? She knows to take some of Mandalay's claims with a good teaspoon of salt. I can imagine that would be a natural impulse, though, can't you?

She's feeling better, less anxious. They've stopped to have lunch, are eating at a North Indian restaurant, a cuisine Cleo hasn't tried before. This is what she loves to do. It's so good to have interesting food, an uninterrupted meal.

Mandalay says: She showed him the social worker's report. From when he was – taken. It said that Bodhi was neglected, mother mentally ill, father ill and sporadically employed and not coping with older children. Garbage on the floor, no food in the house.

That's not true, Cleo says. There was peanut butter and bread. The garbage was in a bucket.

Mandalay says, I'm just telling you. He had a copy of it. I saw it. It said that Bodhi had chronic diaper rash, probably impetigo. He had ringworm.

No he didn't, Cleo says. He must have picked that up in foster care. Pinworms, maybe. Everyone had pinworms sometimes, in Butterfly Lake.

Listen, though, Mandalay says. It said he had scurf. What's that? Like scurvy?

A kind of crust on his scalp, Cleo says. It's common. It's not a sign of neglect. She feels confident, a little angry, but at least united with Mandalay in this. Shared indignation. The basis for a lot of social connection, if she thinks about it.

He had not had any vaccinations and was Vitamin D and niacin deficient. He had baby-bottle mouth, whatever that is.

It means his baby teeth were already decaying, from falling asleep with milk pooled in his mouth, Cleo says.

It said that he did not appear to have any burns, bruises, or broken bones, Mandalay says, and that he was a bit developmentally delayed.

How does Mandalay remember such detail? But she's always been good at repeating conversations, even from long ago, verbatim.

He was not, Cleo says. He was walking. He could pick up objects and say words.

I'm just telling you what he said it said, Mandalay responds.

A kind of dread going through her now. Poison, yes: That's what it feels like. Something curdling the actual blood in her veins. She feels cold, a little sick. I don't know if I want to meet him, she says. It sounds like he's getting a lot of pressure. He's going to feel divided loyalties. Maybe it's not the right time.

He's not a child, Mandalay says.

IN THE LATE AFTERNOON, walking back toward Mandalay's apartment — Cleo must catch the city bus to the terminal, then the Greyhound home — Mandalay says, why don't you stay another day, why don't you stay longer? We never see each other anymore. We'll go out for dinner; we'll see a movie or something.

On the phone Trent says: But what will I feed Sam? And she remembers only then that he's still breastfeeding three times a day, at night and in the morning and before his nap, to fall asleep. She says, not convinced herself, He'll take a bottle; just rock him and sing to him. He'll be okay.

Trent says he'll drive in and pick her up. No, she says. The kids need to go to bed.

She won't be that late if he picks her up now, he says. Nine, nine-thirty at the latest. He says it with such authority that she herself is almost swayed, but she thinks, sensibly, that it could well be later. She remembers that he is always curtailing her time; he is always second-guessing, modifying her plans. No, she says. I don't want to have a time limit. I will stay overnight at Mandalay's. I'll bus home in the morning.

After she hangs up she feels a terrible longing for Sam, and for Olivia too: a desperate nostalgia for them, a panicky regret at her decision.

You shouldn't have to ask his permission, Mandalay says.

She hadn't asked Trent's permission, had she? She was just asking politely.

You're totally apologetic, Mandalay says. You don't take any initiative. You should assert yourself more.

But then Trent gets angry, and there's always conflict. She doesn't like to argue in front of the children. She doesn't want always to be fighting.

It is too difficult to explain this to Mandalay. But she feels, now, the separation pangs subside and a kind of exhilaration run through her, in spite of Mandalay's lecture. She feels free. She feels the next fifteen or so hours of freedom ahead of her, a wide meadow of time.

Mandalay loans her a dress (You can keep it, she says; It's a little short for me) and tights. Cleo will have to wear her own ankle boots. (Your feet are so tiny, Mandalay says). Cleo thinks, taking off her jeans and sweater, that she never wants to see them again. She will buy some new things, she thinks.

On their way to a restaurant, they pause at an intersection, wait on the corner for the light to change, and then suddenly Cleo sees Cliff, on his bike, and so they all stop and talk, Cliff shy and a bit awkward, as usual, herself trying to draw him out. (He has a cut and some bruising on the side of his face, on his left cheekbone, she notices when he takes his helmet off.) They try to get Cliff to go with them to dinner, but Cliff demurs: He has to get home, he says.

And then the really incredible thing happens, the thing that Trent will not believe when she tells him the next day.

Mandalay says, Oh my god. That's *him*.

Who? Cleo can see, on the facing corner, only a small group of young people. Three young guys, almost boys still, and a girl. They're carrying bags, they've been to the liquor store.

Mandalay waves, calls: Ben!

One of the boys looks up, looks directly at Mandalay, grins and waves back.

In Cleo's chest everything seems to seize up: lungs and heart and diaphragm.

The boy says something to his companions and they all glance at Cleo and Mandalay without much interest, and then the light changes, and Cleo sees that he isn't moving with his friends, but hanging back on the opposite curb, as his friends surge forward. And Cleo herself can't move, she is frozen in place, but Mandalay pulls her by the elbow. They cross. It's like walking through mud, through thick cement. Something slows her progress. The pavement stretches before her, a continent wide, and the very air is thick. The sounds of the cars and the other pedestrians and the seagulls are slowed as well, each note taking on a kind of physical weight.

She feels that Mandalay is dragging her across the intersection, up onto the curb. She could not have made it on her own volition.

And there he is, waiting for them a little back from the corner, out of the foot traffic. He's much taller than she is, quite a bit taller even then Mandalay, and she has to look up at him, and at first the sun is in her eyes: He's backlit, only a halo of sunlit hair around his head.

There are a few dozen seconds, maybe a couple of minutes, Cleo thinks, when one meets someone one hasn't seen for a long time, when they appear as strangers, and their faces must be read objectively. And then there is a switch thrown in the mind, and the physiognomy suddenly becomes familiar again, recognized, seen now subjectively as a whole, rather than the sum of its parts. And more significantly, this new face is superimposed in the visual memory over the old, so that it disappears, and only the new now exists in that catalogue or whatever it is of known faces.

Cleo feels this happen: the succession of impressions, the un-known young man with the pleasing, symmetrical, oval face, light hair, slight beard; then, the familiar cast of family features, the family resemblances; then a face that clicks into place as familiar, long-known: *you*. You.

Mandalay says, Ben, this is Cleo.

Cleo puts out her hand. She sees realization (not recognition) openness, curiosity, embarrassment flicker in succession in his eyes.

I was meaning to call you, he says.

It is so inadequate, so paltry, that her heart shrivels a little inside her. It's every flimsy excuse ever made to the one who loves by the beloved, to the one who cares excessively by the one for whom the caring is invisible, or taken for granted, or a small source of embarrassment, something unearned, never longed for.

But of course it is not that. He doesn't remember her. He doesn't know. She can't even resent his oblivion. It's the best fortune he could have had, that he doesn't remember her, has not missed her.

He can't join them: plans. But he'll catch up with them soon. He moves down the street; he is gone.

Cliff bicycles off, is gone, too.

She needs to check up with him more often. She doesn't like the look of that bruising.

THE LAST TIME Cleo saw her brother Che was in the fall of 1989. She was in university, in her third year. She had moved into a new place, a house in Kitsilano that she shared with three other girls – women. The three others were there before her, and when Cleo had answered their ad, she had been worried that they would not want her as their fourth. They all seemed much older than her, grown-up, focused. The house was well-kept; it was the opposite of the grungy student suites she was used to seeing. One of the women was wearing a suit, which seemed awfully sophisticated. As it turned out, the woman in the suit was the same age as Cleo, and was considered the least sophisticated of the group: She worked part-time in a bank to put herself through school, whereas the other two, in their sweatpants and T-shirts, had wealthy parents who were supporting them. But these refinements of class and dress, Cleo came to understand only later. The two wealthier girls were great partiers, and leavers of doors unlocked and pans on the stove and water running, and food and clothes piled up in corners. They, not Cleo, were the classic undesirable roommates. But at the first meeting, they all took pains to appear sensible and responsible, and they accepted Cleo, to her relief.

But then Che had moved to Vancouver, and had started showing up at Cleo's house, always without warning, and after she'd just arrived home, as if he'd been watching her house. She'd made the mistake of mentioning this timing to her roommates, who said it was creepy. One of them insisted that Che was a drug addict. Was he? Cleo didn't know. Certainly he had been dirty, and sometimes hungry in the way of people who have not eaten much in weeks, and had smelled of pot. Had sometimes seemed stoned. He had sometimes been jittery, but he might have been sleep-deprived, starving. He sometimes had no place to sleep, and she'd let him sleep on the floor of her room.

He had changed his name to Shane, and his skin had darkened so much from living out of doors that she hardly recognized him.

Her roommates had said he was scary, he needed help, they didn't feel comfortable with him hanging around. She'd understood. He'd turned up in the middle of the night, was having an argument with someone outside their house, and she'd paid for a cab to take him to a shelter.

Her roommates, though they were partiers themselves, were cross about the middle-of-the-night shouting. They thought they might get evicted. The mother of one of her roommates was a substance-abuse counselor who told Cleo, via her daughter, that as long as Cleo was giving Che money or other kinds of support, she was enabling Che's addiction. Tough love, the roommate's mother said.

Cleo was giving Che money, but not much. She never had much. He never wanted to take it. She did not want to *enable* him, as people said, but she didn't want him to starve. He was but he was not still her little brother.

Cleo had said to Che: It's better if you don't come by here anymore. And he had not. And a few weeks later, he was dead: He had died of a combination of exposure and overdose, hitchhiking back to town from a logging camp he'd been kicked out of.

She could not save both Che and Cliff. She had saved Cliff. She had done that. She had not seen, at that time, how she could save herself and both of them. She had saved herself and Cliff, but not Che.

She had not been able to save Bodhi, but he'd been fine. In the bigger scheme of things, in a world where babies in Third World countries die at the rate of one per minute, or something like that, he'd been really, really fine.

WHEN SHE GETS BACK to her house the next morning, her breasts hard with milk, Sam gives her the cold shoulder. He doesn't seem interested in nursing. She has to express milk, for the pain. In the evening Trent puts Sam to bed while she's still clearing up the dishes, and he still won't nurse, and she has to express again, but there's only a little milk, and in a couple of days more, there's none.

Afloat

THE FLIGHT TO SANDSPIT is scheduled once a day and arrives at three in the afternoon. Descending, Mandalay sees the islands against the sea, more rounded, thickly-forested, than she had imagined. The intense green of the conifers is brilliant against the dark blue-green of the sea. White scrim along the shores. White of boats. Then, a cleared area, roofs of buildings, black strips of road that end suddenly. And near the end of the descent, the waves and gulls visible just above them.

They have a vehicle and driver waiting, a big SUV and a young Haida man called Gerry, who loads their gear — four duffle bags — into the back, and opens a rear passenger door for Mandalay, the front one for Duane. It's an hour's drive still to the bed and breakfast in the bay where they'll stay the night, and set out from in the morning. Gerry is booked to pick them up again in the morning, carry them and their equipment to the kayak rental shop at the government docks.

They have salmon steaks at the only restaurant in town. Eat, Duane says. Might be your last meal for a while. He seems keyed up, a little edgy, not present. She tells herself she won't ask what's wrong, but then she does, and he says he's just anxious about the trip arrangements. I sweat the details, he says.

There's no internet at the bed and breakfast. Their host shrugs, her pleasant round face untroubled. Sometime we'll get it, she says.

Duane seems irritable, or rather, that he's trying not to be irritable. He says, I should have thought about not having internet.

Do you need it? Mandalay asks.

Of course I need it, or I wouldn't be worried about it, would I?

It's the first time he's showed irritation in front of her, let alone towards her. He apologizes. I shouldn't have left this loose end to tie up when I got here, but I was waiting on somebody else to provide some information.

It's okay, she says. She's not sure it is, but she wants him to relax, to let go of work. Maybe you can phone, she suggests. She knows his mobile doesn't have service here, but there are phones.

He spends half an hour in a phone booth near the docks, comes back whistling. Took care of it, he says, and kisses her.

There's a long evening to pass, even after they've walked to the restaurant and back to their bedroom, to the docks and back again. It's very light out. Mandalay has been up since four – she went to the café for the morning – and is tired, but not sleepy, and Duane seems excited too. They walk on the shore, which is steep, rocky, here, and then finally just sit on one of the cedar logs and watch the water. After a few minutes, Duane whispers: Turn slowly. To your left. And she does, and there's a mottled brown bird about as high as a table standing on the rocks, ripping at a good-sized salmon with a beak the bulk and shape of a man's hand, if he were to hold it up in a pincer shape.

Duane's hand is on the small of her back; she feels the pressure increase there as they watch the bird. Immature bald eagle, she knows. The bird's talons shift on the fish as it bends its head for another tear.

Nice welcome, Duane says. The eagle swivels an eye toward them, but it's clear he – or she – has known they were here all along, and not been bothered.

When it's finally getting dark, they walk back to the bed and breakfast, and other guests are there now, who've been boating or hiking all day. The house has a big fireplace in a high-ceilinged log room, and the other guests, two couples from Germany, are drinking and talking. They offer Duane and Mandalay some of their whiskey, in fluent English, and for a little while they all sit and talk comfortably: Where have they gone? What have they seen? Where are they planning to go next?

Then Mandalay can't keep her eyes open any more. I have to go to sleep, she says. You can stay down here. She can see Duane is enjoying himself, relaxing.

She doesn't wake up when he comes to bed, but later, when he shifts position for what feels like the fourth or fifth time. She has the sensation that he's been moving around a lot.

Sorry, he says. He kisses her forehead, tucks the covers around her. Now you know why I don't have you sleep over more.

She wakes again to see him at the room's small desk, typing by the glow of his laptop screen. She's still tired, but now it's about the time she wakes up for work, and her body clock is bringing her to full consciousness against her will. Hey, she says, come to bed, and he does, smiling.

I've got something to make you sleep, she says, and goes down on him, shaking her head when he reaches for her after a few moments, finishing him off. She hasn't done that before: He hasn't asked, and she doesn't think it's a good habit to encourage. Then he falls asleep quite quickly, and she's awake, lying awake, until after dawn. Then she falls asleep, but now he's up: They have to get moving, as Gerry will be there with the truck for their gear.

So we begin the trip sleep-shorted, and not really connected, she thinks.

They're staying in protected areas, mostly, on the lee side of the archipelago, between the islands where the ocean is tempered.

Only twice they'll have to take on potentially rougher water: once crossing a strait that is cut through by a strong current at certain tides, and once travelling from one island to the next in a stretch that is more open.

Duane has planned it so that they need paddle only a few hours a day, and that they can break this up into shorter stretches, with stops. Still, her shoulders ache, and her abdominal and lower back muscles, as well. When they stop for the day, they massage each other, which gives relief, and leads, always to sex. They don't sleep well at night: It's cold and the foam mats are never enough against the rocky places they find to pitch the tent. It rains, or the wind blows things around. The nights are always loud, busy – and short. In the tent, they have only a few hours of darkness. One night they hear someone rummaging through the bag of equipment they've left outside – and Duane sets forth warily, with the flashlight. It's a pair of otters: Mandalay sees them in the beam of the flashlight before they drop the bag and amble off, grumbling.

They see bald eagles and ospreys, and seabirds: surf scoters, with their big bodies, their naked faces; crested mergansers and guillemots and scaups. They paddle over kelp beds and see otters sleeping, as they float tethered to the stipes. They see bears fishing and swimming, and one day a small pod of orcas.

They see other kayakers, and sailors, and hikers. They share a hot pool fed by natural springs with a pair of Finnish geologists who tell them that the archipelago lies on a fault line, that the west coast of it drops off steeply, the edge of a continental shelf, and the islands are bubbling up out of the sea, squeezed out from between the two plates like glue from a mortised joint.

They pull ashore at small villages, where carved cedar poles stand addressing the sea, speaking to the creatures of the sea, telling the story of the people who live on the shore, who have become separated from the sea. In a museum they read about Raven finding, after a cataclysm, the first people, hiding in a shell on the beach.

My brother Cliff would like this story, she says. He would say the shell was actually a spacecraft, and Raven some chief or shaman. He likes origin stories. He would like it here. He watches nature shows almost exclusively, on TV.

My brother Al was like that, he says. He went to the Galapagos when he was in his early twenties.

They buy food, liquor, when they can, at the villages. Duane buys a carving which will be shipped home for him: gift for his parents, he says. It's a replica mask, fierce with teeth and abalone-button eyes. Small children greet them, follow them. They wear warm, bright-coloured clothing.

They eat at a sort of communal barbecue that feeds tourists, and the cooks and servers sit and eat with them at wooden tables in a roofed-over pavilion. A woman asks Mandalay: What are you? Salish? No, you don't seem Salish. You're not practical enough. Dreamer.

Duane has raised an eyebrow, but says nothing. Mandalay says, I don't know. My mother would never tell me.

Where's she from?

Southern Alberta. I think.

Crystal's stories tend to shape-change, but that seems the most stable of them.

Blackfoot, maybe, the woman says. Blackfoot are dreamers.

Then she turns to Duane. You stick by her, now. Indian women aren't for using up and throwing away.

They don't sleep as well at night but they take to sleeping in the afternoons, stacking the two mats and one of the sleeping bags, lying spooned on the narrow space, and in the full brightness of the day through the blue walls of the tent, giving themselves to the luxurious deep sleep of children, while their clothes, which are always damp, hang in the sun and wind.

They catch or gather food for their meals, and Mandalay finds herself constantly ravenous, salivating for the protein and salt and iron before the food is even cooked. They eat mussels and periwinkles and a kind of seaweed every day; these can be gathered from the rocks at low tide, and it's safe to eat them here, so far from cities and pollutants. When they come to a flat beach of mud and sand, they dig small sweet clams and steam them in a pot and eat so many that they leave the beginnings of their own shell midden. That night, they run along the long flat beach, their footsteps glowing with bioluminescence.

In the equipment they have rented with the kayaks are small shovels, a little axe, a spear. For fish, Duane says. In a sheltered cove Duane strips and swims out carrying the spear, one of the equipment nets from the kayaks, which has floats attached, and, in his teeth, a knife. She thinks he's doing it boyishly, laughs. But when he comes in she looks up to see him walking up the beach naked, shedding drops of water, the net full of sea-creatures, which he spreads in front of her: abalone, sea urchins, a couple of rock perch speared through, a giant, menacing crab. He's Neptune, he's Poseidon, he's some more prehistoric god, earlier than Poseidon. His body shines; the droplets of water blaze in the sun. The sea creatures bristle and stir. *Fruits de mer*, she thinks, remembering a restaurant menu. The fruits of the sea. Here they are, truly, in a way she hasn't understood the phrase before. There is something primeval about them, something truer and older than plated seafood. They are living. Although they wall themselves in or menace futilely with spine and claw, she will eat them; they will become part of her. She will be part of the sea, in turn.

There are droplets of sea water in Duane's eyebrows and chest and armpit hair, his pubes. His body is shining, muscular, streaming with water. He has speared two fish; he has pried oysters from rocks with a knife; he has brought her food caught with his bare hands. If this is the peak of it all; if this is the best moment they will have, it will be enough.

He shows her how to crack the sea urchins open and suck out the gelatinous insides. She doesn't want to at first – she's repulsed – but then can't get enough of the salty, slightly watermelon matter. A couple of the urchins have roe and that she eats also, ravenously.

AND THEY TALK. In the tent, in the kayaks, scrambling over rocks and trails, they talk. They talk about things they have never talked about before, or have not dived into very deeply. Duane tells her now not about the cases he has won. But the ones he has lost. He tells her about the mistakes he has made, the ones he has not been able to repair.

She tells him about Butterfly Lake, finally. As she guessed, he has heard of it: He remembers the news stories. That would have been, when, the mid to late seventies, he says. You'd have been a kid then.

Whatever you heard, it was probably exaggerated, Mandalay says.

Of course it was, he says. Later information showed that. It was kind of blown up by the media.

It wasn't even really Butterfly Lake people, Mandalay says. But all people think about now, when they hear Butterfly Lake, is that there were eleven child mortality cases between 1975 and 1978.

Well, that is a lot.

Eleven children. Two had drowned on a raft in the lake. One had fallen down an old mineshaft, and one off a deck with no railings. Three had been left alone in a house that had caught fire when the space heater malfunctioned. The other four had died of pneumonia brought on by malnutrition and exposure.

He says, I remember you told me you were split up, put in foster homes, after your father died. That would have been what year?

She says, it wasn't the same thing. Those other kids — they were outsiders, not taken care of properly. We weren't part of that. But social services was so jumpy, after that.

They overreacted.

Yes. We were fine, really. We had lots of people around us. My mother was getting better. But social services just swooped in. They had an agenda. They made her sign that she'd given us up, so we couldn't go back, even when she was better.

She is telling him this as they lie in the sun, one afternoon. It's warm; they've spread the mats and sleeping bags in the sun, and are lying on them, in a small meadow.

He tells her about his wife as they are paddling. They're trying to cover a few kilometres of coastline in one stretch, to reach the next sheltered cove before late afternoon, when the wind is supposed to pick up. He says, we met in university: We met at a party, when we were twenty-one, and that was it. We both knew right away that we wanted to commit. Of course our families, friends, told us we were nuts. Twenty-one! We still had to finish our degrees, and then we should go to grad school, and not in the same place, as I was heading for law and she was going to do medicine. We both wanted to specialize, so that would add on years. But we did it, you know. We were apart for five years. We saw each other holidays; we wrote letters. There was no email and long distance phoning was really expensive. And we stayed exclusive, and missed each other like hell. We both suffered.

And then we were both done, and I managed to get on with a law firm in Vancouver, with a chance to do commercial law, and she got a residency at Children's, doing pediatrics, which is what she wanted. So we got married: We had the big wedding, and the parents and friends were, I'm sure, all congratulating themselves on their good sense in telling us to be sensible and wait.

And then Ellen got pregnant, and that was wonderful too, though we hadn't even had a year together yet. And then, four months in, she was diagnosed. It was pretty advanced; she'd probably had the tumour for a year. It was so small, still. Pea-sized. She could hardly feel it. But it was in her lymph nodes.

She terminated the pregnancy: She didn't want to, but it was her only chance. I forced her, I think. She had surgery and months of chemo, and she was very sick; she got every side effect possible. And then she was in remission for three months, and then she wasn't: It was in her liver, her bones. Her spine and hips started to crumble like cheese. The pain was unbearable. More chemo, which she hardly survived, but the cancer devoured her, anyway. Her liver stopped and the toxins and pain medication deprived her of her ability to speak or to reason. There was constant nausea and pain and confusion, for three weeks, which was too long. She was gone already.

The last time I talked to her, I didn't know it would be the last time. She was in hospital, and I went to the office to tie up some loose end, and when I came back two hours later, something had shifted. They'd upped the Demerol or something. She couldn't come up to the surface enough to interact, and she never did after that.

It takes him about half an hour to tell the story, around her questions and his explanations. During this time a heavy fog settles around them, and then the wind picks up, and they have to head to shore.

He says: Ellen was my best friend. The only person I ever felt really knew me. Knew me completely. There was no space between us. No gaps.

There is almost no space between *us*, Mandalay thinks. Is there?

The next day they paddle through a shallow tidal zone between two of the islands, a wash of sea so shallow that the seabed is visible under the kayaks for a kilometre. It's speckled with the white of clams and ruffled, bright-green kelp, and with sea stars, purple and ochre, in their scattered thousands. It's like a night sky drawn by a young child, by her niece Olivia, Mandalay thinks.

They have no radio, but at their previous landing Duane picked up the latest maritime weather forecast, which had predicted squalls this afternoon. Now they must stay put until the storm finishes and leaves. The fog vanishes, and they watch the squall build across the water: It looks like an invisible being is moving across the sea's surface, stirring the water into fury. They pull the kayaks higher up the beach, then higher again; the waves keep surprising them with their reach. It's suddenly impossible to put up the tent. They retreat into the forest with their bags, find a relatively dry spot under the spreading boughs of a cedar. The sky darkens, the treetops thrash, the rain begins. Not all of the water runs to the tips of the cedar boughs. They use the tent as a poncho and wrap themselves in the sleeping bags.

Now there is little to say; both of them have withdrawn into themselves a little, Mandalay thinks. But it's okay. It's a comfortable silence. Duane heats some soup mix in water, expertly, with no fuss, on the butane stove, and they drink it, and then have some of the jerked meat and dark chocolate rations that they've ignored so far on the trip. This fare produces intense thirst, though, and Mandalay fills a metal bowl over and over, and they drink it up. It gets dark, or rather darker, and the sound of the waves grinding the gravel of the shore becomes paramount. Then she falls asleep, somehow, curled into Duane, but wakes in the night, has to pee, disturbs him trying to extricate herself from the cocoon they've made, and gets wet just moving a few trees away to crouch in privacy. She crawls back in, and can't get warm enough to fall asleep again for some time.

At one point she feels Duane's watch on his wrist; his arm is around her and her hand in his, and she slowly removes it, presses the button for the light on his watch, reads the time: 2:45.

His familiar arm, his familiar watch.

My man, she thinks.

When she wakes again it's light, and Duane standing a few feet away, his back to her, pissing what seems like a great distance into the rain. He's cheerful, joking. Does she want him to dive for some more abalone? Sea urchins? The sea is still grinding away at the shore, the slap of the waves and the roar of the gravel as it is dragged back filling her ears, and more: taking up a good deal of her attention besides, Mandalay feels. She wonders if she will want to hear the sea for a while after this, or smell it.

They spend part of the day cocooned, again, dozing, talking a little. The rain stops for a while at midday, and they crawl out and down to the beach; the kayaks, pulled up under the trees, are safe, but the beach has actually changed shape during the night. The sea, at the height of the day's light, is glowing grey-green: it must look like the luminescence of something dying, Mandalay thinks. The waves are still terrifyingly high. She can't imagine that they will be able, ever again, to venture out on it in their little shells of boats.

Then the rain starts up again, and they retreat to their shelter under the cedar, their cocoon. Now Duane is sleepy, but she is not, and she sits with her back against the tree trunk daydreaming while he sleeps with his head on her lap, his legs curled around and entangled with hers. She feels at once protective of him and protected by him. She thinks of a poem she used to like when she was younger – in her early twenties, perhaps, she'd written it out and taped or tacked it to the wall above whatever bed she was inhabiting then. *Love consists in this*, the poem read, *that two solitudes protect and touch and greet each other.*

It is not impossible, she says to herself.

Around them the rainforest a temple of green shawls.

12

Jam

JULY AND THEY ARE GOING ON VACATION: going, as they do every
other year, to visit Trent's family, or rather, to stay at Trent's family's
cottage. It's a long way to travel, but it is free. It is worth the trouble
of the trip, flying to Toronto, then driving to the lake, because it's all
paid for by Trent's parents.

Cottage is a misnomer: It's a house, bigger than Cleo's and Trent's
house, and then there are two smaller houses that really are cottages,
that belong to Trent's older brothers, whose children are in their late
teens and early twenties, already. Trent's sister does not have a cottage,
but her husband's family does, only a few miles away. When she is on
the island, she and her two children, who are in their teens, stay with
Trent's parents, as do Trent and Cleo. Trent's parents' house is so large
that they are not at all crowded.

All of these are situated on an island in a lake, on land that is very
rocky, or that consists, as far as Cleo can tell, of solid rock that has
been sculpted by the wind and water so that it looks like cake frosting
spread in long swoops. Frosting made of basalt. In hollows here and
there, enough earth has gathered for plants to grow. The trees seem
to grow out of solid rock.

And then, of course, there is the lake. The first summer, when they reached it, she was confused by its size: She couldn't see the other side. Is this Hudson's Bay, she had asked, trying to put together a map of Canada from her memory, trying to explain what is apparently the ocean. Trent had mocked her for her lack of geographical sense. But she'd never seen a lake of this size. When they arrived at the ferry slip to go to the island, the lake stretched out in all directions, unbroken (except for clusters of small islets), a sheet of crinkly grey silk. There were gulls, pelicans. The wind had blown fiercely off the water, whipping her hair around. She had felt that she had travelled to a new continent, after a long ocean voyage.

Everything was new to her. She bought field guides to the local flowers and birds, the trees and the shrubs. It was all new and exotic.

She listened. She looked around. She took note.

Trent's family told stories — illustrated by an album of black-and-white photographs — of the building of the big house, which entailed trucking beams and planking as well as the logs for the walls over the lake in winter, when it was frozen solid, and then raising the house in spring. Trent isn't present, in these photos. His father is a young boy.

The house is huge and airy, with a post and beam structure, which makes it like a rustic cathedral, with the great beams rising to a star point. The log walls, finished with drywall and plaster on the inside, are hung with real paintings, not prints; stone and wood floors, deep wooden doors and sills, fireplaces, fat leather sofas, rugs and blankets. Outside is a landscape of moss and even little flowers that have grown in the chinks.

The village is small and strange: It's not at all like the villages she grew up in. She can't place what's different about it. Maybe better kept up? There's a hairdresser, a grocery store, a bakery, a liquor store, a few general-purpose shops that sell household goods and clothing and toys and souvenirs, as you'd expect. But she can never orient herself in the village, or find her way easily to any of the shops.

She sees that Trent's nephews and nieces have rituals around going to the village: an ice cream shop they must visit, all together, on the first day, and whose menu they notice minute changes to. They can, it seems, enumerate all of the first-day ice cream treats from successive summers at the lake. They know, also, the history and succession of the buildings in the village, in the form of personal history. (There's the Laundromat, where John fell asleep in a basket of clean towels and we didn't find him for three hours.) Trent's siblings and his parents have similar, longer histories, and these are brought out and recounted, yearly, it seems, during the family barbecues. This year, Olivia recognizes some of the places in the village, and Cleo sees that they will become part of Olivia's history, her sense of who she is.

Then the family: Contrary to Cleo's expectations, and impressions of teenagers from her own experience, Trent's nephews and niece are lovely human beings: polite, respectful, able to engage in conversation with adults, happy to play with and amuse Olivia and Sam. She sees that the teenaged cousins will have very different lives than she has had — that they will walk into university, careers, on paths carefully cleared and groomed for them by their parents. There is already mention of the accomplishments of the older ones, who are at university, who have summer jobs that are more interesting and relevant, Cleo thinks, than the jobs usually available to students, and who drive up sometimes, on the weekends, with or without friends, to be hugged and admired and served.

They are all handsome, healthy, bright, self-confident young people. They are not, she thinks, outstandingly bright or accomplished, but they do excellently, or at least very well.

She thinks: If I and my siblings had had their opportunities.

When she tries to say this to Trent, he's annoyed with her, interprets her comments as crass, envious. Which perhaps they are.

Here at the lake, Cleo may, for the only time all year, find herself divested of children for long periods of time. Olivia and Sam are carted around by careful, affectionate, solicitous cousins, uncles and aunts, grandparents. Some mornings she wakes up to find the sun shining, the two bedrooms she and Trent share with the children empty, and Olivia's and Sam's voices distant in the kitchen, happily chattering to their grandmother. She is encouraged to put her feet up, have a drink, read novels or magazines. When she helps make a salad for dinner, or washes the dishes, she is thanked and praised extravagantly. She and Trent walk to the village, hand in hand, for ice cream. Trent takes her out in the canoe.

She has learned, since, that their trips to the cottage are a kind of bubble in which normal life is suspended, but the first visit, when she hadn't known Trent well, had been dating him only a few months, she had fallen under some sort of enchantment of privilege and lack of responsibility. For the first time in her life, perhaps, there had been nothing that she should be doing.

Now she does not have as much freedom, but is still relatively cocooned. She sits on the beach, watching Sam, who's at an age at which he has to be watched closely near water, and watching Olivia a little less closely. Olivia must wear water wings, but she paddles and dives under with a fair bit of control, of confidence, Cleo can see. She does not panic, if she loses sight of Olivia's purple bathing suit, her neon-orange water wings, for a few moments, in the crowd of children in the water. (There she is, on her cousin Harry's back, having a dolphin ride. Not floating under the surface, caught in weed, lost and gone forever.)

The teenaged cousins spend the afternoons at the beach, too. They helpfully, politely, carry some of Cleo's gear: the beach blanket, the large basket of plastic pails and spades and sifters, the hats and towels and sunscreen and diaper bag with its bottles of juice. They lay out Cleo's stuff in the sand, and then lie a little distance off, marinating. They talk among themselves, in the secret talk of adolescents. They build sand castles with Olivia and let her bury them in the sand and give her rides on their inner tubes and take her across to the beach store to buy popsicles. Olivia is in heaven.

Sam likes the beach less. He cries when sand sticks to his fingers. He curls his toes, draws his legs upward, when Cleo tries to dip him in the water. He cries if one of the cousins comes out of the water and picks him up wet. He wants to sit on Cleo's lap, not on the blanket, which gets sandy and wet. But if she opens a book, if she closes her eyes, Sam might run away at warp speed, toward the water, under the dock, even in the direction of the playground, at the other end of the beach, across a strip of sunbathing and picnicking families.

No, he wouldn't. He will only sit in the sand within her arm's reach, and cry with irritation. Sam won't desert her, as Olivia has, for the glamour of the cousins and the ice cream parlour.

WON'T YOU PUT JAM on that toast? Gwendolyn says.

No, Cleo says. Sam's happy to eat it without jam.

But it would taste better with.

He doesn't need it, though. I don't want him to need sweets.

A little sugar won't hurt you, Trent says. That's all a myth, all of that stuff about sugar. A little sugar doesn't hurt.

Yes, she says, but why develop Sam's taste for sweet things? That isn't healthy.

She must have spoken in too sharp a tone, because Trent's voice becomes impatient. I didn't want to start an argument. I just don't believe in being nutty about food.

Gwendolyn has retreated to the kitchen, not in an unfriendly way, Cleo thinks: just deciding that discretion is the better part of valour.

By "nutty" Trent means someone like Mandalay, who is sometimes vegetarian, who thinks that hot dogs cause cancer, that milk is full of hormones and antibiotics. Cleo is certainly not nutty. She grew up with nutty; she knows what nutty is.

Gwendolyn says, Those little canvas shoes are so cute. When my kids were young, we put them in laced-up leather boots, so their feet would develop straight.

Cleo says, No need for that; their feet will develop naturally, without shoes. Humans haven't worn shoes for most of our history. She says this with more confidence than she feels, and isn't really even sure if this is true.

But won't their feet turn inward, or their arches not develop? Gwendolyn says.

Cleo is struck with fear. Perhaps they will? Sam's little feet are still unformed, fat little pads. Olivia's look fine, but now that she comes to think of it, don't Olivia's ankles lean toward each other, a bit?

Olivia's such a thin little kid, Gwendolyn says. James and Bob Junior were both thirty pounds on their first birthdays.

Olivia and Sam weren't twenty pounds on their first birthdays, Cleo knows. Sam was a pudgy baby, but now that he's walking, he's getting lean, like Olivia.

Trent's mom has given them two rooms, one with a double bed, one with a single and a crib. Cleo takes the second one, so that she can get up with Sam in the night. He still wakes up, needs to be comforted. It would almost be easier if she were still nursing him. But Olivia won't go to bed without Trent or Cleo lying down with her, anyway.

Bob would never have liked me sleeping in a separate bed, Gwendolyn says. Also: My children all slept through the night by the time they were three months old.

In the evenings, she often lies down between both of the children, until they fall asleep, then moves Sam to the crib and reads in the bed beside him.

Don't you watch sports at all? Gwendolyn asks.

No.

And you don't like movies.

I like movies. We don't often get out.

Oh, you have to get out, Lou — Trent's brother-in-law — says, kindly, warmly. He's nice to her; he remembers to try to draw her out. A big man, broad rather than lanky like Trent's family. He's smoking the fattest cigar she's ever seen, though, and she has to turn her head sometimes for air.

If you want to keep your marriage, he says, you have to get out together.

Probably true.

Gwendolyn says, You sleep in pajamas? I always find a nightgown more convenient. She says it in such a way that it seems a salacious comment, though Cleo can't believe she meant it that way.

TRENT'S SISTER BORROWS Sam and Olivia for the afternoon. We miss little kids around here, she says. Cleo's anxious: What if something happens to them? But she can't refuse. There's no way to refuse.

She thinks she might lie on the double bed and read. That's what she might do.

Then Trent comes up. Hey, lady. This is my bedroom, he says, his voice cracking, falsetto. Are you looking for my big brother? Are you Bob's girlfriend?

It's the pubescent boy game. Trent likes this one. She tosses imaginary long hair, pats the bed. Rory's not here, she says. He's so busy with his homework. Why don't you come and entertain me for a little while?

It's a dirty game. She's not sure she likes it, but Trent does, enough for both of them, maybe. It's not about Trent's brother Bob, of course. Bob is grizzled, middle-aged, a judge. He seems dry, sexless, to her. It's about Trent being a little boy, free of responsibility. It's about Trent being innocent. It's about making her, Cleo, responsible for everything.

Tawdry, she thinks. Shameful. Also, the idea of a very young guy doesn't turn her on. She feels a sort of chill, a kind of cold clear dismay.

Why does she agree to it then?

Because it is easy.

Because it relieves boredom, temporarily. It passes the time. Because what does titillate, what does get her worked up a little, is the accompanying disgust – not toward the fantasy, but toward Trent, for finding pleasure in it. Disgust toward Trent. His childish persona gives her a feeling of separateness from him, of superiority and separateness. That's what turns her on.

Disgust at herself, too: yes. But she can suppress that.

It's the sense of distinctness from Trent, the moral and aesthetic rejection of Trent, in her mind, that pulses in her brain, opens her libido.

It's a nasty little game. She has to play a bored and horny and desirable young woman to Trent's pubescent boy. It's a stretch for her: She doesn't think she ever was that young woman. She knows the kind: the high-breasted, willowy girls in their long hair, their miniature jean shorts, their sunglasses, promenading the sidewalks in summer. Town girls, with their radios, their bikini tops.

Working the counter of Hermann's Deli in her powder-blue coverall, her hair bobby-pinned and netted back, no makeup, she had not felt any kinship with those girls, with their confidence, their ease, their ownership of not only the male gaze but the sidewalk. Maybe the whole of the valley.

She had not thought of herself as related in any way to them.

She had not wondered how she could be more like them, had not even asked herself if she could grow her hair long and straight and gleaming. (Mrs. Giesbrecht insisted she keep her thick light-brown hair in a short, housewifely bob, for neatness, for control.) She had not wondered where the girls had bought the gauzy tops, the jeans that hugged their hips and flared at their feet, their sunglasses, their rope sandals. She had not considered that she would ever have exposed her pale, spotty back and shoulders to the sun, or public gaze. She had a farmer's tan, from helping Mr. Giesbrecht in the garden, sun-burned neck and upper arms, cheeks and nose. She didn't imagine that her own torso or shoulders or thighs had the same lines, the same petal texture or golden sheen as the tourist girls. They had walked fully formed off the pages of *Seventeen*, which she sometimes leafed through quickly at the store, which she was not permitted, for various reasons, to buy.

And now she must pretend to be one of them, pretend to get inside one of the pretty heads. She doesn't have a clue how they think, of course. What it would be like to be one of those girls, so it's all pretty mechanical, artificial. Made-up lines, like in comic books: snappy, flirty. She doesn't have to be a real girl.

She asks, What's your name, Tiger? She asks, What grade are you in? Do you have a girlfriend? She asks these in a bored, patronizing voice.

She puts her hand on Trent's thigh, rubs it as if absentmindedly. She brushes his erection, says, Oh, what's this?

Trent, in his little-boy voice, asks, Can I touch your booby?

She doesn't like her breasts touched by Trent that much: He seems to think nipples are knobs to twist, and when she was breast-feeding, she would leak milk. Once when Olivia was tiny, Trent had got some breast milk in his mouth, had pulled a face, spat it out.

She says, Sure, touch my boob. But suddenly, she's tired:

KAREN HOFMANN

▸ 195. ◂

The game seems crass, moronic, again. She takes Trent's penis in her mouth, gives it a businesslike workover. At first Trent's body stiffens — she's not playing the game right — but he can't resist.

After he comes, she gets up to brush her teeth; his penis tastes a bit cheesy, sweaty and maybe not recently enough washed.

When she comes back to the bedroom, he has fallen asleep.

She walks down to the village. She has finished the books she brought with her, has read the stash at the cottage, or at least those she considers readable. (It surprises her that her in-laws, educated, well-off professionals, read mass-market paperbacks, even if it's at the beach.) She dawdles in the village shops, looks at bright yellow and cobalt stoneware, at pastel cargo pants with matching jackets and flower-printed T-shirts and crocheted sweaters. She can't imagine wearing items like them, at home. She tries on a couple of April Cornell dresses — romantic, flowered — but they're too expensive, and maybe not really what she likes, anymore.

Candles, suncatchers, silver-plated starfish, flat metal shorebirds stuck into driftwood bases. It catches her eye; it's pretty, it says buy me. But she doesn't want any of it. She can't see what it's *for*. Though she does recognize some of the objects that she and Trent have been given as Christmas gifts, by Trent's family.

Why the village has always seemed exotic to her: Nothing in the shops is anything anyone actually *needs*. That's the difference between this place and the little towns she knew growing up, Butterfly Lake, Guisachan Falls. Even Powell River, or Abbotsford.

She walks through the village, to the beach. She has not thought to put on her suit, but it's not a warm day, anyway: the sky marled, the lake an opaque moody slab. She could go for a walk, where the bush comes down to the beach, but she can't just head down one of the trails without telling someone; she had done that on her first visit, and the family had been hugely upset.

She's walking back toward the shops – she'll look for *something* she can buy, something she can give someone – when she sees, across the street, her sister-in-law Caroline at an outdoor café table, and with her, Olivia and Sam. Without thinking, she ducks behind a planter of trumpet vine and canna lilies. Through the greenery, she peers at them, the tableau. Olivia's chatting away to Caroline, who's leaning in, attentive, smiling. Sam's looking back and forth; they seem to have made a joke, because Sam is laughing, they're all laughing. Then Sam knocks his drink container over, and she tenses, waiting for his reaction, but even while his eyes go wide, Caroline rights the glass, says something to him, smiling, and Sam's face relaxes again. In fact, he's grinning up at Caroline adoringly.

She peers through the heart-shaped leaves of the vine, and thinks she will join them in a minute, but then sees that she must not.

She walks up the street in the other direction, aimless. In the large café window she catches her reflection, sees a medium-sized woman, neither very old nor very young, with nondescript hair, wearing unobjectionable navy shorts and striped T-shirt, plain canvas shoes. Is that what she looks like? She stops for a moment, wanting to see something more, something she recognizes. The double panes of glass blur the lines of her face, so she can't really make out her own features.

She turns away, begins to walk back to the cottage.

There's her mother-in-law, Gwendolyn, now, moving purposefully toward her, her purse over her forearm.

Don't know what to do with yourself! she calls to Cleo, in passing, an observation rather than a question.

Falling for You

CLIFF IS SPENDING SO MUCH TIME at Loretta's that he's hardly ever at his own place. He misses his apartment, but Loretta doesn't like him to be away from her. She doesn't even like it when he's at work, but he says: I have to work. She doesn't like it when he goes over to his apartment to take care of Sophie.

Sophie's not happy without him, though. When he's there one evening feeding her, the manager comes by to say that Sophie cries at the door all day and night. The other tenants are concerned.

He misses his TV, too: Loretta's isn't working.

He doesn't know what to do. Loretta doesn't like it if he sleeps at his place: She gets into a terrible state. He asks her to stay at his place sometimes, but she says it's a bad neighbourhood. She's scared of the other tenants. She wouldn't feel safe. And besides, all of her stuff is at her place.

He says that maybe it's not going to work, and she says: You can bring your cat to my place.

He brings the cat and the TV.

He knows he should give it some time, not burn his bridges, but the rent is so much and now he has to pay Loretta as well. He thinks he'll give it till the last day of the month, and if things are going okay, he'll give his notice. And they are and he does. But then on the second day of the new month, he and Loretta have an argument and she throws a can of soup at him. Then he has the feeling that he has fallen out of an airplane, and sometimes he can't breathe, but he makes himself go to work. He tells himself that it will work out.

And mostly it's okay. It's nice, mostly. It's nice to cook and eat with someone else and watch TV together and spoon with someone in bed. It's nice when they have sex and Loretta says she loves him and asks him about his day. And she knows how to enjoy herself, how to have fun in simple ways. They're always going for walks in the park or on Granville Island or along one of the ethnic neighbourhoods, just looking at things and getting a pastry or an ice cream cone. It's nice when she tells him about things she's done and people she knows. Because she's older than he is – twelve years older – she has a lot more experience. She's just smarter about a lot of things.

And she *needs* him, he thinks. She has times when she lies curled up on the bed, not talking, her skin looking greyish: when she can't go to her part-time job, and he sees how alone she is, and how much she needs him. He's different, she tells him. He is the first one to really understand her, to be sensitive enough to see the person she really is, and unselfish enough to stick by her during the rough times.

It's a miracle, she says, that the two of us found each other in this big world. We were two half souls searching for each other.

He doesn't know if that is true but it makes him feel like he has a point to his existence, he guesses.

It's only that sometimes he would like to feel that he could do what he wanted.

It's not like he really ever did anything different, he has to admit: His life before was pretty well going to work, eating, watching TV, like it is now. It's just that he is bothered by the thought, which lives in him somewhere like a stowaway, a squatter, and comes into his mind sometimes to remind him that he isn't free. He can't argue with the thought, when it comes up. He isn't. And then the thought takes up residence in his mind and gives him so much aggravation that he can hardly stand it. He'll just be at work pushing the mower or riding his bike home and the thought will materialize: He's not free. He's not free.

Then a tornado of misery, of torment, will swirl through him, through his whole body and his brain, and he'll be choking for air, wanting to tear his heart and lungs out of his own ribcage.

He reminds himself that he's not lacking for anything real. Not anything he could see or touch. Is he? And nobody is free, really.

It's always such a relief when the misery passes, when the thought retreats from his head, leaves him alone again.

What friends? Loretta asks.

What friends? He has few, he has to admit. A few people who have accumulated, he thinks, like pearls, people who have not been so disturbing that he has had to dislodge them (by avoiding them), people who he likes, or whose oddness, whose irritating habits have at least been bearable. He can probably count his friends on one hand, though. Nicki, who he works with, a landscaper like him. She lives in his neighbourhood and he has been to her apartment. Nicki was the one who gave him Sophie. Nicki's girlfriend, Meg, a biologist, who has good conversations with Cliff about animal adaptation and cell function and so on. Maybe one or two of the other people he works with. Not Ray. Cleo, and Mandalay, of course, who are family, but could be invited to a party. And now Ben.

Maybe Mrs. Cookshaw, his boss. His real boss, who owns the landscaping company, who has said to him more than once that Ray is a nasty piece of work, but he's just a bully. Don't mind him too much, but if he ever gives you too much trouble, let me know.

He thinks about all of the people he could invite to the party Loretta wants to have. He does have friends. But then he thinks about them in this room, Loretta's apartment, which is the top floor of a shared house. Her satin pillows that say SEX KITTEN and LOVE ME. (They embarrass him; he thinks they would be embarrassing to his friends, too.) Her posters with rude sayings: I'll let you know when I want your opinion.

Her way of knowing something about everything, which had made her seem really smart at first, but which now he has to wonder about.

He imagines his friends in this room, not knowing where to look. He imagines them getting ready to leave, and then Loretta not letting them leave. Shutting the door and leaning against it. The dull spade-shape of her mouth when she's angry. Her voice high and fake-happy saying, You can't leave — I've just put another tray of onion tarts into the oven. Now who will eat them?

He allows himself to grin weakly, to say, Yeah, what friends?

I'm the one with friends, she says.

That you are, he says. He knows if he can get her into a good mood she'll be fine again: Things will be fine.

But what about your brother? she asks.

What? he says, fearful now.

The night we met, at the UBC pub. That blond boy with the little beard. You said he was your brother.

Oh, yeah, he says. I don't see him much.

Why not? You should invite him.

I don't think....

Her clay-smooth face in his. Invite him! What's the matter? Are you ashamed of our home?

She will hit him again, he thinks. She's hit him a couple of times, not meaning to, she's said after, but her rings cut his cheek the one time, near his eye. It's not her fault, she had a terrible childhood, she has mood swings because of it.

She loves him, she loves him. She can't live without him. When she's in a good mood it's okay.

He doesn't want to explain about Ben. He has resisted telling her his stories, though she has extracted some of them. With each he feels a little bit of himself drain out, lose its shape, turn into something else. It's a relief but he's losing himself too.

I don't know my brother very well, he says. We're not close. We were raised in different families. It occurs to him to say, *You're upsetting me by talking about this.* It's something she says. But he will not; he will not say that.

She cuffs him on the ear, a little harder than playfully. Do you have other siblings you're hiding from me?

He is not good at lying. He doesn't lie. He has not told her about Mandalay or Cleo, but that hasn't been lying: She hasn't asked directly before.

He makes himself small. It will pass, if he doesn't aggravate her further.

Invite your brother, she says. What's his name? I'll call him if you're too shy. I have a friend I know he'd like! Judy! Wouldn't she like him?

He can't remember if Judy is the one with the big varicose veins or the mustache. Both are women in their forties, he guesses. He's sure they are nice women but they are in their forties. Loretta herself is thirty-seven. In her prime, she says.

When he's at work his head clears and he thinks: He will break up with her before the party. He'll move out. But then when he's back he can't think through it. He can't say to her that he wants to move out. It's like his head is full of swirling muddy water, and he thinks in circles. How can he do this to her? She'll be so hurt. She'll be so hurt inside. He can feel her hurt; he can feel the desolation. Another betrayal, another abandonment. She has had a sad life. People have hurt her. He knows her so well; he knows her feelings better than his own. All that he can think of is how hurt she'll be.

And imagining the telling: her rage. What will happen then? He can't imagine what he will do after that. What will happen to him? Where will he go?

All of his possessions are in Loretta's house. Even the things that didn't fit, or she didn't need: Those are in boxes in the basement. He has nowhere to go.

And even when he can calm down these thoughts, when he can stop the swirling for a moment, there is something else: a sort of gaping hole or void when he thinks about what he will do then, because he can't imagine it anymore. He can't imagine things without her there.

When he's home, she fills up everything, and the decisions he has come to while he's at work float away like there's nothing to him. Like the person who made them doesn't exist.

He will have to break up with her after the party. It's too soon, before.

She talks about nothing else. He comes home from work and she's home already, as she always is, with more stuff. Balloons and shiny letters strung together that say Celebrate! Paper plates and napkins. Packages and packages of cookies and chips, bottles of liquor.

He has to give her fifty bucks for his share, she says. When he blinks at that she says, And you've left me to do all of the work for it, so don't complain.

She says, How's your brother getting here? We can ask Judy to pick him up.

No, he says, without thinking, he has a car.

Oh, then maybe he can give some of my friends a lift.

I'm not sure, he says.

You have invited him? This, whirling around, looming, so that his back's against the stove where a vat of chili bubbles.

He hasn't invited Ben. But he says, yeah, of course. He's really excited about it.

He'll have to invent a good reason for Ben not to show up.

He has to leave. He's become a liar.

She kisses him, then, and his body responds on its own accord, like a big untrained dog.

At work, pushing the mower, he thinks: He could take the afternoon off work, tell Ray he's sick. He'll pick a day when Loretta is at her part-time job. He'll have a taxi waiting. It'll take him probably four trips. And then there's Sophie. He might have to leave the stuff in the basement.

Where will he go? He'll have to go to a motel, which will be really expensive.

He has a little bit of money. Loretta had said to close his bank account and just put it all with hers, it would work better that way. But he hasn't done it yet.

The motel will be expensive and he'll have to find a place to rent quickly but he can't do it from here because they always want a phone number. It'll clean him out.

He could hawk his TV.

Yes, he will do that.

At home, though, he thinks of Loretta's panic, her terrible shock at coming back and finding him gone, all of his stuff, just a note. What kind of person would do that to her?

He will have to tell her. After the party.

He reminds himself: Logically, she can't stop him from leaving. He'll call a taxi and he'll leave. She can't really stop him.

It'll be tough but he'll have to do the right thing. If you don't do the right thing, what are you?

CLIFF'S HEART IS jackhammering away in his chest. He comes up the stairs into the main room, where she's sitting with a magazine and a glass of wine. He doesn't take off his jacket, and when she looks up, he says it, all of it, reminding himself as if he were a child: Get it over and done with and it won't be so bad. He wishes he'd thought to pick Sophie up in his arms first.

Loretta comes at him so enraged that he is given the gift, for that moment, of complete certainty that he is doing the right thing. She rises up from the armchair with a sort of scream, her face turning purple. Comes at him. Then she hits at him, and then hits him. He can't hit back. He tries to catch her wrists, to step away. She screams again, and it's a sound like an animal's, a scream of rage or fear or threat, straight from the animal part of the brain. And then she lunges at him with both of her big arms thrusting forward, her hands splayed out, and shoves him down the stairs with all of her weight. He can't believe it, at first, that he's falling. His sense of balance tells him; the drop in the floor of his stomach tells him; the surge of adrenalin through his veins like a flush through a pipe tells him, but he can't believe it. Midair, for so long that he thinks he's flying. Then the impacts, the first and then the subsequent, which he feels only as impact, not pain, and then pain.

He can't move. He thinks: My back is broken. He can't draw in a breath. Then the pain starts in: head hip knee elbows wrist back, each place clamouring. He must get up but his muscles won't move. Loretta is still roaring, looming above him on the landing, her face still distorted and discoloured. No sound from the main floor: Is that good or bad? Good; they'd call the police, surely. Bad; there's no rescue. He finally starts to roll over, gather himself onto his hands and knees. He can't stand, but he begins to crawl backwards toward the outside door, a sidling, whimpering thing. He doesn't care.

Then there's an even louder crash than he had made, a hard sound of shattering and crunching and tinkling. The missile strikes him on his shoulder on the way past him, on its last bounce, then stops. His TV.

He thinks now, Sophie! and hears Loretta say, *and your dumb cat,* but Sophie's too smart; Sophie hisses, he hears her hiss, and then the lunge at the window, the table banging against the wall under Loretta's weight. Another roar. Sophie has got out. The thought gives him a zap of energy or something, and he scrambles for the door. And he grabs his TV on the way out.

Soon, though, he has to put the TV down. It's only adrenalin that has let him carry it down two alleyways. But the screen is shattered, he sees that, and the plastic casing broken in at least three places, and things rattling around inside. He can't move quickly enough to look for Sophie, either, with the TV. He puts it down gently, marking the spot in his attention so he'll be able to find it again. He understands that it is irreparable, but he does not want to just abandon it. He keeps calling Sophie in a hoarse whisper, doesn't dare to yell.

His knee doesn't feel right. He can hardly put weight on it. He has to hobble. His wrist and his skull are sending sharp staccato distress messages. His ankle and hip complaining, too, when he steps. But it's his back that's the worst. He can't draw a full breath. He tries to breathe through the pain but he can't breathe properly.

Blood in his eye, his mouth, the salt taste. He touches the side of his head, feels wetness. Blood on his fingers now, so much that his heart gives a lurch.

Sophie, he calls, low. Sophie. He circles the alleys and side streets around the house, staying out of view of the house and of other pedestrians.

Now dizziness and nausea: the alley going black for a few moments and then he leans forward to vomit on his own shoes.

He needs help. Sophie has gone to ground somewhere. He will find her but he needs to stop bleeding, to stop reeling and retching. Emergency room, he thinks. But if they call the police?

He lies down for a moment, not realizing he has done so, wakes to darkness and the night sounds of the city. Sirens. Traffic quieter. He doesn't know where he is at first and when he moves to stand up, his head spins and his back is a jolt of agony. He's thirsty. But his head is clearer. He needs to call for help. He'll find a pay phone.

He tries Mandalay first but gets her answering machine. Who next. Cleo? But she's an hour's drive away, probably in bed. And he's not sure he remembers her number. He has only one more quarter, will have to go into a store to get change, and there's so much blood and vomit on him that he is avoiding even the more lighted parts of the street.

He calls Ben. He remembers his number, and calls him, and Ben answers.

Ben says, I'll be right there, man! Stay put!

An accident, he'd said. He needs to sit down but there are no benches near the pay phone. It's inside the door of a bar, the lower floor of a cheaper hotel, and he can't stay in there with the throb of the music like someone banging on his head. Outside of the bar there's no bench. He thinks there could be something, a planter box or a bicycle stand or something but there isn't. Only the street and the lamppost. He has to stay here because Ben is coming, now, but he wishes he hadn't said here.

A narrow metal signpost at the sidewalk's edge. He moves to it, sits. No cars here so the sign probably says no parking. He leans on the metal rail that is the post but it is very narrow, with sharp edges. There is no place on his back that can lean against these sharp metal edges. And yet he cannot stay vertical now.

His feet over the curb, so he can hunch over his knees. Better: the back better.

Flashlight in his eyes, now, blinding him except for the sense of the blue and red light strobing very near but in the street. Cop car. Therefore, cop. He tries to sit up and the pain in his back forces out of him a deep, animal groan. One of the cops putting his hands on him, not ungently but touching all of the sore spots, nevertheless. His old fear pulsing in his throat.

One of the cops, and he's not aware till she speaks that she's a woman, says, Jeez Louise, looks like someone threw you down some stairs.

They want to see his ID which he gives them, and to ask if he has been drinking, and if he can count to ten. He can count to ten but his tongue is thick and he's gagging again, the flashlight somehow making him sick. His mouth full of blood. The cop shines the light into his mouth as if holding a glass for him to drink, and says, you've bitten your tongue. He has not noticed before. She's calling for an ambulance on her radio. He spits, his blood and saliva too thick to expectorate cleanly, and says, My brother's coming to get me. He's coming from West Point Grey to get me.

Yeah? she says.

I don't need an ambulance.

We'll see, she says. The other cop has come back with his driver's licence and hands it to him and with great concentration he extracts his wallet from his pocket again and puts the licence back in and puts the wallet back into his pants pocket.

Do you want to make a complaint? the male cop asks.

Do I what?

Make a complaint. File a report. Who beat you up.

Something is pecking around at the edge of his consciousness but he can't pluck it up. Something about his licence, that the cop was going to do something that was dangerous. He wants to look at his licence now to see if it's alright, but getting it out of his pocket again seems too much effort.

Were you hit by a car?

He says, Fell down some stairs, and then has to vomit again.

Have you had anything to drink?

No. He hears a siren now. The ambulance? He says, My brother is coming to get me.

Okay, the female cop says.

People coming out of the pub, stopping. Holy fuck, look at his face, one of them says. There's murmuring. They move off, he can hear them, and then one of them yells back, Pigs! Police brutality.

He vomits again. Now he remembers. The databank. They have a big computer somewhere, and when they put his name in, off his licence, it would show. His record. They haven't said anything, though. Maybe just waiting.

We need you to make a statement so we can make sure this doesn't happen to you again, the male cop says, squatting down next to him. He's wiping Cliff's face, somehow.

The woman says. He can do all of that later. He's not in shape.

The ambulance and Ben pull up at the same time, Ben trying to park in the place the ambulance wants, the woman cop directing him – *Away!* – with an impossibly loud sharp whistle blow, a chop of her arm.

Ben is beside him, his hand on Cliff's shoulder, saying Jesus, man! in a shocked voice, and then, sounding very young, his voice squeaking up a slide, asking the cops: What happened to him?

Overnight in emergency, with curtains, sleep and vomiting and some rousing him at intervals to take his blood pressure and shine a little light into his pupils. In full daylight he wakes again, sees Ben asleep in a chair beside his bed, head back, mouth open, arms thrown out. Then Ben in a split second on his feet, blinking. Then grinning at him, his wide-open, no-holds-barred grin.

Six weeks of rest, the doctors say. In a dark room.

Wreck

MANDALAY ASKS, Will we miss our flight? But he says that he has built an extra day into the trip, and they can take a more direct route back, cutting off the last leg. Thanks for being such a good sport about the weather, he says. You've been an excellent travelling companion, my dear. He folds her into his arms more tightly, but it is somehow a letting go. In his words something ebbing. But she won't pursue it, try to pin it down, not when they are both cold and wet and cramped.

In the night the rain stops, and she hears now only the dripping of the cedars, and then at dawn, the bird chorus. When she wakes again, it's light, the sun sparkling on a calm, limpid sea, and Duane making coffee over the little stove.

It will be a longer day of paddling today, to get back to the village, but they take a break in the early afternoon to spread their clothes and sleeping bags out on a beached tree and to make love on a carpet of moss. Mandalay wants to sleep, after, to stretch her limbs out naked in the sunshine, but Duane puts on his shorts, says he'll go exploring. Then he comes back for her: Come, I want to show you something.

Down a trail is another small cove, and lying on the beach the wreck of a small fishing boat. Not much remains of it but the bowed shape of the hull. The wooden planks have been mostly pried off, and the boat's ribs can be seen, like the ribcage of a whale, beneath the lattice of planks that remain.

She walks into the shell of the wreck. Come in, she says, but Duane does not. She sees him standing a little away, on the beach, through the slats and gaps between the ribs, the lattice of planks, his hands in his shorts, his face in the shadow of his hat.

Now he holds his fingers and thumbs at right angles, makes a rectangle at his face. I wish I had brought that camera, he says. He has not regretted the camera the whole week, even when the humpbacks surfaced only a dozen metres from them.

Why? she asks.

It's a perfect photo, he says. You look as if you're in a bird cage.

THEY PADDLE SIDE BY SIDE; it's their last stretch. They'll reach the docks in the evening, before dark, have a meal, sleep overnight again at the bed and breakfast inn, and catch a ride back to the airport at Sandspit. Duane says, I'm really looking forward to a hot shower and a real bed. I bet you are too.

He says, You've been great. This has been great.

And so have you, she says. Thank you for taking me on the trip.

My pleasure, he says.

Is this how they will finish it? The sudden distance he has created; what is it in aid of? She feels it drag at her, a current.

We make a good team, she says.

Yep, he says. Is it her imagination, or has he speeded up his paddling? She feels she is paddling harder to keep abreast.

Are you really tired? she asks.

I am, he says. But it's a good kind of tired. Mentally, I feel refreshed. Ready to get back to work. What about you?

In his voice, the cheerfulness, the politeness, of a stranger. She reminds herself: Intimacy is a dance of closeness and distance. And he might just be steeling himself against their return, against his return to that other world of work and conflict.

She is sure that if she were to ask, what is wrong? he would not know what she was worried about. She must let go of her anxieties, have more trust. After this week of emotional and physical intimacy, of complete mutual reliance, of the breaking down of all boundaries, of the sharing of intense discomfort – and awe – they can hardly go back to the way they were. They won't slip back into their previous routine of shared meals and entertainment and sex. It's not possible. She must trust this.

And yet, she is not being honest if she doesn't admit that she wants some acknowledgement, some small sign that their bond has deepened. She says, I'll miss waking up with you every morning.

Really? I didn't think you were the kind of woman who wanted to be together 24/7.

It's not her imagination. She's having to paddle very hard to keep up with him. Don't react, she tells herself. Let it go.

He says, then, Yeah, I'll miss it too. You were really great.

She can't do it anymore. She slows her paddling to let the muscle fatigue in her shoulders and back and arms subside, and is quite quickly left behind the other kayak in the couple of moments it takes him to notice she's not with him anymore. When he does, he turns the craft and waits for her to catch up, and then paddles beside her more slowly.

You knew, he says, the distance gone from his voice now, it wouldn't last. The intimacy, the excitement. It doesn't last. If you try to hold onto it, it slips away. And then you try to turn it into something else: You look for a bigger house, or you take salsa lessons together, or you bring home a bag of handcuffs and paddles. But you're just replacing it. You're not reviving it. You can't. We're not capable of sustaining pleasure or interest in each other that long. It's so bound up with novelty.

Maybe it isn't, always, she says. Maybe it can deepen. Maybe it can turn into something better, not cheaper.

No, he says. It can't. This week was amazing, Mandalay. It really was. It was one of the best weeks of my life. And I feel it's brought us closer too. But our relationship isn't going to change now. It's good, being companions, isn't it? Do we really want to change that? We have the best of each other, this way. We get to put into our careers and the other aspects of our lives all of the energy and attention we need to, and then when we're together, it's always fresh and new and enjoyable.

She thinks: There is something wrong with this, but I can't put into words what it is. There's something missing, some flaw.

Everything okay? he asks.

Okay, she says.

As they paddle now into the bay, the water around them is suddenly full of sleek round heads. A party of seals is hanging in the water all around, just watching them.

We have no fish for you! Duane calls to them. No handouts!

The seals' dark round eyes and whiskered muzzles regard them gravely, questioningly.

WHEN SHE GETS BACK to her apartment, messages on her answering machine from both Cleo and Parvaneh: Call me as soon as you get back. And from Bodhi: *Yo. Ben here. Call me.*

Parvaneh isn't in. She calls Cleo, who asks her about her trip, listens, asks the right questions, sighs, and says, I'm so envious. Trent would never consider doing something like that.

Then Cleo says, Cliff's staying with me for a few weeks. He's been hurt....

In a bike accident, Mandalay says. Suddenly, she can't breathe.

Cleo says, carefully, I think he was beaten up. He won't talk about it.

He's badly hurt, then? She's thinking of Che; they both are, she knows.

Skull fracture, Cleo says. A couple of broken ribs. Otherwise I think just bruises. He's told Bodhi more. But there's something else going on, I think. Did you know he had moved?

She had not.

A couple of months ago, Cleo says.

But he loved his apartment so much. He was so happy there. Did he get evicted or something?

I think he moved in with a girlfriend.

Cliff? Oh, dear.

He's not that low-functioning, Cleo says. I keep telling you this.

But he's likely to be exploited or something. You know that.

I know that. Anyway, he's supposed to be quiet for six weeks. For the concussion. He can't work. It's okay; I talked to his boss. The company owner. You know, his supervisor I guess it is, a total creep, had told him not to bother coming back, if he took sick time. After, what is it, four years he's worked for them.

So he's doing okay now? She suddenly feels that she can't process any more today; she just wants to change into sweatpants, do her laundry – all of her clothes are damp and smell like fish and campfire smoke – and sleep.

He's on the mend, Cleo says. He's just worried about his cat. It's lost. Do you think you could go look for it?

Cleo is the most practical and impractical person in the world. You want me, Mandalay asks, to go around a strange neighbourhood looking for a cat? I don't even remember what she looks like.

Tabby. Her name is Sophie.

Are you out of your mind, Cleo? Mandalay says. I am not going to do this.

Okay, Cleo says. I just thought I'd ask.

She doesn't call Parvaneh until later. Parvaneh says, My uncle wants to have a meeting.

Did you mention about the raise? Or opening a second place? Did he say anything?

You need to slow down, Mandalay, Parvaneh says. It's a phrase she often uses. Not everything can happen at once or as you like it to. We will have a meeting Wednesday, okay?

How is the café?

Not as good without you, Parvaneh says. I will see you tomorrow.

SHE CALLS BODHI and a woman answers: Carol York.

She says, It's B- uh, it's Ben's, it's Ben's sister. Mandalay. She had meant to sound authoritative, but here she's stammering and squeaking. She asks to speak to Ben, and the woman says, carefully, I'll get him, Mandalay. I'd like to meet you, and your brother and sister. Maybe we can talk about a get-together.

Okay, Mandalay says. And then, because she doesn't know what exchange this sort of occasion calls for, she says, Thanks.

We'd really like to get to know you all, Bodhi's adoptive mother says.

There's something being offered, an exchange of something for something else, and Mandalay sees that she, all of them, must participate in the exchange. She feels her shoulder blades tighten.

That would be nice, she says.

I'll call Ben to the phone, the woman says.

Ben says, I heard you were kayaking around Haida Gwaii. I did that a couple of years ago. It's intense, eh?

He says, I called to tell you about Cliff. But you might have heard. And I wanted to talk to you, you know, about going to Butterfly Lake. I've been thinking. We should all go together, you know? You, me, Cleo, Cliff. For a week in August. Before my classes start up again.

She's filled with dismay at the thought. What does Cleo think? she asks.

She's not really into it. But you could talk to her. You could help me persuade her.

We'll talk, she says.

Why does this have to be the first thing he asks of her? She can't really take any more time off this summer: Parvaneh wants the whole month of August. And it never works, she and Cleo together at Butterfly Lake, at Crystal's house. They are close when they meet here, every month or so, she and Cleo. And they both can manage Crystal on their own — they've discussed this. Together, though, they just can't seem to connect.

And then there's Duane. Who, of course, she can leave for the week, if she thinks about it. No question. But below rational thought, she feels panic at the thought of being separated from him for that long.

He calls her late that evening. She hasn't been expecting him to. They'd said goodbye affectionately when he'd dropped her off, but she'd had the sense that he was preoccupied, already moving, in his head, into his work, that he'd call her, as he usually did after a weekend together, Wednesday evening. She had expected less contact, rather than more, too, given his distance — his coolness — on the way back from the trip.

He says, Is everything alright?

Yes, she says.

Should we have dinner Tuesday?

If you are free, she says, that would be lovely.

You sound tired, he says.

She is, she realizes. Very, very tired.

Get some sleep, he says.

She doesn't tell him about Cliff.

DUANE CANCELS FOR TUESDAY; she's not surprised. On Wednesday, just after closing, Parvaneh arrives, and then a few minutes later, her uncle, who's technically Mandalay's boss, as he owns the café, signs the paycheques, though doesn't involve himself much otherwise. (And how lucky is that? She and Parvaneh have been able to have a free hand, have creative control.)

She's only met him a few times. He's tall, with slightly olive skin, silvering hair, a large mustache. He's always dressed in linen trousers and a very white cotton shirt. He doesn't speak much English, or maybe he does, but prefers to have Parvaneh transmit conversations between them.

He speaks for a while, and Parvaneh answers him, and it seems that they're having an argument. Then Parvaneh says, My uncle agrees that you're very hard-working and that your ideas and skills have been indispensable to building up the café's profile and clientele. He agrees you should be making more.

That's good, Mandalay thinks. But she has a sense it's not going to be that smooth. Parvaneh seems to be arguing with her uncle again, remonstrating with him. *No, no,* he says. She understands that much Persian.

Parvaneh presses her fingertips to her temples briefly and then turns back to Mandalay.

Okay, she says. The bad news. Two of my cousins, my uncle's nephews, are moving here from Iran. They've finally got their approval and they'll be here in a couple of weeks. They'll be managing the café. My uncle is giving The Seagull to them to manage. They are men and need jobs to support their families.

But what about us? Mandalay only manages to squeak out. It feels as if an enormous metal object has just clapped her on the head.

We are welcome to stay on as staff. Lower pay, shorter hours. Less responsibility.

But the menu! That's ours. We developed it.

My cousins will learn it. They'll be helped by the staff who already prepare some of the things.

All of those recipes that Parvaneh had so diligently typed into the computer, asking Mandalay to be specific, be specific, how long do you chill the dough.

How long have you known about this?

Parvaneh says, Only a few days. Though I knew my uncle wanted them to have some place to work if they ever made it.

Why can't they be staff, and we be managers? And get paid as managers?

I told you, Parvaneh says. In our culture men need more pay.

Mandalay can't believe that this can happen, that this is permitted to happen. It can't be legal.

We have so much business, she says. We've built up so much business. Maybe your uncle could open a second location now, and your cousins could run that? We could train them.

Parvaneh speaks to her uncle. But she knows the answer already; she nods as she replies.

He's already planning a second location, she says. And a third, as a matter of fact. But they will go to my cousins, and there are more men in the family to run them.

What about the art wall? She's set that up; she has the contacts. Only she can do the art wall.

No art anymore, the uncle says, in English.

Her senses finally seem to be coming back to her. She feels light, now, clear-headed. She stands up. Parvaneh, she says. Please tell your uncle that I give notice right now.

She begins to shake, as she walks back to her apartment. She should have said quit, not give notice. Why hadn't she? She has become too practical, too entrenched in the system, that's why.

And look where it's got her. Can they do this to her?

THEY CAN DO THIS TO YOU, Duane says. They are eating steak — or Duane is; she hasn't touched hers.

Duane had said: I think we're tired of seafood, aren't we? and chosen this place famous for its beef. The thought of the meat is making her ill, though.

You don't have a contract, he says. You don't own any part of the business. Your recipes are in the business computer.

It's three years of my life. I made The Seagull — Parvaneh and I did. I came up with most of the ideas, most of the items on the menu. Parvaneh took care of the details, and we bounced ideas around together. But it wouldn't exist without me. And the art wall? That is all mine. I do all that.

It's not ethical, Duane says. But I'm afraid it's not illegal.

So there's nothing I can do?

I didn't say that. Of course we're going to do something.

What?

I'll have to figure that out. I need a few days, to talk to colleagues, to do some research.

But you think I have a hope?

I said that we would do something.

He doesn't seem very sympathetic. It's my life, she says.

And we're going to do something about it, he says. Mandalay, sweetheart. We'll deal with it. Let's just have a nice dinner, now.

Part of her mind is saying that this is reasonable, that it makes sense. But another part is bristling, disgruntled, stirred to slow-burning resentment.

She says, I don't want to. I don't feel like eating.

Okay, he says. Can I order you something else?

She knows that she is being unreasonable, but she is stuck in this groove, now, can't change tracks.

If you drink your wine, at least, you might relax.

She says, I don't want the wine. It's true: Her insides seem be rejecting any food or drink.

Okay, he says. Do you mind if I finish mine? I'm really hungry. He says it so mildly, so calmly, that she's tempted to capitulate, but she cannot, she cannot.

After he pays the bill he says, Do you want to go for a walk, and again she's tempted, because she knows he finds walking, ordinary walking in the city, unappealing.

No, she says, and she hears her own voice, small and thin and knows it's self-pity, it's only self-pity, but she's powerless to stop it.

They would normally, on a Wednesday, go to his apartment for a drink and sex, but she asks if he'll drive her home, instead. And on the short trip there the thoughts that have been swimming around in her head since the last day of their trip now line up, form a pattern.

What is she doing? This isn't going anywhere, is it? The relationship will never be equal – he'll always have so much more income than her, and he'll always be able to choose what they're going to do. And it will never develop into anything else. She can see that. She's finally admitting it to herself. He's never tried to hide it, but he's never going to want a committed relationship. He'll want to leave his options open, to be able to walk away whenever it's not fun anymore. When will that be? Maybe only a few months, or maybe a few years? In the meantime, she will be getting older, and her options will be diminishing. She's wasted so much of her life on dead-end things: jobs and relationships. She can't really afford to do that anymore.

He takes the Granville Street Bridge south – the restaurant is in Yaletown – and turns right onto Broadway, and in the dusk the traffic surges and stops, surges and stops, the headlights moving with some sort of pattern she can't fix. On her street he stops and puts the car in park but doesn't turn off the ignition.

She says, I've been thinking. This can't go on, you know. It's not going anywhere. It's not working for me. You don't want a committed relationship, and I do, and so I'm kind of wasting my time, aren't I?

Are you?

She can't look at him.

Where do you want it to go? he asks.

She can't actually answer that, honestly. She doesn't know. Does she want anything different? But she can't bear the uncertainty, the lack of trajectory, of purpose. It isn't safe for her. It doesn't feel safe.

If it's not moving, it's not alive, she says. Does she believe this? What does she mean by it? She doesn't know. It feels like some kind of hard-won truth.

Is there anything I can do? he asks.

She can't be in the same space with him, suddenly. She opens the car door and is out, has shut it behind her, before he can get out. He does, though, stands looking at her across the top of the car. She can't look at him. She makes herself look at him. She can't read his face; it seems expressionless.

Okay, bye, she says, and turns to go down the sidewalk.

We'll talk, he says after her.

THERE'S SOMETHING MOVING in the little false balcony, the *balconnet*, that projects below the bay window in her apartment. She notices it one morning when she has slept in and draws the drapes later than usual, late enough that the sunlight reaches the dark little demi-cup. A paper bag or some leaves that have blown in, she thinks. But when she opens the sash window to remove it, there's a nest, a messy edifice of twigs and grass, and in it, two baby birds.

At first she doesn't take in what they are: there is naked pink-grey skin, flesh that doesn't resolves itself into a familiar shape; the flesh moves in a kind of spasmodic flop. She screams, jerking her hand back.

It takes a second and a third look to make sense of what she's seeing, and then it still seems monstrous. They are large chicks, their bodies big as her fists, their skin mottled like something decayed, unwholesome. They flop and lurch as if some vital part of their nervous system has been destroyed. At the movement of her hand, though, their blind naked heads shoot upward on stringy naked necks, hooked beaks gaping. Something scaly shifts in the lumps and stumps of horrible skin.

She realizes that they are birds, but still can't make sense of them in part of her brain. Some primal reaction floods her with disgust and fear.

She asks the downstairs neighbour to have a look at them. He squints. Pigeons, I'll guess, by the bills, he says. Here, get me a bag and I'll get them out of there for you.

What will he do with them?

He looks uncomfortable: Clearly she is ruining his attempt at gallantry by asking. Or he hasn't thought it through himself yet. He's one of three downy boys, engineering students, who share the main floor.

Maybe – a bucket of water. Or. Bang their heads with something, yeah.

In her balconnet the hideous babies have subsided into an abject heap, are huddled resting their necks on each other's backs.

Ah, crap, she says. I can't do it. Leave them.

They're disgusting, the boy says. Rats with wings. He's heard that somewhere, she thinks.

You're right, she says. But leave them.

She wants to draw the curtain but her apartment would then be very dark. She finds a shawl, tacks it over the lower part of the window only.

Black Ops

HE HAS TO TELL BEN because he needs Ben to go for Sophie. He has to tell Cleo because he needs somewhere to stay for a couple of weeks, an adult to whose responsibility he can be released because of his skull fracture. So then Cleo and Ben in his hospital room, not exactly arguing but talking too loudly for his head. Cleo bossing Ben and Cliff: Ben with his own ideas. Cliff with mush in his head.

Cleo says, you have to report him, Cliff. Whoever did this to you. You could have been killed. He could kill someone else, attacking them like that. You don't have to protect him or be afraid of him.

He doesn't answer, screws his eyes shut. He had said *roommate*. He doesn't know why it seemed worse that a woman pushed him. He can't report it. She'll just say it was a fight, anyway. That he was beating on her, and she pushed him, didn't think he was so close to the stairs.

And you can't go back there, of course. So we need to go get your stuff for you. How are we going to do that?

Just find Sophie, he says. Never mind the other stuff. Just find my cat.

Cleo says, don't be a moron, Cliff. All of your things. Your work clothes, your equipment. Your books. Your new TV. You can't just let this monster win.

Never mind it, Cliff says. His tongue is swollen. He has stitches in his tongue. He feels he can't defend himself. He feels defenceless already, because Cleo is taking over his life, phoning Ray to tell him Cliff can't come into work, then, when Ray said: Tell him he's here Monday morning or he looks for a new job, yelling at Cliff – not at Ray – that Ray's an asshole, as if it's Cliff's fault, and calling up Mrs. Cookshaw, going over Ray's head.

Ben says that he will collect Cliff's stuff. He'll go with a couple of his buddies. They won't be afraid. They might even teach this bozo, Cliff's roommate, a lesson. Cliff, mushy-headed, lets it go. He can't gather his thoughts, make his tongue work. It's all wrong but he lets go, sinks down into the twilight, the medication, he supposes.

He's at Cleo's then but he doesn't remember the trip there, from the hospital. He's in Cleo's basement, in the finished spare room there. From his cave, his safe dark basement den, he hears their voices, Cleo's and Trent's, the kids'. At first they alarm him. He's not used to them; he doesn't know where he is. He floats: They're giving him pain medication, nausea medication, anti-inflammatories. Cleo brings him his medication, and food and water. For a couple of weeks, time is marked off only by her visits, the knock, the opening of the door that lets in only paler darkness, not really light. Cleo appears and disappears. He floats. The food is more abundant and frequent than he has appetite for. Soup and sandwiches cut into triangles, crusts removed, and baked beans or macaroni and cheese with coins of wieners mixed in. Children's food, comfort food. He sleeps and floats.

He hears Trent's heavier steps and voice in the early morning and the evening, Sam's crying, Olivia's chatter and laughter. Cleo's voice, which changes pitch and tone constantly. The squeak of the stroller wheels, the muffled click of cabinet doors, the sounds of pots and dishes and utensils, of toilets flushing, of the vacuum cleaner, the washing machine. All around him the sounds, a soup.

He hears the change in sound when Cleo is about to bring him food or his medicine: the plaintive voices of the kids, her reply: No, no. He hears sometimes their footsteps on the stairs, echoes of Cleo's, and her whisper: I told you, no!

He gets up one morning or afternoon to use the washroom and sees a white flat object that has been pushed under his door: a sheet of paper folded into a shape that isn't quite a rectangle. When he unfolds it, it says: *Dear Clif, I am yor frend. Love, Olivia.* He understands the letter's intent clearly: Another prisoner has reached out to him.

He says to Cleo, You can let the kids come in.

No, she says. They'll jump all over you. They can't be still for two minutes.

The pain meds or his injury keep him suspended for what he later knows is two weeks and then he wakes up and it's like hitting the ground, like he's been born, an elk onto frozen tundra and expected to run, or like in that movie he saw this spring, Keanu Reeves being dumped wet and naked out of his pod.

He thinks now of Sophie, lost and hungry, maybe hurt, wondering why he doesn't come for her. He thinks of Loretta and his head is split – on one side his worry: How is she doing? And on the other side fear and rage growing like white shoots on a potato. He has to slam that door.

He thinks that Cleo is probably saving his life but he doesn't want it to be that. He doesn't want to be in her debt again, to need her, to owe her anything more.

In the end Cliff has to tell about Loretta, too. He lets himself sink into the shame. He just adds it to the tab. He tells Ben, who has come all the way out to Cleo's, who is sitting by Cliff's bed, in the semi-darkness, on the chair where Cleo leaves his puke bowl. He just tells Ben.

Ben seems impressed, rather than disdainful. Holy fuck, Cliff! He says. As if Cliff has participated in some really stupid extreme sport, the kind guys boast about.

Maybe he has, at that. He has a skull fracture, a concussion, three broken ribs, a chipped hipbone and ankle, a torn tendon in his knee. And a bitten tongue. The rest is just scrapes and bruises. The broken ribs, that's the pain in his back, the injury that's making it hard for him to breathe.

He says to Ben: Don't tell Cleo.

What? She's going to have to know.

No, don't tell her.

She's not going to let it go, bro.

Just don't tell her.

Okay, man. Ben looks pleased, excited. He reaches over with his right hand and punches Cliff lightly on his arm.

It's a game, to Ben: Cliff can see that. Ben takes a sort of delight in it. He seems to see Cliff as some sort of star athlete, an explorer of the unknown and dangerous. It makes Cliff nervous. No good can come of this. No good can come of pretending you're something you're not.

But it's more than that. He cringes when Ben talks about it, uses words like *bitch*. He wants to say to Ben that women aren't like that, that Loretta is an abnormality, and probably broken in some way by somebody else. He wants Ben to know that it's usually women, in his experience and observation, who get thrown down stairs. It doesn't seem good, the glee that Ben is expressing. As if he really wants to believe there are a lot of violent and crazy women. As if he's only too happy to have evidence of their existence. It's not good.

At the same time, he lets it go. He's not unhappy to have Ben's admiration rather than his pity or disdain.

Ben and two of his friends, Coop, the lean-jawed one, and Rav, the Indian guy, cook up a plan. They will pound on Loretta's door. They will demand to come in. They'll barge in. They'll storm the apartment like firefighters. Like ninjas. Like a swat team. They'll kick open the door. They'll hold her down. They'll threaten her with fake badges.

They'll retrieve his clothes, his boxes. The cat if they can find it. His armchair. They'll throw something of hers down the stairs, in repayment for the TV. What does she have that's expensive and breakable? Does she have a computer? They'll throw her computer down the stairs.

No, no, Cliff says. You can't do that kind of thing. They're all speaking in hushed voices in the downstairs room at Cleo's. Cliff is not supposed to be agitated but they're more concerned about Cleo hearing.

Dude's right, Rav says. It's no good, guys. She'll call the cops.

So a second plan, which they like better than the first, which they call Black Ops.

Nothing good will come of this, Cliff thinks.

They'll go in daytime, when Loretta's at work. Let themselves in with Cliff's key. They ask Cliff to make a floor plan of the flat. They put an X on the map for the spot where his things are, where the storage locker key hangs. They make a list of Cliff's belongings. They write down a description of the cat. There's only one cat, Cliff says. If there's a cat, it's my cat.

Cliff feels very tired. They are boys. They are just boys.

They could have set it up on the phone but they drive all the way out to Cleo's and huddle around Cliff and cook it up and make him very tired.

Cleo comes downstairs and tells them to leave. They pat Cliff's shoulders. They're all very excited. Coop's lean cheekbones are red; Ben and Rav are giggling. Cleo frowns at them. They leave.

When they come back, they're less giddy. They have got Cliff's stuff from the storage locker, but not his clothes, his jeans and button-downs, his work uniforms. Those are gone. Threw them out, the bitch! Coop says, and Cliff winces. They have retrieved the armchair. Cleo looks at it like it needs fumigating. She says they can put it in the garage.

No sign of the cat. No cat dishes or litter bin, even, Ben says. I thought to check.

Oh, Sophie.

He's not allowed to get up and look for her. If he doesn't let his brain rest it will take years to get better. He might have permanent damage.

Cleo drives him to his checkup with the neurologist, who tells him: You have an earlier skull fracture. See? He points to the x-ray pinned to his light board. There's a white line sort of on the front and top, to the right and above his eyebrow. You did that as a child, the neurologist says. We can see that it healed while your skull was still growing. There was likely some bleeding, some bruising.

Cleo has come in with him, against his wishes. He feels her grow cold and withdrawn, beside him. Neither of them say anything until they are in Cleo's car. Then she says: You fell a lot. You and Che rough-housed a lot. I don't remember a specific time. Then she bursts into tears, cries hard for about two minutes, wipes her face and starts the car up.

The neurologist has told him: You need to rest more. No exertion, no thinking! If you don't you could be permanently incapacitated. You could have headaches, seizures. You might not be permitted to operate a motor vehicle again.

He has to stay in bed in Cleo's dark basement room. He's allowed to read a little, watch TV a little. That's it. He sleeps a lot. When he sleeps, he dreams of Sophie, and in his dreams she's sentient, and talks to him with a human voice. She reminds him of the girl in his building, the girl with the tattoo. But she's a cat.

He knows where Sophie is. It comes to him one morning as he is waking up. He knows where she is. He needs Cleo to drive him into the city. She says No: it's been only three weeks. He says he'll wear dark wrap-around sunglasses. Sit quietly in the car all the way there. He'll go in and look. Ten minutes, that's all. Ten minutes.

Cleo likes cats. He knows that she'll give in. She does.

HE HAS TO WAIT for someone to buzz him in and then he's going up the stairs, trying not to rush and raise the blood pressure in his brain. The familiar stained and scuffed floors and walls fill him with nostalgia. To the second floor. Along the corridor. He knocks and knocks at her door. Nothing. He had thought she never went out, but maybe she has moved out. It has been a few months, now, since he himself moved in with Loretta. He hadn't thought of that.

But there's still somewhere else, something he didn't mention to Cleo. She'll give him heck but he's in here now. To the back stairs, now: the basement. There's no light bulb, as usual, and he feels his way in, groping, counting steps, worrying about bumping his head against something. Why hadn't he thought of a flashlight? Then the wall, where he was expecting it. Turn to the right, now, and keep going. Which door? His outstretched hands touch things he has to identify: grating, roll of something smooth – linoleum maybe?

At one point his feet hit something immoveable, and he thinks his path is completely blocked, but patting with his hands, he finds tacked boxes of asphalt shingles, the top boxes opened. Only knee high, this barricade, though heavy, and too deep to step over; he has to crawl. The mechanical parts of the building shriek and groan, suddenly. A swath of cobwebs across his face, himself swabbing involuntarily to wipe them clear.

Something he brushes against comes clanking down all around him, clanging and echoing. Metal of some sort. Another turn, a fork in the corridor. Where is he now? A locked door. No. But there was a locked door, he remembers. Door to the electrical room: not the one he wants. The other door will be just a few feet further.

And here it is, the cool metal knob turning in his hand, the door resisting fractionally on its spring.

He calls. It seems there's a listening, or that something has stopped moving. Might be rats. Mice, anyway. He can smell mice, old clothes or furniture, bicycle oil. Then he thinks: light switch, feels inside, pats the wall down. There.

A room of wire cages, lockers. This is the room. He calls again, and realizes: small odds. Such small odds. Something folds up, makes itself small, inside his chest.

And then there she is, blinking in the light. She's thin and covered with dust, but it's her. She walks up to him, mewing a little. She head-butts his shin. He picks her up. She purrs.

Cleo and the kids, grinning, when he carries Sophie back to the car.

The Knuckleheads

ON THE FIRST FERRY Ben buys gift-shop souvenirs: a plush toy otter, supine, with a felt clam between its paws, a wind-up plastic hermit crab with a bright orange plastic anemone riding it. Do you think he'll like these? he asks. Is the stuffed toy safe for the baby? Mandalay understands he is nervous, wants to arrive bearing gifts.

He is distressed that he has nothing for Crystal. You're the gift, Mandalay says. She's being facetious, but really: What can he offer that won't be too ludicrously ordinary for the occasion?

But she understands: The gifts are an act of penance, for something.

On the ferry he plays with the wind-up toy. He'll break it, she thinks, but she doesn't say anything. Sunlight shafts through the big slanted windows, sudden warmth. She closes her eyes: She is tired with the sort of tiredness that must be like battle fatigue. Too many losses, recently. Too many lost battles. She is empty.

She had wanted them all to travel up to Butterfly Lake together: Cleo and Cliff and Ben and herself. But Ben had wanted to go a few days before Cleo: Cleo had wanted to bring the children and Trent, and Trent couldn't leave till the weekend, and Cliff had appointments. She had cried, sitting on the floor of her jewel-box apartment with her telephone. She doesn't drive. She must be a passenger, be carried along by other people's plans.

The second ferry, to Powell River, then the winding drive along the fjord, to Guisachan Falls. I can't believe I've never been up here before, Ben keeps saying. He is enthusiastic about it all: the long drives, the two ferry rides, the small city with its potholes and derelict houses, its smokestacks, its new mall glittering like a squat alien colony on the outskirts, the steep and winding highway leading up to Butterfly Lake, the ascent through the overarching cedar and then dark upright spruce taxing the engine of his little car. He changes gears and the car seems to hesitate and then move into the next grade with a sort of resigned determination. It's, like, *wilderness*, he keeps saying.

Mandalay feels the old heaviness descend on her: the darkness of the forest, the assault of maple and salal and salmonberry on the roadside, the effort of climbing the thirty kilometres from sea level weighing on her as if she were doing the engine's work herself. She has last been on this highway eight years ago, riding pillion on Horst's Harley. Horst, her fiancé. He'd wanted to meet her mother; one of his eccentric, old-world quirks. And he'd had romantic notions about the wilderness. They'd had rain all the way from Powell River, had arrived stiff with cold, soaked through under their leathers. Horst had loved it. She'd developed a stubborn bronchial infection.

And before that, another gap of about eight years since she'd hitched a ride with Danny Jones out of Powell River, followed him to Vancouver.

A perpetual passenger. Maybe she needs to get her driver's licence. Though at least, on this trip, she's riding in a newish car with a working heater and windshield wipers.

Ben asks, Why is it so far? What's up there, in the mountains? Why is the community there?

She has to say that she's not sure, exactly. There's a hydroelectric dam, she says. And a mill.

So the lake wasn't always there?

She doesn't know. It feels to her that Butterfly Lake has always existed, and yet it can't have been there for more than a hundred years. Her sense of its history is muddled, fragmented. The community she remembers from her childhood is one of back-to-the-land types, growing their organic beets and cabbages, holding solstice parties. Macramé and hummus and homemade granola, she thinks.

Maybe there was, like, a rich farming valley before the dam, Ben suggests.

Maybe. But she has never heard that — never heard of people's land flooded, any of the community displaced.

It must have been so cool to grow up out here, Ben says. In the natural landscape. In the wilderness. It must have been so free and healthy.

I was a teenager when I last lived here, she says. I just wanted to get out.

He can understand that, Ben says. But then he's exclaiming at the steep drop now from the guardrails down to the river, the tightness of the turn, the narrow bridge open to only one lane of traffic at a time. Man, extreme! he says. This is wild!

She never comes here, but only sees Crystal at Cleo's house, maybe once a year.

Then the dam, and a few more kilometres to Butterfly Lake. Then they're at the house, and Crystal is running at the car, her off-kilter run, arms and legs moving out of sync. She's dressed up: She has on an oddly girlish dress with a full skirt and puffed sleeves and a floral print. Her lipstick's a strange harsh colour, a bright geranium, and she's wearing pink cowboy boots. Her greying hair hangs down her back in a long braid; it reaches almost to her waist.

And Ben gets out of the car and walks toward her, with his expensive shirt and jeans and his artful light beard, his shining, clean, well-cared-for teeth and hair, and he takes a breath, squares his shoulders, murmurs *Mom*?

Crystal's self-conscious screech, then: *Omigod he looks just like his Dadda*. They embrace, Ben almost towering over Crystal, Crystal hugging him awkwardly, her words coming out in strange artificial-sounding squawks. She can never just be natural. Crystal is never at home in her own skin. Mandalay tries, but Crystal's awkwardness flays her nerves.

Crystal's husband Darrell comes out of the house then, comes up to Crystal and Ben. He gets bushier of beard and bigger around every time she sees him, a demented mountain man, something out of a horror movie involving axes and canoes. She waits for Ben to turn and look at Darrell and startle, and he does. You don't really want to see a man who looks like Darrell coming suddenly into a clearing in the woods.

Ben, says Darrell. Good to see you. He puts out his hand.

My baby boy! Crystal says, and again it sounds false, like bad acting. Why should it? She's sure that Crystal is having some pretty strong maternal or parental response to Ben. Why can't she just let it emerge naturally? It's like she's rehearsed a false response to cover her natural expression. Mandalay winces.

Ben, though, does not seem to be put off by it. He embraces Crystal. He shakes Darrell's hand. He pats the two dogs who have bounded up from somewhere, barking and slavering. His body relaxes. He smiles. He is all grace.

Only she is stiff and unhappy, as if she has been trussed up and delivered to the wrong house.

▼▼▼

CLIFF SAYS from the front passenger seat: I don't recognize any of this.

Cleo doesn't, either. The turnoff should be along here, should appear soon, but she doesn't recognize landmarks. The slopes above the highway have been debrided of their thick forest, and there is raw earth, some red roots and bark, a swag of glinting houses. No landmarks. The highway has changed, too – it's been widened, straightened, and the new detour around the town, which they've just taken, has removed recognizable marks – billboards, streets – and replaced them with overpasses. She has not expected this. She does not know where they are. How long has it been? Ten years, maybe. She has been back only once, about ten years ago.

Do I turn or not? Trent demands, not slowing the SUV. She is supposed to be navigating, but what she's seeing outside doesn't translate into what she remembers. She thinks: I should have been driving. I could do it by feel, the feel of the road, if I were driving.

Quick, Trent says, his voice rising. Turn or not? But he hasn't slowed.

Almost too late, she sees the sign. Turn, turn! she yelps, from the back seat.

Trent yanks the wheel around and Sam's car seat slides toward her on the back seat, scraping her wrist. Olivia, on her other side, squeals and protests. Hey! Daddy! Cliff grabs the door handle.

Next time, give me more warning, Trent snarls. How far now? Quick!

You could slow down, she points out.

Trent slows to an exaggerated crawl. Cliff stares out the window, whether looking for the house or removing himself from the conversation, she can't tell.

But then, a few metres past the corner, things snap into their proper place. The moss-covered trees overarching the road, the thick undergrowth of salal and sword ferns, the dim wet gloom. There's the driveway, at last, the hand-lettered sign nailed to the bole of the enormous spruce. Cleo spots the 70s A-frame, identifies it, though it's been painted blue and disguised by additions, by the mountain rising behind the house — the only part of the landscape that isn't altered.

Turn, she says, turn, and Trent swings the wheel and the vehicle lurches down the unpaved driveway. Yard — a small clearing, in an impenetrable stand of cedar and fir, fronted by maple, filled with cars. Two large dogs, a volley of barking.

This is it? Trent asks. She doesn't answer, at first. She can hear Cliff breathe out slowly through his nose.

The two dogs — one black and white, the other yellow leap at the car windows, barking. Olivia shrieks, laughs. Mom! The dogs are slobbering on the windows!

This is it, Cleo says, but she doesn't move.

The front door of the A-frame opens and Mandalay stands in the doorway. She's wearing a little smocked top, flared jeans, has her hair in a loose ponytail, rather than in her usual elaborate updo. Her arms are crossed; she's smiling the smile that says to Cleo, I am here first. She looks like she might have done twenty years earlier.

It's Mandalay, Cleo says, unnecessarily.

Then Crystal bursts out from behind Mandalay, totters toward them across the lawn, the heels of her boots sinking into the spongy turf. Above the boots Crystal's legs are encased in bright-blue tights. Then there's a flowered dirndl skirt, black with large flowers, a yellow sweat shirt, a flowered headband. Crystal's long hair flying out behind her, witchily.

Cleo registers the open arms, begins, belatedly, to move, but she can't get the door open: The child safety locks are on. It's Trent who emerges from the car first and is seized and embraced, emerging to stand stiffly, hands in pockets, looking around him, hunched like a heron in a sudden rain. He's forgotten that Cleo can't get out of the back seat on her own.

Crystal turns to their car, then, and opens the back doors. Hello, hello, who's this very big person! she says, and unbuckles Sam, scooping him out of the car seat. Sam, like his father, stiffens, arches back from Crystal's kiss, looks appalled. No, he says.

In the other seat, Olivia bounces, then undoes her own harness. Grandma! Grandma! I'm here! Cleo is amazed: She has not taught Olivia to call Crystal Grandma, and Olivia has seen Crystal maybe three times in her life.

So you are, darling! Crystal says, passing Sam suddenly to Trent, taking pirouetting steps around to the other side of the vehicle to capture Olivia.

As she clambers out herself, she sees the house door open again, and Bodhi – or Ben (She must remember to call him Ben) – emerges, wearing a large hat, followed quickly by Darrell, Crystal's husband.

I don't recognize any of this, Cliff, still in the passenger seat, says querulously, not moving to undo his seat belt.

And so they are reunited.

▾▾▾

COME ON! Trent says. Knucklehead Mountain! You're making that up!

Tell him, Mandalay instructs. She's laughing, in top form. Tell him. We can show him on the map.

It's true, Cleo says. It really is called Knucklehead. The Knuckleheads, actually.

Cleo's mouth is pursed up, her voice prim. Mandalay knows that Cleo doesn't like the way she and Trent interact, but it's just a game. It's their ritual. They have a relationship of jokes, of teasing. They each have their role to play. An anthropologist would call it a joking relationship. Trent becomes heavier, stiffer, avuncular, even, though he's the same age as Mandalay. He treats her with a kind of assumed tolerance, incredulousness: What will this outrageous woman come out with next? And Mandalay lets go a little, lets herself get a little loud, a little unbuttoned. Cleo complains that they always go too far. She doesn't like them swearing in front of the children. She doesn't like the repartee between Mandalay and Trent, takes it too seriously. Maybe Trent complains, after, to Cleo. (Mandalay herself complains, sometimes, about Trent, to Cleo.) But it's their ritual. It's a performance. Maybe a performance for Cleo, for Cliff, for Ben.

Mandalay knows she is entertaining. She's got a gift for telling stories. She's funny; she knows how to put a story together effectively, so much so that people always accuse her of making it up.

And all of Mandalay's stories are true, yes. But they are, nevertheless, shaped in some specific ways. Their childhood, their lives, are all apparently a big soft medium that Mandalay can shape as she will.

She is telling them, now, about hiking up Knucklehead. The time Crystal, their mother, took them up Knucklehead and they were caught in the snowstorm. She's told it before, but not to Ben. There's no harm in it. It's true that the story isn't very flattering to Crystal, but sometimes their mother, Crystal joins in the stories, though Crystal says she doesn't remember much of those years anymore. Mandalay thinks, What electroshock therapy hasn't erased of Crystal's memory, pot has.

It was April, she says. Ma decided to take us all out of school to go hiking on Knucklehead, to see the spring flowers. It was too early, of course. Ma forgot it wouldn't be spring yet up the mountain, didn't you, Ma?

They all glance at Crystal, involuntarily, Mandalay thinks. Crystal is smiling, looking down at her plate; when they look at her, she looks up and says, brightly, Can I get anyone anything? More water? Coffee? But they all shake their heads, they all let Mandalay go on.

Ma drove us up the mountain, it's a provincial park, in the old station wagon. Remember that car? What happened to it? You could see the rust holes in the floor. You could see the road going by underneath! It's a wonder we weren't all asphyxiated by the exhaust. And no seatbelts! The boys rode in the hatch like groceries. Remember that, Cliff?

Cliff doesn't look up, barely shakes his head. Cleo doesn't look at Crystal or at Mandalay. Ben doesn't look at her, either. What is he thinking, what is this like for him? But she can't imagine: Her mind throws up a wall.

Ma drove to the park gate, then we went up a trail. We're totally unprepared for the bush, let alone that time of year. We're all in canvas runners and shorts. I think we had along a plastic bag with some trail mix and some apples in it. And maybe an extra diaper. We hiked about an hour, and then the sun went behind a cloud and it got cold. And then it started to snow.

Crystal says, then: Oh, wow — I can't remember....

It's Darrell who interrupts, surprising them. He's a big, silent man whom most of them ignore, or maybe not exactly ignore, but don't remember to interact with. Now he says, through his beard, Well, I don't know as we need to rehash all of those old stories now, do we?

Mandalay feels herself flush. Crystal's smile has gone stiff. Nobody is looking at Mandalay: She can feel the energy of their emotion, all turned against her, all in support of Crystal. Cliff, beside her, makes some sort of grunt, or mutters in agreement with Darrell.

Fuck them all. Especially Darrell.

She has known him all her life. Darrell was ten years older than her, had grown up in Butterfly Lake, had been a teenager when she was kid, a young adult when she was a teen, had worked for her dad, sometimes, or hung around asking for help with fixing his car. When she'd emancipated herself from her foster home and moved back to Butterfly

Lake, when she was sixteen, she'd thought for about five minutes that he was coming around the house to see her. But it had been Crystal, a few years older than him, that Darrell, now in his mid-twenties, was after. She hadn't seen how that was possible. But of course Crystal would have been thirty-four, then — the age Mandalay is now.

She remembers herself taunting him: What's with the moustache? Perv-stache. Looks like two Little Brown Bats copulating on your face. Darrell once pinning her, hands on her shoulders, against the wall, his face darkened, then releasing her, crashing bear-like out of the house.

She'd been a brat, then, and Darrell had taken Crystal's side, had told her off a couple of times. Deservedly, she thinks now. She'd been jealous. She hadn't really been interested in him; already at sixteen she felt herself more sophisticated than Darrell was ever going to be. But he had been good-looking, and had taken Crystal's side.

▼▼▼

THEY ARE HAVING A TOUR of the house. Cleo had tried to time their arrival so that it would be, say, an hour to dinner, and she would be able to help finish the preparations, and then they could all sit down and eat, and it would be a way to have something to do, to avoid the awkwardness of a roomful of people both too closely and too distantly connected. But it doesn't seem that any dinner preparations have begun, at all, so once Crystal and Darrell have exclaimed over the size of the children (itself a silent reproach, an occasion for awkwardness, the unspoken thought that she does not visit, that she does not invite Crystal to visit her very often), once they have had a conversation about the trip up (which takes all day, and involves two ferries), there is not much more that can be said, with all of them there. They sit on the deck, from which there is a view of the mountains that wouldn't have been there when Cleo was a child. Trees have been removed. The sun is starting to move toward the horizon, and slants toward the deck in a spotlight glare, too bright for the eyes. Crystal and then Darrell fiddle with an umbrella, but it's no use: Anyone facing west right now is blinded.

So: a tour.

Mandalay and Ben have already been shown around, so the tour is for Cleo and Olivia and Cliff, Cliff who has never been back at all. Trent stays with Darrell, who says he wants to ask him some questions about his new computer, and Sam. Cleo is glad to have a few minutes apart from Trent, who is going to scold her pretty soon about there not being dinner on the horizon. He'd wanted to stop in the town for burgers, when they got off the ferry, and she had said, don't spoil your appetite.

I don't remember any of this, Cliff says again, as they look around the house, and now Cleo wants to snap at him that he must, that he was nearly seven when they left, he must remember something. In any case, she is tired of him repeating the phrase. What does he mean by it?

It has all been redone, anyway. Darrell has put a lot of work into it, the last ten or so years. The A-frame still has its loft, its cathedral ceiling, but the log walls have been drywalled over and painted – hard clear shades of blue, yellow, pink – and an addition with more bedrooms and a bathroom added onto the house. The kitchen has new fixtures and cabinets – the kind you can buy from Home Depot, Cleo thinks – and the old chipped terra-cotta tile and shag carpeting have been replaced throughout with inexpensive laminate and vinyl.

Darrell and I couldn't make up our minds about the laminate, Crystal says, so we got a different kind for each room! Isn't that fun? Doesn't it look nice?

Yes, it does, Grandma, Olivia says.

Cleo imagines how Trent will smirk, how impossible the floor is, the look of the house with all the different floorings, the amateur finishing. Crystal says, the living room is Denver Pine and the master bedroom is Old Virginia Beech and Darrell's study is Holland Cherry. Olivia dashes from room to room, demanding the names of the flooring styles, repeating them. She'll remember them all, too. At four, she's soaking up language at the rate of a dictionary a day, as Trent says.

In some of the rooms, Crystal has painted, freehand, on the walls: curlicues and flowering vines and birds. The paintings are decidedly amateur, and Cleo wonders what Darrell thinks of them. Olivia, of course, is entranced. Grandma! You are an artist!

Crystal gives Cleo a wink, a knowing smile that throws her for a second. Cliff studies the paintings closely, seriously. What will you do when you have to paint over? he asks. You won't want to lose these!

Oh, well, Crystal says. They're not that good.

All this work, Cliff says. Maybe you can get Darrell to cut out pieces from the drywall, get them framed.

Cleo is glad that Trent is not with them. She says, The pictures are so detailed. And the colours are so pretty.

Crystal says, Oh, I should take classes and learn how to do it properly, I know. Mandalay is always saying that. But I get all seized up, you know, if someone is watching me and telling me what not to do.

Olivia takes Crystal's hand. Me too, Grandma, she says.

Crystal looks mischievous then. Why don't you ask your mom which room was hers?

Is she kidding? But Cleo says: The loft, all of us kids slept in the loft.

Yes, Crystal says. Isn't that funny? Your mom's daddy wouldn't make any more rooms. All of those children were up there, in two sets of bunk beds and a wee little crib, packed in like baby bunnies. I used to tuck them in at night and think, all of my baby bunnies are now tucked in and safe.

Inside Cleo the ground shifts unsettlingly. What is Crystal thinking, bringing this stuff up?

Cliff asks, How old were we then, I mean when we were all living here?

And now Crystal looks doubtful, confused. Hmmm, she says. That's hard to say.

I'm thinking, Cliff says, that it might have been kind of chaotic.

Yes, Crystal says. It was crazy! You can't imagine! But we all had a lot of fun, didn't we?

She seems to be asking Cleo. She never uses my name, Cleo realizes.

You were six when we left, Cleo says to Cliff. I was twelve.

The loft is now Darrell's study. Trent and Darrell and Ben are up there now, looking at Darrell's computer, Darrell asking, What is this Windows 98, Trent explaining about operating systems, Ben contributing computer jargon that is making Darrell more confused.

Crystal points to the pullout couch upholstered in deep sea blue. See, there's lots of room, Crystal says. You could stay here. I could fix an air mattress on the floor for Olivia.

It's okay, Cleo says. Trent's back bothers him. He can't sleep on a pullout.

Oh, well, Crystal says. You could have mine and Darrell's bed, we'd sleep up here.

We're better off in the motel, Cleo says. She can't imagine, even with the extra rooms, how they'd all fit – Mandalay and Cliff, she and Trent and their kids, Ben.

Are you sure? Crystal says. I hate to think you come to visit after all these years and have to stay in a motel.

It's fine. We're fine.

Maybe you and hubby would like to have the motel to yourself? You could leave the little ones here.

Olivia pipes up then: I want to stay at Grandma's!

No, she says. The kids won't actually sleep away from us. I don't think it would work.

Whatever you want, hon, Crystal says, brightly.

Trent has put Sam down, and suddenly he's pushing a chair over to the railing of the loft, obviously intending to climb up and look over, as Olivia is doing now. Cleo catches him, pushes the chair back, says, *Trent!* a little sharply. Does she have to do it all? Nobody else has noticed Sam climbing toward a fatal fall.

I thought you had him, Trent says, and Crystal says, My aren't you quick! But it's not clear if she's addressing Cleo or Sam.

Darrell says, Now, what can you tell me about this Y2K bug? Folks said I shouldn't buy a computer with that coming up but the fellow at the store said there would be a plug to fix it.

Oh, let's go downstairs, Crystal says, picking Sam up. Let's leave them to it.

Cleo has to agree with that. But she wants to linger – she can see Cliff does too – and try, in this room where she spent a good deal of her first decade, to see what remains. What remains of her.

So I slept here, Cliff says.

Do you recognize anything now?

I'm afraid to go near the railing, Cliff says. I have a deep fear of that railing.

▼▼▼

THEY'RE WALKING to the store, the four siblings and Olivia. First the path through the trees, which Mandalay remembers as being much longer, and then along the highway, where there's luckily not much traffic on a Sunday afternoon, just the odd pickup truck.

What do people do here? Ben asks, and Mandalay says: binge drinking, firearms accidents, incest. Ben laughs, but Cleo and Cliff do not.

I mean for work, Ben says. Why is the town here?

Nobody says anything for a few moments. Then Cleo says: Do you remember, Che almost burned the garage down.

There's a new one, now.

Mandalay feels cold: The sun has already set behind the high walls of spruce that guard the valley.

The mill and the dam, Cliff answers, unexpectedly.

Ben asks, and our dad worked at the mill?

Mandalay says: And was pretty self-sufficient. He could make or fix anything. He made that house, and he made furniture for people, and bartered for food.

And self-educated, Cleo says. He read a lot. He told us stories, things he'd read. He knew a lot about history and geography and politics.

He was a draft dodger, Mandalay says. Do you know what that is, Cliff? She sees, suddenly, that she and Cleo can give the boys a real gift: a sense of who their father was. A good role model. There aren't very many men like him around anymore.

Cleo says: I don't think that can be true, do you, Mandalay? Think about the dates. Dad was fifty-four when he died. That means he was born in nineteen twenty-five. He'd have been too old, he'd have been already in his forties, during the Vietnam War.

Can that be true? But she's always known that about Dadda. Draft dodger. Hippie.

She's disoriented.

I think there was a bit of farming here in the sixties and seventies, Cleo says. Sunflowers and – pumpkins, maybe?

None of them really know. It's strange.

And where does the highway go?

To the mine, Cliff says. There's a new road in now, though, from Guisachan Falls.

That's a Native word, right? Ben says. What does it mean?

You'd think so, but you'd be wrong, Cliff says. It's from some Scottish title that David Thompson had.

We've been watching a lot of Knowledge Network, Cleo says.

Cleo has appropriated Cliff again, Mandalay thinks. Cliff obviously thinks the sun shines out of Cleo's backside. And Ben has become obsessed with Cleo's kids, carrying Sam around, playing endless inane games with Olivia, so that he too has become a satellite of Cleo.

How annoying Cleo is, with her round, bland face, her smooth prim hair. Not soft, but implacable, somehow inhuman, disturbing. Termite-queen. She is so analytical; she has to know everything, take care of everyone's needs before they're even aware of them.

But Cleo has been transformed, has transformed herself: She is not just herself but also warrior, defender, and in this role she is consumed by her care for her children, for Cliff: She both wills it and has no say in it. She has taken it on and been taken over by it, both. If there is a Cleo who is all self somewhere in there still, she does not know where it is.

Is it being a parent that has done this, or has Cleo always been like this?

She wants to stalk away from all of them, as she used to, but they have all elected to tag along to the store, again as they used to. She has an entourage, but it's Cleo's entourage. They are walking along the highway, with its narrow verge of vetches and daisies and seedling conifers, to Butterfly Lake's one grocery store.

There are so many more amenities in Butterfly Lake than there had been when she was young. Mandalay can remember the community of Butterfly Lake as it was in the seventies. Then, there was only the gas station with its attached garage, the small mom and pop grocery store, the café, which served Chinese food and perogies and dry ribs and potato salad, the bar, the RCMP detachment, the Roman Catholic church, the elementary school, the community hall where the bookmobile held court on Saturday mornings, all strung out along the highway. Now there's a bigger grocery store, part of a chain, a Tim Horton's, an A&W. (No Starbucks, though, Trent had complained.) And Darrell says they're getting a Canadian Tire soon. Maybe Walmart, in the town, he had said, enthusiastically.

We used to collect bottles from here, Cliff says, suddenly.

That explains something, Ben says.

He would bring pop or beer cans to his parents or nanny. They thought he must have learned to do that before.

He flushes then, telling this, Mandalay notices. He had not thought out completely the implications of what he was going to say. He flushes and the blond down along his jawbones is white against the reddened skin. He is ashamed. No: He thinks that they will be shamed, embarrassed, and that he will look crass for embarrassing them.

We used to make you hunt for cans, Cliff says. Soon as you could walk, we sent you out scrounging. No milk for you till you fill that bag with cans, kid.

A shocked silence, then laughing. They had all collected cans: They could exchange them at the store in Butterfly Lake for penny candy. They all had a sweet tooth, all craved and schemed for and stole sugar, all of the time.

The shop where they had traded pop and beer bottles for penny candy is now about four times as big, not including its adjunct post office and liquor store. It's not very interesting, as a grocery store: the usual mainstream brands. Some sad-looking baked goods – muffins, scones, a limp croissant – strangled in cling wrap. They'll be unbelievably stale. They're brought in from Powell River, the cashier says. Mandalay thinks: Surely Butterfly Lake is big enough to support a bakery.

Immediately she imagines herself rolling out and folding, her fingers with their muscle-memory shaping the perfect rows of chilled pastries, the croissants and butterhorns and sausage rolls. Breads, too. Lots of seed and flax breads, some Danish rye. *Here*? she thinks, then. Could she live and work here? She has not considered it, before. Has never considered leaving the city. But has it turned an inhospitable face to her, begun to wall her out?

What are you going to do? Cleo asks, as if on the same wavelength, and she says: Look for another job in a bakery or café, I guess.

If you don't mind my saying this, Cleo says, I think you should go back to university and finish your degree.

She does mind, she thinks. She is in no mood to be patronized by Cleo. In what? she asks.

I always thought you should do visual arts, Cleo says. They are at the dairy cooler. Cleo grabs a four-litre jug of milk, and Mandalay scans for the brand of yogurt she likes, which is not carried here.

Yeah, that would be practical, she says, letting the sarcasm curl out, snail's cold path of slime. But it's not as discouraging a suggestion as others she's had: that she should go to cooking school, or take business courses.

And then do what? I've just spent two years selling paintings at the café. You can't make a living. You have to have wealthy parents and connections.

Anyway, she says, I wouldn't want to compete with Crystal.

They drift apart then, and when they rejoin, they both see at the same time that Ben has given Olivia a paper bag and a loonie for penny candy – it's a nickel apiece, now – and she is almost swooning with excitement and indecision.

What about your boyfriend, Cleo says. Would he help out? Didn't your ex – what was his name? Horst? Didn't he pay some of your tuition?

Mandalay feels as if she's been hit with a blunt object.

Cleo is staring at her, now, wide-eyed. Oh, shit, she says. Boundaries. I'm sorry.

Under the hard light of the fluorescent fixtures she feels herself penned in, pinned. A snarl curls her upper lip. She opens her mouth, but then Ben is there, draping an arm around her shoulders, a six-pack dangling from each hand.

Can I have these? he asks, making his eyes cat-slant, smiling beguilingly, and Cleo says, Ben! You're not supposed to take alcohol out of the liquor store area, and they all turn to look at the cashier in her brown uniform behind the half-barrier, and freeze. Cleo, Cliff, and she herself, she notices, are all rigid, in flight mode. They are all afraid of people in uniforms.

But the cashier is smiling at Ben. It's okay, she says. We'll let you get away with it this time.

▼▼▼

MANDALAY AND BODHI — Ben — have stayed on the deck, in the two lounge chairs that don't face the sun, Cleo sees. She wants now to talk to Mandalay, to hear about Ben meeting Crystal, to ask her about Crystal bringing up their childhood. That hasn't happened before; it's as if there's been a tacit agreement not to talk about it at the base of their relationship. She thinks: I only have this relationship, tenuous as it is, with Crystal because we have this understanding. I won't bring up what a terrible time we had and that makes it possible for us to spend time together, for my kids to know her, sort of, as a grandmother.

But if Crystal is going to bring it up herself? If she's going to introduce some cute, downmarket women's magazine version?

She really needs to talk to Mandalay. But when she opens the new French doors to the deck, she smells, right away, that Mandalay and Bodhi/Ben, are smoking pot.

Oh, for crying out loud, she says.

Mandalay giggles. Did you really say that?

Cleo steps out, shuts the door quickly, so Olivia can't follow.

You look so stressed, Mandalay says. Just breathe.

She breathes. She sinks into a chair and manages to wriggle it around until the sun is not directly in her eyes.

Pretty bizarre, hey? Mandalay asks.

Cleo is not sure how much they are going to say about Crystal in front of Ben.

Ben's kind of overwhelmed by it, Mandalay says.

No, I'm not, Ben says. He still doesn't really look at Cleo. She feels again the cold trickle of loss.

Mandalay holds the joint out toward her, but she shakes her head. She can feel Olivia's eyes drilling into them through the glass panes of the doors. And she supposes that's another nail in the coffin, as far as Ben's impression of her is going. Prudish, as well as everything else. Well, she's too tired to bother trying to correct the impression.

▾▾▾

IT WAS BLOWN OUT of proportion by the media, Cleo says. The four of them now, sitting around the brazier on the deck, smoking and drinking beer: Darrell and Crystal have gone to bed, and Trent has taken the children back to the motel in Guisachan Falls.

I'm guessing, but eleven kids? In five years? Ben asks.

Cleo says, you have to understand what was happening then. In the late seventies and early eighties, logging had picked up in the areas around Butterfly Lake, and a mine had been opened to the south, and the boom time had swelled the nearest town – Guisachan Falls – creating an acute housing shortage. The town filled up with people with good paycheques, and renters on the lower end of the economic scale in Guisachan Falls had spilled over into the village of Butterfly Lake, fifteen kilometres up the road.

A lot of them ended up living in cabins, shacks, really, or old trailers, that weren't meant for four seasons – they were summer places. And they weren't people who had grown up in the country – they didn't know how to take care of stoves, or what was dangerous for their kids, like the lakeshore, or the old quarry – things like that. There wasn't a doctor in town, even. And there was some alcoholism, some neglect that was harder to see because people lived further apart. So it was a combination of things that led to that calamity, but it wasn't Butterfly Lake itself. If you look at the time before the mine opened, there were no problems at all.

How does Cleo know all of that? Crystal is likely to just say things like: Butterfly Lake was fine until the poor people came there from the town. And Darrell might say worse: might say, It was those welfare cases, the Natives and so on. According to Darrell, the area was doing well, until wiped out by the NDP government's higher corporate taxes and restrictions on logging. And then a flood of non-desirables – Natives and welfare bums and immigrants – even Vietnamese boat people – had poured in, and turned the place into a dump. Drinking, fighting, neglecting their kids, Darrell says. All they were good for. According to Darrell, the new mine and the proposed pipeline are saving Butterfly Lake – turning it back into the thriving resource-based town it should be.

So how was our family part of that? Ben asks. You said our dad had lived there since the sixties.

Mandalay says: It was kind of a hippie place – people did a little fishing, a little farming, a little selective logging. There was a small sawmill. Dad worked there. But after the uproar about the children, the social workers and the police were kind of over-vigilant. They moved in on people much too quickly. They didn't bother to find out if people were making it or not. Really, we were managing fine. It was just a temporary crisis. When Dad died Crystal happened to be in the hospital. But there was a tight community, Dad had tons of friends. You should have been at his funeral. Well, you were sort of. People would have stepped in. The Mounties and the social worker just overreacted.

She has imagined telling Bodhi, or Ben, this story, so many times. She has told it to many people.

My mom says you and Cleo tried to abduct me. That you stole a car and took me away from my foster care into the mountains.

That is not quite true, Cleo says.

I wondered, Ben says. Because you must have been, like, twelve and thirteen? That's badass.

Mandalay notices that Cleo almost smiles, then.

▼▼▼

IN THE MOTEL Cleo dreams that Crystal has gone for a long walk in the bush – she's been gone hours or maybe days – and she, Cleo has to give Bodhi a bottle. She is little herself, in the dream; she has to drag a chair to the stove to reach the knobs, and of course because it's a dream there are no numbers, just squiggles, when she goes to turn the element on. At the same time, she's also her present age and size; she carries Bodhi easily on her hip, as if he were Olivia or Sam, and feeds him his bottle while folding laundry in her own grown-up laundry room. Then, in her dream, she finds Bodhi playing on the back deck in a bucket of chicken guts, and his hands and face are smeared with chicken blood and grease, and he has feathers clinging all over him. It's very distressing, that he has got into the bucket, that she has left the bucket there, that she hasn't been watching him (though she feels that she was just holding him, it's very confusing). But when she lifts him up, he has wings. The chicken feathers have somehow become white wings, soft and downy underneath, smooth and strong above. When she lifts him, she can feel the stretched tendon of the joint, can feel the warmth and moisture and downiness of the hollow, the wing-pit, against her arm. He has wings: That realization is both joyous and worrisome. She feels how marvellous it is that he will be able to fly. It's the manifestation of his specialness, his wonderfulness as a baby. It's proof. On the other hand, now she'll have to be constantly watching that he doesn't fly away.

She wakes first into another dream, in which she realizes quite lucidly that Bodhi hadn't been born yet when she was that small, when she couldn't reach the stove dials. It must have been Cliff. She must have dreamed of Cliff. She feels resigned, but also grounded. It was Cliff, of course. Then she really wakes, and isn't sure.

Caught

OH, NO, CRYSTAL SAYS. They are in the kitchen: Crystal has been playing Go Fish with Olivia, and Sam is banging pans on the floor, and Mandalay and Cleo are sitting side by side at the table with Crystal's photo albums. Oh, it was the fifties. Your dad moved here in the fifties, after the war. Lots of young men immigrated, after the war.

What war? Mandalay thinks, and Cleo asks.

The Second World War. He was sent to work on a farm in Manitoba but he didn't like it. He came here as a logger in the early fifties.

I thought he was from Indiana, Cleo says.

No, Crystal says. He was Swedish. Don't you remember? He had an accent.

Mandalay does not remember that.

Likely you're thinking of Keith Pollard, Darrell says. He was one of those draft dodgers from the States who came up in the sixties. Could have been from Indiana.

Swedish, Crystal says. He swept me off my feet. (Mandalay cringes at the cliché.)

Here was this sophisticated, older bachelor. Everyone said he had lots of money. I was hitchhiking through with some friends, looking for work, seeing the world. Powell River. It was the end of the beating path. (She says that, Cleo notes: *beating* path.) We went to a big Canada Day celebration. I was seventeen. I had hitchhiked from Calgary.

We went with some relatives of one of the guys I was travelling with. It was them who pointed your Dadda out, said he was a rich bachelor. He wasn't. They thought he must be because he had lived there so long, and had worked as a logger and on the dam. They thought he must have saved up a lot.

What about Cliff's name? Cleo asks. Wasn't he named after Daddy's father, back in Indiana?

Nope, Crystal says. My father. Who had just died when Cliffie was born.

But Daddy named the boys and you named the girls, right?

Ha, Crystal says. Your dadda named you all. Even Cliff. I didn't want to name my kid after him; he was an asshole. Your dadda named you all. That's why you all have such goddamn weird names.

The earlier, black and white photos have held up better than the later ones from the seventies, which have bled out their colour, lost their reds and blues. Here are their parents, at what Mandalay realizes must be their wedding day. She's seen this photograph, or a copy of it, before, but now looks at it as an adult. Her father is wearing a little smile and a suit: His hair is receding and he's very much taller than Crystal, who stands next to him with her arm tucked into his. Crystal has on a pale shift dress that stops an inch above her knee, and a sort of beehive hairdo, topped with a little round hat and a big bow. She's very thin, in the photo, her face small under the upswept hair, her eyes huge and her chin pointed.

She looks like a child. She is a child: She's eighteen. Mandalay has seen this photo before but had never seen this aspect: that Crystal is so young.

She says: Don't you have family? Where was your family?

Crystal looks at the photo for a few moments as if she hasn't seen it before. My mom ran off when I was little, she says. I don't know what happened to my brothers. I didn't speak to my dad after I took off, when I was seventeen.

Had Mandalay known that? She can't remember now. She doesn't remember, either, any question of their being taken in by relatives, when her father had died.

Another photo with both of her parents in it: this one, she thinks, taken in the mid-seventies — a group of people, an informal shot. There are a lot of beards, long hair, fringed vests, maxi skirts. She can see herself, a small child wearing only shorts, one of the only figures looking at the camera. Now her father is bearded, heavier, dressed in a loose shirt: He looks the way she remembers him. Crystal, in a different part of the photograph, her hair long, now, rippling down her back, wearing a mini-dress, carrying a toddler — that would be Cliff, she guesses — on her hip. Crystal is half turned from the camera, smiling at someone off to the side, someone who doesn't appear in the photo. One of her siblings? There's a younger child in the background, who might or might not be Cleo.

Who were you looking at? Mandalay asks.

I don't remember, Crystal says, staring at the photo.

What was going on, in this photograph?

Some kind of picnic, I think, Crystal says. She's smiling now, though.

▼▼▼

SHE AND TRENT will leave in the morning, Cleo says.

Oh, come on, Mandalay says. It's a long weekend. You don't have to leave.

We do. It takes us all day to drive back, with the ferries and so on.

No, it doesn't.

Well, Trent needs to do some work.

So why didn't he bring it with him?

Cleo doesn't want to leave, suddenly. Ben and Mandalay are going to be here a few more days. Cliff wants to stay: He will stay longer, he says. And then Crystal is asking again, and Olivia begging. Everyone will be gone, back home. It's August. Trent will be working. What will she and the children do? There's not even a waterpark near her neighbourhood.

It's difficult, here, for Trent to be amused for more than a couple of days. But he can go on home without Cleo, can't he?

It would be good to stay, to not always be second-guessing herself, the way she does when Trent's there.

Trent is annoyed: She can see that. But then, suddenly, he's not. He'll fly back, he says. He's still contriving to sound annoyed, to sound like it's a big imposition, but she can see that at some level he has realized some benefit to himself in going back alone.

You'll have the house to yourself, she says to him. Yes, she can see he is now looking forward to it.

Cliff and Ben will sleep in tents. Cleo and the children will stay in the house.

You'd better keep an eye on the kids, Trent tells Cleo, threateningly.

▼▼▼

MANDALAY AND CRYSTAL are watching Olivia from the deck. She has been riding her tricycle – they have brought it with them in the van – around the plantain-choked lawn, but now abandons it and wanders over to the shed, where she picks up one of the rods Darrell had left leaning up against the shed. He had been showing Olivia how to cast, at the stream, in the morning. Cleo has gone on a hike, with the guys.

Mandalay has persuaded her to leave the kids with her and Crystal and Darrell.

God, Crystal says. You can't take your eyes off her for a minute. Darrell should have put that away. Olivia, honey, she calls, don't touch Grandpa's fishing rod, okay? Put it back.

Olivia is well within earshot, but ignores Crystal.

She's so defiant, Mandalay says. It's amazing that she can be so – autonomous, determined – at her age. She has just an inkling, now, why Cleo seemed so anxious about leaving the kids with her and Crystal and Darrell, going off for a hike with the guys. There are three of us and two of them, she had said to Cleo, but now she has to wonder if that's enough.

The house and yard aren't exactly childproof, Cleo had said.

What, is that like bear-proof? Darrell had joked. It was turning out not to be a joke. Darrell had just finished nailing a sheet of plywood across the top of the deck stairs; before that, Mandalay had caught Sam in mid-air on his way to the bottom.

Che was like that, Crystal says. Your dad tried to beat it out of him, but he just got worse.

Mandalay thinks: One of those Crystal bombshells, as she and Cleo call them, when Crystal says something outrageous without an apparent sense of its impact.

Olivia has thrown the rod back over her shoulder now, as if she's going to cast. Come on, honey, Crystal calls to Olivia. Let's put that down. She starts for the stairs.

Something small flies across Mandalay's vision. There is a tiny, tinny jingle, a light tap on her nose, and then a sudden jab in her left nostril. Crystal says, from the steps, Oh, look out, honey! Olivia, across the yard, stands still, the rod clutched in her two hands, her eyes and mouth perfect Os. And then she begins to turn the handle of the reel.

The scream that comes out of Mandalay, involuntarily, is louder than any sound she has ever made before. It's more of a bellow. The pain is excruciating. That or the tears that start in her eyes blind her. She stumbles forward, puts her hands out, gropes for the filament. Crystal is running toward Olivia, calling, Oh, honey, don't. Then Darrell comes around the corner of the shed.

It's his breaking into a run that seems to panic Olivia. She begins to run, too, but keeps a firm professional grip on the rod and the reel handle. She heads off down the driveway. She does not let go. It takes Darrell, a heavy man not used to running, quite a long time to catch her.

Mandalay runs too, fumbling for a grip on the line, which continues to elude her. She can taste the blood channelling down her philtrum into her mouth. She doesn't understand how her nose is still attached. Darrell tackles Olivia gingerly, the way a man might tackle a porcupine, and then the tension is released and Mandalay stumbles, falls to her knees on the gravel of the driveway. Blood and snot are streaming from her chin.

She has an almost irresistible urge to slap Oliva upside her head, but Crystal is there, lifting Olivia, who is now sobbing (why is she crying?) into her arms, saying, Oh, honey, were you scared?

And Darrell is already laughing. He laughs as he inserts the tip of his wire cutters into Mandalay's nostril, as he extracts the bloody barb with his needle-nose pliers, as he reels up the line and puts the rods into the shed. He's a really silent laugher. His shoulders shake, tears run down the creases of his upper cheeks and the bristles of his jowls, and he wheezes, but does not make a sound. He's still laughing when he asks Mandalay if she thinks she needs stitches.

It's only a small tear. She has packed her nostril with toilet paper, has managed to staunch the blood for an instant, long enough to see that the rip is only half a centimetre or so.

Likely you should have a tetanus shot, he wheezes.

No.

When she goes outside later, there's a trail of blood spots across the deck and the yard and down the driveway. Even on the lawn, the blood spots glisten, clinging darkly to the grass blades and the plantain.

▼▼▼

CLEO WANTS VERY MUCH to lie down and close her eyes. It's partly the sun, and partly that she really doesn't ever get enough sleep. It's so rare to be just sitting. She and Cliff and Ben have been hiking – she is so tired, but they had wanted to go to the lake, and she had thought she remembered the way. Her eyes keep closing. She thinks that she might just fall asleep. It's afternoon; there's sun, a light breeze in the surrounding brush.

They have followed the trail along the hill; the terrain familiar only in segments, like a coded message. She hadn't been entirely sure that they were heading in the right direction: then a lone blackbird warbling its liquid call, flashing its scarlet wing patches, and the path opening out, not onto beach, as it used to, but to black cottonwood and aspen and willow, and then bulrushes.

The lakeshore is inaccessible now: The trees have grown back thickly, this end of it has grown marshy. The land is being reclaimed. There is no getting at the lake, though behind the vigorous hedge they can hear the calls of different birds, splashing that might be something large. Bear or moose, even. They can't get at the lake, anymore, from this path, to see, though. The bush is completely impenetrable.

They stop in a small clearing beneath trembling aspen, at the edge of the bulrushes, where the ground is spongy but not too muddy, throw themselves down on the moss. They have picnic things, not in a basket but in a backpack.

Cleo dozes a little, then is aware of someone moving beside her. Cliff? she asks, but she knows without opening her eyes that it is not. Knows by smell or some other sense that it is not.

She can hear him breathing. She hardly breathes herself, as if she's found herself next to a deer or other wild creature and doesn't want to startle it.

Ask me if I remember you, she wills. Ask me. I will tell you that I remember every single thing about you. That I spent more time with you, that last year before you left us, than anyone else did. That I have thought of you every day. She can't speak; she is too sleepy.

She wakes later: forty-five minutes or an hour; she's not sure. He's asleep; she can tell by his breathing, by the dampness of the hair. He is sprawled half across her, his arm around her, his right hand clutching her breast, his face pressed into her neck. Under the new, young-man smell of him, she can smell something deeper, more intrinsic, more familiar. He is sleeping against her the way he slept so many times, in his first not-quite-two years. In his sleep, he has remembered. He has moved through the doorway of sleep into the little space that they shared, he and she, for those short years. Here he is, now.

She lifts his hand, gently, from her breast and he sighs and shifts, but doesn't wake up.

▼▼▼

MANDALAY SAYS, I met a cougar, once, along this road. Just up at that corner.

They all stop. Cleo looks confused; then she says, You did not. That was me. It was me who met the cougar.

What?

Me, Cleo says. That was me.

No, I swear it was me. I'm positive. (Is she, though? She has told this story so many times that she doesn't know if she's remembering the event or her telling of it, now.)

Maybe both of you met cougars, Ben says.

No, Cleo says. It was only me. It was a big deal. Everyone talked about it for ages.

But she remembers so clearly its yellow-grey coat, dappled, its clear amber eyes watching her as she backed away, backed up as far as the next turn, and then ran.

What about you, Cliff, Ben asks. You meet any cougars?

No, Cliff says, seriously. I don't remember anything.

They follow the loop of dirt and gravel road back down to where it curves by the school. The kids are already shrieking at the sight of the playground equipment. You were here yesterday, Cleo says, but Mandalay thinks: That is why they want to come again.

Only the old swing set remains, of the original equipment. She lifts Sam into one of the bucket swings, and Cleo begins to push him, methodically, almost dreamily.

Cleo says, remember?

And she does. She does. And she has to let this out, now: There has been too much swallowing of emotion the last couple of weeks. She must let it out.

Dadda's funeral, she says.

Then, to Ben: This is how we abducted you.

It had taken the community of Butterfly Lake three weeks to arrange Dadda's funeral. In that time, they had all stayed at different places – Che at Myrna Pollard's, where he spent so much of his time anyway, and Mandalay at a friend's in town. Cleo had had an offer from the mother of a one of Mandalay's classmates, but she had turned it down.

She had said she turned it down because the offer didn't include Cliff. But really, that was Cleo. She always sided with the adults. So

Cleo and Cliff had stayed in town, in temporary care. Neither she nor Cleo knew where Bodhi was. She was allowed to telephone Cleo, twice, and both times they speculated, for as long as the conversation lasted, on where Bodhi was. Mandalay had been confident that he'd be left with her, but that had not happened.

They had been on time for the funeral, which in Butterfly Lake meant that they were among the first to arrive at the community hall.

The children were to sit in the front row. Mrs. Carlson, Mandalay's friend's mom, sat there, too. Che had fooled around, and tried to mess up Cliff's hair. Myrna Pollard sat behind him. Mandalay noticed that Cleo and Cliff had new clothes, though she and Che did not. She'd had to borrow an outfit from her friend.

Cleo was turning around in her seat, scanning the arrivals. Where is Bodhi? she was thinking. Mandalay knew this without Cleo saying anything.

Where was Bodhi?

Then Mrs. Carlson, who had seemed not to be paying attention – who was talking to Myrna Pollard – said, likely a baby would not be brought to a funeral, as if she knew what they were thinking.

Everyone comes to funerals in Butterfly Lake, Mandalay said, which was true.

But the hall filled, and the service started, and there was no sign of him.

There was a lot of talking. A long procession of grey-haired, baggy-clothed men and women took the microphone to tell stories about Dadda. They were really talking to each other, not to her and her siblings – though they all did remember at points to look at the four of them in the front row and say things like "We honour your daddy." It was as if there were two groups of people there – Dadda's friends and neighbours, who the funeral was really for, and his children, who were strangers and due some recognition but who were, on the whole, intruders.

Then one of the old guys said "And that's when he met Crystal, here," and nodded to somewhere at the back of the hall. And Mandalay, Cleo, and Che swivelled around in their pinky-grey metal folding chairs — Cliff wasn't paying that much attention — and there she was, Crystal, sitting by Myrna Pollard. Cleo could only see her head through the forest of people, but it was Crystal alright. What was she doing here? Did she have Bodhi?

After the service they all ran to the back of the room where Crystal was still sitting, but there was no Bodhi. And then Che dived in, crying, to wrap himself around her, and then Mandalay. Hugging and crying. Hi Mandalay, hi Che, hi Cleo, hi Cliff, Mam said, as if she were an acquaintance seeing them at a party. She was wearing a blue dress they hadn't seen before, flowered, with fluttery short sleeves, a fitted bodice, flared skirt. It was a style of dress Mandalay admired, that some girls she knew wore. Crystal's hair was shining and fell in loose curls like a catalogue model's, and she had eyeliner and lipstick on and her skin looked very smooth and clear — it looked translucent, like she was still a young girl. She had no wrinkles, not even tiny ones like Jean the social worker.

She did not look like a person who was in a mental ward of a hospital. Mandalay knew from stories she had read that people in mental hospitals had slack, doughy skin and dull hair. She did not look like a person whose husband had died, either. She did not look like a person who could look after five children.

Someone must have arranged for Crystal to have a visit with her children, because suddenly after the funeral they were all left alone together in the Butterfly Lake Elementary School playground. Or not quite alone. There, on some benches, were Myrna Pollard, Mandalay's friend's mom, and another woman who they didn't know, but who had been sitting with Crystal, and the woman Cleo and Cliff were staying with. When Mandalay looked over, Mrs. Carlson waved to her and smiled and nodded her head, once.

Then there was the sound of a car door, and everyone's eyes turned to the car, and Mandalay looked up to see Jean the social worker walking toward them with Bodhi in her arms.

Now here they all were, the five of them and Crystal in the playground, with five other people watching them from a distance, or pretending not to watch them. They were so oddly here – not at home or anywhere they usually would be together – here in the playground with its swing set and teeter-totter and the chain of the tetherball hanging from its pole. The tetherball was always taken away at the end of the day and locked in the equipment closet. There was only the chain, now.

Mandalay noticed that Bodhi had also got new clothes. He was wearing a little sweater with fake leather elbow patches and corduroy pants, and little suede boots. And his hair, too, had been cut – his shoulder-length white-blond curls cut off. She wanted to cry, because of his clothes and his hair and not looking like Bodhi anymore.

Mandalay had taken Bodhi from Jean's arms, and Crystal was trying to get him to come to her, but he would not. He did not remember Crystal at all.

They all wanted to hold Bodhi – even Cliff wanted to. When it was her turn Cleo put her face in his hair and just smelled him. Then Cleo had put Bodhi in the bucket swing and pushed him over and over, away from her, and he laugh-screamed and tried to kick her when she pushed in front, their old game. He remembered her, for sure.

It looked like Crystal was better. Would they all be going home now?

She took turns with Cleo, pushing Bodhi. He was laughing, his mouth open, his little white milk-teeth in a perfect row, his eyes locked on hers so there was no space between them, even as he advanced and retreated. She saw the tiny shift in his eyeball, the infinitesimal movement, as he moved closer and then further way.

How could their mother look after them all? She was too young. She was not much older than they were. She was not really a grown-up. She was not going to be allowed to have them back.

Suddenly Mandalay knew that. They weren't going home. They weren't going to see Bodhi again. She knew it in the way the women sat, the way Crystal stood, her shoulders slumped, her bright girlish face blank, the way she and the others were being allowed to play together.

It had come to her, what was going to happen, and then right after, what she needed to do.

Mandalay said to Cleo: You need to take Cliff over there and say he has peed himself.

But he hadn't. Cleo was indignant in his behalf.

You need to do that, Mandalay said, get over there and get them all fussing over Cliff, and don't look back at us, do you hear?

Che was grinning. Yeah. Don't look back or I'll shoot you in the eye.

Cleo didn't get it.

Then we split, Mandalay said. We split, and then when they notice we're gone, you take Cliff and run.

Run where?

Home, Che said. Somehow he was connected, telepathically, but Cleo wasn't.

Cleo said that the women, the watchers, would just get in their cars and come after them. They would get there before any of them did.

Not if we cut through the bush, Che said. We can make it home in, like, five seconds.

It wasn't that fast, Mandalay knew. Cleo was right.

The next idea had come to her again fully formed, but so much better than the first.

We'll hide out on Knucklehead for a few days, Mandalay said. We can sneak back to the house and steal food and stuff. Then when they give up, we'll move back there. (How had she thought that it would work? How had she been so ignorant, even at thirteen?)

How would they get to Knucklehead?

Mandalay said, just stay here for a minute. I am going for a little walk. When you hear a car beep, pick up Bodhi and run.

She had made it. She had walked quietly to the edge of the playground, and slipped into the trees, and then had sprinted home. She knew where the spare keys were, knew how to drive the car – Dadda let her drive it as far as the highway, all the time, if he gave her a ride to school in it. She started it – it had coughed a couple of times, but she remembered how to give it a little gas, not too much. She was taller than Crystal; she could easily reach the pedals and see. She lurched out of the driveway, then got the feel of it back as she coasted along the road.

She'd felt like Faye Dunaway, in *Bonnie and Clyde*, which they had watched on TV. She'd felt, those few moments between the house and the schoolyard, that she knew what it was to be totally, terribly free. It wasn't like being a bird or butterfly, as kids in her class wrote. It was like being a hollowed-out log, completely hollow, and the air just blowing through.

She slowed the car, not as smoothly as she wished, beside the playground. Go, Mandalay thought to Cleo and Cliff. Don't over-think it. Just go. And Cleo did. She picked up Bodhi and she walked over to the car and got in before anyone noticed.

It was Che who spoiled it, of course, running, looking back and laughing, as if it were a game. Carol the social worker and the woman who was accompanying Crystal had run toward them then, faster than Mandalay had known grown-ups could run. She'd hit the gas and taken off, leaving Che still running after them, now shouting.

Cleo said, Che and Cliff! But she could not stop, now. It was too late. The air was blowing through her, she had no body of her own, and she could not stop.

She tells an abridged version of the story to Cliff and Ben, Cleo jumping in occasionally. She leaves out the part about leaving Cliff and Che behind. Why? She doesn't know.

Cleo says: That's why we were all taken so far away from Butterfly Lake. Myrna Pollard kept Che, but Mandalay ended up in a sort of reform school, didn't you, Mandalay?

It wasn't really, Mandalay says. Kind of a group home. All of the other girls were cutters. It was a pretty sad place.

And I went to live with the Giesbrechts, who had a foster home in Abbotsford, a farm, really, that was for troubled youth.

And Cliff, too? Ben asks.

Cliff came later, Cleo says.

But Cliff is asking now: Where was I, when you abducted Ben? I don't remember this. Did you abduct me too?

She looks at Cleo. She has left that part of the story out, but Cliff has picked up on the gap, anyway.

Cleo doesn't meet her eye. Mandalay says, of course, Cliff. You should remember. I said run! And you just ran, on your little seven-year-old legs. You just ran. You beat Cleo to the car. It was amazing. Don't you remember it?

Cleo is shaking her head, but she won't contradict Mandalay. Cliff is smiling. It's a tour-de-force. Mandalay didn't know she had it in her.

How far did you get? Ben asks, admiringly.

Not far. She had thought she knew the way to Knucklehead, but she hadn't ever driven it. She'd missed the turn, had gone down a dead-end road. There had been sirens, pretty quickly, and the police – the same ones, again. She hadn't tried to run; the spirit of Faye Dunaway had left her suddenly. She'd stopped the car and got out and cried, and they'd been pretty gentle with her.

Cleo says, And then they put all of us in the police car, and one of the cops drove Crystal's car back to the house.

Cliff says, I think I remember being in the back of the cop car.

Yes, Cleo says.

Mandalay remembers, now, the howls Cleo made when Bodhi was removed from her arms, back at the school: a groaning howl, in the voice of a mature woman. She remembers something about how Cliff came to be at the Giesbrecht's with Cleo, some story about that.

What they all can't forgive Crystal for, she thinks: not having that will, that unselfishness, that fierce maternal instinct or whatever it is, that has possessed Cleo. But if it is possession that is required, that unpicking and restitching of the self, who can be expected to undergo it, to succumb to it, to be capable of it?

It's in that moment, emerging from the ammoniac-smelling path into the clearing around the house, that Mandalay realizes what even her cells have been trying to tell her for the past week.

▼▼▼

BEN/BODHI has travelled through France and Turkey and Vietnam and Cambodia. He plays soccer for fun and snowboards and has a bicycle and an old Saab that he loads up with friends' furniture on weekends. He has never tree-planted but has friends who have. He plays in a band and he has read *The Brothers Karamazov* and *A Farewell to Arms* and his favourite movie is *Reservoir Dogs*. He likes micro-brewery beer and punk music and doesn't like celery. He has a wet suit and he has slept with at least two girls.

His teeth are very white and straight, unlike Mandalay's or Cliff's, or even Cleo's.

He used to collect pop cans, beer cans, when he was little. If he saw a can on the ground he would bring it to his parents, or his nanny.

His nanny.

A procession of nannies, he said. French girls in their late teens, early twenties. They lived in the suite over the garage.

Ben/Bodhi is taller than all of the rest of them, his legs and arms especially longer in proportion to his body. He has probably never had a bad haircut.

He has a scar on his upper lip, left side, from trying to skateboard down the front steps when he was nine.

He had probably always worn a bike helmet and had been buckled into a regulation car seat. He had bookcases full of books and he had riding lessons and nobody ever slapped him or shouted at him.

Mandalay or Cleo had always carried him around, except for when he was at Myrna Pollard's. They had known everything about him, everything he liked and disliked, what he was afraid of, what would make him laugh until he couldn't breathe.

He had nannies. She thinks about the nannies, now: they would have been girls her own age. Lying beside Ben, now, under the aspens, at the edge of the rushes, she feels it as a new hurt. Girls her own age, but not her. She had not been allowed to see him.

His parents were lawyers and in their early forties when they adopted him. They couldn't have kids. Then they got Bodhi, a little golden toddler not talking yet, not toilet trained. He could be theirs.

Or so Cleo imagines.

They were intelligent and they had worked through all of their shit. But their arms, maybe just the woman's arms, felt empty. They were sad at seeing families in the park. Maybe the wife cried every month when she got her period. Maybe she'd had an abortion when she was young and wondered. But she'd been a student from a poor family on a scholarship; she'd had to choose. Or maybe she thought she'd still have good eggs after she got established in her career and then it took longer and she didn't. Or maybe it was him, mumps when he was fourteen, or something. In a doctor's office with a little bottle and a *Penthouse*, the microscope slide. Swimming. Not enough.

Cleo had known above everything else that she wanted children. If Trent had been infertile she'd have got a donor. If Trent had been infertile she wouldn't be with him and that was the truth. They wouldn't have made it the first year. She was pregnant with Olivia by the time she had known Trent a year.

She had not been able to see Bodhi, the social worker had told her, because she was a flight risk: because she and Mandalay had tried to abduct Bodhi and couldn't be trusted. But she knows, she has always known, that it was because his adoptive parents wanted to believe that he was theirs.

Ben's adopted parents had been together a long time, maybe. (Mandalay would know if this was true.) They had been together for years. They were still passionate and they knew each other's bodies so well. They worked too hard but they sometimes talked about their cases before they fell asleep. On the weekends they went to Granville Island and bought figs and goat cheese. They cooked together, or he cooked, and they had really interesting new dishes. They went on holiday and held hands on the beach. For birthdays they always knew what to give each other, a new camera lens or a hammered silver bowl or windsurfing lessons. They had everything but not a child. They had blond Danish furniture and a Volvo but no child.

Ben woke in the night and cried and they were both wrecked from work. Or she finally went and lifted him out of the new hand-turned birch crib and brought him into their bed, and the husband got up with sharp movements and went to sleep on the couch. The spare room. Or maybe the other way around. Or she took some leave, maybe her firm was very progressive that way, and took the child out in the Perego Peg and bought toys at the expensive little shop in the village, a maze of coloured wires and wooden beads, wooden puzzles from Germany with prints of intelligent, logical-looking rabbits, and a gaudy, rainbow-coloured plastic Fisher-Price xylophone, because who hadn't had one of those as a kid? And she sat on the floor with him for hours, just watching him, because he was so beautiful and fascinating and hers, though after a few months of it, of watching him and banana ground into everything and not being able to go for a jog or haircut until her husband got home, she'd had enough. She was glad to go back to work.

They had not witnessed his first words or steps, but they saw him grow up into a person, like them and not like them. They had thoughtful conversations about discipline and preschool and music lessons and French immersion, and if Bodhi was a name that would set him apart too much, draw attention to him in the wrong ways. They dressed him in tiny checked shirts and cords from baby boutiques which they bought too big at first because they couldn't get their heads around how small he was.

They gave him his first bath together, because she was scared: The baby cried, wailed really, at the water, the shampoo; he wouldn't sit in the tub, but fought and tried to climb out and slipped, banged his head, and howled so loudly that they couldn't think, and the husband just wrapped a towel around him and lifted him out, shampoo still in his hair, and held him against his chest until he'd stopped, though his shuddering sobs went on for a long time. Clearly he was terrified of the bathtub.

The child didn't want to touch them; he didn't *like* them, and because of their sleep deprivation they just looked at each other and thought, what have we done?

And *what have we done* might or might not surface again and again. It would depend on what sort of people they were. It would depend on how stable their little boat had been before they had brought in this third person, more than on the child himself.

There were times when he brought them an egg-shaped stone, at the beach, or when he looked up from his crayoning and said, this is a backpack for a hippopotamus, or looked around at them when they were all watching a street entertainer in Paris and just *grinned*, and they felt their chests explode.

There was the first time he came to her, or maybe him, for a cuddle, on his own, and nestled in, and maybe fell asleep, and they knew that he had claimed them.

Maybe the nanny because he would be better off in his own home, he'd had enough change. Because they wanted him to be bilingual, they wanted him to go to the Montessori preschool and kindergym. Or because she would stay late, they both worked long hours, and would do some housework so it was more economical, really, in the long run.

The nannies were French girls who wanted to see another part of the world: They were chic and saucy with the husband, pragmatic, promiscuous, socialist, opinionated. They met other nannies in the parks and spoke in French. They did not like to cook or clean or look after children more than any other twenty-year-olds, but they liked pushing strollers in a leisurely way through Point Grey. They liked being in charge of their own time. They liked bossing around their young charges. When they left they were demonstrative, weeping, kissing, or angry, voluble, their hands slicing the air. (A succession of strangers had looked after him, when it could have been her. But his parents had looked after him, had loved him too. She understands that.)

Bodhi/Ben falls in love with them but learns not to get too attached. He learns it is better not to be too attached. He learns to let go.

He wears a uniform to school, navy shorts or trousers and a grey long-sleeved knit shirt with a collar and placket: a Rugby shirt. His parents go to all of the parent events. Their friends are there too. They walk home together in the dusk, the wet streets, the child between them in his navy duffle coat, holding both their hands, chattering about the teachers. He says things that they recognize as foreign, not coming from them or the French nannies, but the teachers, and they feel the first pang: He is not all theirs. But they are okay with that because they are liberal people and it is a very good school.

This is the school Cleo will pass on the Number Four bus on her way to the university each day. She will see the groups of boys in their navy trousers, their grey shirts, their blazers and caps. One of them will be Bodhi, but she will not suspect that.

Sometimes groups of these uniformed boys will get on the bus she's riding, on field trips, maybe, to the anthropology museum. Maybe Ben brushes by Cleo, in the aisle. Maybe he says excuse me or sits in the seat next to her. She will not suspect: In her mind, at this time, Bodhi is forever a year-and-a-half old, and lost.

Because this school is expensive and prestigious, it might be very progressive, there might not be gold stars on spelling tests, arithmetic, maps. But there might. It might be very traditional. A lot of the students would be privileged and the standards would be high. Ben might not seem especially bright. He might struggle to do fractions. He might be mischievous, be part of a group that sets a wastepaper bin on fire. His parents called to the headmaster's office. Wondering maybe what is in the package that is their son, what genetic proclivities, what time bombs. Will he fall into addiction, will he be limited intellectually, will he be a boy who never thinks about consequences, impulsive, destructive?

This is what Cleo knows about Bodhi. That he is sociable, good at sports, well-read for his age, sure of himself. He is kind and appears to think things through, not react. He has a sense of humour, by which she means not that he's always joking or teasing, like Trent, but that he has distance from things, that he sees the absurdity in things. That he doesn't take himself too seriously.

That he likes to play Nintendo too much, that he is sometimes more boy than man, that he drinks too much beer and forgets his wallet. That he is not sensitive but not afraid. That he is not afraid to take risks with his heart, to be wrong, to try, to reach out.

That he is okay. He has grown up fine.

Salmon Returning

THEY WERE LYING, those girls. Cliff knows that. He can remember, he wasn't that young. He can't remember much, but he remembers two things: sitting in the back of the police car, and running after Cleo and Mandalay, running after their mom's car as it drove away. Che running beside him, swearing: Stop the car, you cunts! Che had a filthy mouth for a ten-year-old, everyone said. Even in his dreams, sometimes, he's running after that car, watching it disappear into the cedars.

They are lying and he sees why but he doesn't want them to. He wants things clean and sharp. He has to build his whole life now from the start and he wants everything to be clean and clear and true.

People think they lie because they love you and maybe this is true but it is also true that the lying puts you in a box. It cuts off some of the world and puts you in a box. How is that a good thing?

He will not lie. Even if he has kids someday, which it looks like he won't, he will not lie. He won't go out of his way to be cruel, but he will tell them the truth, even if it makes them hate him.

He says, now: I don't want a party.

They are all on the deck. The weather has turned hot again. A last kick of the can, Darrell says. The air is hot to breathe and tastes of toast: fires, somewhere. It's comfortable only in the morning and evening, when the lake and land breezes rise.

Cleo has said, only Cleo remembers, and she has said: It's Cliff's birthday this week. Of course Mandalay has picked it up. Let's have a party. And now everyone is planning it and he doesn't want a party.

It's the last thing I want, he says. A birthday party. It's the last thing I want.

Okay, okay, Crystal says. You don't have to have a party. Everyone is suddenly sad. His fault.

Then Darrell says: Let's just have a party anyway. Can we do that? Not a birthday party. Just a reunion party. A coming back together party.

Crystal brightening up then. She's like a kid, Crystal, sometimes. Not always, though: that's the tricky thing. Darrell seems to get that, but not the others.

What would you call Darrell? He thinks not *stepfather*: that's for if you are raised by someone. Not dad, no. Mr. Giesbrecht had wanted him to call him dad but he wouldn't. Cleo had said, just do it, but he wouldn't.

In some countries, he's seen this on TV, older male friends, even if they are not family members, are called *uncle*. And women are called *auntie*. He likes this idea but it wouldn't work here. He couldn't really call Darrell uncle, could he? That would be confusing.

Cliff is an uncle, to Sam and Olivia. He had not thought about that before, but living with them for a few weeks, he has got to know them and he has figured out some things. For one, it's maybe better to be an uncle than a parent. He doesn't care what Sam or Olivia do, as long as they don't hurt themselves. So immediately that improves things. Though already he can see things he would do differently if he were a parent. He would not keep all of the toys and the TV in the basement room, for one. He'd make a hidden room in the basement where an adult could go to be quiet, that's for sure. But he'd take that big room upstairs, with the leather couches, where the kids aren't supposed to play, where nobody goes all day, and he'd put something washable on the floor, something like they have in kitchens but maybe softer, and he'd hang paper all over the walls, maybe chalkboards.

At his work, in the main office where they all have their cubbies, there's a wall that's painted in chalkboard paint, the whole wall. He had not understood it, had wondered where they had got a chalkboard that big, but Nicki had said: It's just paint, Cliff. You can make anything into a chalkboard.

He'd get some of that paint and paint a wall with it and just let the kids go to town. He'd make a kitchen, kid-height, with running water but maybe not a working stove. He'd dig up the yard and let them play in the dirt. Cleo should do that: should dig up some of that lawn and just let them play in the dirt. Too many cats, she'd say, but the cats should be inside anyway. They don't get it about cars and they kill too many birds. He keeps Sophie inside, at Cleo's.

He doesn't know if little kids should have a cat. Olivia's fine, she gets it, but Sam wants to squeeze the hell out of Sophie.

He hopes that Trent is looking after Sophie. Cleo told him he had to. He's not sure that Trent will.

If he ever has kids, he will not be like Trent, who says, I'm tired. Go off and play now. Though that at least is not lying. Now he has to think about it, because Trent doesn't lie to be nice, but maybe he should. Trent will say, this steak is tough, or, I don't like cauliflower, or, I really dislike this new cushion. While Cleo, he sees, Cleo pretends things all day long: She pretends that she wants to read *Scuppers the Sailor Dog* again, that she isn't tired, that she doesn't want to just lie down and read her own book. He can see that. But what would happen if she didn't?

Maybe he had just better decide right now that he will never have kids. Like Mandalay. Mandalay seems to have decided that. Mandalay can do and say what she likes, it seems.

But it was good that he said he didn't want a birthday party, because they're all happily planning a party anyway, and he doesn't have to feel stressed about it. Doesn't have to worry about what he wants, or about being the centre of attention. The party will happen, and he can move in and out of it as he likes.

Or not. Here's a job for you, Cliff, Darrell says. I'm going to need you to get up and clear out those tent caterpillars from those maples there across the yard. They're just too creepy hanging there now, thinking about that lawn being full of guests eating and such. I'm going to need you to get up there with the twelve-foot ladder and cut them down and burn them up. You know how to do that?

Yeah, he knows how to do that. He has to do it all the time. Clients that don't like spraying. It's his least favourite job, probably. Afterwards, he can't ever seem to feel clean.

They all have jobs, already. It seems he has been assigned the most disgusting one.

Mandalay's and Ben's is to drive around and borrow lawn chairs. Mandalay has to do that because she's the only one who knows the neighbourhood; she lived here for a while, in her teens. (Why hadn't he been allowed to come back, then, when his mom was better and Darrell was living here? That has never been satisfactorily explained to him.) Ben because he can lift the chairs into the truck. He could do that. But no; he has to do the caterpillars.

FIRST HE HAS ANOTHER JOB. Crystal wants the rock garden weeded. He'd noticed it, long rock bank holding back the ferns and salal, the dusty miller and creeping phlox choked with dandelions, with plantain, but figured they were letting it go back to bush. Crystal says, I keep meaning to get to it but I just never seem to. He doesn't mind it, kneeling on the ground, pulling the weeds out by hand with a dibber, with his thumb and forefinger. He's not on the clock. He can relax into it. Crystal gets them both some sacking to kneel on, and gloves, but he likes to feel around with his bare fingers. He can do a more accurate job that way.

They go out in the morning, when this side of the yard is still in shade, the sky still sort of iridescent, like a thin Chinese bowl. He can hear birds in the trees, several kinds, but he doesn't know their names.

He'd like to know their names.

I want you to tell me something, Crystal says. I've never asked you this and you can tell me to go to hell if you want. But Cliff, at that place you and Cleo lived – I can never pronounce it, started with a G – was there something funny going on there?

Cliff's body stiffens, though he has tried to stiffen himself against stiffening.

What do you mean, funny?

What everyone means. No. What people used to mean. Not funny ha-ha. Funny peculiar. Stuff with kids.

Someone has inserted an inflated balloon into his chest, and it is gently but inexorably squeezing out any possible inflation of his lungs. The wall of roaring rears itself beyond his eardrums.

Molestation, Crystal says.

He shakes his head. I don't know. Then: Why would you even ask that?

I don't know, she says. You hear so much about it on the news. I just wondered. Did someone hurt you, Cliff?

He's paralyzed; he's hardened into some dense lifeless material.

Crystal reaches for him then, puts her hands, covered in garden soil, on either side of his head. He so does not want her touch but she has not touched him like this before and he feels he can't pull away; he has to give her this gesture. But she moves her hands away.

It doesn't mean there's anything wrong with you, you know that, she says. It's not something you did. You know that, Cliffie?

She's all wrong, she's got it all wrong. And he can't talk about it. He says, I'm fine, Mom. I'm fine.

You're the only one who ever calls me Mom, you know that? Crystal says. He glances at her, then. He doesn't mean to but he looks at her, and sees that tears are spilling down her cheeks, and she has wiped at them with her loamy fingers, and left muddy dabs across her cheeks. Tribal marks, he thinks. Like in shows about the Amazon. How people paint their faces when they are going to be part of some big ceremony. Some ritual of transition.

He reaches over to her with his own dirty hands, draws more lines of earth across her forehead, down her nose and chin.

Hey, she says. Hey! Cliff!

When they stop throwing the garden dirt at each other, they're covered in it.

He gets the ladder from the shed. Fourteen-foot aluminum: He won't be able to get all of the bugs, but he'll try. Olivia now in the yard, hanging out, watching him set it up. Are you going to kill all of the worms?

They're not worms, he says. Caterpillars aren't worms. They have legs. They're baby moths.

Stay back now, he says. Things could fall. You stay on the deck.

I want to help, she says.

No you don't, he says. He gets the pruning loppers. Up the ladder, he's used to that. He's not supposed to be climbing yet, technically, but he sees a hard hat in the shed, puts it on. Also goggles.

I want to do that, Olivia says. Lift me up so I can do it.

No, he says. And then he has an idea. He climbs down the ladder, carrying the loppers, which are big ones, three-footers, leaving the hard hat on, and swinging a pair of goggles with a nose filtration cone attached from his arms. He goes in through the deck doors, past Ben, who's on the computer, toward the kitchen, moving slowly, deliberately. Just getting a glass of water, he says to Crystal. Ben looks up.

Oh, man, he says. Hey, I want to do that. Give me that gear.

Then a little show of reluctance, so that Ben almost tussles him for the hat, the loppers. Better take the goggles, then, he says. When you dislodge a caterpillar nest, you get a shower of bug shit.

He doesn't mind picking up the lopped branches with their pouches of translucent silk, the crawling inside, as much. It's when they're above his head, falling around him, that he doesn't like them.

He gets the can of lawnmower gas, an old spray bottle. He lays the branches out on the gravel driveway, well away from the shed, and sprays each lightly, as if he's one of those women standing inside the rounded glass part of The Bay downtown, with their perfume bottles. The caterpillars don't like the gasoline; they start to move more vigorously, inside their tent. His hair rises. There's nothing creepier than a mass of something wormy, moving. Moving behind a translucent membrane, especially. It curdles something inside him. What's that called? Atavistic.

Ben coming around the house now, the odd caterpillar hanging from him still, brushing at himself spasmodically. Ben has the matches. He tosses the box to Cliff.

Nah, you do it, Cliff says. You earned it. He feels good.

He catches Olivia as she brushes by, steps back a few feet, keeps a good grip on her. Ben tosses the match.

Even from this safe distance they can see the caterpillars writhe and shrivel in the flames. Olivia bounces and laughs.

Holy shit, Ben says. And then to Olivia: You're a bloodthirsty devil, aren't you?

Thin black smoke from the burning curls upward. Cliff wonders, too late: What eats the tent caterpillars? Something, now, will go hungry.

THEY'VE PUT THE STEREO OUTSIDE: Ben puts on Darrell's and Crystal's LPs and CDs and tapes. Darrell says, Look at this, they sure know how to make things obsolete, don't they? Ben plays Cream, The Doors, CCR, Led Zeppelin. He puts on Blondie and Pat Benatar and Rush and Journey, 54-40 and April Wine. Bob Dylan, Joni Mitchell and Ian Tyson. U2 and Green Day and Shania Twain and Jay-Z.

There are five kinds of salad and a laundry basket full of rolls. There are tubs and tubs of beer on ice, and people bring even more. There are pies: All around Butterfly Lake, fruit and berries have ripened and people have made pies with the glut. There are two huge roasts of pork that have been cooked for twenty-four hours and then pulled apart and doused with barbecue sauce. There are Sockeye salmon, grilled on the brick barbecue, the silvery planks of them bursting out into coral meat.

There must be three hundred people, Cliff estimates. He doesn't think he knows any of them, and then after a while he isn't sure. People keep coming up to him, saying things like, I was a year ahead of you at school, or, I used to babysit you. Sometimes they look familiar.

When it gets dark, the strings of white lights that Darrell and Cliff have strung along the edges of the yard are turned on, and people dance. Cliff has not seen people dance on a lawn before. They dance all together, the shaggy oldsters who tell him they were friends of his dadda, the middle-aged people with their weighty bodies, the younger adults who claim to know him, the troop of small children. He sees Ben dancing with Cleo, and then Mandalay, and then Crystal, and he figures he might do that too. He takes off his shoes, because other people are barefoot and it seems disrespectful to wear shoes here.

He sees some people about his own age dancing together, slowly, in a circle, their arms around each other's shoulders, and when he tries to move by politely one of them sees him and pulls him into the circle. They're smoking; they pass the joint to him but he says no, as he always does, even though he feels that this group might be offended by that. One of the guys says, hey, Cliffie, you stay clean, now, and he thinks it is mocking and affectionate, both. They are also all weeping, he sees, or the women are and some of the men. One of them says, then, as if they've been interrupted and are just continuing on: Che, it's Lisa, I'm remembering you and me swimming naked all the time. Hope you're doing okay, wherever you are. And this is very weird for a moment, until the next person speaks, and says, Che, buddy, I guess you always knew it was me that lifted your Black Sabbath tape, I hope you've forgiven me, and Cliff understands that this is a kind of private wake, a remembrance. And when it's his turn, he says, Che, my brother, I wish you were here, which is true at that moment, anyway.

After that a girl pulls him over to dance, a girl or woman, he can't quite tell. She's wearing her hair loose, down her back, and a white top with tiny straps, and cut-off denim shorts, and she reminds him of someone else, but also doesn't. He's nervous, though, when she puts his arms around her waist, and her arms around his neck, and he says, How old are you? And she says, *Thanks*! and, *twenty-five*. Which seems okay. She smells like apples, he thinks, or roses, or something, and the grass touches his bare feet in a way that's on the border between pleasant and tormenting.

Then he gets bold enough to try to pirouette her, to spin her around by one hand, and she dips her head and her hair falls back and he sees the butterfly tattoo on her shoulder.

He touches it. I saw one just like this before, he says, on a girl.

Oh, then it was on a Butterfly Lake girl. We all got them, one year, all of us that were apprehended and came back, that were high school age. The same tattoo, in the same place. And we had it specially designed. Nobody else can have it.

He thinks of the girl in the apartment building, the one who found Sophie. He is almost sure it is the same tattoo.

In the morning everyone sleeps in, and when he gets up it's bright, bright, and he thinks: Drank too much beer.

The house is quiet, as if everyone has a headache. He finds coffee made in the kitchen, and follows the sound of a voice to the deck, where Cleo is stretched out on a lounge chair, on the phone, Sam beside her playing with some rocks. When she sees him, Cleo beckons him over, says into the phone, just hold it up to her again, and then to Cliff, listen. And he does, he holds the receiver to his ear, and there is Sophie's purr, loud as a bulldozer, the purr that sounds like it's going to burst out of her pigeon chest.

SO NOW EVERYBODY WANTS a piece of him. First Crystal and Darrell, who sit him down with a formal proposal: He can move back and live with them. Pete McCurdy up the road is looking for someone to take over his backhoe and landscaping business. Learn the ropes. Lots of work now, did he see all of the new houses on the way in? He could live with them for a while, see how he likes it.

He says, But I have a job.

But this. Get in on the ground floor. Own your own company in a couple of years. Your own house. Whole house here for the price of an apartment in the city. Anyway, talk to Pete.

He will, he says.

Then Ben: Let's stick around another couple of weeks, drive up the coast. Do some hiking and camping.

My job, he says. And your job.

I quit already, Ben says. They wouldn't give me the time off to come up here so I quit. Anyway I have enough for next year. My parents cover my tuition.

I miss my cat, Cliff says.

You really need a girlfriend, Ben says.

No, Cliff says. I think I don't. He touches his head where the shaved part, the new scar, still surprises his fingertips. But he laughs.

Think about it, Ben says. You can get some more time off.

Cleo says: We're leaving tomorrow. I need to get back for an appointment.

Maybe I'll stay a bit longer, he says. Get a ride back with Ben.

Cleo says, sharply: I was counting on you to take turns driving and help with the kids.

He doesn't know what to say. It's Mandalay who answers: You should have asked him earlier. Did you even ask him? You can't just spring this on him. It's not always about you and your kids.

Then Cleo in tears, and he feels like he ought to go back with her, but suddenly knows that he doesn't want to leave, not just yet. He hates it when people are pulling him in different directions. He doesn't want to make Cleo mad at him or to feel that he is letting her down. For so much of his life he has struggled with the things people have wanted of him: wanting to go to play pickup hockey after school but not wanting to displease Mr. Giesbrecht, who always needed him to do farm chores; wanting to tell Ray off but not wanting to lose his job; wanting to ask a girl out but not wanting to risk some sort of trouble.

Wanting to leave Loretta's and to stay.

But now he wants what he wants so strongly that there's no contest. He wants to stay much more than he wants to please Cleo. For once there's no contest. It makes everything clean and safe. He says, no, Cleo, I don't want to go back with you.

Okay, she says. Then he does feel sorry for a few moments. He knows that he owes Cleo everything, not just for giving him a place to stay and feeding him the last few weeks since his accident, but also because she saved him before. She got the Giesbrechts to take him in and raise him and that was the best thing for him.

He can remember the time before, the foster home before, as a series of corrections: an obstacle course of a thousand inexplicable rules. Don't butter the toast that way. Don't put your shoes there. Don't teach the little kids to pretend they are puppies. Don't touch the books. He remembers lots of children, all or some slow, or deaf, or blind. The woman who never quite looked in his face, but made sure everyone was clean and fed and went to school in her little van, walked the gauntlet to the special needs classroom, holding hands, her big huffs of relief when she saw the teacher, Mrs. Barber. Here we are again, she always said, like she was putting down a big load. He made no friends but sat in the corner, tried to do as he was told, to stay out of trouble. On the playground tried to slip away, to join in games with the other kids but Mrs. Barber was vigilant: She kept them all together where she could watch that they didn't get bullied too much by the normal kids. Sometimes when he tried to join in a game the kids would call out, Mrs. Barber, here's one of the special kids.

He was stupid, of course. He was stunned, his mind curling up inside his head like a hibernating animal, that first year. He had forgotten how to talk, to read even the baby books inside Mrs. Barber's classroom.

Then Cleo came and visited him and talked the Giesbrechts into asking for him to come and live with them. That he knows from Cleo, rather than remembers. He doesn't remember leaving, moving: only then being with Cleo at the Giesbrecht's, on the farm. Always Cleo. He has so many memories of Cleo: how she'd sit with him at the kitchen table, helping him read or do his arithmetic, showing him with raisins: three groups of five is fifteen. Her own books, thick and dense, spread out. Cleo making dinner, her job, the big roasts and piles of dumplings, the steaming potatoes. Cleo burning her fingers, her arms, on pots, the oven, the ironing board, swearing if nobody but him was there, running her hands under cold water, showing him: *see?* The red blistered triangular mark on her wrist.

How Cleo softened everything, found a way for him to do everything. He had been like a little spring freshet rolling from obstacle to obstacle, and she'd been there guessing at what he had needed, smoothing out his way. Always in that big warm sunny kitchen, with her books, her patience, her attunement to him. Whatever happened at school — and it was hard; he was in a regular classroom, he was often, it seemed, the worst at everything — he could shed it all, shake it off like the farm dogs shaking off the pond — when Cleo was there.

And at night he slept in her room. He had his own little room but it was next to Cleo's and at night he would lie awake until he heard her springs move — that meant she had stopped studying and gone to bed — and then he would knock softly as she had asked him to and come in, close the door without a sound, feel his way with his bare feet across her room and into her single bed, and she would put her arm around him, so that he could spoon into her, and he'd fall asleep.

He was always falling asleep in class, when he was small.

So he owes Cleo everything but now he also sees that living at the Giesbrechts, growing up there, he had missed out on a lot too. Watching Ben, listening to Mandalay talk, being here in Butterfly Lake, he sees that. Listening to rock music and hanging out with friends, girls especially. Being able to have his hair the way he wanted it and more than those things, the chance to figure things out himself, like what he wanted to do for a career or what he liked to think about some things.

And it was true that Cleo had taken care of him and been like an extra skin, a shell, for him. And the Giesbrechts had been a family, the older boys that lived there and did the farm work; Mr. and Mrs. Giesbrecht themselves, grey and doughy and happy when they were all around the table, the gravy and the dumplings piled up, or taking up that whole pew at church, himself leaning into Cleo, allowed to colour, the older boys in their white shirts they only wore on Sunday falling asleep in a row, their heads going back, mouths open, or leaning forward, head on hands, as if praying but really asleep.

But he has started to think now about how Mandalay knows people in Butterfly Lake and how everyone here knows Che (and claims to remember him). And he has to wonder – not being ungrateful to Cleo, just wondering – if maybe, if he'd been left where he was, not taken to the Giesbrecht's, he might have been able to come back home. Because he had not known before that Crystal was living here, that she had left the hospital and had come back and was living here with Darrell, all that time.

He can see that Crystal would not have been the most organized parent. She wouldn't. But he would have grown up here, and would have had Mandalay and Che, and the forest, and the water. Maybe it would have been better and maybe it wouldn't, but it would have been his. His own.

IT'S A PLACE THAT HAS been logged, and logged again, and flooded. Once there had been a lush valley with a river running through it and nine-hundred-year-old cedars creating, in their arched red boles and roots, their own microclimate. Streams had descended the thick forest, spawning streams to which salmon had returned year after year for millennia. The forest had comprised not only cedar but maple and spruce, hazel and beech and fir, salal and swordfern and moss thick enough to muffle any sound. Fourteen varieties of fish had navigated the river and streams, and a dozen species of large mammal – black bears and grizzly, cougar and bobcat, fisher and mink and muskrat and otter, hare and white-tail deer and elk and moose – as well as dozens more of smaller mammals and amphibians. And birds! Bald eagle, osprey, heron, dipper. Several species of duck. And of the small singing forest birds.

It was logged at the last turn of the century, and then logged again with bigger equipment through the forties and fifties. In the sixties the river had been dammed at Butterfly Falls, the narrow neck of the valley, named for both the many species of butterfly that passed through the gap to their summer breeding grounds – and the three species endemic to the valley – and also for the shape of the falls, the gauzy wings of water that fanned out across the granite pincers at the valley's end. The valley had been flooded to make a hydroelectric dam. Technically, few species had been lost with the flooding. The government had commissioned studies. Most of the animals had disappeared with the loss of their habitat – the forest and streams. There had been only a great bowl of stumps and fireweed left, and a river from which most of the fish had already been extirpated – their spawning streams scoured out by the rains, after the clearcutting.

Then a little community had grown up along the lakeshore, at the point where the land was flat enough to be accessible – a community of sawmill workers and some would-be homesteaders who, in the sixties and early seventies, obtained grants of crown land on what was left of the logged-out slopes above the lake. For a decade or two the community had eked out a living, logging and milling the few remaining almost inaccessible stands of trees, trying to grow crops in the washed-out soil, picking blackberries and blueberries and mushrooms.

Then the economy had gone bad, in the early eighties, and people had moved away – moved back to Powell River or to Vancouver, or the oilfields. Cabins and mobile homes had been left derelict. The forest had begun to grow back. Fish ladders built in the seventies had finally started to make a difference, the salmon finally returning. With the salmon and forest, other wildlife had begun to reappear.

There is lots of forest now: The salmon are carried from the streams into the forest by bears and eagles and other predators and scavengers, and the nutrients of the bodies enrich the soil. But none of the trees are older than forty years, and there are nowhere near as many fish as there once were. They have started to return to spawn in those streams that have the right flow, the right kind of gravel bed, but it will never be the same. It has revived. It will never be the same.

Deal

IT'S HOT IN THE CAR. The air conditioner doesn't seem to be coming on, and Cleo remembers, faintly, Trent telling her to do something – was she to take it to the shop, or fill something with some fluid? – something about the air conditioning, but she isn't sure. The details elude her, small movements on the periphery of her memory. Worry over Trent's displeasure with her settles in her mind, further clutter. He'll be angry; he'll say, I *did* tell you. Why hadn't she done whatever it was? There must have been a reason, but she can't quite remember that, either. Anyway, maybe he could have done it himself? Defences stack up. It was not exactly easy for her to get the car to a shop, in Butterfly Lake, with two small children.

She winds down the window, but Olivia roars: The wind hurts her ears. Well then, Cleo says, you'll have to put up with being hot. Sam, at least, has fallen asleep. She should have taken the jacket off him, though. His face, when she glances in the rear-view mirror, is red and moist-looking, his hair damp. He'll be so uncomfortable, so cranky when he wakes. But he is sleeping, so she won't wake him now.

She sees, on one of her glances, Olivia reaching across to shake Sam's seat. Don't you dare, she says, hissing it between her teeth. Don't you dare!

What? Olivia asks. I was just.

Don't you dare wake him up.

I'm so hot, Olivia says. I don't want to be here. I want to go home.

We are on our way home, Cleo says. But Olivia's misery fills up the car, beating at Cleo. She thinks of the couple she had overheard in the school playground, talking about how they had bicycled through France with their two little girls, aged one and three. How could that be done? She can't imagine it. More placid children? Perhaps the husband, Greg, took on the kids more, or more enthusiastically: She remembers him putting the younger child into her jacket, adeptly, with good humour. Of course, that wasn't evidence that he was always helpful. Trent tends to pay a lot more attention to the kids at other people's houses. People that know them probably think he is a pretty hands-on dad, pretty easygoing.

She rolls down her window again, gets a few kilometres of fresh air before Olivia's howl. I'm so thirsty, Olivia moans. She must look for somewhere to stop. Gas station, maybe. She doesn't remember seeing one along this stretch of highway but she doesn't know the new road that well. She doesn't really have a sense of where she is, or what is up ahead.

I know, I know, she says, soothingly. I'll stop soon, I promise. She should have bought more to drink. She had intended to, had even put a case of bottled water in the cart at the grocery store, but Mandalay had said, you don't need that; you can fill some bottles from the tap. Of course she had forgotten to do that, in the scrum of packing up.

Let's sing, she says, and starts in: *Skinnamarinky dinky dink*, but the words trail off feebly and Olivia says, Not now, you're hurting my brain.

Then the blue sign, the silhouette of plate and pump, and the exit, the largish painted clapboard building blooming into view just off the road. There are a couple of other vehicles in the parking lot, a minivan and a newish sedan. It should be okay to stop. In the store there is an ATM, yes, and big cooler cases of drinks.

Can I have anything I want?

Anything, she says, feeling expansive, wise. Sam is groggy and hot and limp. She'd have liked to have left him in the car, with a window cracked – she parked in the shade – but since that time at the convenience store in Abbotsford, she has been afraid to do that. She has to sit him on the restroom floor so that she can use the toilet. How unhygienic is that? she says to him. Just don't lick the floor. She buys cold bottled water and iced tea and chips and cookies. Anything to distract Olivia, to have a couple of hours of uninterrupted driving.

Outside are a picnic table and a path leading through the aspens and cottonwoods. She can hear the river nearby, the cool gurgle of it. Hear that? she asks Olivia. What do you think that is?

River, Olivia says. Let's go down and see it. Do you hear the river, Sam?

They walk down the path. There are others down there, on the river's gravelly shore: an older couple, a couple of boys around ten or twelve with their father. They're all wading, paddling. Of course Olivia wants to go in.

You'll have to swim in your panties, Cleo says. I'm not going back to the car for your suit.

For once Olivia doesn't argue, but strips off her pants and T-shirt, her shoes, and wades in. Don't go past your waist, Cleo says. She strips Sam down, holds his hands as he steps into the water, gingerly on the stones. His round little bum looks red; his diaper is soaking. He wants to walk in further, to follow Olivia. She levers off her own runners and socks, off-balance while she tries to hold Sam up at the same time. A stork, she is. Flamingo.

The man with the two sons is playing with them, chasing and splashing, and laughing in the river, further out. They're like three boys together, she thinks. Hard to imagine Trent like that, into the game, unselfconscious.

Olivia is up to her waist now and pushing out further into the river. Cleo stands up, calls her to come back. Olivia turns, smiles, stops. The older couple are both smiling at Sam, who is slapping at the water with his free hand, crowing. She dips some water, pours it over his sweaty head. He gasps and then laughs, and she pours more. How delightful, how easy, that he is fearless of water.

And then glances up for Olivia and sees her neck deep, more than neck; she's holding her chin up to keep her mouth out of the water, and in that second Olivia bobs under, comes up paddling, already moving with the current, her face swinging around to look for Cleo's, her eyes and mouth perfect circles of surprise.

How long does it take before Cleo starts after her? A split second, an eternity. She must let go of Sam, sit him on the gravel edge, say, firmly, stay, start running through the water, over the slippery round stones. She doesn't take her eyes off Olivia, watches her expression change from surprise to fear. Feels Olivia's terror in her own mind. Cleo slips, starts paddling, realizes she should have headed toward the point Olivia was going, not the point where she had been.

Olivia opens her mouth, screams: Mummy! Cleo doesn't know if she has answered: She keeps moving. In an instant Olivia will have been carried past this little widening of the river, this shallow beach, to where the banks are steep and the current moving faster.

Swim! Cleo shouts, and Olivia does swim. Her paddling doesn't take her anywhere, but it keeps her afloat.

It's the older gentleman who reaches her first, running, as Cleo should have done, along the shore to intercept Olivia. He leaps in past her, plucks her out of the water, holds her up, laughs. You went for a swim, he says.

Olivia on the border between anger and relief. She is poised for a moment, Cleo sees, watching her rescuer's face, then decides to laugh. When the man hands Olivia to Cleo, his eyes say: Make it light. And so Cleo laughs too.

Only then does she remember Sam, and turns with an explosion of adrenalin, but the older woman has picked him up, is holding him safely in her arms.

How did they manage to do that, to be so calm, to do the right thing?

They are a group now, the eight of them, the older gentleman laughing as he holds his dripping wallet, takes bills out, dries them on his wife's scarf, the younger man with the sons making a joke to Olivia. They are acting as if it was nothing. How do they do that?

She forces herself not to rush off – to get dry clothes out of the suitcase, to buy hot dogs for the three of them from the store, which they eat at the picnic table, because Sam could choke on a hot dog if she weren't right there, if she were driving and he in the back seat. She is shaking, but she makes herself not shake, makes herself smile.

When they're back on the road, Olivia says, severely: You don't know how much danger I was in.

Why do you say that?

You laughed, after. You weren't scared.

I wasn't scared because you were already safe.

But did you think I would drown?

Cleo feels the conversation is carrying her off in a dangerous direction. Then she is inspired.

I was scared for a second but then I saw how brave you were.

Olivia considers this for a moment, then says: I was brave, wasn't I?

Yes, and I saw that you weren't panicking. That was the important thing. You kept your head. You didn't panic. You thought it out, and you knew that if you just kept swimming like you learned in your Sunfish and Dolphin classes, someone would get to you and pull you in.

I did see that, Olivia says.

So it was an adventure. You had an adventure. And you learned something.

Then she feels that she has done something very powerful, and also very dubious.

She'd thought, when Olivia was in the river, that she was gone. And also when Sam cracked his head, at the Jensen's. And she lies awake, often, imagining the terrible things that could happen to her children. There are so many levels and types of bad things that can happen.

It occurs now to her, though, that everybody must worry. Everyone must, and some people are less careful, less alert, less diligent, less intelligent than others, but everyone must worry, all the time.

She is not sure what is to be done about that.

She cannot do this anymore. But she will.

NOW THE LATE AUGUST DAYS are getting shorter, but are still long enough, and warm, and Cleo sometimes takes the children to the school playground in the evenings, the long light evenings after dinner, when Trent just wants to have peace and quiet. It seems like a good idea, to be outside. Healthy for children. (Cleo is dying to be outside.) Their backyard is not much use: It's in shadow, sloped, nude of toys or anything to play on.

On the way back from the playground, she takes different routes, winds through the residential streets. There's one she likes more than the others; it's older, from the eighties, and the houses are bigger, with wood siding stained rich, earthy colours: spruce green, oxblood, marine blue, and the street has mature trees, maple and chestnut and chokecherry, that spread their new green canopies, their

candles of blossoms, and are full of birdsong. In driveways parents –
mostly dads – shoot baskets with half-grown offspring, and in lighted
windows bend over tables where children sit with books. She stays out
until dusk, sometimes, to see the lights come on.

One evening a woman in a window raps, and then beckons to her:
She crosses the street, pushing the stroller with both of the children
in it, and the front door – which is painted purple – opens, and from
it emerges the dark-haired woman from kindergarten registration,
Mira. Come in for tea, come in, Mira says. And she does, surprising
herself. She lifts Olivia and then Sam from the stroller and follows
the woman inside.

The front hallway is wide and decorated with a wall-sized collage
of framed photographs: She glimpses some posed, black and white;
others coloured, informal. Family photos: some recent, some in styles
of other decades, back to the 40s. The wide hall opens to a great room:
The entire main floor of the house is open. Two-thirds of it seems to
be kitchen: a huge open kitchen, with miles of cupboards in whitish
distressed wood, with open upper shelves, painted Mediterranean-
style tiles, the fruit gleaming in rich subtle colours, a gas range, an
enormous refrigerator, a heavy table of rustic-looking reclaimed wood
that must seat ten easily, unmatched, but related, chairs.

Sit, sit, Mira says.

She sees that there are stacks of clean plates and cutlery on the
table. But you're just about to eat.

Not for half an hour, Mira says. Jim won't be home for half an
hour. Will you have some tea? Or maybe a glass of wine? Wine might
be better, this time of day. I'm going to have a glass of wine. Betts
(she says to a girl of about twelve drawing at the far end of the table),
Betts, that's enough for tonight, I'm sure, take the baby and the little
girl – Olivia, isn't it? – up to the playroom. I think Mariah is up there.
Keep an eye on the baby.

Cleo is dazzled. She has fallen into another country.

Excuse me for not taking you into the living room, Mira says. I just have to watch this pot of pasta and finish the sauce.

Cleo glances into the living room, which is filled with a fireplace, a deep sofa upholstered in a soft olive and green and wine velvet. There is a fireplace, made of carved antique-looking oak, an armchair upholstered in gold and one in wine, solid, old-looking tables and footstools. And in an alcove, an upright piano, on which a small boy is playing a recognizable melody. And a window seat, on which a girl a little younger than the first is reading.

It's almost too much to take in. Mira gives her a glass of wine, and pours one for herself, but remains standing at the stovetop which is on an island, facing the table. She is wearing a long loose dress of some sort of very soft rich fabric — actual wool, maybe — in a deep blue and teal and purple print, and with it leggings, and little soft embroidered slippers, Indian, Cleo thinks. Her long curly hair is held back with a gold-lamé band.

This is lovely, Mira says. I love this time of day, when everything is starting to slow down, don't you?

Cleo thinks of the dead time after their supper: her struggle to clean up and get the kids ready for bed. She doesn't answer.

Then she begins to ask Cleo questions about herself: How long has she lived here? What does she do? What does her husband do? Where did she grow up? Does she have siblings? Where did she go to school? — and with more and more branching and detailed sub-questions, so that answering them, Cleo feels that this woman knows more about her than maybe anyone else in the world.

And Mira presses for detail, not in a judging or nosy way but with what feels like genuine curiosity. It's a strange experience, to meet someone who is so interested. The even stranger thing that Mira does is question. Often when Cleo makes a certain kind of statement, what she'd call a statement of opinion, Mira will pick it up – not in a critical way, but again with that tone of simple curiosity. Why do you think that? she'll ask. So things that Cleo has ceased to question, or has not questioned, are shaken down and turned around: She has to look at them anew. By the time she's sat there an hour – at which point a car is heard in the drive and the girl who was reading jumps up to put the plates around the table, and Mira calls up the stairs, and Cleo's children are delivered back to her – Cleo feels like her brain has been doing sprints.

Mira works part-time giving music lessons. Her husband Jim is a dentist, and works eleven till seven, to accommodate people who want later appointments. He gets the kids off to school in the morning so Mira can sleep in. They knocked out two walls in their house to make that one great room and the big kitchen. They use their living room as a family room. The two older girls sleep in the master suite, and have their toys and computers there, Mira and Jim have one of the smaller bedrooms. They do a two-week bike trip every year with Mira's brother's family. Even when the children were small, they did this. Jim runs every morning to keep in shape. The children all take piano and play soccer. They all go to the symphony. Mira reads the *Globe and Mail* every morning. She listens to the CBC; she has the radio on while she cooks, cleans, drives kids around. She can talk knowledgeably about anything. She is genuinely interested in what other people think. She makes you think about your opinions.

Come back any time, Mira says, as she leaves. I'm usually here, after school and evenings. If I'm busy I'll tell you.

Cleo feels, walking home, as if she has been dreaming. She wonders if a week is enough time to leave before arriving on Mira's doorstep again.

HERE'S THE DEAL, Kate says. You work two-and-a- half days a week. Twenty hours. You can spread it over three days or five. You get one sick day or daycare-issue free card per month, on top of your legal sick days. You have to make up anything else you miss. More about that later. You're on probation for three months, then you have a review. Your salary is eighteen thousand plus pro-rated benefits until your review. If your review is successful your salary goes up to twenty-one. If you're not successful — well, you won't be working here, so it's a moot point. You wear business attire every day. We don't do casual Fridays. You can take lunch or not; you don't get paid for lunch breaks. You have to attend biweekly office meetings, but you are paid for that.

Kate is her age, Cleo thinks. Dressed in a suit. Cleo will have to buy a couple. This isn't a suit like women wore when she was a grad student applying for jobs, with their padded shoulders and pleated trousers, but a slim outfit: sleek charcoal-grey flared pants, almost like yoga pants, a silky blue shirt, a jacket that looks like a motorcycle jacket, with zippers and snaps, except that it's made of some matte black fabric she's never seen before. Kate has a no-nonsense haircut, a short bob that looks like it has just been cut straight around and tucked behind her ears, though Cleo suspects it takes a very expensive stylist to get that look. She wears little or no makeup, has striking features, a strong, cool, even hard manner.

Mira had warned her about the manner, which is a good thing. Kate is a friend of Mira's sister-in-law. Kate has her own home design business, which she runs on equitable and green principles. She likes to hire women with young children, to give them an entry back into the workforce. She makes sure they're paid properly; she gets them benefits. She is flexible about hours so that people can work around daycare.

You have to be in the office twenty hours, Kate says. I realize you could do this from home on your computer, but I feel people produce better when they get out of their pajamas and come to the office. I also like the interchange of ideas. If you want to do some work at home, you can do that too, and for that you can achieve bonuses. But not during your probation time, and not unless you're producing up to expectations during the salaried part of the week.

It sounds fair, and ideal. It's only the coldness that scares her. Even when Kate wrinkles up her nose and crinkles her eyes in a twinkly way while she says "get out of their pajamas," she seems frighteningly focussed, in charge.

You'll find I'm fair and consistent, though firm about deadlines and expectations, Kate says. Also. If I have to give you negative feedback, which I will, especially the first few months, don't take it personally, okay? It won't be meant personally.

About the making up time, she says. Kids get sick. I have kids, I know that. You can't take them to daycare when they're sick. So you can stay home then. But you will have to make that time up in hours on site, over the next billing period. So if you miss a few days one week, you might have to work forty hours the next. It's not negotiable. How you manage it is your business. I don't want to hear daycare excuses or sick child excuses, ever. That's why I'm flexible. But I need people to produce, too. To give to the job. I'm generous and supportive of hard work and initiative. But I'm not running a charity.

It's very odd. She has never met a woman so impersonal in her life. And yet what is being offered her seems the most fair – and yes, generous – situation she could imagine. She feels like her perspective has altered, as if a strong cold wind has blown in, blown away all of the dust and heaviness of late summer.

Will she take it?

She'll take it.

Olivia starts kindergarten in a week. She'll have to make arrangements for Olivia and Sam, but she's already talked to Lacey Lennox about taking turns, already contacted the daycare Lacey uses about spots for Olivia (occasionally) and Sam. She'll see what's available; she'll plan her workday.

She'll leave an afternoon or morning a week, at least one, for herself.

She won't always be there to meet Olivia after kindergarten, which is only half the school day, less than half. She will be apart from Sam, her baby, who has just started to engage with her verbally, to follow her around babbling words, to lie beside her before his nap just looking into her eyes, holding her gaze, sometimes for ten minutes, until his eyelids close, to play with her. Just this week, he has started bringing her folded up pieces of paper with crayoning on them: mail. She opens them, reads them. Has to guess what they say. Has to guess right. Sometimes he includes a gift: a piece of crayon, a penny. She'll be apart from him now at least twenty hours a week, not including travel time.

Maybe she won't take the afternoon for herself just yet.

Trent sees it all in terms of money: He's pleased with her salary. She should have let him think she negotiated it, but it hadn't occurred to do her to do that. He is pleased that she will make enough to contribute to the household. That's what he cares about. (No, that isn't fair. It is a lot for him, to carry them all financially.)

She knows it won't be really exciting work. She'll be drafting, on a computer, designs for home renos, for people wanting to put an extra bathroom or a suite into their attic or basement. But she can do it. And she had thought she might end up stocking shelves at night, or cashiering, or waitressing, for minimum wage. She'd thought maybe that's all that she could get.

When she gets home she tells Trent that she is going out, he can feed the children. (But you just got back, he complains.) She marches down the milky late August streets, fast and hard until she finds the entrance to the wooded park. Inside the park, well in where the trees arch over to form a kind of green cathedral, she stops, sits on a mossy rock.

She wants to howl that it is unfair, that she takes care of everyone and no one takes care of her. Nobody has ever taken care of her. But the park is surrounded by houses; really, it's quite a little park, though it had seemed formidable when she'd found it, with the children, in the spring. It's a very small park. If she were to howl, she'd be heard; people would come.

And maybe it is not true. Maybe she's been as lucky as anyone else. And who knows what will happen? Anything can happen. Look what she has imagined, and set her mind to, and caused to come into existence.

She cries a little then out of the tension of the day, sparingly, as if letting a little pressure out of a tire. It will be alright, she tells herself. She doesn't know that, but she can't see that it will make much difference to think it, and saying it actually makes her feel better.

Then she hears the whir of bicycle wheels on the path, and wipes her cheeks, and is dry-eyed and smiling by the time the riders pass by.

No Deal

MANDALAY HAS BEEN PREGNANT twice before. The first time by Tomas: There had been no question of her having a baby, at twenty, or of Tomas wanting that life. He'd taken her to the clinic, showered her with affection and gratitude after. A realist, but a romantic realist. The second time with Benedict. She hadn't realized until she got back to Canada. She'd been on birth control pills, but they must have gone straight through her when she had dysentery. Then, when she'd still been deciding what to do – she'd been almost thirty then, had thought she might have the baby, raise it – she'd miscarried – bloodily, frighteningly, but – the gynecologist had assured her – not with permanent damage.

After that she'd got the job at The Seagull and had not looked at any men, until Duane.

She is the type of woman men want as a girlfriend or lover, not wife, she has to admit. Well, that's not precisely true. Horst had really wanted to get married. And Christopher had said he did, though she doubted it. Or doubted he wanted to marry *her*.

Maybe it was just that the men who she liked the most – Tomas, Benedict, Duane – were not interested in marrying. Or in marrying her.

It didn't have to be wife. Life partner? She was good with that. Maybe even exclusive companion? Maybe not.

And now this.

Cleo says she has to tell Duane. Even if you're not planning to keep it, Cleo says. Even if you want to raise it on your own. You have to tell him. It's a question of ethics.

She doesn't see that. It's a bit of his DNA. How does that affect him?

Cleo says, I think family bonds are mysterious things. You can't always estimate their importance. And think about the child. Look how upset Bodhi was at being lied to about Crystal.

That is a good point. She can imagine a child – she imagines it as a boy, an older teen or young adult, she can imagine him saying, in shock, You never told my father I existed? – and turning to look at her with disappointment, with resentment, with hatred even.

She thinks, all the way back, on the bus, the ferry, about how she will tell him. On the phone or face to face? She could ask to meet. Or email him. She has forgotten that she can email now. Breaking the ice, that's what she has trouble picturing. Initiating that first contact, as if they are two countries that don't acknowledge each other's existence.

But when she lets herself into her apartment (dusty, curiously cold) her answering machine is signalling furiously, and the messages are all from Duane. Where are you? Please call me. I have some news about your case. Please get back to me, Mandalay. I suppose you're out of town. You really need to leave messages about where you can be reached. Okay, Mandalay, please call me as soon as you get this. It's about The Seagull. It's good, I promise.

She calls.

We should meet, he says. Her heart speeds up at his voice; she thinks: Flutters, though that's a cliché, isn't it? What it is, she thinks, is fear, trepidation. But then is all romantic love partly fear? Is that the rush, the excitement that fades? Fear?

Yes, she says. Okay. And hears it in his voice too, a kind of tremolo.

They end up meeting at a restaurant they have often gone to, The Golden Horn, which specializes in little medallions of beef, rare and tender; tiny octopi and large prawns, *ceviche*, baby vegetables, little birds roasted with herbs. She lets him pour her wine before it occurs to her that she should drink less, or maybe not at all? – those posters in bus shelters – and maybe not eat raw fish. Is that it? Cleo will know. The restaurant is finished in black marble and blond wood, and she feels a homesickness for it, as a place from her past.

She says, Butterfly Lake. He has scolded her again for not answering her messages, but as if she's endangered herself, not as if she's inconvenienced him.

Family reunion?

We found my younger brother, who was adopted as a baby, she says. Or he found me. In the spring. This was us all getting together.

You never told me about that.

You said you weren't into family occasions.

Not the same thing. But okay.

He has something for her: a phone, a cell phone. How small it is, like two packs of cards, maybe, end to end. It's actually my old one, he says. It's pretty clunky. They're getting much smaller.

She doesn't want it, doesn't want to take it. I will just toss it, if you don't, he says. Have it.

No, she says. I don't need it. No.

Suit yourself, he says. She thinks she can read him enough now to see when he's repressing irritation or disappointment, and he's not.

He says: The Seagull has agreed to settle. For a moment she doesn't know what that means.

We talked to them, he says. My colleague and I. Remember? They don't want to give you your job back, and really, I don't recommend that you try to fight for that, though of course you can if you want. You'd be in a hostile environment. They've offered a decent payout, though, and I advise you to take it.

She's still having trouble getting her head around what he's saying: It's as if she's let go of The Seagull in her mind, as if it's receded to a far shelf. How much?

He gives a number: It's a year's salary, basically. She doesn't know, can't calculate, if that's a lot or a little. But Duane thinks it's a good amount, he said that.

It's not really generous, he says. But I think it's the most you'll get, without going to court, which will be expensive.

He says, you can do something with this. Live on it while you look for another job, which I think you'll find easily, with your reputation and experience. If you get another job right away, invest it. It'll be a nice nest egg.

Ha.

She still feels confused, disoriented. She says, making an effort to focus, Thank you, thank you so much. This must have taken a lot of time and energy. Thank you.

Nah, he says. A letter. That's it. We mentioned the article about you from *Aloft*, though: that was helpful.

She hasn't thought about that article for months, it feels like.

If she gets another position, cooking or baking, maybe, right away, she can put the payout away, use it to live on when the baby is born. It's the cushion she has needed. She can do it, now. She can see how to do it.

He says, I've missed you. I really enjoy your company. Any chance you'll reconsider? Maybe just give it another few months? Unless you're – unless you have – other – plans, now?

And she thinks, realizes, an *èclat*, as her old lover Benedict would have said, though she doesn't trust these sudden epiphanies, that if circumstances were different, she might reconsider. Because it was good, it was. And what was she giving up, really? A kind of ownership, a possessiveness that she doesn't believe in, anyway. A claim on the future, and she doesn't even believe in living for the future. She doesn't really believe in monogamy and nuclear families and all of that. She was happy, when she didn't think about what he was not offering. And was that, what she thought she wanted, all an illusion? So what was her objection to the arrangement? It was working out so felicitously for both of them.

She had been happy, in the moments of it, in all the moments of it.

But now, of course, she can't go back to it. Well, she could: She could make that decision, terminate, it's early days yet. She could do that, tell him or not tell him, and do that. And then they could have it back, this thing they have between them, which is more than just a social and sexual arrangement, which is really the most connection she has experienced with a man, the most intense and clear and joyful connection she has ever had. It's as if all of the other relationships she's had have been trials for this, experiments in which she's learned what she wanted, what she didn't want. In which she's learned, maybe (her brain, she feels, is zizzing with these realizations) how to be the person who doesn't get in the way of having the best relationship possible for herself.

She could do that. She could move on. She'll have other chances: she's only thirty-three. Maybe even with Duane. He might change his mind. People do.

Does she really want to have this baby?

An image comes to her, then, unsought, not of Cleo's sweet clean cherubic babies, whom she had held and smelled and wanted; yes, admit it, wanted, at least in those instants, but of Crystal: Crystal, it must have been after Bodhi's birth, Crystal in a stained, sour-milk-smelling T-shirt and dirty sweatpants, lank hair, smoking over the baby's head as he nursed, and her eleven or twelve-year-old self recoiling, feeling disgust, disdain, saying, You're a mess, you're not supposed to smoke around babies. And Crystal saying, You wait, see what it's like.

Her mind now saying: Is that what it's all about? Recognizing her competitiveness with Crystal, lining up examples from her whole adolescent and adult life, pinning them up for her, warning her not to keep making decisions based on that useless need. Crystal! She doesn't want her whole life to be shaped by her need to define herself against Crystal.

She doesn't need to have a baby. Nobody needs to have a baby, really.

But she wants it. It is hers, and she wants it. She is not seeing it in any romantic, rose-coloured way, she thinks. She has been around babies and children enough. She actually knows that they are only appealing about five percent of the time: The rest is sheer hard work and loss of freedom and loneliness and, likely, ultimate rejection. But she wants it: She has come over the past week or so to want it with something that is not part of the package of her emotions about Crystal or other people's kids or her picture of her life as a woman. It is something deeper in her gut; it is something from her primal self.

Something that is in her, wants this baby to grow, and says, damn the consequences. Maybe it is hormones. Maybe self-protective hormones sent out by the baby itself. Maybe just some prescript to breed. Maybe the need to commit to something that only she can take on.

Duane is looking at her with something that is a mixture of vulnerability and self-irony and – yes – tenderness, and she has taken so long to answer that his expression is starting to change, the thing she thinks of as vulnerability erasing itself from the eyes and mouth. She takes her hand out from under his – she hadn't noticed it there – and says, on the last of an exhale, says, I have to tell you something. I'm not asking you for help, okay? I know you don't want this. And I hope you know I didn't plan this: You must know how it happened. On our trip. Anyway I'm not asking you for anything, okay? I'm just letting you know.

And she tells him.

He becomes very formal, but she doesn't feel hurt or angry at that: It's his defence, she knows, against shock or surprise; it's his way of pre-empting any reaction in himself that he might regret or that might offend. He says, very formally, that indeed he knows how it must have happened; it was partly his responsibility, and he wonders if she has really thought out what she wants to do. It is her decision, he says, and he'll talk to her about fiducial matters. (She wonders: Is that fair? On an individual basis, maybe not; in a larger social context, yes?) It is her decision, he says, and of course he is speaking from self-interest; he'll admit that, but he wonders, under the circumstance, if it wouldn't be better also for her not to take this on.

The food comes and they do not eat, and then they both eat hungrily, aggressively, as if it's a last meal, or as if they are grinding each other up in their chewing.

She says she'll cab home but he drives her, and then waiting for a light to turn, a light that's taking its time, he cracks: His voice stays soft and neutral, in the way it is when he is formal, businesslike, but he says: When I read that article about you, I thought maybe you were more — *career-driven.*

You're making a lot of assumptions here, she says. She says it in a cold, hard voice, so that she will not cry.

When he pulls up outside her building, he says, We'll talk about arrangements.

Whatever, she says. I don't need you, you know.

She had meant to say, I don't need your help, but she lets it stand.

SHE BEGINS TO LOOK for a new job. This is done over the internet now, she discovers: She has to be grateful for Duane's gift of his old laptop. She makes up résumés, different ones for different kinds of jobs. She wants a management-type job in a café or restaurant or bakery but there are not so many of these at her level: mostly cashiers or *baristas* or waiters are wanted, at minimum wage. She looks also for jobs in marketing and office management and personnel, and writes careful cover letters that bullet her management experience, but the ads ask for diplomas or degrees she doesn't have (and really isn't interested in getting: When Trent suggests she take a business degree, she realizes that's the last thing she wants to do.)

Cleo says single moms are often hired as nannies, so she answers some ads for nannies, which are initiated online, and gets a reply from "Academic Couple" that turns out to be from Christopher, her old boyfriend Christopher, now married with two young children. (Is that you, Mandalay? Will you meet me for coffee? No, she says. She can imagine, now, where that might go.)

And then the truly miraculous, the undeserved, the impossible thing happens: Buying vegetables, she bumps into Belinda, the visual arts instructor who had helped her organize the art wall at The Seagull (gone now, of course), and Belinda says that she's just heard that day that someone she knows is looking for an assistant in her gallery, and Mandalay would be perfect for it: She'd been about to telephone Mandalay. I told her, Belinda says, that you have everything: the aesthetic, the curatorial skills, the business skills.

They go for coffee, then, or rather, steamed milk. Belinda says she has just found out she is pregnant. She and her partner have been wanting this for some time. She's in her late thirties; she has always wanted to have a child. She says that she and Mandalay should do prenatal classes together. She says that Mandalay should take some art classes herself; she can use Belinda's studio.

Then Mandalay thinks: See, it was meant, and then laughs at herself for thinking that. Whatever *meant* means. It is luck that this opportunity has come up, but it is also a step, the culmination of thousands of steps: the years of hanging around galleries, of struggling through those first-year drawing and painting courses she'd convinced Horst were necessary, of working seventy-hour weeks at The Seagull, of coming up with new recipes, of taking the initiative to organize that art wall, the hours and hours of her own time to maintain it, to get the payments back to the artists. She had not envisioned, really, where it was all going, but she had put the work in, hour after hour.

So she will start over again, but not quite from the very bottom. She'll have a lot of work: It looms before her now, a mountain. But she is not unhappy. She feels in herself finally a lightening: No, that's the wrong word. It's more a deepening, a sense of rootedness, as if she has gained gravity, as if her feet have sunk into the earth. It is not unhappiness: It is more as if she has grown larger, more substantial, and sadness can now roost in her, and she is not afraid of it carrying her away.

And then, two weeks after their meal, Duane calls. She is home; she picks up thinking that the call is going to be about the cheque from The Seagull, but it is not.

He says: I have been thinking.

She can hear it in his voice, what's coming. She waits, then, for her *self* to dissolve, to become vessel, to find herself once more in the loose floating enchantment of the stream. She does not know if it can happen again. The stream calls to her to put off whatever is binding her, to step in, to allow herself to flow with it. She does not know if she can. If she will. It is too late, maybe. Something has changed.

Latitude

BEN COMES BACK FROM the counter with a red flush on his cheeks. Problem, Bro, he says. He's angry or embarrassed or both: Cliff thinks that this is the first time he has seen Ben not cool.

Did they lose our reservation? he asks. He has heard of this happening. Ben shakes his head. Oh, man, he says. They won't let me rent a car. I'm not fucking twenty-five yet.

You have to be twenty-five to rent a car?

Apparently. Of all the motherfucking....

He's never seen Ben like this. He feels unnerved, but then intrigued, and a curious calm settles on him. Not a dissociative calm, but an alert, steady kind of calm, like when he knows exactly what to do, at work, and Ray's not there.

Are you allowed to put it on your credit card?

Yeah. That's not the problem, Ben says, impatiently. I've got the money. It's my fucking ID.

He can see the mechanical structure of Ben's understanding, his assumption that it is Cliff who has misunderstood, as if it is a clock-work in a glass dome. He sees its structure but he is not caught up in it.

I meant, he says, keeping his voice easy, soft: I mean I can drive, no problem.

You have a driver's licence? Again, there is Ben's assumption, which might be insulting, in the space between them, but Cliff can see around it, just at this instant, and there's that glass case around it, between it and Cliff's feelings about it.

Yeah, I do. I have to for work. I drive the equipment between job sites. It's true that Ray mostly does the driving, but Cliff does have to drive, and had to take classes and get his permit, at Mrs. Cookshaw's insistence. He pulls out his wallet, flips open to the windowed pocket where he keeps his card.

Oh, man, Ben says, slapping him on the shoulder. You are one surprising dude sometimes.

And so they have a car. Ben wants to rent a jeep, so they do. It's just like CHIPS, now, Cliff thinks. The two of them on the highway winding alongside the ocean, the palm trees, the warm air and sun. He puts on the aviator sunglasses he bought. Let's roll, he says.

What's that? Ben laughs at him.

Just some show, Cliff says. He understands that he doesn't have to go into detail. You wouldn't have seen it.

They were going to go camping up the west coast, north of Powell River, but then the weather had turn really stormy, and Ben's parents, his adopted parents, had said, Why not go to Maui, use the condo, nobody rents it the last week of August. And they had paid for Cliff's flight, too, which he can't quite understand, but Ben said: They won't miss it.

He wishes, now, that everyone he knows could have this trip. The air is warm and smells like flowers. There are lizards on the garden walls. The sea is everywhere.

They drive up to the west part of the island and go snorkelling: It's the thing he has wanted to do most. He pulls on the snorkel and mask, the flippers, and figures out how to get into the water in them. It's difficult, getting through the shorebreak. He falls, then decides it's easier, if not very cool, just to paddle out through the shallow surf. He has worried that he won't be able to swim well enough or get the hang of the equipment, but it's easy; it feels as if he were born to it. The flippers, the goggles, the mouthpiece, feel almost instantly like parts of his body that his brain already knows how to use.

Then he wonders when he will see the reef: All that he can spot is big dark lumpy rocks. But like magic, he sees this *is* the reef: He sees first an angelfish, yellow and black and white, and then a blue and yellow fish with what looks like protruding front upper teeth, and then suddenly he's surrounded. The tropical fish are everywhere. Their names start coming into his head, and he realizes it's from all of the nature shows he's watched on TV: convict fish and parrot fish, surgeon fish and trumpet fish, in their multiplicity of shapes and colours, all around him, beneath him, a hundred or more species in all the brilliance and variety the mind can take in.

He thinks that he will die of happiness.

And then Ben pointing to the left, and when he paddles over, a large dark oval shape that resolves itself into a sea turtle as long as his legs and torso, which swims past him, turns its head slightly, looks at him, eye to eye.

First they drive through flat fields of some kind of shrub: taller than a man, with long spiky leaves. What is it? Ben doesn't know. Pineapple, Cliff thinks. There are acres and acres of the stuff. He can imagine, for some reason, trying to move through it. Hiding in it. He thinks the leaves would cut a man up. He sees a sign: Sugar Museum. Is it sugar cane? But Ben doesn't know. He has to let go of it, quit worrying it.

They drive through a tiny town set close up on the shoulders of highway. It's like Butterfly Lake, Cliff thinks. The highway narrows here to a thin two lanes. The posted speed limit is twenty but Cliff slows even more. People of all ages, little kids and guys and women around their age, and sinewy men with grey dreadlocks, people in swim trunks and sarongs and bare chests and bikini tops, with deep tans, sunbleached hair, are walking along, crossing the street randomly. Some are carrying surf boards.

Look at that, Ben says. Cliff has stopped to let a group of three girls, very fit, with long rippling hair, bikinis, cross the highway. One of them turns and gives Cliff a fast, light smile and he realizes that he's been smiling all along. He feels her smile light down on him, touch him briefly.

Ben says, Come on, man. You gotta like that!

There's a question, a challenge, behind his words, maybe.

I respect women, Ben, Cliff says.

Ben groans. Yeah, so do I, man. But dude, you gotta, you gotta want to: He holds his hands out in a gesture Cliff has often seen Ray make, a cupping of two round things, an inclination of the head. It always embarrasses him when Ray does this. Now, in the open sunshine, coming from Ben, it's somehow cleaner, more natural. Cliff laughs. He hears David Attenborough's voice, not hushed now but slightly mischievous. *The male resorts to an incredible variety of gestures to attract females and to signal his territory to other males.*

He thinks of Loretta, of her two huge breasts like piñatas, his head between them. He thinks too of the sensation of falling down the stairs, his fear that he was going to be paralyzed. Somehow the memory has receded a bit: It doesn't fill up his body and brain anymore. It's not like he's watching it happen to someone else; it's just that it has a border, a container, around it now. He can walk around it in his mind. He can see it with a kind of wonder, see the fall as part of the same package as the great full globe of Loretta's breasts. Can see her moon face, now. Think her name without the roaring starting up in his head.

What? Ben asks, and Cliff realizes that he has laughed out loud.

The road to Hana is fifty-six miles and has six hundred and fifteen turns, Cliff has read. Driving, he has to get into the rhythm of it, slowing, then accelerating slightly into the curve. It's a kind of slalom, he thinks. The jeep starts to become part of his body. He's glad they're on the inside lane, against the upper rise of the cliffs, not the outer, though he wishes he could have more view of the ocean. It will be reversed on the way back. There is a curtain of thick green, too, between the highway and the ocean, but occasionally he can see the loops and turns ahead, and it seems sometimes that the highway is cantilevered out over the sea.

Beside him, Ben is gripping the roll bar, closing his eyes. You okay? he asks.

I always get sick on this road, Ben says.

Do you want me to drive slower?

No, Ben says. I just forgot. I get sick.

Stop at the next lookout? Cliff asks. He is the driver. It is his job to do this.

A couple of bends after that, there's a break in the trees, a sign, a widening where Cliff can pull over, and he does, and Ben vaults from the jeep and lies on the ground on his belly, breathing deeply. Cliff can hear the surf pounding. They don't seem to be as high up. There's a narrow dirt road leading downward through the green curtain, and also a footpath. I'm going to walk down there, he says.

The trees, palms and others, are all strange to him. Their trunks and bark and leaves are all strange. He thinks that some of them are like hothouse plants, like potted plants in the greenhouses where he has to go sometimes to pick up the trays of annuals for planting out. Philodendrons and hibiscus and rubber plants: hothouse plants that have suddenly grown to giant dimensions. Also the path has stairs, like the path down to Wreck Beach, and it is like climbing down the cliff through the rainforest. Only here the air is warm and humid and it feels very old. This is what the world was like in the Mesozoic era, he thinks.

When the path stops descending, there is an opening in the trees and there is the ocean, stretching out as far as he can see, a clear pure blue. The rollers look huge, high as houses, and their motion is hypnotic after a while: It's perpetual, repetitive, but not quite rhythmic.

It is doing something to his brain, he thinks. There is something about the sound or the amount of ocean, something about scale. In the mile upon mile of sea, the billions of creatures: not just the fish and mollusks and jellies, the singing humpbacks, the hunting dolphins, but the billions of phytoplankton and zooplankton, all of their lives. The ocean a million, million times the size of him.

He reels and nearly falls. The size of it. His own smallness. It makes him feel a lightness, a sort of freedom, as if he could lift off, hover, fly. *Insignificance*, he thinks. He is insignificant, which means, he doesn't matter. But that realization is what is making him feel free. His legs his body his guts and veins and bones, his brain: all small enough to escape attention in this world. To not matter. To be only a particle among billions and trillions of particles. *To not matter.*

And yet to have the right to exist among every other life form. That is it. He runs along the beach. He runs from one end to the other, his arms in the air as if he could take flight. He runs back up the long stairs, back up the cliff, lightness in his heels, his shins, his knees and thighs.

Back at the jeep, Ben is still lying on the ground, but on his back now. He has somehow procured a bag of grass: He holds it up, without saying a word, as Cliff walks up. He says: There are little farms all along the highway, hidden in the bush. Handmade signs. You didn't notice?

Cliff didn't notice. His eyes were on the road.

Dad used to buy it, Ben says. I wasn't supposed to know what it was. They never smoked in front of me but by the time I was twelve or so I knew what the smell was.

Cliff feels anxious now. Should we save it for later, he says. After the drive.

It's good for motion sickness, Ben says.

I don't get much out of it, Cliff says. He has had pot a couple of times, at parties. He's always been worried, though. Last thing he needs, to get caught.

You haven't smoked enough then, Ben says. You need to develop the receptors in your brain or something. What's the beach like here?

Rollers, Cliff says.

Rocky?

Some, Cliff says.

I know a good one, Ben says. Should be just a little further.

When they find the turnoff, Ben isn't sure it's really the right one, and to Cliff it looks all the same as the rest. It's like Butterfly Lake, here, though, he thinks in a kind of wonder. For some reason he had thought that Maui would be completely covered with hotels and resorts. He knows too how in Butterfly Lake only the locals can find the good places; some roads aren't marked. You just have to know.

This beach is a long crescent of sand that's the same colour as Lucerne brand vanilla ice cream. The waves rise to a translucent pale green curl, like glass, before breaking into foam. Palm trees lean out over the beach, where it meets the forest. It's like a picture in an ad. Only it is alive, more than alive.

They dive in to cool down, testing the tug of the current, the slam of the shorebreak, then lie on the sand. They flop on the sand. The sun kneads Cliff's back and shoulders. The breeze off the water licks him cool. If he did not ever leave this spot, for the rest of his life, that would be completely fine.

They are smoking the pot now and what happens is that Cliff feels that same feeling he had getting out of the jeep and walking down to the ocean on the road to Hana. Everything is bright and he is lighter and he is connected to everything. That is a feeling he has had before and he does not know if he needs to be smoking pot to have it, but he is glad to be having it again.

Ben says, One year my parents let me bring my girlfriend. That was the best. Everything was heightened. It was like being high the whole time. She was my first girlfriend. My first serious one. It was, I don't know, kind of like everything was new. Innocent. Like being Adam and Eve or something.

Blue Lagoon, Cliff says. That is a movie he saw on TV once.

What? Ben says. Never saw it. My parents left us pretty much alone, and the two of us, Diane and me, we just were so free, so into each other. So — attuned, yeah. On the same wavelength. We didn't have to say anything. We were just two happy people at the beginning of world.

There's something about this story that makes Cliff feel old, much older than Ben.

What happened to her? he says.

Oh, we were just too young, Ben says, laughing. I was seventeen, Diane was younger. Fifteen, I think. It can't last when you're that young. I don't think we made it through the next school term.

Cliff feels shocked. Fifteen? And her parents let her go with you? Here?

Oh, they sort of knew my parents, Ben says. They were cool with it. Actually, it was only Diane's mom, now that I think about it. But she was cool with it. She was only worried about Diane being on birth control.

But *fifteen*, Cliff says. He knows he's being uncool but he can't help it. He's that shocked. Isn't that illegal?

Only if I were some old guy, Ben says. Like, old as I am now, even. This isn't the fifties, man. Anyway, it wasn't like that. She was just as into it. I mean, she wasn't immature. It was the first time for both of us, and we were kind of innocent together, you know?

Fifteen and seventeen, Cliff thinks. That is not so different. Not so different from almost fourteen and eighteen. Is it?

What about you, man? Ben asks. You remember, you know, your first time?

Cliff is not usually comfortable with this kind of talk. He gets enough of it from Ray. Dirty talk. But now, lying here. And there is still that feeling in him from earlier in the day, still that lightness and freedom.

Do you think eighteen and fourteen is bad, though? he asks.

You mean, too much age difference? Depends on the girl and the guy, I think. Some girls, they're pretty mature at thirteen, fourteen. Mentally, too, I mean. They can think circles around a guy a few years older than them. I guess there has to be a cut-off. Thirteen and twenty, that would be creepy, yeah. Fourteen and eighteen, grey area. Depends on the couple. Why?

Cliff can't think how to answer.

You like little girls? Ben asks, as if he doesn't really care.

No, Cliff says.

Not that there's anything wrong with liking adolescent girls, Ben says. I mean, evolutionarily, it's probably natural, right? It's just a legal problem, really.

I don't, Cliff says. And this is true. He thinks now surprisingly of the girl in his building, the girl on the floor below him, with the tattoo, who had brought Sophie back, that time. He had looked at her face and seen that *youngness*, seen that she was only eighteen or so, and had felt something like protectiveness, and not been able to think of her in a sexual way after that.

KAREN HOFMANN
▸ 327 ◂

It's the other time that is the problem. The thing in the past. Don't remember it now, he instructs himself. Though now he can see her, the way she took his hand, laughing in that way, pulling him. Her white top, its little buttons. The fine tendrils of her hair. Her name, which he hasn't let even his brain say in years. *Caitlin*. There.

You know, Ben says. It wouldn't be surprising if we were attracted to really young chicks, you and me. Because of being, you know, taken care of, basically raised, by our sisters. By Mandalay and Cleo. I mean, our first experiences, being fed and washed and held, you know. By adolescent girls.

Now Cliff is completely shocked. You're saying – our sisters taking care of us – set us up...?

I don't know. Ben's suddenly embarrassed. I heard my mom talking about it to a friend who's a psychiatrist, actually. It's probably all crap. You know shrinks.

No, I don't, Cliff says.

You have had girlfriends, though, Ben asks.

Cliff hears himself say: Yes, I've had girlfriends.

Oh, of course. Ben says. Large horrible tatas.

What?

Sorry. It's a rude nickname. Sorry.

Loretta?

Ben is silent.

Cliff thinks, again: He is much younger than I am. Sometimes.

Sorry, man, Ben says.

Large horrible tatas, Cliff says. He gets it. If you take the name Loretta apart and put other words in. L-hor-tata. Loretta.

Sorry, Ben says again.

You are so immature, Cliff says.

But then they're both laughing their heads off.

He asks: Why did you ditch me, that day in the pub?

You ditched me, Ben says. You went to the can and then didn't come back, and I finally found you on the other side, the lounge side, with Loretta.

No, Cliff says. When I came out of the can.... What lounge side?

Oh, man, Ben says. Oh man. You know there's two bars, right? They're pretty much the same but one side has a piano and we call it the lounge? And the washrooms are between them; they have doors both ways....

Oh man, Ben says.

Okay. He needs to work this through his thoughts.

I was in the wrong bar, he says. I came out of the can and I was in the wrong bar. That's why I couldn't find you guys.

Holy shit, eh, Ben says. Talk about random. Like stepping into an alternative universe.

He doesn't know whether he's more relieved or angry. Or whether he just feels stupid.

THE WAVE SEIZES HIM and tosses him over and slams him down. There's a sharp tug on his wrist: The sea is trying to tear off his hand. No: the board, which is being sucked backward, away from the beach. His hand strikes the bottom and he scrabbles with his feet but the sand is being sucked away; his feet won't stay under him. Another wave slams him then: He's being tossed like a seal pup by an orca. He's helpless. He squeezes his eyes shut and tries to hold pressure in his nose but the water shoots into his nostrils. His chin scrapes along the sand.

Then the tether goes slack, and he thinks: I have lost the board. But the water stills, he stands up, he can see the board, still attached. Ben zips by him, whooping, gives him a high-five. He gets back on the board.

Again and again he swims out, tries to sense the ripeness and the angle of the waves. Too late, and they break closer to shore, and he bobs uselessly behind. Too early, and they crash down on him, so that he is slammed, churned, roughed up. Each time the waves catch him, he feels himself helpless, and then his knees or elbows or ears connect with the sand or the board and he is bruised and scraped, and each time he feels the salt water scour out the inner channels of his brain. And always the fear, when he is tumbled, of being pulled under too long, of being sucked out to sea, of drowning, of annihilation.

But the water is warm, and he does not drown, and he learns to give himself up to it, to let his shoulders and spine soften into it, to let the surf have its moment of power over him. And then it seems to relent, to thrash him less fiercely. It bats at him; it strikes him without claws. Then his fear diminishes, and he feels in its place an opening, a respect, a curiosity.

When his body tires so that he can hardly stand, he rides the board in, lying on it prone, hanging on with all his grip. It's like an incredibly fast sled ride. It's like he's tobogganing down the spine of the planet.

On the beach he flattens himself and it's a relief to just breathe, and Ben comes in and lies down too.

Ben says, You're doing great, man.

No, he isn't. He has barely stood up for a few minutes, in all that time. He has managed to stay upright, to ride a wave for a few seconds, consecutively. But I have learned a lot about wiping out, he says.

Even lying on the hot sand, he can still feel the rhythmic pull of surf on his body, his torso and legs correcting for it. It's the oddest sensation. It feels as if something has changed inside him, at the cellular level. Something has been replaced. This is a new body, with new senses, new knowledge, new power. He thinks: Nothing will ever be the same.

He remembers again Caitlin's face, the *prettiness* of it, how it had just made him happy. How she had drawn him into the field, into the tall corn. She had pulled off his T-shirt, undone his jeans, put his hands to her breasts, then into her underwear. He can still feel, see her: the softness of her face and hair, her nipples, which he has not seen anything like since, the size and texture and colour of the little wild strawberries that grew in the meadows, but not really: Really they were just like themselves. He remembers the silkiness of her, between her legs, the small warm slippery space that he had come to want, with every cell, to be one with. It had felt as clean and natural as rain. His first time, and she had guided him, and said it would be alright. Innocent, Ben had said, and he had felt that, innocent.

But at the same time, he had known better. He had known he shouldn't. That she had been in trouble and the Giesbrechts were her last chance, and he should not fool around with her. He had been told, not in so many words, but let know, that she was off limits.

He had not known that she was just shy of her fifteenth birthday, not then. But even if she had been older, sixteen, he should not have touched her.

But the silkiness of her, the softness, the way she took his hand.

It was okay and not okay. That was the thing. It was okay and not okay at the same time. That is the thing he has never been able to understand until now.

What Mr. Giesbrecht and the others had done, though: That was not okay. He felt, still, the deep shame of that. He sees himself, now, at eighteen, in the circle of their dark suits, their heavy men's bodies. He does not want to think about that but he makes himself look at it. The shame makes his mind shut down but he calls it by its name, shame, and makes it smaller. He makes himself hold the shame in his arms like a sack of feed and look closely at himself in that circle. Their heaviness, which he tries also to name. Anger. Disapproval. And fear, the thought comes to him. How fear, though? The force of them, in their complete authority, their complete belief that they were right and he was wrong. How fear, when there were so many of them (but were there? Was it not just three: Mr. Giesbrecht – Elder Giesbrecht, he was called at church – and his neighbour, also a farmer, and the other man, who might have been – but his mind won't let him see that right now). So even three of them: their weight, their force.

Had they beat him, pushed him around? His heart is beating so quickly, right now, his nerves are telling him to stop thinking about it, but he holds himself steady. He breathes and he hears the surf and feels the land breeze touch his cheek and he holds himself steady, as if lowering himself carefully, carefully, into a well. Had they beaten him? No: He can say that. Had they threatened to beat him? He has to listen, now. He had once heard the neighbouring farmer threaten to staple someone's balls together. His own son's. Cliff had been sent over to borrow some tool, had come around a corner of a truck and heard that. I catch you doing that again I staple your balls together.

But he had not heard the neighbour say that to him. No: They had worn their dark suits and talked to him about God and punishment. That kind of threat. Which he hadn't really believed in anyway, but he thought they all did and that gave it force.

But he knows there was a threat. Something that had scared him, had come down on him like a great mountain of rock and dirt, had crushed him so he couldn't think.

He lets himself feel the safe harness that's holding him, lets himself down the well a little more. Looks at the circle. Where is it? It is in one of the Sunday School rooms at the church. He sees now the pinky-brown curtains at the window, the silver-coloured latch, a semi-circle with a little tab, the lower half of the window open. He'd thought about diving through but the opening was too small. And there was a heavy-duty screen, anyway. The walls were cinderblock painted thickly white, the floor was white tile of some sort of rubber or plastic, with streaks in it. It had never occurred to him, staring at that floor Sunday after Sunday, that it was meant to look like stone but he sees that now. The green chalkboard, with the metal ledge below and the rolled projector screen above. It was a classroom. The door, heavy pinky-brown painted metal, with a silver metal grill at shin level. The door is shut: two of the men between it and him. The painted metal folding chairs. Two of the men, Elder Giesbrecht and the farmer, they were large men, and sat with their legs apart, the bulges of the Sunday-suit crotches and their white-shirted bellies heavy, substantial. (Who was the other man?)

He also in a white shirt, dark pants. His tie in a roll in his pocket. He had been walking out of the chapel, after the service. A hand on his shoulder. Come this way, please.

Then the talk of trust, of generosity, of opening their hearts and homes. Like a son. He had not seen what was coming, still, then. Only after that, the swerve in the conversation, the going down a track he hadn't foreseen, couldn't see the end of, only that he was likely not going to get off it in once piece.

Confess, they'd said, but he had not. He had not admitted it. Stronger than his fear of them had been the conviction that what had happened between him and Caitlin was private, none of their business. He'd just sat there and said nothing.

For a while he'd blamed her, Caitlin. For the first little while. He's been angry at her, wondered why she'd told them. Why she'd got him in trouble, set him up to go through that misery. But then he'd seen her: They'd sent her somewhere else but he'd seen her briefly, at the bus depot, and seen in her his own fear, and known. Then he hadn't been angry any more.

What had they threatened her with? Why had she felt it necessary to tell? How had they even known to take her into a little room and question her? He didn't know that. But he had remembered, later, seeing her come out of a room, the three of them around her. After youth group, that had been. Tuesday night. Not really unusual but that she didn't look at him. And that Ed Dyck's hand had been on her shoulder, and her twisting slightly under it, and he'd wanted to knock it off, but she had looked away from him, turned her back to him.

That was the third guy. Ed Dyck. Yes. Always at youth group, Tuesdays. Always taking them to the pool or to Dairy Queen, giving one of them a ride in his pickup cab. The rest had to sit in the back, the bed of the truck. Always one of the girls in the cab.

Where is his mind going now? He is not going in a useful direction, for now.

So, Ed Dyck in that room. Yes. His brush cut, his reddened face. A cop. No, not a cop. Security guard, maybe. It was him, though.

Your name is going on record, do you understand? You'll always have a record. If you get so much as a speeding ticket, a parking ticket, the police will look it up and they'll see that you have committed a felony. That's what it is, Cliff. It's a felony. Statutory rape. And you should be going to jail. It's the mercy of these elders here that you're not, but that's what will happen if you ever get in trouble again.

He sees now that there are a few holes in this threat. He's never thought it through, never let himself really think about it, but he sees now. First of all. There was no record. He wasn't arrested. There would not be a record. He's watched enough crime dramas on TV to know that. Second of all. They didn't really want to know. They didn't want to go too deeply into it. Because who knows what Caitlin would have said. What other girls would have said. They really didn't want to know.

This he sees in images, rather than thoughts, lying on the warm cream-coloured sand. He's sweating and the breeze from the ocean washes over him, cooling him, wicking the sweat from his face and chest. He's splayed on his back, open and helpless under the great blue sky. And the very air is drying him, bathing him with coolness and light.

It had been wrong and it had not been wrong. Inside a small dark circle on a small farm in a small community in a scarcely populated corner of a country, it was wrong. And maybe it was wrong in other ways, for other reasons. But under this huge blue sky, in the warm sea, it is not wrong or right, and it no longer matters. The warm sea has washed it from him.

The fear that has followed him – uniforms, handcuffs, court, jail – is suddenly not the problem, he sees. It's smoke: It dissipates in clear air. As he looks at it. He feels that his mind has cleared, is ticking along better than it used to. Like a big whack of matted wet grass has been shaken out.

He feels the damp and cool, now, through the sand: feels the earth beneath him, pressing up at him, holding him, just the right shape and temperature for his body. The planet is very large, and there is room for him on it: room for him to live, and to not be under anyone's jealous eye.

After

THE SECRET COLOUR of the forest is orange. That's the colour it is if you don't listen to the green. If you listen properly with your eyes shut. All around you is orange light.

She is colouring the orange trees and Mariah says: Trees are green. But Mariah doesn't know everything. She makes the trees orange and she presses harder on one side to make the shading, like Auntie Mandalay showed her. She makes the bark scribbly and she makes the branches come down like arms, even though Mariah says: Tree branches go up like *this*. She draws them down like sweaters with too-long arms. She colours softly with a different crayon to make the light, the secret light around the trees.

It's a forest fire, Jacob says but she tells him it is not. All around the edge she makes the blue light that the trees keep out. And at the bottom, the browny-red roots of the trees, which Uncle Cliff says are as big as the trees. She has forgotten to leave enough room, so she draws just some of them.

When she is a grown-up or maybe twelve she is going to go live in the forest. She will have a pointy blue house in the forest. She has drawn this house lots of times, so she knows exactly what it will be like. In the forest the food grows on the bushes and in the stream and you cook it outside with a campfire. (Yes it does, Mariah. You don't know everything.) Blackberries and salmonberries and chanterelles and salmon and bannock on a stick.

She will have a wildcat called Sophie and it will be her best friend. Her best animal friend. Claire will be her best person friend. And Mariah too, but only if she stops being so bossy.

She has to get another piece of paper for the blackberries and chanterelles. The teacher is Miss Doucey. She says, a fresh sheet, Olivia? But she is smiling.

They are drawing their summer holidays. Mariah is drawing lots of tall houses with rows of windows. She makes the lines very straight and careful. It looks like Mummy's work drawing. Mariah has made the row of houses march across the page, and it hardly slants at all, but she's sniffing because there was not enough paper and she has to make the last house too skinny. Olivia says, you could tape on a new piece of paper. Or you could make half a house. Like it's a picture in a camera.

Claire is drawing people very carefully on her paper. She won't run out of room. She won't even use up most of her paper. The people are very small and very real. Olivia can tell who they are, exactly: Claire's mom and dad and her granny and her little brother. Olivia can even tell what clothes they have on: her granny's skirt with the zig zags, and her mom's red shorts, Claire's polka-dot dress. She knows Claire is going to draw a ferry next. That's why she has left so much room. She, Olivia, could have drawn a ferry too but the forest was better.

Mariah is drawing Paris. She did not get to go on a ferry on the holidays.

Olivia makes the chanterelles. She can taste them while she's drawing them, the taste like the forest, and butter, and a flute playing. The chanterelles look perfect on her paper, their hats and stems yellow like eggs yolks. And blue for the crispy bits. But then the teacher is talking, five minutes before centre time, and she can't taste the blackberries she is trying to draw, and they get all messed up.

You don't have to cry, Mariah says. You can just try another day. But Claire hugs her.

At centres she and Claire and Mariah get the house, and it is her turn to be the mom, but Mariah says she has to go to work and Mariah will be the stay-at-home dad. So Mariah gets to be the boss and that is very sneaky and mean. A boy called Oliver wants to play too and they let him, but he has to be a kid. She doesn't like Oliver because his name is too much like hers.

When she is grown up she is going to change her name to Crystal. That's her secret plan. She won't answer if people call her Olivia. Not even her dad.

Well, maybe her dad. She will send emails to her dad. She will have her own computer and she will send emails to her dad and her grandma Crystal. And she'll play video games. She is only allowed to play Reader Rabbit now on her mom's computer but she will get some games like Mariah's brother has.

Her dad said: When you're a teenager everyone will have a computer. They'll be so small you'll take yours to school in your backpack. And her mom said: Yeah, and a flying car. But that was silly.

She will send emails to her uncle Cliff and her new uncle Ben, and to her auntie Mandalay. She will invite them to visit. She will tell them what presents to bring her. She will tell them how to get to her pointy blue house, because it will be hard to find, in the forest.

She will make them come inside, and she will tell them her new name, and they had better remember to call her that, or she will not invite them anymore.

Don't call me Olivia, she will say. I am somebody different now.

She will show them her paintings, and she'll teach them how to paint, too, if they like. She will let them stay up late and see the comets. She'll bring them blankets and popcorn. She will make sure they go to sleep, and she will give them blueberry pancakes, as many as they can eat.

And then she will show them how to get home.

ACKNOWLEDGEMENTS

Thanks to family and friends, who forgive my disappearances into the manuscript.

To my tireless editor, Anne Nothof; to Matt Bowes and Claire Kelly and the NeWest team.

To Thompson Rivers University, for time and financial support.

To Susie Safford for brilliant early feedback; to Susan Dumbrell for two decades of walks and conversations; to Sue Buis for mindfulness and poems.

To Sharon Nash for the seed.

KAREN HOFMANN lives in Kamloops, B.C. She has been published in *Arc, Prairie Fire, The Malahat Review,* and *The Fiddlehead.* She has been shortlisted for the 2012 CBC Short Fiction Contest, and won the Okanagan Short Fiction Contest three times. Her book *Water Strider* was shortlisted for the Dorothy Livesay Prize at the 2009 BC Book Awards, and "The Burgess Shale" was shortlisted at the 2012 CBC Short Fiction Contest. Her first novel *After Alice* was published by NeWest Press in 2014.